Praise for *The Versions of Us*

'The literary love child of *One Day* by David Nicholls and *Life After Life* by Kate Atkinson'   Fiona Wilson, *The Times*

'Excellent . . . Barnett's clever and sophisticated plotting weaves the three outcomes seamlessly over a 60-year period . . . An affecting and thought-provoking read, *The Versions of Us* will keep you gripped until the tear-jerking conclusion'
Mernie Gilmore, *Daily Express*

'Barnett renders an irresistible concept in sweet, cool prose – a bit like a choose-your-own-adventure book in which you don't have to choose'   Hephzibah Anderson, *Observer*

'Clever, but not showy, romantic but not schmaltzy, it's clear that the buzz around this book is justified'
Deirdre O'Brien, *Sunday Mirror*

'Truly enthralling – I simply adored this wonderful novel'
Jessie Burton, author of *The Miniaturist*

'It is an unusual and lovely thing to watch an entire romance develop across a novel, not just the fun early bits, or unpleasant mid-life startings-over, or male midlife crises disguised as literary novels. Its very scope is a joy, the technical achievement seamlessly done, and the ending – all the endings – suitably affecting'
Jenny Colgan, *Guardian*

'A classic summer read. *One Day* meets *Mad Men*'   *Metro*

'I absolutely loved [*The Versions of Us*]. It's so elegantly and beautifully written . . . a really wonderful book'
Esther Freud, author of *Mr Mac and Me*

'Well written, deftly crafted and constantly surprising . . . an utterly convincing love story about two people destined to be together somehow, no matter what' Kate Saunders, *The Times*

'The tantalising "what if?" theme keeps all three stories going at a cracking pace. It is to her credit that youthful Barnett invokes the power of love and loss among both the young and old with equal tenderness' Christena Appleyard, *Daily Mail*

'Both brilliant and astonishingly good'
Elizabeth Buchan, author of *I Can't Begin to Tell You*

'A deeply moving and emotional story that has the ability to make you evaluate your own life' *Stylist*

'Everyone's talking about *The Versions of Us* by Laura Barnett. Eva and Jim's first meeting has three possible outcomes. Barnett interweaves the resulting love stories with their beautifully drawn characters into an elegant, touching tapestry'
Fanny Blake, *Woman & Home*

A clever, romantic debut' *Grazia*

'An exciting and clever novel. It marks the emergence of a major talent in literary fiction. I can't wait to see what Barnett does next' Viv Groskop, *Red magazine*

'Thought-provoking and moving' Cathy Rentzenbrink, *Prima*

'Each strand is distinct – and equally captivating'
Good Housekeeping

'Written with intelligence and warmth' Natasha Cooper, *TLS*

GREATEST HITS

Laura Barnett was born in 1982 in south London, where she now lives with her husband. She studied Spanish and Italian at Cambridge University, and newspaper journalism at City University, London.

Her bestselling debut novel, *The Versions of Us*, was published in May 2015 and has been translated into 23 languages. TV rights have been optioned by Trademark Films.

As a freelance arts journalist, features writer and theatre critic, Laura has worked for the *Guardian*, the *Observer*, the *Daily Telegraph* and other national newspapers and magazines. Her first non-fiction book, *Advice from the Players* – a compendium of advice for actors – was published in 2014 by Nick Hern Books.

@laura_jbarnett
www.laura-barnett.co.uk
www.versionsofus.com

GREATEST HITS

Laura Barnett

WEIDENFELD & NICOLSON

First published in Great Britain in 2017
by Weidenfeld & Nicolson
an imprint of the Orion Publishing Group Ltd
Carmelite House, 50 Victoria Embankment
London EC4Y 0DZ

An Hachette UK Company

1 3 5 7 9 10 8 6 4 2

Lyrics by Laura Barnett and Kathryn Williams
(Except 'I Wrote You a Love Song' and 'Living Free'
by Laura Barnett, Kathryn Williams and Romeo Stodart; 'Road of Shadows'
by Laura Barnett, Kathryn Williams and Polly Paulusma; 'Home' by Laura
Barnett, Kathryn Williams and Michele Stodart)

Quote from Stevie Nicks is printed with the kind permission of Stevie Nicks.

From MA RAINEY'S BLACK BOTTOM by August Wilson, copyright © 1985
by August Wilson. Used by permission of New American Library, an imprint
of Penguin Publishing Group, a division of Penguin Random House LLC.

A CIP catalogue record for this book is
available from the British Library.

ISBN (Hardback) 978 1 474 60020 0
ISBN (Export Trade Paperback) 978 1 474 60021 7
ISBN (eBook) 978 1 474 60022 4

Typeset by Input Data Services Ltd, Somerset

Printed and bound in Great Britain by Clays Ltd, St Ives plc

www.orionbooks.co.uk

For Andy, of course

Each song is a lifetime. These songs are the memories.

Stevie Nicks

You don't sing to feel better. You sing 'cause that's a way of understanding life.

August Wilson, *Ma Rainey's Black Bottom*

So it wasn't a failure after all! It was going to be all right now – her party. It had begun. It had started. But it was still touch and go.

Virginia Woolf, *Mrs Dalloway*

8 a.m.

The day has begun slowly, gently, with a steady creeping into life. The dawn hazy – thin bands of cloud lifting into a pale blue sky – and the sun low and yellowish, promising warmth but delivering only deep, angled shadows.

A series of planes has made a steady procession up towards nothingness, or the unidentifiable place over the English Channel where each, as if by some ancient instinct, will turn its nose towards the Atlantic and pick up speed.

In Cass Wheeler's garden, partitioned from the Tunbridge Road by a series of high dry-stone walls, two rangy, sharp-faced foxes have emerged from their den behind the shed and curled up, doglike, in a patch of sun. At the narrow, blind turning that leads to her house – its sign, Home Farm, almost entirely obscured by thick coils of ivy that Cass hasn't cared to remove – a man, new to the village, has paused while out walking his dog, drawn by the faint outline of a memory. And then, after a moment, he has walked on, re-immersing himself in the shape-shifting cares of the moment, the dog shadowing his heels.

Cass has known none of this. She has been rising reluctantly from sleep, ignoring her alarm, chasing the vague, receding image of a dream. A hall somewhere – not a large room; a school auditorium, perhaps. Shining parquet and the smell of chalk. Black plastic chairs arranged in expectant rows. Silence, measured by the metronomic tick of a wall-clock. The uncomfortable, tightening sense that there is something else she ought to be doing, somewhere else she ought to be, and she can't for the life of her remember what it might be.

The alarm shrills out again. She lets it ring, opening her eyes,

I

abandoning the ghostly image of the hall. Here is her bedroom, her dressing-table, the soft pressure of her cat, Otis, stretching and yawning at her feet. Here is the pillow, cool against her cheek, which, on other mornings, has carried the weight of Larry's head; from which he has turned, on waking, and gathered her to him, and she has thrilled to the strangeness of his long body, his warm hands, after so many years of sleeping alone.

She thinks, *Where is Larry?*

She thinks, *Chicago.*

She thinks, *I could forget today, couldn't I? Just lie here, under the covers. Draw them up over my head and sleep.*

She thinks, *No. You have done too much sleeping. Today is the day you wake up.*

Downstairs in her kitchen, she makes coffee. Toast. Stands at the window eating – she can still hear her mother's voice: 'Sit *down* at once. Anyone would think you were born in a barn' – and watches a pair of foxes on the lawn, black-nosed and long-tailed, sleeping under a weak beam of sun. One wakes, lifts his head, and looks back at her. His eyes are impassive, dark-pupilled; there is, she thinks, something uncommonly human about his stare. She looks away first, sips her coffee. When she turns back to the window, both the foxes have disappeared.

Kim has left a note on the counter; she must have written it after Cass had gone up to bed. She'd stayed for dinner, made lasagne. *How often*, Cass had thought, *have I sat and eaten Kim's lasagne, and yet I never tire of it?* Well, that wasn't quite true: on one of the worst days, Cass had taken a tray of lasagne from the fridge and the stench of it, that oozing, gelatinous gloop, had suddenly been more than she could bear. She had let the tray drop from her fingers, left the whole broken mess where it fell. Kim, later, had simply cleaned it up, and said nothing more about it. They can laugh about it now – had done so last night, as Kim had placed two steaming plates on the dining-room table.

'Won't smash these, will you, Cass?' she had said, and Cass had poured them both a glass of wine, and loved this woman: the woman who has seen so very much and never flinched from it; the woman who could stand to look at her even when Cass couldn't stand to look at herself.

Hope you had a good sleep, Kim has written. *I'll be round about three. On the mobile if you need me. Callum's calling at ten about the masters – he'll try the studio line. The caterers will be there at five, but I'll deal with them. Otherwise, you're on your own. Enjoy it, Cass, all right? There's no hurry. Take your time. Kx.*

That was a song, wasn't it? Cass can almost hear it, as if from a radio, turned down low. A deep-bellied chord, a man's voice. *Take your time, girl. It's only you and me.* Whose was it? Not Ivor's – not that reedy, fluting tenor. She closes her eyes; she can feel the answer lurking in a distant, shadowed corner of her mind. That's how it is, so often, now: the clear Technicolor of memory fading to sepia, recollection a deliberate act. An act of deliberation. *Take your time, girl.* Damn it, it won't come.

Cass slams her mug down, sending a cool sluice of coffee spattering across the worktop. Otis, methodically washing himself at the window, shoots her a disdainful glance.

Forget it, she thinks. *It probably wasn't any good anyway.*

In her bedroom, as she dresses, the answer suddenly appears.

A pub – dingy, gleaming with horse brasses, men glowering over glasses of stout. A man with a guitar, pale and thin-faced, curly hair creeping down over the collar of his jacket. Ivor beside her: the tall, beloved outline of him, leaning down to whisper in her ear. *We're up next, Cassie. Don't be nervous.*

But she had been nervous, had felt the fear washing through her with each sip of shandy. She had wanted that song to last for ever – *Take your time, girl*, the man had sung, and she had wanted to say, *No, you take your time* – *just keep on playing, and don't ever stop.* But he had stopped, and Ivor had placed a hand

3

on her shoulder, and she had reached down for her guitar. The men and the walls and the horse brasses, all of it had seemed to turn and buckle around her, and if she could have turned and run, she would have done so, and not looked back. But Ivor had pushed her forward, gently, and the fat man with the black, tufted beard had put down his beer and stood up on the stage.

'Ivor Tait and Cass Wheeler,' he'd announced to those who cared to listen, and then there had been no turning back.

What had they sung that night? She can't recall. 'Scarborough Fair', probably. Something by Joan Baez, perhaps, if she'd been feeling particularly brave. And she *had* felt brave, in the end: her fear had evaporated, as it almost always did, in the moment she sat down on the stool, settled the reassuring bulk of her guitar upon her knee. Then it had begun: their slow, dancing courtship, over and under, under and over, as the strings of their guitars bowed and curtsied to the will of their darting fingers.

Slipping on her shoes, Cass thinks, *My God, I loved Ivor then. How could I not?*

She opens the curtains to the morning. Across the garden, the tiered glass and concrete of the studio roof is catching the sunlight, casting long, geometric patterns across the lawn. She had designed it herself on graph paper, accurately measured: the architect, Luke Bennett, looking over her plans, had peered at her over his black-framed glasses and said, 'Impressive.'

Anna, ten years old – gap-toothed and tousle-haired, her knees thin and bony below her cut-off denim shorts – had said, 'Wow, Mum. It looks like the *Starship Enterprise*.'

Anna. Cass stands for a moment at the window, one hand on her dressing-table, steadying herself. Down on the lawn, one of the foxes emerges from behind the shed, lifts his snout to the air, and sniffs.

She thinks, *Now. I am ready.*

*

The studio is cool and calm, quiet but for the monitors' steady electric hum. Callum and Gav have left the live room tidy: coiled cables, folded mike-stands, removed beer-bottles and ashtrays – not that there's so much of any of that now. Even Gav's only vice is working, in the course of each session, through a small packet of Golden Virginia Light. Cass has grown used, in recent months, to seeing the shadow of him outlined against the sliding doors to the terrace, hand cupped around his latest slender, hand-rolled cigarette.

The computers in the control room are at rest, blank-screened and silent. The console sleeps. Beside it, on the desk, lies a sheet of paper lined with notes in Callum's angular, boyish hand. *'When Morning Comes'* – *boost cello going into chorus by 3dB. 'Gethsemane' – repeat coda to fade. Javier – play softer.*

Cass smiles. He's a good man, Callum: careful, thoughtful, unlike some of the producers she's known. It was Alan who'd suggested him for the new record: Callum Sutherland had, he said, faced down a few demons of his own.

'Demons?' she'd repeated, smiling at the thought of them, swish-tailed, maniacally grinning.

'Well,' Alan had said, smiling back, 'you know what I mean.'

Cass had known exactly what he meant – had seen it for herself when Alan had brought Callum to Home Farm for dinner. He was thirty-eight, good-looking in a stubbled, brooding sort of way, with an actress wife, Andrea (he'd brought her, too), three Grammys and a shiny new 'Producer of the Year' award from the Guild.

His last job had been with an American pop starlet – or whatever they were called these days – whose album cover pictured her in a skintight white rubber suit. Looking at it – they were in the garden, smoking, 'talking business' while Alan poured Andrea another glass of wine – Cass had been unable to conceal her distaste.

'I know what you're thinking,' Callum said. 'But there's more

5

to her than you'd think. She's strong-willed – knows what she wants, definitely doesn't take any crap. And you should have heard her singing voice before they brought me in.'

'Fair enough.' Cass drew deeply on her cigarette. 'At least you're honest.'

'Always,' he said. 'Learnt that the hard way.'

Later, over coffee, she'd invited Callum to her next rehearsal session with the band. A few days after that, she'd told Alan that this might, indeed, be the man she was looking for. The man who would treat her gently, and her new songs even more so.

'All right,' Alan had replied, studiedly casual, reaching into the pocket of his jeans for his mobile phone. He was glued to the thing, these days – said it was impossible to imagine *ever* having managed anyone, or anything, without it. And yet they had got along just fine without any of that for so long. Letters and telegrams and long-distance phone calls; LPs and hit parades and the slick-haired kids queuing outside the record shops. It was a different world now. What was the phrase Callum had used to describe it? An *analogue world*. That was the world she belonged to; who knew why this shiny new one should have any use for her?

Watching Alan's stubby, calloused fingers moving with un-customary grace across the glass screen of his phone, Cass had felt the old fear rising, asserting itself. Her irrelevance. Her un-importance. Her new songs, so unexpected, so precious to her, as quiet and timorous as whispers, passing unnoticed amid the brash, ruthless, deafening clamour of the young.

She had spoken none of this aloud, but Alan had looked up, met her eyes with his.

'You don't have to do this, Cass,' he'd said softly. 'You don't have to do any of this. The greatest-hits record, the new tracks – all of it can wait. Or go to hell, if you want it to. It's up to you. It's always been up to you.'

6

She'd held his gaze for one second, two, three.

'No,' she'd said. 'I do want this. I need it, Alan. Please.'

At the open door to the listening-room, Cass waits for a moment. Alan and Kim have arranged it all for her: the stack of records on the table; the bottles of San Pellegrino arranged neatly in the fridge; the fresh mugs warming on the coffee machine. On top of the pile of albums, she finds another note from Kim. *Happy listening. Like I said, take your time. Kx.*

Beside it is a square white envelope. Cass slides a finger under the seal, draws out a Henry Moore sculpture printed on glossy card: bulbous, eerily smooth. Two women seated; beside one of them, a child, her hand resting on the woman's knee. Inside, in his oversized, square-angled hand, Larry has written, *Today, Cass, find a way to forgive her. And then – please – find a way to forgive yourself.*

He must have left the card with Kim, or posted it to her, from Chicago. Cass stands still, the card in her hand, picturing Larry's face. It had been to him, first, that she had described the idea that was gradually forming in her mind, assuming the shape and colour of firm intention. She was thinking, she'd told him, of putting together a compilation of her greatest hits, to accompany the new material. Not, she'd said, the obvious songs – the label had put *that* record out long ago – but the songs that meant the most to her. The songs that tracked the arc of a lifetime.

They had been sitting side by side on the living-room sofa, after dinner, sharing a bottle of pinot noir. It was October, late evening, and they had not yet turned on the lamps: the colours were leaching minute by minute from the room, the grey shadows thickening around them, but neither of them, each intent on the other's face, had noticed.

She had told Larry that she had in mind one single day – an ordinary day, a day like any other – in which to listen to her music and make her choices. There was a simplicity, a crisp

efficiency, about the plan that appealed to her. No fuss, no ceremony, just a portion of time allocated to the act of listening. At
the end of the day, a party. Old friends, musicians, journalists,
comrades-in-arms. She would play the new songs to them for
the first time: make her new music known, as she must again
make herself known to them, after so many years of isolation.

She had told Larry that she wanted this, wanted all of it, but
she was afraid. Afraid of what she might hear in her past: in
those songs with whose sound and structure she had so confi-
dently framed her comprehension of everything that had not,
in the end, proved comprehensible. Afraid of following the trail
that must surely lead to what had happened. To all that she had
won, and all that she had lost.

And Larry, throughout, had said nothing, sat listening, intent,
expressionless. When he saw that she had said all she needed to
say, he'd drained his glass, leant forward, and wrapped her in his
arms. They had held each other, two lonely old fools embracing
tightly in the darkness; and that, Cass had realised then, was the
only answer she'd been looking for.

Now, alone in her studio in the clear-skied freshness of an April
morning, Cass sets Larry's card down on the coffee table, in
front of the stack of LPs. She takes a record from the top of the
pile, slides it onto the turntable, and sits down to listen.

'Common Ground'

By Cass Wheeler
From the album *The State She's In*

It was early morning when she left
And the city, under a grey sky was still sleeping
A note left on the table lying flat
Held the secrets she'd been keeping

We have no common ground, my love
We have no common ground
So I am leaving with the dawn, my love
And I never will be found

Ooooooooooooooooooooooo

Crossing that dirty green London common
As the sky turned from grey to blue
A suitcase, a long-distance airfare
And a life to start living new

We have no common ground, my love
We have no common ground
So I am leaving with the dawn, my love
And I never will be found

Ooooooooooooooooooooooo

RELEASED 13 September 1971
RECORDED June 1971 at Union Studios, London NW10
GENRE Folk rock
LABEL Phoenix Records
WRITER(S) Cass Wheeler
PRODUCER(S) Martin Hartford
ENGINEER(S) Sean O'Malley

She was born Maria Cassandra Wheeler, in the back bedroom of the vicarage that faced the common, and the tall white cupola of the church it had been built to serve.

It was April 1950. Through the three hard days of her labour, the baby's mother, Margaret, watched the blossom bowing the branches of the apple tree outside the window, and prayed for release. But when it came at last, it was at a price: a small, damp-headed creature, ugly and mottled, screwing up its face against the light.

'Your daughter,' the midwife said, placing the warm bundle in Margaret's arms.

'She's beautiful,' Margaret said, though she did not think so. *All that*, she thought, *for this*, and closed her eyes.

Francis, the vicar, took the newborn girl from his wife's slackening grip.

'Cassandra,' he said under his breath: it had been his mother's name, and he'd have liked to pass it to his daughter, but a Christian baptismal name had seemed more fitting. Expected, surely, by the congregation, several of whom were downstairs now, making tea, occupying themselves with whatever it is women do at such a time; brisk, busy wives and mothers, who had arrived, a whole chattering, hatted flock of them, three days ago, when Margaret's torture had begun, insisting he remove himself to his study.

'You mustn't worry about a thing, Reverend,' they had said as one, and yet how could he not worry, confined to those four walls, pacing up and down while his wife's cries travelled through the thickly carpeted floor?

And now here she was: his daughter. Alive and well, though surely her colour was a little alarming. The baby stirred, opened her eyes, and he saw that they were a deep shining brown, just like his own.

Hello, little one, he said silently, and he felt something for which he had not been quite prepared: love, of course – sharper, more visceral, than his love for Margaret, though that had its own particular piquancy; clearer, more focused, than his love for God – but also fear. The terror that he, alone, would not be strong enough to protect her.

'I'll put her down now, Reverend,' the midwife said, and Francis looked up at her in surprise: he had, for a moment, quite forgotten she was in the room. 'Your wife needs to rest.'

'Of course.' He handed his daughter over, and his arms, without the small weight of the child, seemed suddenly redundant. 'I'll be downstairs. There are women . . .' He trailed off, unable to quite define their purpose. 'If Margaret needs anything.'

'Yes, Reverend.' The midwife was already turning away. 'We'll be just fine, won't we, little Maria?'

Cassandra, he thought disloyally as he closed the bedroom door behind him. *Her name is Cassandra*. And then Francis went back downstairs to his study, where his unfinished sermon was waiting.

Maria grew quickly. At six months, she was crawling; at ten, lifting herself unsteadily onto her feet.

She hated sleep – resisted bedtimes, and found, once her motor skills permitted, increasingly ingenious ways to vacate her cot, and draw her mother from her bed. Margaret – delirious with exhaustion and her own inchoate, private pain – began to lose patience with her daughter: she had a lock installed on the door of the child's room, and drew the bolt across after laying her down to sleep.

'Leave her, Francis,' Margaret said when they woke in the night to the sound of the child's distress, the beating of her tiny fists on the locked door. 'She'll grow out of it.'

Most nights, Francis buried his head deeper in the pillow, and obeyed. But there were times, in the early hours, when he simply couldn't bear it any longer, and then he would creep from the room and cross the landing, open the door to find his daughter hoarse, exhausted, her cheeks wet with tears. He held her, then, as he had held her that first April morning, and walked up and down before the curtained window, telling her the stories he dimly remembered from his own childhood. Mowgli in the jungle, the panther Bagheera; Tom, the chimney sweep, who fell into the river and lived there, among the otters and the reeds.

Maria would grow calm, then, and watch him. Those moments in the night – his own soft whisper; his daughter's staring eyes and tiny hands, opening and closing like the buds of some strange, exotic flower – became so precious to Francis that sometimes he went to her even when she hadn't begun to cry.

By day, too, Maria could not sit still. New outfits were ruined within hours, marred by grass-stains (she loved to slip from her mother's hand and roll across the churchyard turf), or the masticated remnants of food. In church, if left to her own devices, she would run up and down the nave, scattering the embroidered hassocks, offering the loud, inarticulate, wordless tune that, at eleven months, she had begun to carry with her everywhere.

'She's running wild, Francis,' Margaret said. 'I'm at my wits' end.'

And she was: the church ladies began to voice concerns, to mount delegations that would arrive at the vicarage most mornings, insisting they take charge of Maria for a few hours 'to give poor Margaret time to rest'.

Under the ladies' care – mothers, most of them, and proud, capable housewives; certainly nothing like Margaret, whose long-held fear that she lacked some essential aspect of the maternal instinct was, she felt, being confirmed with each passing day – Maria was transformed. With them, she sat quietly, absorbed in her game: an abacus; a doll; a set of building-blocks. Sometimes, the ladies brought their children with them, and then they played together, Maria and whichever toddler was placed before her that day.

'See,' the ladies said. 'There's nothing wrong with her – she just needs the company of other children. Perhaps if she had a brother or sister . . .'

But no second pregnancy was announced. Privately, the ladies suspected it never would be; there was talk that the reverend's marriage was a troubled one, that he and Margaret no longer shared a bed. This was untrue – the spare bedroom was pristine, kept only for guests – but it was clear, even to the infant Maria (though she was not, of course, yet able to give voice to such knowledge) that happiness had eluded them. And Margaret herself was elusive, too: her mother seemed to shrink from her daughter, to have no interest in her at all besides the basic desire that she be clothed and fed. So Maria sought that interest – demanded it, in the only ways she knew how.

One morning, returning from the vicarage kitchen with a fresh cup of tea, Mrs Harrison found her son, Daniel, set down to play with Maria just a few moments before, screaming at the top of his voice, a red mark on his cheek that surely must be a bite. That was too much: Mrs Harrison called the vicar's wife down from her bedroom. (Margaret wasn't sleeping, just lying silently, watching the shadows shift across the ceiling, and wondering how much more of such a life she could possibly endure. *Surely*, she was thinking, *there must, somewhere, be more for me than this*.)

Downstairs, Margaret confronted her daughter. 'Did you bite Daniel, Maria?'

The child stood frozen, motionless, staring up at her mother, her dark eyes huge, sorry, full of the questions to which she could not yet place the words. *Why won't you play with me? Why won't*

13

you touch me? What is wrong with me? What am I doing wrong?

Margaret stepped forward, then, and drew her right hand, quick and hard, across Maria's left cheek.

'You're a vicious little madam,' she said, 'and I wish I'd never had you.'

The room was silent for a long moment – the girl open-mouthed, the livid bruise already blooming on her skin; Daniel confused, reaching for his mother, whose own voice had stilled in her throat. Then Maria began to cry, and Daniel did the same, and Margaret turned on her heels and ran back upstairs, slamming the door behind her.

Later, home from evensong, Francis asked his wife what had happened to their daughter's face.

'I slapped her, Francis,' Margaret said. 'Do you expect me to pretend otherwise?'

Things seemed to improve once Maria started school. She liked it there, tripped off uncomplainingly each morning towards the imposing Victorian building with its high, narrow windows and lingering smells of floor-polish and boiled carrots.

She had a teacher named Miss Meller, who was young and pale and nervous and spoke quietly, in a small, melodic voice that seemed to well up from somewhere deep in her throat. One day, when they were studying world flags, Miss Meller told the class that she had been born not in England but in a country called Poland, far, far away.

The children considered this.

'Why did you come here, then?' a boy asked. His name was Stephen Dewes; Maria found him dull and silly, with his neatly ironed blazer and the stick insect he'd brought to school once in a cardboard box. *Not much of a pet,* Maria had thought. *If I could have a pet, I'd keep a tiger.*

'Because of the war,' Miss Meller said, and she looked so miserable that even Stephen Dewes – whose uncle had, like so

14

many, gone off to war and never returned – knew better than to press her further.

Maria was intrigued by Miss Meller, after that: by her pink-rimmed nose (she seemed always to have a cold); by the fine slivers of thread that trailed from the sleeves of her cardigan. Miss Meller wore her hair in a bun, which would begin the day at the top of her head, and slowly work its way down, pulled inexorably by gravity, until, by afternoon registration, it was sitting right on top of her collar. She liked 'Art' – she said the word so, grandly emphasising its initial letter – and gave the children sheets of thick, coarse paper on which to draw their families, their pets, their holidays.

Maria drew tigers, ferries to France, a smiling phalanx of brothers and sisters.

'But you don't have any brothers or sisters,' said Irene. She was six and had three brothers and a hamster called Hammy, and was Maria's best friend.

'It doesn't matter,' Maria said. 'It doesn't have to be *true*.'

'She's very creative,' Miss Meller told Margaret at parents' evening. 'But tell me – does she have a tendency to make things up?'

At home that night, Margaret caught Maria by the wrist, held her in front of the hallway mirror.

'See that face?' she said. 'That's the face of a liar, Maria. A naughty little liar. Don't *ever* let me catch you lying again.'

Her mother's grip was tight on Maria's arm. She began to cry, her crumpled face reflected back at her in the glass: dirty-blonde hair, brown eyes limpid, damp, under her uneven fringe. When her mother let her go, she fled upstairs to bed, where she made a nest under the covers, and sobbed until no more tears would come. Then she took out her pad of paper and drew an aeroplane, aiming its wingtips towards a shelf of sky, a wide, smiling beach ball of a sun.

After that, Maria preferred to keep her stories to herself.

Irene lived in a house on the other side of the common. It was smaller than the vicarage, and on just two floors; two of her brothers shared a room, and Irene and the third brother – Max, who was nine, and always muddy – had bunk beds. Her father went to work in an office, and her mother was pretty and friendly; she would sit the girls up on the kitchen counter as she made their tea, and ask them what they had done that day at school.

'Arithmetic,' they would say, or, 'spelling.' Then Irene's mother would ask them which subject they liked best, and Irene would say, 'reading,' and Maria, always, would say, 'art.'

Irene's mother had a piano. It was in the front room, which was painted yellow, and was never quite tidy. Sometimes, after tea, and before Irene's father came home from work, Irene's mother would let the girls sit on the sofa and listen while she played.

Maria loved that room: loved the colour of the walls, which seemed to her like pure sunlight, trapped and held fast; loved the rough and tumble of it, the toys waiting where the children had left them; the brown rug, soft and thick as a bear's fur, on which she and Irene were sometimes allowed to lie and roll around, as if on a patch of warm grass.

But, most of all, she loved listening to Irene's mother's piano. It sounded nothing like the dusty, unreliable instrument the church organist, Mr Raynsford, kept in the vestry, or the ancient baby grand old Mrs Farley thumped about on during school assembly. Irene's mother didn't play hymns – 'When I Survey the Wondrous Cross'; 'There Is a Green Hill'; 'Dear Lord and Father of Mankind': all the tunes Maria had heard since infancy. Irene's mother played music with no words. Music that rose and surged and soared, and then fell away to nothing. Music that seemed to pour from Irene's mother's fingers as they moved over the keys: forming first one pattern and then another, according to no will, it seemed to Maria, other than their own.

Often, as her mother played, Irene would grow restless; she would shift and fidget on the sofa, or lean over and whisper in Maria's ear, 'Let's go and play with Hammy.'

Maria would shake her head. 'No. I'm listening.'

Sometimes, when she had finished, Irene's mother would sit quietly for a moment, her head bent forward, resting against the cool wooden body of the piano. Then Maria would want to ask her to play again. But Irene would ask for ice cream, or one of Irene's brothers would appear in the doorway, and Irene's mother would get up from the piano, close the lid, and Maria would be filled with a strange sense of loss that she was too young to understand.

One afternoon, while waiting for Irene to retrieve her dolls from her room (she had four, each with a different hairstyle and outfit, and would usually permit Maria to play with the second prettiest, a blue-eyed blonde named Sylvia), Maria stood in the hallway, watching the piano through the open door to the front room.

Suddenly, she found herself walking in, lifting the lid, and fitting her small hand-span to the cool ivory of the keys.

She didn't press down at first, afraid of making a noise – the children weren't supposed to touch the piano, or to enter the front room alone. But then her fingers seemed to move without her permission, and a fractured blur of noise came up from the belly of the instrument.

Maria jumped back. Irene, coming in with the dolls, let out a gasp. 'What are you *doing?*'

Irene's mother came in then, too. She walked up to the piano; gently, she closed its wooden lid.

Maria hung back, waiting to be scolded, but Irene's mother bent down to her, took her hand. 'I did ask you not to touch the piano, Maria. But I can see that you're drawn to it. Would you like me to teach you to play? I tried to teach Irene, and the boys, but they all got bored and gave up.' To Irene, she added, 'Didn't you, love?'

Irene shrugged, and looked cross.

'Would you like that, Maria?' Irene's mother said again. She was still holding her hand. Maria nodded, and in that moment, she was filled with a love for Irene's mother so pure, so strong, that she wished she could stay there for ever, in that yellow room, with the warmth of Irene's mother's hand in hers.

'We must ask your mother, then, when she comes to collect you,' Irene's mother said, and Maria's spirits plummeted: surely her mother would say no. And indeed, when Margaret arrived at six o'clock – barely greeting her daughter, standing awkwardly in the hallway, impatient to be gone – she tried to do just that.

'Well,' Margaret said, 'that's very kind, Mrs Lewis. But I should think you have enough on your plate with all these children, don't you?'

Maria felt her heart slip into her mouth.

'Oh, they keep me busy,' Irene's mother said lightly. 'And I can't promise to turn Maria into the next Myra Hess. But I'll teach her a few scales. Then, if she takes to it, perhaps you might like to find her a proper teacher?'

Margaret gave a tired smile. 'Well, as I say, that really is very kind of you. Thank you. If you're absolutely sure you can spare the time.'

That night, after Margaret had tucked her into bed, Maria imagined it was not her own mother crossing the carpet, closing the door behind her, but Irene's: cool-skinned and sweet-smelling, and drawing after her the soft, pealing music of her piano.

Maria liked watching her father in church. She saw him, there, as a man distinct from the father at home, with his slippers and reading-glasses, his *Daily Telegraph*, the sweet, bemused expression he wore as Maria's mother crashed and thundered around the kitchen, or fell into implacable silence, lying motionless for hours behind the closed bedroom door.

It was the unpredictability of Margaret's moods – there were also weeks when she would rise each morning humming to herself, clear-headed and capable, steering her way through days marked out with meetings of the flower-arranging committee, the ladies' prayer group, the parish council – that defined the atmosphere of the vicarage. There, Maria's father appeared blurred, not quite in focus: a quiet man, watching his wife as he might an animal of whose reactions he could never feel quite assured.

In church, Francis was different. He grew taller. On Sundays, he wore a white surplice over his black cassock – he had taught Maria the correct nomenclature, showed her the garments hanging, starched and pinned, in the vestry – and a white stole tipped with gold. She watched him process along the nave, his head lifted towards the altar, and above it, the great north window, which sent shards of coloured light scattering across the heads of the congregation, and she felt her pride swell and thicken in her chest.

When he spoke from the pulpit, he did so in a fine, warm baritone, and the worshippers looked up at him, and listened. Maria, herded back into the church with the other children from Mrs Harrison's Sunday school, would stand beside the arched entrance to the lady chapel, and watch her father, and believe that he was speaking only to her.

She remembered nothing, consciously, of the nights when Francis had lifted her, pink-faced and bawling, from her cot, and walked her up and down, speaking of stories she didn't yet comprehend. But he still liked to read to her, even now that she was eight years old and happily spent hours reading by herself. It was a special treat: after tea and homework, Francis would call Maria into his study, close the door, and take down the book they were reading together from the shelf. They were grown-up books – *Great Expectations*, *The Thirty-Nine Steps*, *A Pilgrim's Progress* – and they would read until Maria's eyes began to close, her head to fall back against his chest, though she always did her best not to allow herself to dive headfirst into sleep.

Sometimes, Margaret would open the door, and stand there watching them.

'I don't know why you bother, Francis,' she'd say. 'They're far too old for her. She doesn't understand a word.'

But I do, Maria wanted to cry out, though her father would only reply, mildly, 'It's as much for my pleasure as for hers, Margaret. Leave us be.'

Once, during one of these reading sessions, Maria dared to ask her father, in the slender portion of silence that fell as he turned the page, 'Why doesn't Mummy like me?'

Francis looked down at her, his gaze frank, clear.

'What a question, Cassandra,' he said. He used her middle name sometimes, when they were alone, and she thought of it as their own, private code. 'She's your mother. Of course she likes you. She *loves* you. But she feels things more deeply than most people do. Her skin is . . . thinner than most people's. She's not as strong, so we must be strong for her. Do you understand?'

Maria did not, but she nodded and said nothing, so that her father might continue to read. As he did so, she settled back against his chest, enjoying the slow music of his voice: its comfortable cadences, its resonant rise and fall.

There was a photograph on Margaret's dressing-table, in a silver-plated frame.

Maria saw it only a handful of times through her childhood, on the occasions her mother permitted her to sit on the edge of the double bed – unmade, the pillows still bearing the faint, rumpled impressions of her parents' heads – while she applied her face-cream, her powder, her perfume.

So rare and special were these moments that Maria experienced them with a particular intensity, each sense seeming sharpened, more acute – the sweetish, floral cloud of scent; her mother's face reflected in triplicate by the three-leaved mirror – and the framed photograph etched itself indelibly on her mind.

A slim, smiling, clear-skinned woman in a knee-length cotton dress; not beautiful, or particularly glamorous, but carefully, painstakingly, put together – her hair neatly curled and set, her legs shining in immaculate, unladdered nylons. Margaret Lyall, nineteen years old, couched in a deckchair on the back lawn of her parents' house in Colchester, the looming silhouette of a man's head just visible above the bottom left-hand corner of the frame.

Decades later, Maria – Cass, by then, of course – would find the photograph among her father's papers and puzzle over it, wondering who that ghostly disembodied shadow had belonged to. Cass's father? Her grandfather? Or an old boyfriend, later tossed aside by her mother in favour of the new curate, Francis Wheeler, almost twenty years Margaret's senior?

For Cass would be familiar, by then, with the details of her parents' unsuccessful marriage, as her childish self had never been. At thirty-two, she would be able to see them clearly. Margaret Lyall, the ordinary suburban girl, swayed by the interest of the man – the vicar, no less – to whom she could look up from the pews, watching his spare, unhandsome features rendered glorious by the dual magic of authority and conviction. Francis Wheeler, the older man, settled on the priesthood after an unhappy decade in the City, looking about him for a woman to make his wife, to root him to a parish, a home, a family. The couple's move to London; the gradual realisation of how ill-suited they truly were; the slow onset of Margaret's black moods, her rages, her lassitude.

No name was ever given to her mother's malaise – at least, not in the child's hearing. And so Maria was left with the assumption that she herself was the author of her mother's un-happiness – that if she could only be different, better, somehow *other* than herself, her mother would be happy once more.

On those rare mornings, then, when she was alone with her mother behind the closed door of her parents' bedroom, Maria stayed absolutely silent, concentrating so hard on not moving that her limbs would ache with the effort for a good while after-wards. And it seemed to her that with each dab of the powder puff, each spritz of scent, her mother was transforming herself, turning back into the young woman in the photograph: easy, unburdened, free.

In the year Maria turned nine, whole months passed during which Margaret did not take to her bed. She was busy again, frenetic with activity: committees, cooking, laundry, church bazaars. And other, private engagements whose object she did not divulge to her daughter, and which began to draw her away from the vicarage for broader and broader stretches of time.

Several times, on her return from school, Maria found the house empty, the front door locked, and was forced to cross the busy road to the church to find her father or Sam Cooper, the handyman, and ask them to let her in.

After this happened for a third time, Margaret presented her daughter with a set of keys, tied together with a length of string.

'You can be a good girl, can't you,' she said, placing a kiss on Maria's cheek, 'and let yourself in after school?'

In truth, Maria didn't mind those hours in the afternoon, alone in the cool kitchen, spreading thick slices of white bread with butter and strawberry jam. In her mother's absence, the house was quieter, free of tension; and sometimes, if Margaret were still not back in time for evensong, Maria and Francis would improvise a rudimentary tea – boiled eggs and soldiers, or ham, lettuce and salad cream, eaten at the kitchen table with a rather rakish, celebratory air – as if they were enjoying a picnic, or a holiday.

On the occasions when Maria did arrive back from school to find her mother at home, Margaret's mood was breezy, even affectionate.

'Not to worry,' she said when Maria nervously showed her the ink-blot on the sleeve of her new school blouse. 'I was terribly clumsy at your age, too.'

Another afternoon, finding Maria reading in the living-room (she was working her way through the adventures of Nancy Drew), Margaret lingered for a moment in the doorway, watching her. When Maria looked up, self-conscious, bracing herself for criticism, she saw her mother grinning at her.

'My bookworm,' she said. 'My little reader.'

And then, one bright Saturday in late autumn, Margaret announced at breakfast that she was going to take Maria shopping.

'A ladies' outing,' she said. 'Won't it be fun?'

Francis, looking up from his *Daily Telegraph*, caught Maria's gaze, and smiled. 'What a lovely idea, Margaret.'

And they *did* have fun: riding the bus across the common, stepping off outside the big department store, pushing open the heavy brass-handled doors to enter the crowded, brightly lit lobby. For Maria, Margaret bought two dresses, a skirt, a jumper and a pair of navy patent Mary Janes; for herself, a Revlon lipstick in a frosted-pink shade called Raspberry Icing, two blouses and a set of mysterious undergarments shrouded in white tissue paper.

Then they had tea, lemonade and iced buns in the café, and Maria looked around her, swinging her legs, watching the other mothers sitting with the other daughters, and feeling, finally, that she had done something right.

Afterwards, in the ladies' toilets, Maria watched her mother apply the new lipstick, blot it carefully with toilet paper, and then draw her head back, taking the measure of herself, and smiling at what she saw.

For Maria's tenth birthday, Margaret organised a party in the church hall.

Maria, Irene and their other friends from school – girls whose names would soon slip entirely from Maria's mind – were set to work making paper chains, while Margaret and the other mothers laid out sponge cakes, prepared sandwiches, poured jugs of orange squash. Mr Raynsford's piano was brought through from the vestry, and the children played musical statues, and pass the parcel, and when they had tired of their games, Margaret – flushed and exuberant in her Raspberry Icing lipstick – hushed them, and announced that the birthday girl was going to play them all a tune.

Maria had been practising; as she walked up to the piano, she caught sight of Irene's mother and her heart quickened its beat. It was some years, now, since her first tentative assaults at the piano in Irene's front room, and they had not come to much: each time Irene's mother tried to sit with Maria, to guide her fingers through the major scales, Irene would appear, sulky and wheedling, or one of her brothers would come through from the garden with some new boyish demand. And so a teacher had been found for her – Mrs Dewson, a whiskered, elderly parish-ioner, whose house, a few streets back from the common, smelt of damp and wet dog – and Maria had been permitted, once a day, to practise on Mr Raynsford's piano. And though her hands were still lumpen and fumbling on those slippery, treacherous keys, those hours in the vestry, and in Mrs Dewson's front room, were precious to Maria; and as she practised, she heard Irene's mother playing, and it was Irene's mother's face that she held in her mind.

That day, at her birthday party, Maria played Bach: the Prelude and Fugue in C major from *The Well-Tempered Clavier*.

Reading the name on Mrs Dewson's sheet music for the first time, Maria had pictured a kindly, red-faced German – a publican, smiling at his customers over beer-pumps of polished brass. *A man of good temper.* And the prelude did seem to soothe her spirits: after several weeks of missed notes and broken chords, Maria found that she could play it, if not well, then at least fluidly, and its arpeggios, rising and falling, began to follow her through her days, and to spool unbidden through her mind in the sweet, unguarded moments between sleep and dream.

At the party, she played the piece through almost from memory, looking only once at the sheet music propped on the stand. When she finished, the silence in the room seemed deafening; and then there was clapping, and the babbling murmurs of the other children, and she felt her mother's arms around her, and heard her voice in her ear. 'Very good, Maria. Very good. Happy birthday, my clever girl.'

She felt her mother's touch, the echo of it, for a long while after Margaret had let her go. As Maria found Irene and her other friends, and danced to the record somebody – Margaret, she supposed – had put on, a great happiness rose in her. So it was true, she thought: that other hard-faced, angry mother had disappeared, and this kinder, prettier one had come to live with them for ever in her place.

Two weeks later, a Saturday, Maria came downstairs to find Mrs Harrison and Mrs O'Reilly preparing breakfast.

'Your father has been taken ill,' Mrs Harrison said.

Maria stared. 'Where's Mummy?' she said, and the women exchanged a quick, furtive glance.

'She's gone away on a little holiday,' Mrs O'Reilly said. 'Nothing for you to worry about, dear.'

She laid a plate of scrambled eggs down on the table. Maria looked at the yellowish mass, fighting a rising nausea – she hated scrambled eggs – and said, 'Aren't Daddy and I going too?'

There was a short, tight silence.

'Eat up, child,' said Mrs Harrison. 'Don't let your breakfast get cold.'

Maria ate as much as she could bear. With each mouthful, she pictured her mother as she had been at the party: bright, animated, moving quickly around the room with the platters of sandwiches and cake. She wondered where she could have gone, and why she would have left the two of them behind. She would ask her father, of course – he would know. How could he not?

Setting her plate aside, she said, 'Where's Daddy? Can I see him now?'

Mrs Harrison placed a hand on her shoulder. 'Don't ask so many questions, Maria. Your father needs to rest. You can see him later.'

Through the course of that long, peculiar day, Maria stayed upstairs, listening to the noises from the rest of the house. The front door opening and closing; footsteps on the stairs; women whispering in the hallway. She tried to draw, to read, to continue with the game she and Irene had devised in recent weeks – Maria's new Sindy doll had fallen out with Irene's, and was now attempting to win back her friend through a series of impassioned letters of apology – but she couldn't concentrate. There was a picture in her mind: her mother, packing her dresses and cardigans into a case, and stepping off alone across the common while Maria and her father slept on. And her father himself, downstairs behind the closed door, wrapped in his mysterious suffering.

By mid-afternoon, Maria could bear it no longer: she slipped from her room, went down to the first-floor landing, and stood outside the door to her parents' bedroom. She placed her ear to the door, and heard a low, inarticulate, shuddering sound. Was her father hurt? Was he in pain? Ought she to go in to him? She placed a hand to the brass doorknob and was just

26

about to turn it when Mrs O'Reilly appeared at the top of the stairs.

'What are you doing, lovey?' she said softly. 'We said your father needs rest. Now, is there a friend you might like to stay with tonight?'

When Irene's mother came to collect her, she spent a while with the church women in the kitchen. Maria waited outside, but the women hadn't quite closed the door, and snatches of their conversation floated out through the gap. *A terrible thing. None of us had any idea. Just upped and left this morning. A note on the table. The reverend's beside himself.*

Irene's mother was the first to emerge. She saw Maria standing there, beside the door, but she didn't chide her. Instead, she knelt down and pulled Maria into her arms. 'Come on, love. Irene's so excited you'll be staying the night. Max is going to sleep in with the other boys. We'll have a party.'

She was true to her word. There was fish and chips for tea – real fish and chips from the chip shop, still wrapped in greasy newspaper – and jam roly-poly. It was all so exciting – so deliciously out of the ordinary – that Maria was able, for a time, to forget the strange, unsettling events at home.

After tea, they played a game where each person wrote the name of a celebrity on a piece of paper, and then stuck it to someone else's forehead, and that person had to guess what was written there. Maria guessed hers quickly – she had Elizabeth Taylor – but Irene's mother took an age with hers, which was somebody called Charlie Parker. When she finally got it, she pretended to be cross.

'Trust *you* to come up with that, Tony,' she said, and kissed Irene's father on the lips. And then Maria remembered her own father, lying in the vicarage all alone, making that horrible sound. She wondered again where her mother had gone, and felt a dizziness come over her, as if she was standing on a very tall building, and looking down at the long, long drop below.

'I think my mother's gone away,' Maria whispered into the dark, when she and Irene were tucked into their bunks.

'Where?'

'I don't know.'

'Are you going too?'

'I don't know.'

'Oh.' Irene was quiet for a moment. 'Well, if not, maybe you could come and live with us instead. But I suppose your father would be lonely.'

In the morning, Maria woke early, and dressed while Irene was still sleeping, expecting that Irene's mother would take her home in time to change for Sunday school. But when she went downstairs, nobody else was up. She sat quietly for a time in the kitchen, watching the clock inch towards half-past seven.

At a quarter to eight, Irene's mother pushed open the door, her long hair hanging loose over her cotton robe. 'You're up early, love,' she said. 'No church today, all right? Let me make you some breakfast, and then we'll have a little chat.'

While the rest of the family slept on, Irene's mother made Maria toast with strawberry jam, and told her that Margaret had decided to go and live somewhere else.

Maria stared at the wall. She had the incommunicable sense of an emptiness opening in some deep part of herself: a void, a fissure, on whose edge she might so easily lose her footing and fall. She swallowed. Her voice was unsteady as she said, 'What do you mean? Are Daddy and I going to go and live there too?'

'No, Maria love.' Irene's mother's voice was low and gentle. Her face, in the grey morning light, looked very young – as young as the woman in the photograph on Margaret's dressing-table. She reached across the table for Maria's hand; her own was warm, soft, with two faint whitish circles on the fourth finger, where she had removed her rings.

'For now, at least,' she said, 'I think you and your father will be staying here in London.'

Months later, just before she went to Atterley for the first time, Cass – then still Maria – found a note on her father's desk.

She shouldn't really have gone in – she wasn't allowed to enter her father's study alone – but Mrs Souter, the new char-lady, had been dusting and sweeping, and left the door ajar while she stepped out into the garden for a smoke.

Dear Francis, the note said. *Len Steadman and I are in love. My happiness has come as a surprise. I feel, with him, that I really might be able to live a different kind of life.*

We are moving to Canada, the note said. *Toronto, we think. Len has a sister there.*

There is no common ground between us any more, Francis, the note said. *I did try my best to love you – both of you – but I have never felt that either of you really loved me. You're as thick as thieves, the two of you. So close. So full of secrets. And Maria will be better off without me, I think. I know I have not been a good mother to her, though I have tried. Please believe that I have tried.*

I have written to Lily, the note said. *You must know how diffi-cult that was for me, and I hope that you will accept the help she is offering.*

I will try, in time, the note said, *to earn God's forgiveness, but I will not dare to ask for yours.*

Maria hadn't quite finished reading when she heard Mrs Souter coming through into the hallway. She put the note back where she found it, and never saw it again.

9.45 a.m.

In the listening-room, the record has eased its spin; the needle returned to its cradle.

'Common Ground.' It was not the first song Cass wrote – there had been screeds of them before that, begun in a burst of enthusiasm, and then fading, for the most part, to a pale imitation of the sounds she could hear in her head. But it was the first song that had really made sense to her.

She can remember exactly where she was when she wrote it: in her bedroom in Atterley, under the watchful postered eyes of Joan Baez and the Animals, and looking up, from time to time, at the large framed photograph that hung above the fireplace.

The photograph was one of her aunt Lily's. A woman – Lily had told Cass her name, but it had quickly slipped from her memory, and so, silently, Cass had awarded the woman her own special, private name, 'Cassandra' – standing beside a brick wall, steadying herself against it, her face cast in extravagant blocks of shadow, like an actress from a black-and-white film. Marlene Dietrich, perhaps: Lily and John had taken her to see *The Blue Angel* in Brighton earlier that year, and the chiaroscuro planes of Dietrich's face – the pencilled eyebrows; the shadowed cheekbones; the thin, painted lips that seemed to brook no argument – were still present in Cass's mind, long after the film had flickered to a close.

As Cass had played through 'Common Ground' for a second time, she had looked up at Cassandra, that anonymous woman in the photograph: not Dietrich, but like her, with the same stern-faced, uncompromising gaze. *Here I am*, the woman seemed to be saying, *and you will take me exactly as you find me.*

30

Cass had thought, then, of her mother, in Canada; had wondered how it was that Margaret had found the strength, so suddenly, to remove herself from the frame of her life, like an article torn from the pages of a magazine. And in that moment – she recalls it so clearly now – she had found herself admiring her mother, almost, for the force of that determination, and the courage it must have taken to begin her life again.

Otis is pawing at the door; his small, fine-boned face is a picture of supplication, and he has risen up on his hind legs to scissor his front paws against the glass.

She can't help smiling. 'All right. I'm coming.'

When Cass lets him in, the cat stands motionless for a moment in the doorway, as if unsure, now that his aim has been achieved, whether it was really what he wanted. She kneels down, rubs his head almost roughly, in the way he likes, and he arches his back, his eyes narrowing to slits.

How tiny he was when she found him, he and his four brothers and sisters, out in the garage on a pile of old carpet offcuts, blind and water-slicked and emitting their piteous high-pitched cries. The mother – she was a farm cat from somewhere round about; Cass had seen her prowling around the garden many times – was exhausted. She had barely found the strength to look up and offer Cass an unemphatic croak of protest before diving back into sleep.

Cass had brought the whole brood indoors, lined a box with a blanket, given the mother water, brought in cat food from the village shop. She'd asked Sally Jarvis whom the cat belonged to – the shopkeeper seemed to know everybody in a ten-mile radius – and she'd said, 'Oh, she's Fred Hill's cat, from up at Dearlove Farm. But he won't thank you for taking that lot up to him. Drown them, most likely.'

It was possible that Sally had been joking, but Cass had taken her at her word. After a month or so, when the kittens were starting to lose their scrawny, alien look, she'd written out a card for the shop window. *Kittens: free to good homes.*

'Are you sure you want people coming to the house?' Alan had said. 'I'll call the RSPCA for you, if you like.'

But Cass had refused: she'd grown attached to the litter of kittens, with their tiny mewling mouths and unsteady legs, and she wanted to see to their rehoming herself.

The people who came looking for a kitten were, for the most part, friendly, punctual, sincere. If Cass had seen recognition slowly creep across their faces – and she had, on some of the older ones – then they'd been far too polite to make any mention of who she was, or, more pertinently, who she had once been.

Otis had been the last animal left. He was not the runt of the litter – that tiny, wriggling scrap of fur had been one of the first to be chosen; out of sympathy, she'd supposed, and the thought had cheered her. But he was certainly the least attractive, with an oversized head and strange, uneven markings: he was black all over but for patches of ginger on his face and belly, like puddles of spilt paint. Cass had looked down at him, alone in the blanket box – the mother cat had unceremoniously departed a few days before, her weaning duties done – and realised, though she had not been planning to keep any of the kittens for herself, that she didn't want to let him go.

The kitten had looked back up at her, his expression weary, resigned. In her mind, she'd heard a familiar refrain, a voice cracked by sunlight and hard living. Not a song of hers, or the incipient budding of a melody, demanding to be heard. But still, it was something.

'Otis,' she'd said aloud. 'I'll call you Otis.' And the little cat, unmoved, had yawned, and stretched, and settled his head back on his paws.

Now, he is stepping away from her touch, streaking out onto the terrace, where the morning sun is rising over the wrought-iron table and chairs; the wooden bench; the pots of bay and thyme and rosemary. Cass steps out after the cat, out of the cool shadow, into a strip of sun, and closes her eyes.

Silence, or something like it. An arpeggio of birdsong. The low rumble of a car. The distant diminuendo of a plane. Such are the sounds that have, over so many years, formed, for Cass, their own kind of music. The only kind that sounded right inside her head; that didn't thud and clash there, ugly, discordant, deafening.

It ought to have terrified her, the loss of music: that gaping hole, that place where once there had been joy, sadness, anger, fear, made manifest, transmuted into sound, now empty, purged. How she had hated silence, before. She had flooded each room with music – her own, and that of others; she had felt, in the sudden shock of quiet that followed the last note of each song, a voiceless fear wash over her, and gone at once to turn over the record, to replace the disc, to switch stations on the radio.

When Anna had been small, Cass had surrounded her with music: placed a mobile above her cot that chimed with the breeze; strummed her Martin guitar for her; settled her on the belly of the Steinway, her little legs tapping out a stuttering rhythm as Cass's hands moved over the keys. No wonder her daughter had woken so often in the night, her cries drawing Cass – never Ivor – from her bed. The child was unaccustomed to silence; her tiny ears had held in them, shell-like, the echo of music, the shimmer of guitar strings and the pulse of drums, and her mother's high, lilting melodies.

Yes, the loss of music had come upon Cass so suddenly, and almost without her noticing. They had been in the early stages of preparing an album, her first in two years. A producer had been found: a Nashville man named Hunter Forbes, who had worked with Mark Knopfler and Black Francis, and had agreed to decamp to England for the sessions. Musicians had been secured, her own band having long since scattered to the winds.

33

All that work had had to be abandoned. The label had been beside themselves; and even Kim had been worried – *really* worried.

'Are you sure about this, Cass?' she'd asked. 'Are you really sure this is what you want?'

Cass had been sure.

She had told Alan to make everything good with Hunter and the musicians, and then lock up her studio. She had asked Kim to take all her records away: her own; Ivor's; the hundreds she had acquired over so many years.

And then she had been left alone with that silence, and she had understood, for the first time, that it wasn't really silence, but its own creeping, layered symphony of sound. And that this – for now; for ever, maybe – was all that she could stand to hear.

The telephone rings at ten o'clock: Callum, calling about the masters. The new songs, polished and smoothed, ready for their long-anticipated launch into the world.

She takes the call in the green room. 'Callum?'

'What are you – psychic?' He sounds amused; she pictures him smiling that slow, lopsided smile of his. He'll be sitting at his desk in his studio – larger than hers, and so it should be, given how much more use it has had. He'd suggested they run the sessions there, but Alan had quickly, discreetly, intervened. 'Cass would really like to record the new songs at home,' he'd said. 'For reasons I'm sure you can understand. She's comfortable here.'

Now, holding the receiver, she laughs. 'Some have said so. But no, Callum, I'm not psychic. Kim left a note.'

'Good old Kim.' Funny how much stronger his Scottish accent sounds on the phone. A trilling, island lilt: he was born in Tobermory, on the Isle of Mull. Perhaps that, too, was why she had warmed to Callum so quickly: the soft echoes of that voice, that place; that house before the shingled beach where she and Anna had spent so many weeks; the rocks and the peat and the sea eagles slow-dancing against strips of cloud. 'You took your time answering. I thought maybe you'd given up already.'

'No. I'm not one for giving up, Callum.'

'That I know.' A pause. 'So I've got the masters back.'

'How are they?' That strange trepidation, knotting in her throat, even after all this time. *Is this any good? Do these songs we have made bear any resemblance at all to the music I can hear in my head?*

'Great. *Really* great.' The knot loosens. She sits down on the nearest sofa: battered brown leather, picked up by Kim from a junk shop in Canterbury.

'Fantastic on the studio monitors,' Callum goes on, 'and pretty damn good on the MacBook, too. I'll give them a try in the car later, and then on the mobile. That's how the kids'll hear them, after all.'

'Kids.' Cass smiles. 'Can't imagine many of *them* wanting this record.'

'Well, you'd be surprised. The Twittersphere, as they say, is abuzz.'

'God. Simon's got an agency dealing with all that.'

'Probably best,' he says. 'You don't want to be bothered with all that stuff. It's another world out there now, Cass. Another world.'

She says nothing, pictures Callum leaning forward in his big leather studio chair, reaching for his cigarettes.

'How's it going, then?' he asks. 'The listening.'

'All right. I've only just got started, really.'

'Oh, I'm sorry – I didn't mean to disturb you. Kim said it would be OK to call.'

'It was. It is.' Cass puts a hand to her forehead, where she can feel her tiredness pressing. She did not sleep well – kept waking in the night, reaching for Larry, and finding only empty space.

'Of course it is. I'm just . . . tired, Callum. And it's strange, listening back. It's been so long.'

'I know it has.' There it is: the soft sound of his first puff of smoke. Perhaps that would steady her, too; she thinks longingly of the small stash of tobacco she keeps in her father's old metal tin in the top drawer of her bedside table. Officially, she gave up smoking years ago, along with so many other things, but there are times when she longs for nothing more than to draw in that first, delicious drag. 'I find it hard to listen to my own old recordings, and I didn't even write the songs. Must be doubly weird for you.'

She takes a breath. 'Yes. It's weird. But good, too, I hope. Like meeting myself again. Or the person I used to be, anyway.'

'You could try writing about it for the sleeve notes.'

'I could.' She can feel herself starting to withdraw. He's right: she doesn't really want to be disturbed, not even by him, not even for this. 'I'll go now, Callum. Thanks for calling. Come round early, OK? About five. Let me have a quick listen before everyone arrives.'

'OK, Cass. I'll see you then. And enjoy today, all right? There's a lot to be proud of in that music of yours.'

Callum's voice echoes in her head as she crosses the lawn a moment later, heading back to the house for her tobacco, and to sneak a look at the mobile phone she has left upstairs in her bedroom, in an effort to avoid distraction. It is four-thirty a.m. in Chicago, but still, absurdly, she allows herself to hope that there might be something from Larry, something other than that card. Something to let her know that they might still have a chance.

The Twittersphere, Callum had said, *is abuzz. It's another world.*

Another world indeed. It had been Simon's idea for Cass – or a carefully curated version of her, anyway – to join Twitter, the press manager the label had dispatched to Home Farm as soon as the plans for the greatest-hits record had been finalised. Simon was a lean, athletic-looking man in his late forties, with short, brindled hair and a handsomely weather-beaten face; greeting him on the doorstep, Cass had felt a rush of affection for him, and embraced him like the good friend he had once been.

'You're looking good, Simon. Really good.'

'So are you, Cass. I couldn't believe it at first, when I heard about the retrospective and the new tracks. It's bloody brilliant news. We've been without you for too long.'

She had offered him a beer, but Simon, it turned out, no longer drank: a fact that, at first, Cass found impossible to reconcile with the lingering images she had of him, blind-drunk, vomiting champagne (and worse) into the gutter outside some industry party. So they had drunk coffee after coffee, and he had outlined the interest that her decision to return to music was, it seemed, already generating.

'Pieces in *NME*, *Rolling Stone*, the *Guardian*,' he'd said, 'and all over the blogs, and we haven't even announced it yet.'

'How did it get out?'

He'd shrugged. 'Someone at the label must have shot their mouth off. We're trying to find out who, but these days, it's like trying to contain a bushfire: nobody under thirty thinks twice about putting anything and everything out on social media. It's annoying, but it works in our favour, really. The main thing is, people are excited. Very excited.'

'Social media': a new concept – one that sounded foreign on Cass's tongue, but was not entirely unfamiliar to her. Over the last few years – the years during which, very slowly, Cass had seen the colours begin to bleed back into the world, had begun to want to look beyond herself, her house, the small patch of land on which she had so deliberately and carefully barricaded herself away – she'd read articles about it; had asked Kim to show her the profiles she had created on Instagram, Twitter, Facebook.

There was Kim, in miniature, sun-warmed and smiling. (She was using a photograph Bill had taken on their last holiday to Nassau.) There – Kim had scrolled slowly down her Facebook page – were the messages from the fans. Hundreds of them. *Dear Kim, I know that great art takes time, but could you please tell Cass to hurry up already? Kim, I've heard that Cass might be back with new material, is this true?? Kim, I am in Tokyo, I LOVE Cass Wheeler, please tell me, is she OK??!* Kim had shown her another profile, too – not her own, but one called 'Cass Wheeler Fan Club – Unofficial'. There was a photograph of Cass, long-haired, impossibly young, her mouth open at the microphone. Cass had squinted at it, trying to place it, but could not.

'Look.' Kim had pointed out a figure in bold type. 'Seven thousand members, all wondering where you are. All wanting you to come back.'

Simon had confirmed that this was so. 'You're the one that got away, Cass,' he'd said. 'Everyone wants to know what you're doing next – and why you've been away so long.' And then Cass had felt a fresh rush of fear: for how, she thought, would she explain it to them, when she could hardly begin to explain it to herself?

Now, pushing open the kitchen door, she thinks, *I believed in it all once, didn't I? That hunger. That energy. That faith. Surely I can find a way to believe in it again.*

'Architect'

By Cass Wheeler
From the album *Snapshots*

I was an architect
I changed my name
With just a pencil and line
I'm going to knock it down
Build it back up from the ground

Oh, a pencil and a line
So beautiful and fine
Just a pencil, a pencil and a line

My windows open like a smile
I paint my walls teeth bright white
And then I rest a while
Rest a while I rest a while

Like a pencil and a line
A pencil, a pencil
Oh, a pencil and a line
So beautiful and fine
Just a pencil, a pencil and a line

Just a pencil, pencil

A blank page
A flag on a ship
A sail full of wind and
A blueprint print print print

Oh, a pencil and a line
So beautiful and fine

Just a pencil, a pencil and a line

Oh, a pencil and a line
So beautiful and fine
Just a pencil, a pencil and a line

RELEASED October 1988
RECORDED August 1988 at Hightop Studios, New York City
GENRE Folk rock / synthpop / soft rock
LABEL Lieberman Records
WRITER(S) Cass Wheeler
PRODUCER(S) David Reiss
ENGINEER(S) Todd Wallis / Leon Brown

The first time Cass saw Atterley, it was almost dark.

She had slept most of the way. They'd left the vicarage after lunch, Sam Cooper helping Aunt Lily carry the bags out to the boot of her car. Her father had not come down to wave them off, but Cass had gone in to him that morning in his study and kissed his cheek. He had held her hand for a long time and said, 'It's only for a few weeks, Cassandra. I'll be right as rain in a few weeks.'

As the car had swung out onto the road, she'd looked up at the house, and fancied that she saw a shadow moving at the window of what had once been her parents' room. But the curtains had not been tugged back, and nobody had waved.

It was three months, now, since her mother had left; three months since everything had changed. Cass had believed, for the first few days, that what Irene's mother had told her couldn't possibly be true: that Margaret would return, that she would come home from school one afternoon to find her there, making tea, or stretched out silently on her bed. But her mother did not return, and though her father returned to work – gave his sermons, conducted his church business – Cass could see that he was not fully recovered. A light seemed to have gone out in him: he was dimmed, shadowy, and would not speak of what had happened, or of why Margaret had left no note for her daughter, and had still not been in touch. No letter, no postcard, no telephone call.

It's true, Cass thought for the hundredth time, there in the car beside her aunt, *I really do mean that little to her. And I always did.*

Aunt Lily reached across the space between them, squeezed her hand. 'You must be tired, lovey. Why don't you close your eyes for a bit?'

Cass was asleep almost at once. The next thing she heard her aunt say was, 'Maria. We're here.'

She opened her eyes. She saw black brick, and dark thickets of ivy, and a grey cat, its eyes glinting yellow at her as it slunk off into the dusk.

'Daddy calls me Cassandra,' she said. It seemed vital, suddenly, that Lily should know this, as if it were the one thing that still bound her to her father.

'Well.' Aunt Lily turned to look at her from the driver's seat. 'Then that's what John and I shall call you, too, if you like. But on one condition.'

Cass blinked. 'What's that?'

'That you call me Lily. "Aunt Lily" makes me feel ancient. And I'm not that old, am I?'

Cass considered her aunt's face. She had a long, hooked nose, like Francis's, and dark brown eyes, like Cass's own. Her black hair was cut into a fringe that sat high on her forehead, above inches of pale skin, which, in the semi-darkness, seemed almost luminous.

'I don't know,' Cass said. 'You look quite old to me.'

And Lily, then, opened her red-painted mouth, and laughed, and said, 'You and I, Cassandra, are going to get along just fine.'

In the morning, Cass saw that Atterley was built of red brick, not black. It was an unusual shape – she spent a while, after breakfast, walking around the garden, exploring. The house was larger than the vicarage – much larger – and made up of several wings that jutted out at odd angles, each one surmounted by a steep slate roof that crept low over the supporting walls, giving the building a rather squat, narrow-eyed look. The windows were odd, too: some of them wide and square and ordinary, and others tall and thin, like arrow-slits, or small and round, like a ship's portholes.

'What do you think?' Lily said. She had come out from the kitchen, carrying an enamel mug of tea; she wore a loose green dress, and a yellow scarf knotted over her hair, like the one Mrs Souter put on when she was cleaning. 'Do you like it?'

Cass nodded. 'It's like a castle. Or a house in a dream.'

Lily beamed at her. 'Exactly, Cass – can I call you that? It seems to trip off the tongue better than "Cassandra".'

Cass nodded again, and Lily took a sip from her mug. 'Yes, it's a funny old place. But we love it here. John, especially. It's his house, of course. His grandfather built it. Arts and Crafts style. All that faux medievalism and worship of the exalted craftsman. John can't get enough of it.'

Cass, at ten years old, naturally had no idea what her aunt was talking about, so she said nothing. Uncle John, as yet, was just a name, and a photograph hanging on the landing, outside the bedroom to which Lily had led her the night before: a man shown in profile, his shirtsleeves rolled to the elbow, bending low over an angled desk, a pencil clasped tightly in his right hand.

'That's one of mine,' Lily had said when she saw Cass looking at it. 'I took it soon after we met. Wasn't he beautiful? He still is, of course. He'll be back tonight. He'd have come with me to London to get you, but he's been stuck up in Norwich. Client can't make up his mind.'

Lily spoke quickly, in fast-flowing bursts, and without pausing to explain or simplify. She seemed not to have noticed that Cass was a child, and that she knew almost nothing about her aunt or her uncle: their jobs, their histories, their strange, exotic lives. Cass had met Lily only once before, and years ago, before she had even started school; she could remember little of the visit other than her aunt's colourful dress, and her heady perfume, and being sent upstairs to play very soon after Aunt Lily had arrived. She couldn't recall John being there. She thought she remembered the visit ending prematurely, and not being called down to say goodbye – watching the dark circle of her aunt's unhatted head as she walked quickly off down the front path to her car – but she couldn't be absolutely sure.

After that, her aunt Lily had rarely been mentioned again – certainly not by Margaret, who would screw up her face on the rare occasions that an incautious visitor alluded to the existence of her sister-in-law. Francis, in their private moments, had sometimes spoken to Cass of his sister – she was a photographer, he said, and Cass had thought of the man who came once a year to her school, lined the children up in regimental rows, and then disappeared under a canopy with his camera. But her aunt had remained a vague, indeterminate figure that Cass seldom thought of – until a fortnight ago, when Mrs Harrison had informed her, over tea, that she would be spending the summer at her aunt and uncle's house in Sussex.

Cass had opened her mouth to say that she would really rather stay here, at the vicarage, with her father; that she and Irene had made all sorts of plans – chief among them, the construction of a wigwam under the apple tree in Irene's garden, with the old bedsheets Irene's mother kept in the airing cupboard for the children's games. And a part of her – though this she would not admit aloud, even to herself – still hoped that something might come for her from her mother: a letter, a call or (yes, she couldn't deny that she imagined it), Margaret herself, remorseful, returned. The soft, caring mother: the mother who had thrown the party, not the one who had once gripped her tightly by the arm, or left a livid red mark blooming across her face. This mother would put down her suitcase and embrace her. This mother would say, 'My darling girl! How could I ever have left you behind?'

But she had barely begun to speak before Mrs Harrison interrupted. 'There'll be no argument, Maria. You're to be a good girl and go and stay with your aunty, and have a lovely time.'

Uncle John arrived just in time for dinner. He was a tall, thickset man, with a wild crop of sandy-coloured hair, and cheeks that flushed pink as soon as he saw Lily coming through into the hallway from the kitchen. He looked, Cass thought

– she was hanging back in the doorway, suddenly shy, watching them embrace – more like a farmer than an architect, although an architect, she had just about been able to gather over the course of the day, was what he was, and that meant that he drew pictures of buildings, and then asked other people to build them.

When he and Lily finally broke apart, John looked over at his niece, and smiled a smile that seemed to stretch from ear to ear, like the Cheshire cat in Cass's illustrated edition of *Alice in Wonderland*.

'Maria!' he said, quickstepping across the flagstones towards her. 'You're here, little thing.'

'Cass,' Lily said as he bent down to Cass's height, placed a hand on each of her shoulders. 'We're to call her Cass.'

John's smile broadened even further. 'Well, of course we are. It's an excellent name. *Far* more interesting than Maria.'

He looked Cass squarely in the eye. His were blue, pale blue, the colour of the Wedgwood china Cass's mother had kept in the sideboard in the vicarage dining-room, and rarely taken down to use. It struck Cass, in that moment, that the china must still be there, along with all the hundreds of other things Margaret had left behind.

'I'm very pleased to meet you, Cass,' John said. Looking back at him – at his handsome, open face, his pink cheeks, his easy smile – Cass saw that he really was; and she felt herself relax, in a motion that seemed almost physical, like a breath long held, and then, quite suddenly, let go.

That summer, Cass and Irene exchanged letters – a long series of them, composed in careful, rounded cursive. (Their last teacher, Miss Doyle, had been a stickler for presentable handwriting.) Irene wrote on pink notelets that carried the faint, not unpleasant whiff of Hammy's unemptied cage; and Cass wrote on sheets of deliciously thick, creamy paper, without lines (she had to rule them in herself with a pencil), under a printed letterhead that read, in fat, bold type, 'John Wiseman, Architect, BSc DipArch RIBA.'

Yesterday, we built the wigwam, Irene wrote. *Max got one of the sheets stuck on a tree branch and it tore and now there's a hole in the roof. We tried sleeping out under it last night, but it got cold, so Mum brought us in and made us cocoa. I miss you, Maria.*

My aunt Lily takes photographs, Cass wrote. *Yesterday, she showed me her darkroom. It's not really dark, but it has a strange red light in it that makes your skin look blue. It smells funny, too, because of the chemicals. She put the photograph paper in a tray and we watched it change and in a few minutes I could see Lily's picture there. (She doesn't like me calling her 'Aunt Lily'.) It was like magic, Irene. Or like seeing a ghost. I miss you too.*

PS, Cass wrote, *Lily and John are calling me Cass now, and I like it. Please can you call me that too?*

Well, all right, Irene wrote. *But I don't see why you should get to change your name and not me. So please don't call me Irene any more. I'll be George now, like in the Famous Five.*

But Irene's alias didn't stick: a few days later, she was back to signing her letters under her given name, while Cass remained, resolutely, Cass.

There were many things Cass did and saw that summer that she didn't write about to Irene – or, when she did try to write about them, they seemed to lose something in the recollection, to turn into hazy facsimiles of the lucid images projected in her mind.

The party her aunt and uncle threw one night: the garden crowded with people, and her uncle's jazz records drifting up to Cass's open window. Duke Ellington, Miles Davis, John Coltrane: John had played them to Cass over the previous weeks, one album each evening, as the three of them sat out on the terrace after dinner, Cass's usual bedtime apparently forgotten.

That night, while the moon rose clear and full over Atterley, she had leant out over the sill, and watched the people talking and dancing and drinking below, until she'd finally slipped into bed and fallen asleep to the high, lonesome wail of a solo saxophone.

The day Lily took her to Brighton: the tall, white buildings and the seagulls and the lady they saw striding along the pier in a tight red dress, a white poodle bobbing at her heels. Lily had bought ice creams, and they had sat on a bench and watched men on motorbikes scoot along the seafront in their leather jackets like a flock of noisy black birds. Lily had her camera with her: a Nikon (Lily had shown Cass the letters etched above the lens), with four cogs across the top that whirred and clicked under Lily's fingers, and a black case that was rough and leathery. So often was this camera lifted to Lily's face that Cass was beginning to think of it almost as a part of her: a third eye, opening and closing like some strange, fantastical creature.

While they ate their ice creams, Lily put down her camera, and talked to Cass as she always did, as if they were the same age. Cass was coming to love their conversations: the words streaming unchecked from Lily's scarlet mouth; the way her aunt would lean in close, her eyes fixed on Cass's face, as if willing her to understand. And when she didn't understand – which she often didn't: she was only ten years old, after all – Cass would do her best not to let on. Like then, on the pier, when Lily said, with uncustomary bitterness, 'Your mother couldn't stand me – but you know that already, of course. She couldn't ever forgive the fact that John was married when we met. *Was* married – he's married to me, now, not that we need a piece of paper to prove it to ourselves. But we got it anyway. Bowed to conformity.' She sighed. 'So holier-than-thou, Margaret Wheeler. The vicar's wife. Funny, really, how it turned out.'

Remembering herself, Lily looked across at Cass, who was concentrating on her ice cream. 'Well, not funny, really, lovey.

47

Not for you. You must miss her a lot. And of course Francis is in pieces.'

Francis is in pieces. Cass pictured her father, then, as a china figurine, lying smashed on the carpet in the front room. She kept on licking her ice cream, which was melting rapidly into its cone.

'I don't miss my mother,' she lied, between licks. 'She didn't like me. Or Daddy. I'm glad she's gone.'

Lily reached into the pocket of her skirt for her cigarettes, not lifting her eyes from her niece.

'Of course she *liked* you, lovey,' she said. 'And I'm sure she loved you very much, in her way.'

In the last week of August, Cass wrote to Irene, *I'm coming home next week. Not long till school starts now.*

The weather was still warm. She spent her last few days at Atterley sitting out on the terrace, under the wide wooden shade, drawing (John, after noticing the sketchbook Cass had brought with her from London, had come home one day with a sheaf of fine draughtsman's paper), and drinking tall glasses of Lily's sugary mint tea.

She drew the house, or parts of it – the ribbed framework of the shade above her head; the ivy inching across the brickwork; the round porthole windows that ran across the upstairs landing. She drew the grey cat, whose name was Louis, after Louis Armstrong, and who had taken, in the last few weeks, to curling up at the foot of her bed, and sleeping there until morning; he would often wake her, ever so gently, by nuzzling his soft, ticklish face against her chin. She would miss Louis, she thought. She would miss Lily and John. She would miss this house, where music played, and people said exactly what they thought, and there were no locks on any of the doors; and no lingering images of her mother, whose features, when summoned to Cass's mind, were beginning to fracture and dissolve.

On the last day of the holidays, Lily helped Cass pack her bags, and carried them out to the car. On the drive home, she left the radio on, and they sang along to Lonnie Donegan and Elvis Presley and Ricky Valance as the hedgerows and the fields turned back into the high walls and dusty pavements of the city.

Outside the vicarage, Lily turned off the radio.

'You can come back whenever you like,' she said. 'Anytime at all. You just telephone and I'll come and get you right away. Your father, too, if we can persuade him. It's not good for him, wrapping himself up in his work.'

Cass said nothing. There was a tight, uncomfortable feeling in her chest.

'Right.' Lily's voice was falsely bright. 'Let's get you home, then.'

Inside, the vicarage hallway was cool and dim, and the only sound was the offbeat pulse of the grandfather clock.

'I've laid your tea in the front room,' Mrs Souter said.

Lily thanked her, and removed her light summer coat. They went through to the front room, and Cass looked around her, and wondered how it was that she could feel like a guest in her own home. As her father came into the room – looking tired and drawn, but smiling when he saw her, coming over to clasp her in his arms – she realised that a part of her had remained in Atterley, with its red brick and its low, pitched roof, and its music climbing softly up the stairs to her room as darkness fell.

Her new name didn't stick: not in the vicarage, where Mrs Souter came every day to cook and clean, and to give Cass her tea.

She collected Cass from school now, too. Cass would come out into the playground, expecting to walk home with Irene – she'd been permitted to do that, most days, before her mother had left – and find Mrs Souter waiting, thickly upholstered in her woollen greatcoat, her frizzy hair covered by that ugly yellow wrap.

'That's quite enough of your silly business,' Mrs Souter said a few days after Cass's return from Atterley, when she refused to answer to 'Maria'. 'Your Christian name is Maria, and that's what it will remain.'

Oh, how Cass hated Mrs Souter, with her red chilblained hands and perpetual stench of bleach and carbolic soap. How she hated the way Mrs Harrison, with her thin, wrinkled face and her white gloves, regarded her with a blend of pity and frustration that, to Cass, made the woman look as if she was struggling with trapped wind.

'You poor thing,' Mrs Harrison said frequently. 'You poor, poor little motherless thing.'

Cass, then, would grow quietly furious, wanting to shout back, 'I'm not poor at all! She never cared about me. I don't *ever* want to see her again!' It would seem miraculous to her, later, that she managed to restrain herself.

Irene she still loved, and Irene's mother, and even doddery old Mrs Dewson, whom she still visited for piano lessons, now the happiest hour in each passing week. And she loved her father, naturally; but the sense that had come over Cass as she sat with him and her aunt Lily in the front room – the unnerving feeling that she was watching her father disappear before her eyes, like a pencil drawing gradually erased – grew stronger over the next few years. In church on Sundays, Francis no longer walked tall and proud: he was a faint, shrunken man, a shadow of his former self. (Cass heard this phrase many times on the lips of the church ladies.) His voice no longer boomed and commanded from the pulpit; it lurched and fell away, and the worshippers grew bored, and shifted in their seats. Some of them even decided to take their communion elsewhere; by the year Cass turned twelve, she was growing accustomed to seeing half the church pews empty.

At home, too, Francis remained distant, remote. He no longer read to her – she was too old now, perhaps, for that, but still she longed for those sessions in his study, the book in his hand, the soporific rise and fall of her father's voice. She was simply longing, in fact, for him – for the nearness of him, for their old familiar intimacy, and the comfort she might take in the knowledge that he, at least, loved her; and that she might offer him in turn. Margaret had left them both, had she not? And so why could he not turn, in the face of their shared loss, to his daughter, and draw her close?

During the evenings, then, and on long Saturday afternoons, she took to following her father from room to room – from the kitchen, where they sat in near silence, eating the meal Mrs Souter had left out for them (the dining-room was hardly ever used any more), to the living-room, where Francis might sit for a half-hour with his *Daily Telegraph* and his mug of tea. Cass would take up a book, sit opposite him in her mother's armchair, looking up at her father from time to time; and after a while, he would return her gaze, and gently, kindly, say, 'Cassandra, haven't you something to be getting on with? Homework, perhaps? I do hate to think of you getting bored.'

How close she came, so many times, to voicing the words that gushed and gathered in her throat. *Why did she leave us? Why didn't you try to stop her? Why did she leave me behind? What are we going to do now?* But each time, fear gripped her – the fear that her father might collapse under the weight of them, and it would be her fault. *Your father is in pieces*, Lily had said. She saw him, now, as something fragile, in need of protection; and so she said nothing. With each dismissal, she slunk off upstairs to her room; and a few moments later, she would hear the door of her father's study swinging shut.

He was spending much of his time in there, and she was at a loss to understand what he was doing – writing his sermons, she supposed, as he always had, though when he stood up in church, his thoughts, once so lucid and clear, seemed poorly organised, scattergun. And when she knocked on the study door – she would sometimes have to rap two or three times before he answered – she would often find her father sitting in silence behind his desk, simply staring into space.

There had still been no communication from Margaret other than the note she had found on her father's desk, and Cass was beginning to doubt that there would ever be. But Lily telephoned once a fortnight or so, and wrote Cass letters, usually with a photograph enclosed: Louis, snoozing in the sun; the front façade of Atterley, rendered in stark monochrome; a blue-and-white china bowl on the kitchen table, sunlight seeming to pour into it like honey. Cass treasured these photographs, and lined them up along her bedroom mantelpiece.

She went back to Sussex for other holidays. Their first Christmas without Margaret, when her father came with her, and his presence there seemed jarring, like a character from one book stepping into the pages of another. And the following summer, though just for a week, as John and Lily were to spend the rest of August with friends in the south of France.

Each time she caught sight of Atterley – those high redbrick walls; those tall arrow-slit windows and round portholes – Cass felt the same rush of excitement, the same sense that here was light, and colour, and noise, while in the vicarage there was only sadness, and shadows, and silence.

On Cass's thirteenth birthday, she received a package from Canada.

It was evening when she opened it. Irene's mother had hosted a birthday tea at her house, with finger sandwiches and cake, and 'Please Please Me' by the Beatles – Irene's present to Cass – playing on repeat in the front room.

Her father had not been invited – it had been a girls' party, really, though Irene's brothers (grown tall and handsome by now) had hung around, causing much fluttering and preening. And when Cass arrived back at the vicarage, she found that another tea had been laid out. Sausage rolls, and salted crisps, and a Victoria sponge studded with thirteen silver candles.

'Thank you,' Cass said, wondering how on earth she would eat another thing. 'But I had tea at Irene's, Dad.'

'Well.' Francis was hovering in the doorway, holding a present wrapped in blue paper. 'Perhaps you can manage a little something.'

She smiled: it was so much more than she had expected, and she would not let him down. 'Of course, Dad. It looks wonderful.'

She cut herself a slice of cake, and another for her father, and then opened her gift: a handsome edition of *Great Expectations*, bound in tooled green leather. Inside, on the ornate frontispiece, Francis had written, *For my daughter, Cassandra, on her thirteenth birthday. From her loving father.*

'I know how much you enjoyed it when we read it together,' Francis said.

'I did, Dad.' Cass held the book for a moment, feeling its weight in her hands. 'It's really beautiful. Thank you.'

He disappeared out into the hallway for a moment, and returned carrying another package. 'This came for you today, too.'

The parcel was the rough size and shape of a shoebox; and indeed, when Cass opened it – discarded the brown paper wrapping, with its unfamiliar foreign stamps, and the address of the vicarage written in her mother's looped, oversized handwriting – that was what she found: a dark blue shoebox, with the word 'Eaton's' emblazoned in gold letters across the top. Inside, there was a bottle of perfume; a jar of maple syrup; a sketchbook, its cover printed with the Canadian flag; and a white envelope. From the envelope, Cass drew out a letter, and a photograph. The photograph was of her mother and Len Steadman – Cass would not have recognised him had he not had his arm around Margaret – sitting on a bench on a broad, white-painted porch.

In her mother's arms, there was a small, blanket-wrapped bundle, its tiny hands just visible.

She turned over the photograph. On the back, Margaret had written, *Your sister, Josephine. She looks so much like you did when you were born.* Underneath, with a different pen – black ink, rather than blue – she had added, simply, *I'm sorry, Maria. I really am.*

Cass tried to picture her mother, pink-painted lips drawn taut as she resolved, at the last moment, to add that message – so small, so inadequate – and found that she could not quite summon the precise composition of her features.

She placed the photograph back inside the envelope, and the envelope inside the box, alongside the perfume, the syrup, the sketchpad. And then, quite calmly and clearly, she said to her father, 'I don't want any of this, Dad. Please throw it all away.'

After that, something changed in Cass; something inside her seemed to thicken and harden. She can remember it so clearly, even now, all these decades later: that new sense of distance; the way she began to see herself moving ghostlike through the days, impassive, impermeable.

She no longer answered to the name Maria. She would simply ignore Mrs Souter, and Mrs Harrison, and her teachers (she and Irene had gone up to the girls' grammar school two years before) until they all eventually gave up, and were left with no choice but to adopt the name she wished to use.

She tugged her school skirt shorter, tucking the excess fabric up over the waistband. She practised applying kohl pencil in the loos – thickly, with an upturned flick at each corner – and learnt to smoke, and stopped bothering to listen in class. She perfected an expression of slow-lidded indifference, as if her teachers were of no more interest to her, now, than a chorus of yapping dogs.

She still applied herself in art lessons. Her art teacher, Mr

Evans – a sweet-natured, rather rumpled-looking man in his early thirties, with whom several of the pupils believed themselves to be in love – said she had 'real potential', and despite herself, she remained thirsty for his praise.

She continued to visit Mrs Dewson for her piano lessons, and did not give up her place in the school choir. But she shifted her position to the back row, rolling her eyes as the choir mistress handed out the song sheets. A hymn, inevitably – Cass no longer found any comfort in the sacred songs of her childhood – or some crass reworking of a big-band number from thirty years before. 'Chattanooga Choo-Choo'; 'Blue Moon'; 'Tea for Two'. How tedious it all was – how *obvious*. Nothing like the music she had begun to listen to in her room on the radio, after her father had gone to bed. Bob Dylan. The Beatles. The Kingsmen. That music – its beat, its urgency, its frenetic hue and cry – seeming to be the only thing that could stir her to feel anything at all.

In 1964, the year she turned fourteen, Cass began spending less time with Irene. A coven of girls in the year above invited her to join their lunchtime sessions smoking at the bus stop on the east side of the common. Chief among them was a slender, almond-eyed girl named Julia Adams, who wanted to be a model, and was rumoured to have already gone all the way.

It was with Julia that Cass met the boy they called Nanook of the North. (She never did learn why: his real name was Kevin Dowd.) He wore a green anorak with a fur-lined hood, and Hush Puppies, and rode a scooter to which he had attached sixteen wing mirrors, eight on each side, so that when Cass rode pillion, she could see sixteen fragmented reflections of herself, her long blonde hair flying out behind her.

Kevin was eighteen, and no longer went to school, so he could see no reason why Cass should keep going, either. He took her to rhythm-and-blues clubs – he disdained the rock bands she was beginning to love – where Cass drew from the palm of Kevin's hand a series of small, round tabs he called 'purple hearts', allowing them to dissolve like sherbet on her tongue.

Some days, Kevin would come to meet her from school on his scooter, and she would feel the other girls staring as she slipped onto the back, her arms snaking around his chest. Then they would go somewhere and park up – Kevin still lived with his mother, and Cass certainly had no intention of taking him back to the vicarage – to kiss, and Cass would let him sneak his hands up under her school blouse, and feel the warmth of them spreading over her skin.

Did she desire him? She wasn't sure; she had nothing against which to measure her feelings, other than the breathless, whispered accounts of sexual adventures offered by Julia and her coterie, much of which she was wise enough to recognise as pure fantasy. But she knew that Kevin desired her – that he *loved* her, even though he had not yet said as much – and the awareness of his desire was thrilling, dizzying, glorious; and she sought it, and kept the knowledge of it to herself, as a precious, secret thing that was hers, and hers alone.

One day in April, when they had parked the scooter in the middle of the common and were locked together against a tree, Kevin looked over at her father's church, rising white and stately across the grass, and said, 'Take me inside.'

Cass shook her head. 'I can't.'

Kevin's mouth tasted of chewing-gum and cigarettes. Cupping her neck with his hand, he said, 'Go on.'

Perhaps it was the pill that Kevin had pressed against her tongue an hour earlier that made her say yes: later, Cass would never quite be able to understand under what other circumstances she could possibly have decided to get back on Kevin's scooter, let him bring it to a screeching halt in the churchyard, and then push open the heavy wooden door of the church.

Inside, all was coolness and silence. The fresh flowers, the polished wood, the dust motes floating on shards of coloured light were exactly as Cass had always known them; and a terrible sadness suddenly seemed to well up in her, and threaten to overflow.

'Come on,' Kevin said; he didn't bother to lower his voice, and the sound of it echoed up towards the high vaulted roof. Then he drew her by the hand, down the nave, towards the altar, which was covered with the starched white cloth that Cass had, for so many years, watched her mother iron in the vestry. Now, she supposed, it was ironed by another woman's hand.

It was there, in front of the altar, that Kevin suddenly clutched her to him, and covered her mouth with his. It was there that his hand began to creep up the inside of her bare leg. And it was there, just a few minutes later, that Mrs Harrison found them, and all hell broke loose.

When Lily came to take Cass to Atterley a few weeks later, she said, 'Got yourself in a right little pickle now, haven't you, lovey?'

She was wearing her red lipstick, and cropped navy-blue trousers, and a white-and-blue striped top, like a Frenchman's. She leant against the doorway, regarding Cass with an expression that was half angry and half amused. Cass loved her aunt in that moment, felt the full weight of that love settle over her shoulders, though all she said was, 'I know.'

Lily leant forward, took Cass's hand in hers. 'Well, I'm not saying I wasn't rather taken aback. I mean, what could you possibly have been thinking?'

Her aunt's hand was smooth, warm, her nails smooth slivers of scarlet lacquer.

'I wasn't thinking, I suppose,' Cass said. 'I just wanted to feel something. Something real.'

Lily sighed. 'Too real by half, I fear. Now, let me have a word with Francis, and then you can help me load the car.'

Cass waited in her bedroom while her aunt and her father talked downstairs. She had packed all her things – her books, her clothes, her stack of sketchpads, her radio and her collection of LPs – into two ancient trunks that Sam Cooper had dragged down from the attic.

She sat on her bed, stripped of its sheets, looking around at the bare shelves, the empty chest of drawers, and heard, quite suddenly, a melody, as clearly as if somebody were standing right beside her and singing into her ear. A high, pure tune, plain and unvarnished as a church pew. Something by Paul or John or Mick, perhaps, caught on the radio she still listened to most nights; or by one of the bands she'd danced to with Kevin in the clubs. Howlin' Wolf. Georgie Fame. Booker T and the MGs.

She closed her eyes and listened. No. This tune was different. This tune was her own. There were no words to it, yet; she had the disconcerting feeling that if she only listened hard enough, the words would come.

But there would be no more time to listen, not then: her father was calling her downstairs. Lily made herself tactfully scarce as Cass stood before him in his study, where she had stood so many times over the last few weeks, as the lectures were issued, the plans set in place. Her father had been angry, of course, and she had understood his anger, had accepted it as her due – at least, it had occurred to her as she'd stood before him silently, chastened, her eyes downcast, he was feeling *something*. At least, now, there were words between them, even if these were not the words she had longed to hear.

But Francis was not angry now. He got up from behind his desk, came round to stand beside her, encircled her with his arms. Into her hair, he said, 'I'm so sorry, Cassandra. My darling. My girl. It's all my fault, of course. All of it. But you'll be better off with Lily and John. I know you will.'

'I'll miss you, Dad,' Cass said, so quietly that in the long silence that followed, she began to think he hadn't heard.

But then he said, 'I'll miss you too. More than you can ever know.'

When she stepped away from him, she saw that his face was wet with tears. She reached up, brushed her father's cheek with her hand, and said, 'It'll be all right, Dad. You'll see.'

Once they were on the road, Lily lit a cigarette and passed it to Cass.

'If you're going to smoke,' she said, 'you might as well do it properly. Watch and learn.'

She drew another from the packet, lit it, and took a deep drag. From her aunt's lips, Lily watched a series of smoke rings emerge, hang for a moment in the air, and then rise up to break against the roof of the car.

At Atterley, they found John in the kitchen, surrounded by a jumble of pans, herb-jars, packets of flour and butter. Louis was coiled on the windowsill, licking his paws.

'Dinner's almost ready,' John said, and he came forward to kiss Cass on each cheek. 'I'm sure we ought to be telling you off, but I suspect you've had quite enough of that. Anyway, I hope this can be something of a new start for you.'

Cass smiled. 'That smells good. What are you making?'

After dinner, John heaved the trunks out from the boot of the car and up the stairs to Cass's room. The door was closed; as she went to open it, he said, 'Let me.'

Lily came up behind him. Cass saw them exchange a glance.

'Actually, darling,' Lily said, 'why don't we let Cass go in first?'

Cass pushed open the door. Inside, she saw the same room she had already begun to think of as hers: the white walls, the green gingham curtains, the bare floorboards covered with a thick white rug. There was something new above the fireplace: a large black-and-white photograph of a woman, standing beside an easel, her chin tilted towards the lens.

'Oh,' she said. 'Did you take that, Lily?'

'I did. She's an artist. Dinah Frith. She reminded me of you, somehow. You as you might be one day, anyway. But keep looking, Cass. What else can you see?'

And so Cass kept looking, and there, laid out on the bed, she saw it. Long-necked, round-bellied, its polished wood treacly and shining under the electric light.

'We know how much you'll miss playing the piano,' John said. 'We thought this might be the next best thing.'

Cass walked over to the bed. The guitar was heavier than she had expected. She held it to her, ran a hand over its thick steel strings, and heard a low, responsive hum.

'It was John's idea,' Lily said. 'He thought it might give you something new to focus on. Something' – she smiled, her tone softening – 'dare I say it, more *constructive* than a mod with a scooter, however handsome I'm sure he must be.'

Cass adjusted her position so that her left hand was holding the guitar's neck and her right was cradling its body. In her mind, she heard the same melody that had appeared in her bedroom in the vicarage: or the echo of it, like some half-remembered tune.

'You don't have to play it, of course,' John said, clearing his throat, 'if you don't want to.'

She looked up at him then, at both of them, her aunt and uncle, watching her carefully, offering her this gift that was surely so much more than she deserved.

'Of course I want to,' she said.

At the record's end, Cass sits for a moment in silence, her eyes closed.

She can hear Larry speaking, as he had in the living-room two weeks ago, just before he'd left – his face stiff, his voice stern, raised, rendered unfamiliar by anger. *Of course I know you, Cass. Of course I know what you've been through. But do you think you're the only fucking person who's ever suffered, who's ever made a bloody mistake?*

Her solipsism, her accursed tendency to look inside herself, rather than outwards, to the world: it had brought her everything, and it had taken everything away.

There had been an interview, sometime in the early years. A pub room somewhere: wood-panelled, dimly lit. The journalist young – barely older than she was – with a suede donkey jacket and a round, boyish face. His name was Don Collins; he'd been flirting with her, making Ivor glower and scowl.

'Cass,' Don had said, his tone changing. 'Tell me – why are your songs so autobiographical? The world's in chaos – Vietnam, civil rights, Ireland. Other singers are responding, trying to make sense of it all. And here you are, writing only about your own life. About yourself.'

He'd leant towards her, smiling, almost in apology, as he added, 'Isn't it a little bit, well, short-sighted? Do we really need to hear your nice little middle-class songs, when there's a much bigger world out there, calling for our attention?'

Ivor had stood up then, leant forward, his fists clenched. 'Hey, whoever you are. That's *enough*.'

Don Collins had looked from Ivor to Cass, his smile broadening. The intention to offend, of course, was deliberate, a stick poked through the bars of a tiger's cage. But Cass had simply smiled back at the round-faced man in his suede jacket, and said, sounding calmer than she felt, 'It's all right, Ivor. Let me answer the question.'

With a huff of protest, Ivor had sat back down. Slowly, quietly, Cass had said, 'I don't know whether the world needs my songs or not. That's not up to me, is it? Maybe I should be writing about politics, or grand ideas. But, you see, I just pick up my guitar, or sit down at my piano, and these songs are what comes out. If people want to listen to them, and it seems they do, then that's wonderful. But really, I suppose, I write for myself. I write to make sense of my own experiences, my own life.'

The journalist had looked up from his notebook. 'And have you?'

'Have I what?'

'Made sense of it.'

She had laughed. 'Oh no, not yet. But then I've only just got started, haven't I?'

Cass stands up from the sofa, slides open the doors to the terrace.

The cool air is a relief. Otis is nowhere to be seen; crossing the lawn, she looks for him, and sees a flash of black and ginger among the hydrangea bushes, still bare and spindly, only just coming into bud. She calls his name, but the cat is set on his own, private business, and does not respond.

Across the grass, Home Farm looms square and solid, the watery sun throwing pale light across its symmetrical rows of white-framed Georgian windows; its red brick; the wisteria bush climbing across the left-hand side of the façade. When she first saw the house, its colour had reminded Cass of Atterley, though this house was a good deal smaller; smaller, too, than any of the other houses she, Kim and Anna had been shown so far. It wasn't as well appointed as those houses, either: the interiors were large, light and airy, but in dire need of redecoration, and the kitchen hadn't been touched since the fifties: the carpet, tiles and cupboards covered a dingy spectrum of brown and beige, and the stovetop was thick with ancient grime.

Kim had been unimpressed: to the agent, a brittle, hard-faced local woman with a mane of blonde hair set in an aggressive perm, she'd said, 'Come on. You'll need to do better than this.'

But Cass had followed Anna – only eight, and not fully apprised, as yet, of the fact that her father would not be coming to live with them – out into the garden. She had stood on this lawn and taken in this view – it was rather forlorn back then, the exterior brick chipped and cracked in places, the paint flaking from the windowsills. Yet she had liked what she saw, and had felt – as she had all those years before at Atterley – that this was a place in which the spring that she had begun to imagine lying, coiled and tight, at her core, might just begin to loosen.

Much to Kim's surprise, Cass had told the agent, there and then, that she would take the house. And despite everything that would happen here – everything Home Farm would come to represent – she has never once regretted that decision.

Up in her bedroom, Cass changes into her running clothes: leggings, trainers, a loose sweat-proof top. She wants to feel the wind on her face, the narrowing of focus that comes with the steady deepening of her breathing, the slow drumbeat of her feet on the road.

It was Kim who'd suggested she take up running: nobody called it 'jogging' any more, it seemed, though that term seemed better suited to Cass's ungainly, lurching pace. Kim had been going out in her Lycra gear each morning for years, and had the long, lithe body to prove it – but then, Cass had reminded herself, Kim had always been naturally slim, even when they'd been out on the road for months, living on hamburgers and fried chicken and champagne.

Kim had broached the subject of exercise not long after Cass had come out of hospital for the second time.

'You never know,' she'd said. They were in the kitchen, drinking coffee, eating Kim's homemade Jamaican ginger cake. 'It might feel good to get out in the fresh air.'

Cass had been sceptical – and, frankly, embarrassed. She knew she had put on weight – two stone, the doctor had told her in the hospital, on the morning they had set her free.

'You'll want to do something about that,' the doctor had said, not unkindly. She was young, as they all were, with flawless mid-brown skin and an ironed sheet of black hair. 'Healthy diet, plenty of exercise.'

Easy for you to say, Cass had only just managed to stop herself from snapping back. *You don't have to see hideous photographs of yourself splashed across the tabloids every time you put on a pair of trainers, do you?* And there in the kitchen, with Kim, she had imagined herself in three inches of inky newsprint, sweat-stained and grimacing. 'Reclusive star in blubbery running shame.'

But gradually, remembering her room in the hospital – those plain magnolia walls; the way she had felt, in the worst moments, as if they were closing in on her, ready to crush the breath from her lungs – Cass had decided to give it a try. Kim had gone out with her, easing her in gently – two minutes' walking, two minutes' running. They'd traced a slow circuit around the Home Farm grounds: from the house, across the lawn to the studio; down to the old barn; past the walled garden and the threadbare copse of trees that the frizzy-haired estate agent had, with defiant optimism, called the 'arboretum'. Then back past the kitchen garden to the house, where Cass had finally been permitted to collapse, pink-faced and panting, on the living-room carpet.

After a few months, though, it had grown easier; they'd begun to venture out into the village, to the road that led up over the high ridge of the Weald. The photographs had inevitably followed – Sally Jarvis had spread the papers across her shop counter, arranging her features into an expression of concern – but by then, Cass had found that she didn't care. She was coming to love her running sessions, the way the frenetic chattering of her mind seemed to still, and fall away; the view that unrolled below her as she climbed the ridge. The valley, dipping gently away towards the silver thread of the river. The dark thickets of trees, the ribboning hedgerows and, above them, the fine white gauze of the sky.

Soon, she was going out alone most days, despite Alan's concerns for her safety. Cass had, over so many years, grown accustomed to the strange, unpredictable behaviour of her more obsessive fans. The old army man Richard McGregor, who'd kept pitching a tent on the front lawn at Rothermere, over and over again, no matter how many times he was carried away by the police. The threatening letters Alan and the security team had tried to keep from her, but about which she had insisted, as a mother, that she must be kept informed.

All that had more or less petered out since her retirement, but had not altogether disappeared. A few years ago, a woman had broken into Home Farm one morning, made herself a cheese sandwich, and then gone upstairs to Cass's walk-in wardrobe to take a knife to several of her gowns. Cass, thank God, had been in London with Johnny; Alan had come to the house to pick up some papers and found the woman with the knife in her hand, slicing through a green floor-length dress Cass hadn't worn since the late seventies. Cass had been upset, of course, but not excessively so: her first reaction, on seeing the mutilated silk, had been to think, *My God – did I ever really manage to fit into that?*

Alan had renewed the alarm system, brought in a new security detail to guard the house. But after a few months, Cass had insisted that she didn't want to live like a prisoner, and the guards (though not the alarm system) had been dismissed. On her right to go out running alone, she had been similarly insistent.

'If they're really so interested,' she had told him, 'in a fat old woman puffing along in her smelly trainers, then let them at it. I don't care any more, Alan. I really don't care.'

Alan had opened his mouth to protest, and then laughed with her, knowing that it was, in any case, useless to oppose her: that once Cass was set on something, there was nobody, nobody at all, who could persuade her to change her mind.

Cresting the ridge – the black tarmac spooling beneath her feet; keeping to the hard right of the road, beside the grass verge and the tall screen of trees; the Weald spreading its green-gold colours out before her – Cass thinks of Larry.

He had taken, in recent months, to coming out with her on her runs: insisting – out of some anachronistic gallantry that, despite herself, Cass had found she rather appreciated – on leading the way, the better to protect her from oncoming cars (or, perhaps, from curious camera lenses).

She had grown used to watching him, bobbing and dipping a few paces in front of her; his long legs, skinny and bare in his running shorts; his arms moving back and forth like the mechanism of some precisely calibrated machine. He ran gracefully, and this had come as a surprise to Cass, for graceful was not the first word that would spring to her mind to describe him. Six foot four in his bare feet, with his mane of white hair, and the large, rough-hewn features that, the first time she saw him, had reminded her, curiously, of Abraham Lincoln: they shared the same thick, emphatic brows, the same direct, expressive gaze.

They had met in May 2014, in Washington, DC. Cass had flown over with Alan and Kim to attend a concert given in her honour at the Library of Congress. Hopes had been expressed that Cass might take to the stage herself, but she had drawn the line at that, and concentrated her energies on surviving the flight.

It was years since she had last flown – this was the first invitation abroad that she had accepted in almost a decade – and the full depth of her hatred of flying (the loss of control, the aircraft's unpredictable bucking and juddering) had returned as soon as they had stepped into the business-class lounge at Heathrow, and she had seen the plane waiting below them on the tarmac. 'Get me a whisky, won't you, Kim?' she had said. 'Dutch courage.' And her old friend had quickly obliged.

She had survived the flight, and as the plane had nosed its way down towards Dulles Airport, Cass had felt a rising sense of elation: there, below her, was dry land; the land that she had travelled so often, for so long. And it had struck her, then, just how much she had missed America. The dusty freeways; the beer-and-sawdust back rooms where they had waited, she and Ivor and the others, to go out and face the unfamiliar crowd. The empty prairies, stretching endlessly beyond the windows of the tour bus on the mornings she had woken early, drawn back the curtain, and wondered where on earth they were heading next.

The Library of Congress concert, however, had been a strain. Cass hadn't known, until she was sitting in the front row in her evening dress (something navy blue, structured and flattering: Kim's choice), how strange, how painful, it would be to hear her music sung by other people, rising from other people's guitars and pianos and mandolins. Then Cass had felt the old fear draw over her – the tightening of her throat; the odd acoustic tricks that muffled sound, making the music seem muddy, over-loud, and setting off that dangerous ringing in her ears. She had stiffened in her seat, gripping the velvet arms of her chair as tightly as she had clasped the metal armrests inside the plane.

Kim, sitting next to her, had taken her hand, leant in close, and whispered, 'Are you all right?'

Cass had nodded uncertainly; and then, quite suddenly, the tightness had eased, the sound levels had returned to normal, and she had begun to sense that she might be able, finally, to hear the songs for what they were: a record of her past. A diary. Nothing to fear or hide from – just her life, as she had lived it, day to day, without foreknowledge of the consequences of her choices.

For who, she had thought then, *could live with such knowledge?* And there, sitting in state in her blue gown, Cass had felt the burden of her guilt begin, if only by a fraction, to ease its heavy weight.

Afterwards, at the drinks reception, she had grown rather drunk on champagne. There, standing away from the crowd, she had seen him.

He was wearing a collarless white shirt and linen trousers, both a little crumpled. Catching her eye, he had smiled, and raised his glass; and she had found herself moving over to him, without quite knowing why.

'Gaudy, isn't it?' he said. She looked up, followed his gaze to the distant, ornate ceiling, an Italianate riot of creamy marble and gold leaf, studded with six broad panes of blue stained glass. 'A grand monument to bad taste.'

'I don't know. That glass is rather beautiful, really. If you want bad taste, you should see inside Buckingham Palace.'

He renewed his smile. His accent, she noted, was well-educated American, with a Midwestern twang. She was good at guessing accents: it was a game they used to play, she and Ivor, when they were out on the road.

'Well,' the man said. 'I guess I must have mislaid my invitation.'

He extended his hand. Cass could feel Kim watching them from across the hall. 'Larry Alderson.'

The name was faintly familiar. His handshake was firm, even vigorous, and this, for some reason, pleased her.

'Cass Wheeler,' she said.

'Of course,' Larry said. 'Who else could you possibly be?'

Now – damp-faced, exhausted; pausing to catch her breath at the mouth of the narrow turning that leads to Home Farm, the sign almost obscured by overgrown ivy – Cass thinks of Larry as he had been two weeks ago, before he left.

Stiff-backed, distant, his lovely mouth set in a grim line, his bright blue eyes – the precise colour, she had decided, of faded denim – looking everywhere but at her.

'I guess,' he'd said finally, as the taxi waited out on the gravel drive, 'I had a different idea of where things were going, Cass. I might be an old man, but I can't say it doesn't hurt.'

She'd wanted to run to him, throw her arms around him – tell him she was sorry, that she would set it all aside and try again, try harder than she had ever tried for anything. But her fear had been too great, too welcoming, too familiar.

She'd sat on the sofa, waited for the dull slam of the front door. And then, only then, had she allowed herself to cry.

'Living Free'

By Cass Wheeler
From the album *Songs From the Music Hall*

I met a man who said he was living free
Nothing before him but the open road
He said, 'Why don't you just leave it all
And come with me?
Who only knows, who only knows
Where it will lead?
Just leave it all behind
Give me this sad old world, I'll set it free

'You know it looks different when you're living free
The sun rises higher in the deep wide sky
The wind it gets stronger, and the air so sweet
Oh, who only knows, who only knows
Where it will lead?
Just leave it all behind
Give me the sad old world, I'll set it free'

And so I followed him and I tried living free
Who could believe that open road was mine?
The wind it grew stronger and yes, the air was sweet
Who only knows, who only knows
Who we can be?
Let's leave it all behind
Give me the sad old world, I'll set it free

Living free

RELEASED 10 September 1973
RECORDED July 1973 at Château d'Anjou Studios, France
GENRE Folk rock / soft rock / pop
LABEL Phoenix Records
WRITER(S) Ivor Tait / Cass Wheeler
PRODUCER(S) Martin Hartford
ENGINEER(S) Luc Giraud

It would seem to Cass, later, that her life only really began once she came to live at Atterley.

Of course, she missed her father: he visited when he could, and she returned to London to visit him just before term started, and about one weekend a month after that. But, disloyal as it was, she began to dread those weekends in London. She was not allowed out to meet friends, and Francis was usually busy with preparations for the Sunday Eucharist. The hours dragged terribly, and the evidence of her father's loneliness – the lone eggcup left to dry on the draining-board; the disarray into which the vicarage was falling, despite the best efforts of Mrs Souter and the church ladies – was almost more than she could bear. She began to invent reasons not to go: she was too busy with homework; she felt it would be better if she could settle fully into life at Atterley.

There, time was skittish, fleet-footed. All was busyness and action: John's new building project; Lily's latest assignment for a newspaper or magazine. Both of them woke early, and seemed to exist in a state of perpetual animation. It was only after dinner, sitting together with a brandy before the wide brick fireplace, playing records, chewing over the matters of the day – a friend in hard times; a tricky client; the civil rights protests unfolding on the television – that Lily and John would fall still, his arm resting loosely around her shoulders, her head lolling gently back against his chest.

Cass would sit with them most evenings, too, Louis asleep on her lap, nursing her own small dose of brandy, made almost palatable with a few drops of water. (It seemed babyish to admit that she'd have preferred a cup of tea.)

She liked to watch her aunt and uncle, coiled together on the sofa; so easy in each other's company, so utterly assured of the other's affection. She had never, it occurred to her, seen her own mother and father exchange more than the driest and most peremptory of kisses. And she was grateful for the fact that Lily and John didn't treat her as a child: they always included her in their conversations, sought her opinion on politics, art, culture, encouraged her as she stammered out her tentative replies.

It was there, in the living-room at Atterley, that she began to have an intimation of another kind of life: one in which she might escape the long shadow of her mother's flight, and her father's reticence. She kept this feeling to herself – treasured it – as she listened to the lovely, meandering plainsong of their voices, rising and falling over the urgent, staccato undertow of her uncle's jazz.

Lily's taste in music ran in a different direction to John's. One Saturday afternoon not long after Cass's arrival, her aunt took her aside and showed her a stack of her own records. Joan Baez, Shirley Collins, Ewan MacColl and Peggy Seeger.

The cover photographs showed intense-looking young women holding guitars and banjos, and a man with a full Father Christmas beard cupping a hand to his ear. Cass wasn't quite able to stifle the desire to laugh, and Lily, laughing with her, said, 'Just listen, Cass. Just listen.'

And so they had listened, sitting before the brick fireplace with a pot of mint tea. The women's voices were high and breathy and unpolished, and sang of maidens and shipwrecks and cruel lords. Cass closed her eyes and experienced the curious sensation that she was drifting back through time, watching lives as they had once been lived.

'Your grandfather used to play the banjo, you know,' Lily told her. 'He taught your dad, too. He was pretty nifty.'

Cass couldn't imagine this: even before her mother had left, she had only known her father listen to hymns, or classical music. Vivaldi. Mozart. Beethoven, when he was feeling particularly exuberant. She couldn't imagine he played much Beethoven now.

'Why did he stop?' she said, and Lily replied, 'I don't think your mother ever cared much for music.'

Margaret: pink-rimmed eyes and downturned mouth, reflected in triplicate; the flowery afterglow of her perfume. Already, her mother's image was losing clarity in Cass's mind, and yet she was always present, a faint outline hovering at the limit of conscious thought. And there, too, hung the questions to which Cass still did not dare give voice. *How long had she been planning to leave? Why didn't she take me with her? Why wasn't I worth staying for?*

In London, she had felt that she might choke on the effort of swallowing these questions; had channelled her curiosity, instead, into anger, alternating with cool remoteness, that sense that nothing that was happening to her was quite real. It was, she was coming to understand, a dizzying seesaw; but then, she was her mother's daughter, and the thought left a bitter taste on her tongue.

Aloud, Cass said, 'I don't think my mother cares for anyone but herself.'

Lily, standing by the turntable, drew the needle down onto a fresh disc. The hiss and crackle of static, subsumed by a fast-swimming shoal of notes plucked from the strings of a guitar.

'Of course you're angry, Cass,' Lily said, turning to face her, 'and you have every right to be. I'm pretty furious with Margaret myself. But nothing is as simple as it seems, especially when it comes to marriage. One day, you'll understand that for yourself.'

Cass felt brittle suddenly, taut; she closed her eyes, and listened to the singer's voice. That high, urgent soprano, singing of a mother, a silver dagger, a bride.

'Joan Baez,' said Lily. 'Isn't she something?'

'Yes,' Cass said. 'She is.'

*

74

Upstairs in her room that night, Cass took up her new guitar, settled it on her knee, fitted her left hand to the neck, and let her fingers dance across the fretboard in silent imitation of the music she had heard.

They had listened to the Baez album, in its entirety, twice through, while Cass studied the album sleeve as if searching for clues. The blood-red lettering, and the bleached, grainy photograph of the exotic Baez. Her features lost in monochrome, her mouth half open, her guitar strapped high across her chest.

The song titles, with their hints of violence and foreign lands: 'Silver Dagger'; 'Mary Hamilton'; 'Donna Donna'. Cass had read them over and over, drunk them in; had allowed herself to believe that if she only willed it hard enough, the songs would somehow pass in one easy movement from her memory to the fluid motion of her hands. But Cass's fingers were clumsy, useless as claw-hammers, and the sound that came up from the instrument's belly was a deep and tuneless jumble.

She thought of Irene's mother's piano, of the discordant smudge of noise she had made all those years ago, back when the keys were still just nameless slivers of ebony and ivory. And she felt, for all her anger and disappointment, sitting there with the instrument she couldn't yet play, a sense of essential rightness: an as yet inexplicable feeling that to sit, holding this guitar, with all its mysteries and secrets, was to see the blur of the world shift, and come, quite suddenly, into focus.

The postcard was a cartoon. Two women – one blonde, one dark – leaning, unclothed, over a hole in a garden fence; the blonde brandishing an oversized pair of scissors, and the brunette a butterfly net. Above the brunette's right shoulder loomed a wooden sign – 'Nudist club' – while the caption read, 'If that smart Alec tries it again . . .'

In black biro, Julia Adams had scrawled a name next to each of the figures – *Cass* above the blonde; *Julia* over the dark-haired woman. On the reverse, she had written, in her looped, uneven scrawl, *London's dull, dull, dull without you, Cass. Still can't believe they've sent you off to the sticks. Went to Margate yesterday on Stan's Lambretta. Wore my new navy bikini. Kevin sends his love.* Next to the word 'love', Julia had drawn a fat, bulbous heart, pierced by an arrow.

She had not expected to hear from Julia. Even as their new alliance had begun to form, Cass had not thought of it as a lasting one; she had, as the months wore on, begun to find Julia hard work, and her card seemed to be addressed to another person entirely – one Cass had left back home in London, with Kevin and his scooter and his purple hearts melting on her tongue.

Kevin, on the other hand, she had expected to write to her – even, in the wilder regions of her imagination, to ride up to Atterley from London on his scooter. His silence, at first, rang loud and reproachful. But Cass did not write to him, either, and made no attempt to flee the vicarage to meet him during those weekend visits to her father. And as the weeks wore on, and those visits dwindled, she realised that Kevin did not mean much to her, now, but the faint remembered pressure of his lips on hers, of his hands on her skin. The fading pleasure of the memory was undercut, anyway, by her acute embarrassment in recalling the moment in which Mrs Harrison had discovered them, and Cass had found herself unable to explain what on earth they had thought they were doing.

And so Cass preferred to put Kevin from her mind. And she did, together with Julia Adams, and, more painfully, Irene, whom she truly missed, but to whom she simply couldn't conceive of a way to reach out, to spool back through the months to the time before Cass had, so casually and thoughtlessly, cast her old friend aside.

In those early months at Atterley, then, Cass was quite alone, and there were moments when the knowledge of this made her head spin. Waking in the morning, not quite yet remembering where she was; returning from her weekends in London, when her anger (with her mother, for leaving; with her father, for not doing enough to make her stay; with both of them, for being the sorry, broken, flawed people she now knew them to be) resurfaced with such violence that she often found herself, on the car journey home, lashing out at Lily, turning her fury outwards.

Her aunt, at first, did not retaliate – she kept her eyes on the unspooling road before them, her lips drawn into a firm line, waiting patiently for Cass's mood to turn. But Lily's silence served only to stoke the fire: Cass grew shrill, vicious, hardly knowing what she was saying, seeking only to provoke. *Why do you want me here with you anyway? Why do you even bother? You didn't bother with me for years, did you? You're only doing this because you feel guilty. You're only doing this because you don't have any children of your own. Well, you can't just walk in and start behaving like my mother. You're not my mother. My mother's on the other side of the world. My mother's mad. She's always hated me, and I hate her, and I hate Dad, too.*

Finally, then, a reaction: Lily shouting, drawing the car to a sudden halt by the side of the road. 'That's *enough*.'

Cass opened the passenger door, stepped out. 'Fine. I'll walk home, then. Not that I've got a home to go to.'

A few moments of stunned silence: the throbbing of the car engine as it cooled, the raucous cawing of crows circling above the fields.

Cass turned from the car, leant against the hedgerow, breathed in its musty scents of grass and warm earth. Then she began to cry, her shoulders heaving. Lily wound her arms around her, and said into her neck, 'No, Cass. Not like this. This isn't the way.'

Gradually, as the months passed, Cass began to understand that this was true: that she could choose, if she wished, to release the grip of her parents' unhappiness, and her own.

She was not alone. She had her aunt and uncle, the parties

they threw, the friends that came to Atterley for one night or two, or even, in one case, a fortnight: that was Harriet, a university friend of Lily's, now working for a publishing house in London, where her fiancé – Lily explained to Cass in whispers the night Harriet arrived – had just broken off their engagement.

She had her drawing – Cass would often sit on the terrace in the late afternoon, as she had that first summer, sketching whatever was before her: a jug of water, a slice of lemon hanging suspended like a sliver of sun; Louis, curled on a cushion; Harriet, stretched out on a wooden chair, her eyes hidden by her white-framed sunglasses.

And, above all, Cass had her guitar. She played for hours up in her room, the strings raising welts on her fingers that turned, gradually, into callouses, and then softened, until they seemed to have become one with the wood and steel of the guitar.

Now, of those months, that is the memory she has most clearly retained. The brightness of her white-walled room; Lily's photograph staring down at her from above the fireplace, fierce-eyed, resolute; her first guitar settled on her knee. The intensity with which she willed her fingers to shake off their clumsiness, to acquire the ease, the fluency, that was becoming her sole focus, the thing that drew Cass from her bed in the morning, and that she was still thinking of last thing at night, when she closed her eyes for sleep, her fingers throbbing, marking out against the counterpane the strange new chord-shapes into which she was forcing them.

In the last week of August, John and Lily took a trip to Brussels – there was a new housing development that John particularly wanted to see – and Cass went with them.

They stayed in a small, dark, cobwebby hotel on a narrow street not far from the Grand Place; drank beer in the evenings (Cass was permitted a raspberry shandy), accompanied, inexplicably, by plates of cubed cheese doused in a delicious spicy salt;

and toured the housing development, which was built of wood and white-painted brick, with roofs swooping off at sharp angles, and concrete canopies connecting one building to another.

'Isn't it beautiful?' John said, while Lily's camera clicked and whirred. Days later, in her darkroom, she would show Cass the photographs, with their textures and contrasts and slices of shadow, and Cass would see the beauty, and understand. But there, under the fierce midday sun, she only smiled, and nodded, and thought, for the twentieth time that day, of how she longed to get back to Atterley, to her room, and to the guitar waiting for her there.

And then, in September – quite suddenly, for in this new quick-march version of time, the summer seemed to have spun past almost without her noticing – there was school.

Cass had seen the place once already, in June, when the headmistress – a kindly woman, youthful and rather chic in a powder-blue seersucker suit – had smiled at her beneath her cat's-eye glasses and said, 'Well, young lady, you'll be welcome here next term. Your reports, until very recently, were exemplary. I'm sure you'll give us no trouble, now, will you?'

Unlike her old school in London, with its high Victorian turrets and dim, shadowy corners – just right for hiding in with packets of stolen cigarettes – this place was newly built, the buildings square and boxy and studded with wide panes of glass that, on the first day of term, were freshly cleaned and shining as the girls gathered for morning assembly.

Cass found herself standing next to a tall girl with a friendly, freckled face.

'Linda Saunders,' the girl whispered as they opened their hymn books. 'Do you like the Beatles?'

Cass nodded. 'Yes,' she whispered back. 'But I like the Stones, too. I can play "Carol" on the guitar.'

'Really?' Linda's eyes widened, impressed; and then a pretty blonde girl whose name Cass didn't yet know, but who wore a

79

shiny red badge – 'Class prefect' – pinned prominently on her blazer lapel, leant over and put a finger to her lips. Linda met Cass's eye, and stifled a giggle; and then the hymn started – 'Dear Lord and Father of Mankind' – and it was all so familiar, and yet so different, that Cass knew that it was going to be all right.

By the spring of 1967, when Cass turned seventeen, she had grown her hair long – so long it almost reached her waist, and she usually wore it, Rapunzel-like, in a long plait, coiled across her left shoulder – and learnt, after many failed attempts in her bedroom mirror, to paint her lips red.

She had acquired ten O-levels – six of them at grade A – and was taking music, English and art at A-level, with the aim of applying to art school.

'You should really take a humanities subject,' her form tutor had said after Cass had announced her choices. 'History or geography. You're narrowing your options.'

But Lily had shaken her head, and told her niece to take no notice. 'Choose the subjects you're really passionate about, Cass. The art schools won't care a jot whether you've taken history or geography or astrophysics if they can see you're any good. And you *are* good.'

Cass could, by now, speak passable French – decent enough to make stilted conversation with the pair of local boys she and Linda had sneaked out of their host families' homes to meet each evening during their fourth-year exchange visit to Amiens. She had read four Shakespeare plays in their entirety, and several sonnets; a stack of novels by Thomas Hardy, George Eliot and Graham Greene; and, on her aunt's advice, *Bonjour Tristesse* (in translation: her French didn't stretch quite that far). And she had acquired a boyfriend, Stephen Lomax, who was in the upper sixth at the boys' grammar, and had the pale, consumptive look of a Romantic poet.

They had met the previous summer, on a camping trip to Chanctonbury Ring. Linda and Cass had begun to spend a good deal of time with Linda's older brother, James, owing to the fact that he was permitted to drive their parents' car, and was their most accessible conduit to the other grammar-school boys. James had heard that Chanctonbury, once an ancient burial ground, was haunted – possibly even by the devil – and had got it into his head that he wanted to spend a night there. With a reluctance they did their best to conceal, Linda and Cass had agreed to go with him, on the condition that he bring along his best-looking friends. Stephen Lomax was one of these friends; and with his black eyes, and his long brown hair just inching over the collar of his jacket, Cass had to admit that James had been true to his word.

Stephen had kissed her as the sun rose, after a night that had begun with the boys running seven times anti-clockwise round the tall circle of beech trees, summoning the devil. Lucifer had not chosen to respond; but an hour or so after they'd all bedded down – the moon already high and full and seeping down through the densely knitted branches – they'd been woken by a series of high-pitched shrieks that nobody would admit to having made. The sound – unearthly, searing – had raised goosebumps on Cass's skin, and Stephen, taking advantage of the general hysteria, had shifted over to her in his sleeping-bag, rolled a joint with swift, practised fingers, and offered her a smoke. Hours later, when he'd reached for her in the cool bluish morning light, Cass had tasted the grass on his breath, and her own, as they kissed.

Stephen's interests lay in science – he'd won the school founders' prize for biology four years in a row, and he planned to become a biomedical scientist, specialising in haematology. But he loved music, too – he worshipped the Byrds, Pink Floyd and a new band from San Francisco called Jefferson Airplane, whose debut LP he had managed to acquire, on import, through a record dealer in Brighton. His intention, after A-levels, was to apply to Stanford, and immerse himself in the California scene.

Stephen's parents disapproved – they couldn't see what on earth was wrong with Oxford or Cambridge – but Lily and John considered his plans eminently sensible.

'It's all happening over there, Stephen,' John said. 'Why not go and be a part of it?'

'Your aunt and uncle are really something,' Stephen said later as they lay on her narrow bed. (Lily and John didn't mind the two of them spending long periods upstairs, either, as long as they were, in Lily's words, 'careful, responsible and respectful. After all,' her aunt had added the first time they'd discussed the matter, 'I'd rather you were here with him than off who knows where. Just don't, for God's sake, tell your father.')

'They are, aren't they?' Cass said, and she fitted her hip to his, and ran her hand down the narrow expanse of Stephen's back, feeling the sharp ridge of his spine beneath her hand.

Stephen was the only person – apart from Linda, Lily and John – for whom Cass would play her guitar.

She still spent hours practising, her long fingers moving easily now over the fretboard and strings. And she had begun to write songs of her own – songs that seemed to pour from her, unbidden and unstoppable, in the time it took to race home to her guitar and transfer to her hands the music only her mind could hear.

Most of these songs, she knew, were no good – piteous, embryonic things that, after emerging one day in a rush of enthusiasm, would, by the next, have lost their lustre and be set aside. But there were a few – perhaps three or four, in all – about which she felt differently; moments in which the words and the music seemed to have caught hold of each other, and circled, hand in hand, around a thought she wouldn't quite understand until the song was finished. And then, playing the song back to herself, she would recognise it, and think, *Yes – that's right. That's exactly what I meant to say.*

But Cass still thought of her playing as a private thing: too intimate, somehow, to expose to others' eyes and ears. She did not perform at school – except in her music examinations, which she completed on the elderly piano in the hall – or at the parties she went to with Linda and Stephen and their other friends, when an acoustic guitar would at some point be produced for chorused renditions of 'Hey, Mr Tambourine Man' and 'Blowin' in the Wind'.

But for Lily and John, Cass would, when the mood took her, play; and for Linda, sometimes; and, now, for Stephen. And Stephen, when she played, would watch her, a small, stoned smile lifting the corners of his lips.

'That's really special, Cass,' he'd say when the last chord had died away. 'You should record your songs. I could play them to my guy in Brighton. He knows everybody. He could send them to a label.'

She would shake her head. 'No. God, Stephen – I get scared enough just playing for you. How could I ever play in front of anyone else?'

He was kind to her, Stephen: kind, and considerate, and careful. Never more so than the weekend in the autumn of 1966, when Lily had asked them both to come downstairs, made a pot of her mint tea, and told Cass that she had some news. Her father had failed to turn up to the church to celebrate the previous weekend's Eucharist. He insisted he had simply mixed up the days, been sure it was Saturday, not Sunday – an easy mistake; surely anyone could make it? The bishop, however, was unconvinced. It wasn't the first time this had happened, and there had been complaints – incoherent sermons, lateness, an overall sense, as one of the lay clergy had put it, that Reverend Wheeler was not fully *present*. It had been decided that it might be better for all concerned – for the parish, whose number of regular worshippers was still dwindling; for Francis himself – if he took early retirement.

Francis was to move, Lily told Cass, to a flat in Worthing – a nice little block, church-run, with a warden to keep an eye on things, and only a short distance from the sea. 'I'm also,' Lily said, 'going to make sure he sees a doctor. As you know, your father hasn't been himself for a long time, but this feels like more than that. We'll wait to see what the doctor says, but I am concerned about him, Cass, and I feel you are old enough to know.'

She had nodded, held Stephen's hand. Upstairs in her room, she had thrown herself onto her bed, sobbing for her father – for his humiliation, for his loss and her own, and for her fear of what might lie ahead. Stephen had eased her head into his lap, stroked her hair, and said, 'Don't cry, Cass. Don't cry. I'm here. I'll always be here.'

And so, the spring Cass turned seventeen, she was starting to feel that she might very well be falling in love with Stephen Lomax. And then, one evening as that spring was just starting to slip into summer, Ivor Tait walked into the garden at Atterley, and she realised that she knew nothing about love at all.

It began with a man named Jonah Hills, who arrived at Atterley one afternoon unannounced, a knapsack slung across his right shoulder, and a guitar – long-necked, with a steel plate covering its sound hole, and two cross-hatched metal circles hovering above like a pair of unseeing eyes – hanging from his left.

It was half-past four; both John and Lily were out at work, and Cass was only just home from school. Stephen had driven her home; he had his own car now, a battered Vauxhall Cresta that frequently broke down, but had managed to cough and splutter its way along the narrow country lanes to Atterley. He'd wanted to come in, but she had homework to do – an essay on

Piers Plowman, already several days overdue – and she could feel the faint, hovering presentiment of a song.

Cass had just poured herself a glass of lemonade – it was one of the first warm evenings of the year – and was sitting out on the terrace, considering this as yet formless, tuneless song, when the man appeared: a looming presence, bearded and ancient, moving across the gravel path towards her.

She stood up, trying not to give the impression that she was alarmed. As he came closer, she saw that the man was not as old as he'd seemed: his beard was dark, with no trace of grey, and the deep lines across his face that she'd taken for wrinkles were, in fact, dirt. He stopped a few feet away from her, allowed his knapsack to swing heavily to the ground, and smiled.

'Hey there,' he said. He was American, and spoke with a deep, rounded drawl. 'This John and Lily's place? They around?'

She relaxed a little: if he knew John and Lily, he was probably not, on balance, planning to rob them. 'Yes. I mean, yes, this is their place.'

The man nodded, still smiling, and drew his guitar from his shoulder. 'Back's killing me,' he said. 'Walked all the way from Brighton.'

She stared at the instrument, with its steel embellishments. Its strings, she noted, were raised higher on the fretboard than the strings on her own guitar.

'That's a long way to walk,' she said.

He followed her gaze. 'You play?'

After a second's hesitation, she nodded.

'Well, then, missy,' he said, 'why don't you let me get cleaned up, and then maybe we can have ourselves a little jam?'

Upstairs in the bathroom, she set the hot water to run, poured in a little of Lily's bath salts (how long had it been since the man last had a wash?), and then realised that she hadn't even thought to ask his name.

She peered out of the little porthole window that overlooked the front terrace. He was sitting where she'd left him, drawing a leather pouch of tobacco from his pocket. He certainly seemed harmless enough – but still, she went up to John's study under the eaves, found the number for his London office on a sheaf of headed notepaper, and dialled it into the phone. His secretary, June, answered, and said her uncle was out on a site visit all afternoon. Back in the bathroom, Cass glanced out of the window again, wondering what she ought to do; and then she saw Lily's little car coming up the driveway.

That night, Lily made one of the spiced, fragrant casseroles she called tagines, and they sat out on the terrace to eat, just warm enough in the blankets John had brought out from the living-room, the garden lit by candles. Cass learnt that Jonah Hills was from a town called Clarksdale, Mississippi; that he had spent a good portion of his late parents' life savings on the boat fare to England, where he'd been living for the last year, playing around London bars and clubs; and that it was in one such club, a few months ago, that he had first met Lily and John, and they had issued him with an open invitation to visit Atterley.

Cleaned up, wearing one of John's loose-collared shirts, his black curls drying from his bath, Jonah had an easy, weathered handsomeness that rendered Cass uncustomarily shy: she barely spoke through dinner, sipping her glass of red wine and trying as hard as she could not to be caught in the act of staring.

After dinner, John rolled a joint, and Jonah took up his guitar, and from it he drew a sliding, plangent wail, deep-bellied and resonant, over which his voice swooped and plummeted, raising each tiny hair on Cass's arm. When he finished, she found herself still quite unable to speak. Then Jonah said, 'Well, now it's your turn, missy.'

And so, emboldened by the wine and the hazy light of the candles, she played for him: first 'The Trees They Do Grow High', which she loved, and which she had transposed to a new tuning – one that, to her ear, was more sinister, more unsettling, than the version she had learnt from Lily's Joan Baez LP. And then, not pausing for applause or to allow her nerves to reassert themselves, the song she had begun writing the previous year, and that, secretly, she was proudest of: 'Common Ground'.

When the performance was over, Cass sat with her eyes closed, not daring to open them. There was a brief silence, and then a chorus of cheers. When she allowed herself to look at Jonah, she saw that he was grinning, displaying a set of only slightly yellowed teeth.

'My, my,' he said, taking the joint from Lily's outstretched hand, 'if we aren't in the blessed presence of Miss Joan Baez.'

Cass smiled and looked down at her hands. Jonah leant towards her, the tip of the joint glowing amber in the semi-darkness. 'I'm not messing, Cass. We need to get you out there. Folks need to hear this. They're going to love what you do.'

'That's what we've been telling her,' Lily said. 'But she's shy, you know. Doesn't really like playing in public.'

Jonah, still staring at Cass – his dark eyes fierce in the candle-light – said, 'Plenty folks feel that way. Just got to find a way through it – or find someone to share that fear with you.' He drew deeply on the joint, then handed it back to Lily. 'I know a guy – a great musician – looking for someone to work with. A woman. Needs a voice to blend with his. Harmonies, that kinda thing. Why don't we get him down here? Meet the missy here, see what he thinks. See what *she* thinks, too.'

Cass looked from her aunt to her uncle, her pulse quickening.

'Why not?' Lily said. 'We were going to have a party next Friday, get the summer started. Why don't you stay on for it, Jonah, and see if he wants to come down? What's his name, anyway? Would we have heard of him?'

'His name,' said Jonah, 'is Ivor Tait. And if you haven't heard of him yet, you damn sure will have soon.'

'I Wrote You a Love Song'

By Cass Wheeler
From the album *My Loving Heart*

I wrote you a love song
But I forgot all of the words
The melody in my head
Just sounded like all the others I've heard

So I started again
And wondered how I could tell you
That life looks so different
Now I'm under your spell
I need to tell you
How deep and far I fell

There's just something about you
And I don't know what it is
Your face in the morning
And the taste of your kiss

And the shape that your body
Leaves in our unmade bed
Your hand in my hand
And your voice in my head
The look in your eyes
Says it's better left unsaid
Ahhh ahh ahh ahh
Ahhh ahh ahhh ahhh

So this is your love song
It's simple, I know

Cast your spell on me, darling
And don't let me go
Don't let me go
Don't let me go
Don't let me go

RELEASED 15 March 1976
RECORDED November 1975 at Harmony Studios, Los Angeles
GENRE Folk rock / soft rock / pop
LABEL Phoenix Records
WRITER(S) Ivor Tait and Cass Wheeler
PRODUCER(S) Bob Wright
ENGINEER(S) Bill Freeman / Isaiah Jones

Ivor Tait at twenty-two. A man with long, dark hair – almost black – brushing his shoulders, and often, when he plays, half covering his face in a way the women who admire him – and there are already many such women – consider impossibly alluring.

A man who stands six foot tall in his brown suede boots. His eyes not quite green, not quite brown, and framed by thick, patrician brows. His cheekbones two sharp ridges defining the topography of his face. Beneath them, shadows gather and pool, lending him a rather gaunt, skeletal look, especially when he is tired, or high, or both.

A man whose appearance, and his voice – low, a little faltering, so that those he is speaking to often need to lean in close to hear him – and the music he draws from the strings of his guitar all seem to speak of a sensitivity, an intensity, a tenderness. And yet at the core of him there is an emptiness, an inviolable absence, a void, and he knows it, and he is afraid.

A man who hasn't spoken to his parents in four years, not since the day he left for London, closing the door behind him on that tense, impossible, suffocating house – the house in which the words his father did not say rang loud as bells, and his rages were almost silent, white-knuckled, fist on bone, blood on linoleum as his mother's gasping, voiceless cries floated out through the party walls.

A man who had walked off up the road to the train station at two o'clock on a Friday afternoon, with two suitcases and the Martin D-28 Dreadnought he'd worked evenings and weekends in the White Hart for eighteen months to buy. His mother, Susan, had written to him once a week for a year, on her blue-lined Basildon Bond, and had come up to see him at his hall of residence, wearing her best Sunday dress. Ivor had asked a friend to tell her that he wasn't there, and had sat at his window and watched her walk away. And then, after a while, he had moved on himself, and instructed the university not to pass on his address.

A man who had first heard *The Freewheelin' Bob Dylan* in his room in that Bloomsbury house, on a grey, damp, windless Wednesday when he was meant to be reading Chaucer, and was instead transported to the streets of Greenwich Village with that skinny slip of a musician. Just four years his senior – an older brother, really, and that tough, ugly, boot-leather voice ringing loud as a siren call.

What can Cass remember, now, of that night in May, almost fifty years ago?

The dress she wore – stiff white cotton, with a paisley print, and a hemline so short she'd had Linda come into the changing-room to check whether anyone would be able to see her underwear. (They would, Linda decided, if Cass bent, knelt, sat or crossed her legs, so she would pretty much need to remain standing at all times.)

The way she wore her hair – loose, brushed straight and smooth across her back – and the thick strokes of kohl she painted around her eyes.

The bonfire John and Jonah built at the bottom of the garden, where the lawn stretched away to meet the stream. Its flames rising, red and gold and blue, into the sky as the dusk gathered its shadows around them.

The two joints she shared beside the bonfire with Stephen, Linda and James. The way she grew sleepy and sad, and her thoughts turned to her father in that little flat in Worthing: to how wrong it was, surely, that she was here, surrounded by people, while he was alone, with nothing to look forward to, and nobody but God to comfort him.

The sudden silencing of the record-player. A man stepping out onto the terrace with a guitar in his hand, and a crowd gathering to watch him. Moving to join them, hand in hand with Stephen, as Jonah appeared beside her and whispered in her ear, 'That, missy, is Ivor Tait.'

The way she listened – the way all of them listened – as the man on the terrace said, in a low voice they had to strain to catch, 'This is a song called "Living Free".'

And then he began to play, and Cass watched the quickstep of his fingers across string and fret, absorbed the deep, roiling warmth of his voice, and felt, for one crazy, intoxicating moment, that he had somehow reached inside her own mind, and brought out of it a song that had been hanging there all along, formless and inchoate, just waiting for the moment to be born.

The second in which Ivor looked up, still singing, and met her gaze, and she saw something there that she had never seen before – some kind of recognition; some unspoken knowledge of her that she herself had not yet fully acquired. And then she let go of Stephen's hand, and moved alone across the grass towards the terrace.

When Ivor had finished playing, he looked up at her again, and bridged the small distance between them. She watched the slow, graceful movements of his body as he approached. 'I hear you play.'

It was dark now in the garden. His face, outlined against the kitchen window, was steeped in shadow.

'I do,' she said.

His gaze was frank and level; she had the unsettling feeling that he was sizing her up. She stared back at him, unblinking. After a moment, he said, 'So why don't you get up there and show us?'

Perhaps it was the grass she'd smoked, or the firelight, or the fact that, there in the garden, she couldn't offer him a satisfactory response. Or perhaps she had sensed, in this stranger, a challenge, to which she was determined to prove herself fit:

later, she wouldn't quite be able to decide what had made her go upstairs to her room, pick up her guitar, and bring it back down to the terrace.

The crowd that had gathered to watch Ivor had drifted back. Some were standing, others sitting cross-legged on cushions – she saw Linda, Stephen and James among them, passing a freshly rolled joint from hand to hand – as Jonah's fingers moved over those tight steel strings, and his voice sent its rough Southern blues shimmering into the Sussex air.

At the song's end, Jonah stood for a moment with his eyes closed. Opening them, he saw Cass, and her guitar. 'And now, would you all please welcome to the stage our very own Miss Cassandra Wheeler!'

At that moment, her courage almost failed her. She shook her head, prepared to run, but Lily placed a hand on the small of her back, and across the terrace she saw Stephen nudging Linda, and beaming his encouragement.

'Go on, darling,' Lily said, and she went.

Yet it was not Lily, Stephen or Linda Cass saw as she stepped into the centre of the circle, slipped the strap of her guitar over her neck, and settled its weight across her shoulders, but that tall, long-haired man who had played so beautifully, and who was watching her, now, with that same assessing stare. Her opening chord was an affirmative answer to that stare, but as the song grew and swelled, she forgot him, forgot everyone around her. She was alone, with her guitar, and the music that had come to her, up in her room – and that now, for the first time, she understood would only ever really exist in the act of sharing: in a moment such as this, with the upturned faces of the people she knew – and many she didn't – watching her, and listening, drinking her music in.

She played four songs straight through, without pausing for breath. At the last chord, applause rose from the crowd. Stephen got up from the floor, kissed her on the mouth, and reclaimed her hand. But Ivor kept his distance, and through the rest of the night, she made no effort to approach him, though she was constantly aware of his presence, as if of a radio frequency to which she had only just become attuned. And then, hours later – it was three a.m. and the party was winding down – Ivor was suddenly there, in the hallway beside her, placing a hand on her arm.

'You're good, you know,' he said. 'Really good.'

'Thank you.' She looked down at his hand.

'I've been on the circuit a few years. Heard a lot of singers. You've got something, Cass.'

Her name sounded different on his lips: that of a woman, not a girl. His face had seemed hard-angled before, out there in the garden – stern, even; certainly not friendly – but his expression seemed to have softened. His hair was dishevelled, as if he had only just woken up, and she saw that there was a tiny scar, barely wider and longer than a penny turned on its side, running from the corner of his right eye. He was, she noted, a little stooped – he carried himself like a man not entirely at ease with his height – and his skin, in the dim light of the hallway, had a rather sickly pallor. And yet it occurred to her, suddenly and clearly, that she had never seen anyone so beautiful.

'So do you,' she said.

'What are you – sixteen?'

She was indignant. 'Seventeen.'

Ivor nodded, removed his hand from her arm, then placed it, quite gently, on her face, as if mapping the curve of her cheek. And then, just as quickly as he had appeared, he was gone.

He returned the following weekend, with Jonah. It was Sunday, late morning: Cass was in the kitchen with Lily, peeling potatoes for lunch, when a white Morris Minor came lurching up the drive. The car was even older and grimier than Stephen's Vauxhall, its bodywork pockmarked with rust and dirt.

'Whose is that, now?' Lily said, and went to find out.

Cass watched the two men as they clambered out of the car. When she recognised the driver, unfurling his legs in their blue jeans, she took off her apron, smoothed a hand over her hair, and checked her reflection in the windowpane.

They stayed to lunch, of course: Atterley so often played host to unexpected guests that Lily almost always over-catered. John talked about the house he was designing for a businessman in Middlesbrough – an ugly pile, faux-classical, with a pillared entranceway and a five-car garage.

'I've tried to push him towards something a bit more modern,' John said, 'or, at least, tasteful, but he won't budge.'

Jonah described the house he had grown up in, over in Mississippi: a two-storey colonial, with a wide wooden porch where the family would sit out on summer evenings drinking iced tea. 'And a fair bit of bourbon, too,' he said.

Cass thought of the cards her mother still sent her from Toronto at Christmas, and on her birthdays, with photographs tucked inside. That high, broad house with the white veranda and the twin dormer windows tucked into the grey sweep of the roof. Her mother and Len Steadman smiling, always smiling, and her half-sister, Josephine, growing taller – once a waddling figure in a padded snowsuit, now a blonde, gap-toothed child in a yellow dress who looked just as Cass herself once had. She could not disagree with Margaret there – the resemblance between them was striking – and she had studied each photograph for some time, filled with a strange, uncomfortable blend of envy and fascination.

With the exception of that first card, Cass had kept all the letters and photographs in a box under her bed, but she still could not bring herself to compose a reply.

'And what about you, Ivor?' Lily said. The meal was over, and they were sitting in front of the fireplace with mugs of coffee. 'Where did you grow up?'

Ivor stared down into his mug. He was sitting on the floor; Cass was a few feet away, on the sofa beside her uncle, and was acutely aware of the precise distance between her leg and his. All through lunch, she had done her best not to look at him, and he had not looked at her; but she knew he was here for her, and the knowledge was like a wonderful secret that only the two of them shared (though of course, she would acknowledge later, it must have been perfectly obvious to everyone else why he had come).

'Nowhere worth talking about,' Ivor said, and Lily shifted a little on her seat, and said, 'I see.'

Later, they took out their guitars, and began to play: first the three of them together – Jonah, Ivor and Cass. After a while, Jonah slipped away, as he had surely intended to do all along, and Lily and John followed him out into the garden. And then they were alone in the living-room, each reading the movement of the other's hands, tracking the rise and fall of the other's voice; absorbing his strange tunings (she was fascinated); her picking style (he had never heard anything quite like it); his angular figure bent low over his guitar (she couldn't lift her eyes away); the pale fabric of her hair falling across one eye as she sang (he wanted to take a bolt of it in his hands, and draw her face to his).

'Hey,' John said when they finally fell silent, and Cass gave a start: she hadn't realised that the others had come back into the room. 'You sound incredible together.'

'Yes,' Lily echoed. 'Incredible.'

Cass looked up at her aunt, then, and saw her watching Ivor with an expression that wasn't quite a frown but certainly wasn't a smile.

They fell into a routine, that summer. Ivor would drive down from London on Saturday morning, and stay until Sunday night. John gave up his study to them for the weekend, and that high-raftered attic, with its wide skylights and angled draughts-man's desk and books on William Morris and Charles Rennie Mackintosh and Le Corbusier, became their music room.

They worked on Ivor's songs first. He had dozens of them, some no more than fragments – a lone melody, a lyric to which he hadn't yet fitted chords. Others, like 'Living Free', were almost finished – she contributed a chorus, harmonies and a chord pattern she'd been working on for some time, transposed to a new tuning.

Ivor scribbled all his ideas and lyrics in a battered black spiral-bound notebook that he carried with him everywhere. One Sunday morning, while he was in the bathroom, Cass reached into his jacket pocket for the book and thumbed through its pages, with their smudges and pencil scores. She saw doodles and crossings-out and, on one page, a drawing of a woman, long-haired and full-lipped, frozen in the act of turning away. *Ursula*, Ivor had written underneath.

The name rattled around in Cass's head, long-vowelled and sibilant, through the rest of the morning (she had quickly slipped the notebook back into his jacket when she heard his tread on the stairs), until she could bear it no longer.

'Who is Ursula?' she said.

Ivor looked up at her; he was tuning his guitar, and his eyes, resting on hers, were distracted, remote. 'A woman I used to know.' He didn't ask how Cass had come across the name. He turned his attention back to the neck of his guitar. 'You have a guy, don't you?'

Stephen, with his ambitions and his pale poet's looks and his declaration of love: he had told Cass he loved her, a few days after the Atterley party, and she had not known how to re-spond; she had thought of Ivor, remembered the heat of his skin on hers as he'd placed a hand to her cheek, and felt a shiver of guilt. She hadn't wanted to lie to Stephen, but neither had she wanted to be cruel; she'd told him she cared about him, deeply,

97

but it had not been enough. Stephen's hurt still lay between them like an unexploded mine. She was avoiding seeing him, making excuses when he telephoned, or drove over to see her. She was busy with her music, she said to him, and it was true – she was busy with her music, and busy thinking about Ivor, and already it was becoming difficult for her to separate the one from the other.

'I'm not sure,' she said to Ivor now, in a voice she hoped sounded casual, worldly-wise. 'I think it's over between us.'

Ivor didn't look up at her, but his hands, fiddling with the machine heads, lay still. And then he said, 'Let's take it again from the top.'

The relaxed attitude Lily had displayed when it came to Cass and Stephen's sharing a room did not, it seemed, extend to Ivor: the first weekend Ivor came to Atterley without Jonah, Lily made up the spare room for him, and that was that.

Their long days together in the music room were, for Cass at least, charged with an electricity to which she couldn't believe Ivor was immune. But he hadn't made any move to touch her since that moment at the party, and she hadn't dared. And then, one Sunday in July, when the heat in the attic was sweltering – they had thrown open the skylights, and still the air was humid, sticky, their faces slick with sweat – they played 'Common Ground' through from start to finish, and then Ivor put down his guitar, came over to her, took her guitar from her arms, and drew her up onto her feet.

He was barely an inch from her now. She could feel the warmth rising from his body.

She reached up, placed a hand on the nape of his neck, and drew his face down to meet hers. There, where there was no space left between them, he said, 'I can't stop thinking about you, Cass. It's driving me mad.'

She started to say, 'Me too,' but her words were swallowed by his kiss.

That night, Ivor didn't sleep in the spare room. In the morning, they woke early: it was already bright and hot, the gingham curtains throwing a tessellated pattern across the painted wooden floor. They lay together on Cass's bed, skin on skin, her ear pressed against his chest, tracking the slow, steady rhythm of his heartbeat. It occurred to her that this – their love-making, the easy, quiet proximity of their bodies – was also, in its essence, musical. It was as if they were running through a song they already knew: a tune both familiar and strange, in which their voices melded and soared.

He left at lunchtime: he had a job house-painting with a friend, and a gig the following night in Milton Keynes.

'I wish I could go with you,' she said, and Ivor placed his lips to her ear and whispered, 'So do I.'

After dinner that night, John took a brandy up to his study, and Lily made mint tea. It was a beautiful evening: golden and still, the flagstones of the terrace still holding the heat of the day, and a wood pigeon calling somewhere in the trees.

'Be careful, Cass,' Lily said after a while.

She did not have to say with whom. Cass stiffened. 'You don't like him?'

Lily put down her cup, and turned to look at her niece. 'I'm not sure if I do. But that doesn't really matter, does it?'

'No.' She could feel the heat of her anger gathering, as it had that other summer, three long years before. Lily's car shuddering to a halt at the roadside. The smell of warm grass and exhaust, and her tears fresh and briny on her cheeks. 'I'm not a child, Lily.'

Her aunt was silent for a moment. Then she said, 'You're not a child, no. And I hope you'll appreciate that I've always done my best not to treat you as one.'

'So what are you doing now?'

Lily sighed, and closed her eyes. 'I don't know, Cass. What am I doing? I'm making a mess of it, whatever it is, I can see that. I suppose I'm just trying to tell you, because I care for you very much, to be careful with him. He's not . . .'

She trailed off, and Cass seized her aunt's hesitation. 'He's not *what*, Lily? What are you saying?'

Another silence, longer this time. Cass watched the side of her aunt's face – her long nose, the smooth, dark pelmet of her fringe. She loved her, and she hated her, and her anger was bitter on her tongue.

When Lily spoke again, she did so quietly, calmly. 'You know, I sound just like your grandmother. She gave me the exact same lecture when I met John. And did I listen to her? No, I did not.' She turned to Cass. 'I like Stephen. I like him a lot, and, more importantly, I know you do, too. Ivor . . . well, of course he's glamorous, he's handsome. He's a wonderful musician. I know you don't see what I see when I look at him – his restlessness, his self-absorption. I understand that, Cass, but I wouldn't be any sort of friend to you – any sort of *aunt* – if I didn't try to warn you.'

Cass's heart was beating fast. 'I thought you were meant to be on my side, Lily.'

Lily reached across the table for her hand. 'I am . . .'

'No.' Cass snatched her hand away. 'Not when you say those things about Ivor. Not when you start bringing Stephen into this. I didn't promise him anything. I didn't know any of this would happen.'

'But how would you feel,' Lily said in that same small voice, 'if he was doing the same thing to you?'

'How would *I* feel?' Cass got to her feet; she was shouting. 'Why don't we go and ask John's ex-wife how *she* feels about what he did with you? You're a hypocrite, Lily. And you're not my mother. You can't tell me what to do.'

She couldn't stand to look at her aunt a moment longer; she set down her glass and ran from the garden, up to her room, the room that seemed so empty, now, without him: without Ivor's slim, cool body stretching out beside hers on the narrow bed; without his warm breath on her neck as she fell into a fitful, overheated sleep.

And though, by the next morning, Cass was flushed with shame for what she had said to Lily – came down to breakfast meek and remorseful, and was forgiven – she had already, carefully and deliberately, put her aunt's advice from her mind. It was only years later that she would remember what Lily had said that night, and understand.

Weekdays, that summer, were a torment: Cass wandered listlessly from room to room, interested in nobody, in nothing, other than the spectral presence of Ivor Tait. Even in his absence, she could still see him sitting on the terrace, drawing his long, elegant fingers across the strings of his guitar.

'What's it really *like*, Cass?' Linda asked. She had a boyfriend now – a blond rugby-player in James's class at the boys' school – but they had not gone any further, yet, than kissing on the back seat of his father's car.

It was a Wednesday afternoon, and Lily was home early from a shoot; Cass and Linda were stretched out together on the living-room sofa, playing records, drinking tea. Cass thought for a moment, looked around to check that her aunt wasn't within earshot. In a low voice, she replied, 'Amazing, Lin. So much *more* than I'd thought it would be, somehow. With him, it's just . . . natural. Easy.' And then, though she hadn't yet said this out loud to anyone, she added, 'I just love him so much. I really do.'

Linda stared at her. 'Bloody hell. You haven't told him that, have you?'

Cass shook her head.

'Well, make sure you don't, all right?' Linda was firm. 'If

there's one thing I *do* know, it's that you'll make him run a mile.'

So Cass didn't tell him – though she voiced the words, silently, each time she caught sight of Ivor's Morris Minor spluttering up the drive; each time they sat together in John's office, and their music floated up to the ceiling and seemed to hang there, suspended and shimmering. And if she was disappointed that Ivor didn't reach for those words first, to offer them to her like a gift – and she *was* disappointed; she couldn't deny that, even to herself – then she put that disappointment from her mind, and made sure it didn't have the air to breathe, and root itself, and grow.

And then, one day in August, he said, 'I think we're ready, Cass. Do you?'

She looked at him, and loved him, and said, 'Yes.'

He booked them a slot at a pub in Lewes for the following weekend. She knew the place: she'd been there with Linda and Stephen and James for pints of shandy. (The landlord turned a blind eye to the small matter of their being underage.) Sometimes, there'd been a musician on the tiny stage – a shifting line-up of men with long hair and pale, anaemic-looking skin, playing Dylan and Donovan and Simon and Garfunkel.

She had, it was true, dared to picture herself sitting up there with her guitar, playing her own songs – offering them to an indifferent crowd: flat-capped locals at the bar, staring into pint-glasses; other kids from school, yawning, fiddling with sticky beer-mats – and she had felt fear unfurling at the pit of her stomach, and creeping upwards towards her mouth.

But then, that night just a year or so later, there she was: standing beside the bar, guitar in hand, Ivor by her side. Lily and John were there; and Linda and her rugby-player, Tim. Jonah had come up from London for the night, and even Stephen was standing alone at the back, clutching a pint of cider. She had finished with him a few weeks ago, over the telephone. 'It's because of *him*, isn't it?' he had said bitterly, and because she felt that the least she owed him was honesty, she'd replied, 'Yes. I'm so sorry, Stephen. I really am. I didn't mean to hurt you.' After a silence, he'd said, 'Perhaps you didn't. But you have.'

Now, in the pub, the fear was there again – snakelike, sinuous, threatening to slide into her throat, and swallow sound – but Ivor bent down and whispered to her, 'Ready?' and then Cass knew, quite suddenly, that she was. They sat up on their stools on the small, raised platform, beneath the framed sepia photographs of nameless, smiling people standing proudly beside freshly ploughed fields; lifting beer-glasses in the bar; processing, their faces blackened with soot, through the Lewes streets on Bonfire Night. And it was as if the rest of the room, and everyone in it, had receded, and she and Ivor were left alone together, their voices weaving over and under each other in a way she believed was special; not only because she loved him, but because she had never heard anything quite like it before, and neither, she knew, had he.

They played 'Living Free', and 'Common Ground', and 'I Wrote You a Love Song', which they'd written together the previous Saturday, up in John's study, in the space of a few heady hours.

Afterwards, their friends whooped and cheered, and one of the old men at the bar gave a wolf-whistle.

'Doing all right for yourself there, mate, aren't you?' he called out.

Cass blushed, and looked down at her hands, resting on the belly of her guitar; while Ivor looked up, blinked at the man, and said, in that slow, quiet drawl of his, 'Well, I can't disagree with you there.'

Ivor lived in a house in Gospel Oak: a tall, wide, Victorian building, set over three floors, with stained glass in the windows, the paintwork old and flaking, and a long garden overgrown with weeds and wildflowers.

'Our wilderness,' Ivor said. 'Nature left to do her own thing.'

His bedroom was on the first floor, overlooking the road; if you stood on his bed, you could see over the houses on the other side to the heath, reaching green and wooded up to the peak of Parliament Hill. They walked up there, the first time she came to stay – Cass and Ivor and a flock of other people whose names hadn't yet lodged themselves in her head, and most of whom, it seemed, lived in the house on Savernake Road. One of the women – Cass thought her name was Serena; she had very long, very straight brown hair, and a dress that brushed the ground – had brought a bottle of Mateus rosé. Someone else spread a blanket on the grass, and they sat and drank, passing the bottle between them.

Ivor settled himself behind her, his arms around her waist, her head finding the space between his collarbone and his chin. The whole of London was displayed before them: the white dome of St Paul's; the stacked crates of office buildings; the shining, space-age spire of the new Post Office tower. Somewhere, miles to the south, was the vicarage in which Cass had been born, and the church in which she had disgraced herself, and her father. What, she wondered with a flash of something like nostalgia, was Kevin Dowd doing now? And Julia Adams, and her old friend Irene?

'I've missed it,' she said. 'I've missed London.'

Ivor lowered his face down to meet her ear and whispered, so that only she could hear, 'I've missed *you*.'

That night, they played a gig in a subterranean bar near Leicester Square. It was a dive – condensation running in rivulets down the black-painted walls, the floor sticky with spilt beer, and the barmaids haggard in their skimpy tops, eyes ringed with dark make-up and tiredness. But it was also a place where, when the music started, the punters quietened down. They sat at round tables, drinking wine or whisky or pints of ale, and they smoked, and they listened, and they saved their conversations for the breaks in between.

Cass looked down at them from the stage, and then at Ivor, sitting beside her, and felt her nerves – always that same, fork-tongued snake, slithering up in the hours and minutes before a gig – recede. She opened her mouth wide and sang, and in no time at all, it was over, and the people at the round tables were clapping and smiling, and Ivor was taking hold of her hand.

Some of Ivor's housemates were in the audience – that girl Serena, and a tall, bearded man named Bob who Cass thought must be her boyfriend (they shared the room on the top floor of the house), and two other men and a woman whose names still hadn't stuck. (The one thing she was sure of was that the woman wasn't Ursula.)

Ivor and Cass stepped down from the stage to join their table. Bob was pouring each of them a glass of wine when an immense hulk of a man, grey-bearded, blue eyes shrewd in his fleshy face, stepped out of the shadows and said, 'Hey, Ivor, that was bloody great.'

'Thanks, Joe.' Ivor nodded, took up his glass. 'Been working hard. Lots of new stuff in there.'

'So I heard.' The man, Joe, fixed his eyes on Cass's face. 'And who's this lovely young thing here?'

'Ah, this is Cass,' Ivor said. 'My girl.'

Cass smiled, and Joe said, 'That last song, "Common Ground" – was that one of yours?'

Cass nodded, and was about to reply, when Ivor said, 'Mine, actually.'

He looked at her, and she stared back at him, waiting for him to correct the error, but he did not. 'Well, Ivor, it's bloody good,' Joe said. 'I want you guys back here a lot. A *lot*, all right – every week, if you can make it.'

'All right, Joe.' Ivor threw an arm around Cass's shoulders. 'Of course.'

They sat down at the table, and Bob handed Cass her wine. Serena leant across and kissed her on the cheek. 'That was *really* good, Cass. You know, you're a far better singer than Ursula ever was.'

Ivor shot Serena a warning glance, and then placed a hand on Cass's knee, and left it there as he talked to the woman on his other side. She sat silently, drinking her wine; but the knowledge of the lie he had told Joe – of how easily Ivor had dismissed her – had settled in her mind like a stone, and would not be dislodged.

Back at Savernake Road, she sat up with everyone in the living-room until dawn, playing Love and Jimi Hendrix and the Doors, and smoking something called 'sputnik', which Bob said was hash mixed with opium, and which made the walls sway and the ceiling buckle.

Cass lay on her back on the carpet, running her hands over its rough weave. Above her, bright and shining, she saw the face of her mother, reflected in triplicate: a three-headed Cerberus, each one narrow-eyed and snarling. *I wish I'd never had you*, the faces told her through pink-frosted lips, and she felt her old anger flare and catch, put out her arms to push the heads away. And as she did so, she saw their features shift, dissolve, into Ivor's: three sets of green-brown eyes, three mouths denying her, claiming her song as his own.

'No,' she said aloud. 'No.'

Ivor, stretched out beside her, took her hand in his. 'Are you all right, Cassie? This stuff's pretty strong . . .'

She turned to him, put her lips to his cheek, and then, sharply and quickly, unsheathed her teeth and sank them into his skin.

He yelped, drew his face away, put a hand to his cheek, where a small semi-circle of blood was already welling. 'What the *fuck*, Cassie? What was that for?'

'That,' she said, 'was to remind you that I exist. So don't you ever forget it again, Ivor. Not with Joe. Not with anyone.'

Mrs Di Angelis was wearing a pale green sleeveless dress, and silk court shoes of the exact same shade.

Cass watched those shoes moving, as if in a slow, silent gavotte, under the desk, as the headmistress crossed and recrossed her legs, and said, 'I'm afraid, Mrs Wiseman, that we're very disappointed in Cassandra.'

Lily, on the chair next to her, reached into her handbag for a cigarette.

'If you don't mind,' Mrs Di Angelis said, 'I'd rather that you didn't smoke.'

'Well,' Lily said, and snapped her handbag shut.

Mrs Di Angelis uncrossed her legs – another step in her solo dance – and planted them firmly on the floor. Cass looked up at her teacher, at her cat's-eye glasses with their jaunty, upturned frames; at her red hair, backcombed and pinned into a high beehive style that, Cass felt, did nothing for her face, which was pretty, and slender, and currently wearing an expression of grave disappointment.

It was a shame: she had liked Mrs Di Angelis, with her smart clothes and her warm, elocuted voice and her handsome Italian husband. (The couple had met while skiing in the Dolomites, a fact of which the headmistress often liked to remind 'her girls', to demonstrate that they never knew when they might meet the man of their dreams.) And now, immersed as she was in music, and Ivor, and the exotic, sunlit hinterland between the two, Cass no longer felt anything for her at all. Mrs Di Angelis, and school, and her A-level examinations – only a few months away now – seemed insubstantial in comparison: dull shadows of the London life she was living with Ivor at Savernake Road.

'I just don't understand it, Cassandra,' Mrs Di Angelis said, looking her firmly in the eye. 'You are such a clever girl, and you were doing very well. We had high hopes for you, and I know your heart was set on art school. But at this rate, you'll be lucky if you scrape passes in any of your subjects. That is, if you even decide to turn up.'

'I'm sorry,' Cass said, and in that moment, truly was.

'She's been distracted,' Lily said. 'And of course, it has been hard for her, moving out here from London, coming to live with us, and her parents being . . . well, not being around. Perhaps we haven't done enough for her. Perhaps we've been too lax. We're not great sticklers for rules, and we've preferred to treat Cass as an adult, allowing her to make her own decisions.'

'Well.' Mrs Di Angelis's feet shifted again, the toe of one shoe scraping back against the heel of the other. 'Perhaps therein lies the problem, Mrs Wiseman – for an adult she is not. At least, not one who is taking her responsibilities, and her education, seriously.'

'But I *am* eighteen,' Cass said. 'Doesn't that make me an adult?'

Both Lily and Mrs Di Angelis looked at her.

'Yes,' Lily snapped, her patience wearing thin, 'it does. Though if you believe you're behaving like one right now, Cassandra, then you're nowhere near as clever as you think.'

A few days later, Cass packed her things into boxes – there wasn't much, really, other than her books and clothes and records and photographs, and, of course, her beloved guitar.

Ivor was waiting on the drive, by his Morris Minor, wearing his brown suede jacket and his blue jeans. When she opened the door to him, she felt a burst of happiness so pure and true that it occluded the guilt she had been carrying with her all morning – for the last fortnight, actually, since she had finally made her decision to leave Atterley.

It was Ivor who'd suggested it, weeks before – early on a

Sunday morning under the covers, half dozing in a warm tangle of limbs.

'Don't go back tonight, Cassie,' he'd said into her neck. 'Who cares about school, and exams, and all that? We're different, you and me. We don't *need* any of that stuff.'

She'd made a murmur of protest – she didn't mind school, not any more; and what about her plans to apply to art college? Her father would be furious, and as for Lily and John . . . well, it didn't bear thinking about. But a seed had been sown, and in the days she was forced to spend apart from Ivor – those long, colourless days of assembly and essays and choir practice – it began to root itself, and grow. Perhaps Ivor was right: they *were* different. They had music. They had each other. What did she care, now, for art school, when it was music she wanted to pursue? And not the music they sat dissecting for hours in her A-level class – Haydn and Bach and Holst, with its strictures and conventions, its fusty gentility. The music she and Ivor made was real, true, answerable to no rules other than its own. She didn't need an examination to prove that. It began to seem very clear to her that she didn't need an examination to prove anything.

And so, gradually, she came to a decision – one that her disastrous interview with Mrs Di Angelis served only to confirm. She told no one other than Ivor what she was planning to do – not Linda, certainly not her father or Lily and John. She carried the secret with her, and hoped that when the day came, she would be brave enough to follow it through.

And then, on that bright, fresh, cloud-swept morning in May 1968, it seemed that she was. Ivor carried the boxes out to the car, and Cass placed the letter she had written for her aunt and uncle on the table. A letter of thanks, as much as apology; a letter assuring them that there was nothing else she'd rather do, nowhere else she'd rather be, and that she was grateful to them for everything they had done for her. Then she climbed into the car beside Ivor, and began the slow, winding drive back to London.

It occurred to her, as the miles slipped by, that her mother had done much the same thing – packed her cases when no one was there to stop her, left her coward's note on the table, and set off towards another life.

She thought of her father, finding her mother's note that terrible Saturday, eight years before: Margaret's words slowly asserting their true meaning, sharp-edged, irrevocable, and that animal sound welling up from the depths of his throat.

She thought of her aunt opening the letter, running upstairs to find the bedroom she and John had so carefully, so generously, prepared for Cass suddenly lying empty. Dear, kind, exuberant Lily, who had given her so much, without expectation, without once making her feel the weight of that debt.

Guilt rose again in Cass's throat. She put out a hand to Ivor, to tell him to stop the car, to retrace the route to Atterley. But then he looked at her, and smiled, and she knew that she would not turn back. And so she said nothing, and closed her eyes, and let the steady forward motion of the car carry her away.

1 p.m.

Lunch. A bowl of thick homemade vegetable soup; a slice of bread sawn from a loaf of wholemeal sourdough, layered with Fred Hill's good, salty butter.

It is only in recent years that Cass has begun to take a real interest in food: in its quality, its preparation, its capacity to invigorate and console. She certainly hadn't cared much about it as a child. Of the meals her mother had prepared at the vicarage, she can remember only two, served on rotation. Roast chicken, dry and tasteless and accompanied by potatoes that were either soggy and undercooked or charred to tooth-cracking cinders; and liver and onion, a slippery, blubbery confection that turned Cass's stomach, and which she had usually refused to eat, going to bed hungry and with an ear full of Margaret's complaints.

Lily, of course, had been a good cook. Those tagines she had served, and the fragrant curries she'd produced at a moment's notice for tablefuls of people: how exotic they had seemed to Cass then. Now, of course, such fare is quite normal, even ordinary. The Royal Oak on the High Street – once a bastion of 'traditional English home-cooking' – has started to serve a Thai menu in place of those heavy earthenware dishes of shepherd's pie and toad-in-the-hole.

Anna used to love the Royal Oak: they'd gone there often for lunch, after they'd first moved to the village. The publican, Roy, was of the old school: a towering, bulky man, with fists that had seen their fair share of action (he and his wife, Sheila, had moved out from Tooting in the late sixties, trailing rumours of some sort of altercation with the Richardson gang), and he had no tolerance whatsoever for what he termed 'funny business'.

The first time Cass had taken Anna in for lunch – it was a

Sunday, and early; the pub had only just opened, and Roy was polishing glasses behind the bar – he had looked up, performed only the most discreet of double-takes, and then swiftly poured a glass of white wine for Cass, and an orange juice for Anna.

'On the house,' he'd said, pushing the glasses across the bar towards them.

After that, they'd been welcome in the pub anytime. And if anyone attempted to approach Cass – to disturb their quiet little circle of two, at their usual table beside the fireplace – Roy would be close behind, his fists opening and closing by his side, to suggest, quietly but firmly, that whoever it was might be more comfortable elsewhere.

Cass loved him for that, and she loved Sheila, who was fat and permed and good-natured, and always gave Anna an especially large helping of apple pie. And she loved their daughter, Angela, who was almost as tall as her father, and was saving to go to college to be a nurse. As an act of kindness, Cass sometimes asked Angela to come and clean Home Farm, though the girl was easily distracted, and spent most of her allotted time exclaiming over the furniture, and Cass's dresses and jewellery, and the framed photographs on the walls: Cass backstage at the Albert Hall, among flowers; Anna as a baby, waddling unsteadily across the Rothermere lawn; Lily and John on the terrace at Atterley, shading their faces from the sun, the ivy-covered house rising tall and solid behind them.

Yes, they had been good to her, Roy and Sheila. He'd died of a heart attack five years ago. Sheila had followed two years later, and the pub, with its Thai food and its freshly painted walls, is now run by people Cass doesn't know. Indeed, it strikes her now that the whole village is peopled by strangers, or almost-strangers. All of them living in such close proximity, and she barricaded away behind these high stone walls. Is it fame, its inevitable distancing, its sheen of unreality, that has done this to her, or something else, something deeper? Her own desire to retreat from the world, to cut herself off from a network of relationships, of simple, daily interactions that seem to come so easily to others, and that once, surely, came easily to her, too.

She remembers a warm September Saturday in the Royal Oak. Anna bending over her drawing. The pub collie, Timmy, curled up on his cushion in the empty grate. And then, without warning, Ivor pushing open the barroom door and walking in.

Anna had looked up, set aside her drawing, and run across the bar to greet her father. Roy, at the bar, had met Cass's gaze – seen her desperation, she supposed, and understood its source. He'd offered her a small nod, marched over to the door, and gently prised Anna's hand from Ivor's. 'You, sir,' he'd said, 'are not welcome here.'

She can remember, so clearly, how Anna had looked then – her mouth gaping, her eyes narrowing, preparing for the onset of tears – and how Ivor had stared at Roy, stupefied, his reaction dulled by whisky. (She could see perfectly well that he was drunk.)

'I suggest, sir, that you leave,' Roy had said, his voice calm and even, and Ivor had looked to his daughter, whimpering, reaching for him; and, beyond her, to Cass.

'Bitch,' he'd said to her – quite softly, even tenderly. 'Crazy fucking bitch. Don't think this will be the end of it.' And then he had turned and left.

Anna had begun to wail. The bar was silent but for the sound of her tears, and the low, tinny burble of a Madonna song – 'Like a Prayer': Cass can still hear it in her mind – from the radio.

Roy had looked around at his customers. 'Well, then,' he'd said to everyone, and no one. 'Looks like the show's over, doesn't it?'

He'd placed a hand on Anna's shoulder. 'Come on, love. Your mum's waiting for you. And Sheila's done her toad-in-the-hole.'

Back at their table, Anna had let Cass wipe her face with a napkin. And then she had bent her head low over her food, while Cass met Roy's eyes again over her daughter's head and mouthed, silently, 'Thank you.'

The flowers arrive just as she is finishing her soup.

She has turned on the radio to catch the news: the high-pitched chime of the doorbell cuts over the announcer's low, politely modulated voice, with its tidings of suffering and horror and disaster. *See, Larry,* she thinks. *I'm still listening. I'm not turning my face away.*

He had been appalled, on his first visit to Home Farm, to discover how ill-informed she had become, how cut off from the cut and thrust of politics and current affairs – 'of life, in short,' was how he'd put it. 'You can't live in a vacuum for ever, Cass,' he'd gone on, fixing her with those pale blue eyes. And so it is for him, now – for Larry, whatever he's doing, however furious, or disappointed, or hurt he may be – that she still switches on the radio each day.

In the hallway, Cass checks the security camera: a woman in a short-sleeved polo shirt, bearing an enormous bouquet.

'Birthday, is it?' the woman says, with only the faintest flicker of interest, as Cass opens the door, signs the woman's tablet computer with a blunt-tipped pen. She is young – twenty-five, at most; impervious, clearly, to the significance (such as there still is) to Cass's name. *So much for the Twittersphere being ablaze,* Cass thinks, and smiles.

'No,' she says aloud. 'It's not my birthday. Thank you.' She takes the flowers from the woman's outstretched arms, and closes the door.

White roses, set among the tall, slender stems of orchids, and white freesias just coming into bud. Their scent is heady, glori-ous: she stands for a moment in the hallway, holding the flowers, breathing them in. *Larry,* she thinks, and then corrects herself, acknowledging, with a sharp stab of disappointment, that this is not Larry's style. And sure enough, laying the bouquet on the kitchen counter in its silver box, she finds a card, nestled among the blooms.

To Cass, the card says, in a stranger's anonymous, rounded hand. *Thinking of you today, and sending love and joy for your playback party. Omar and I are so looking forward to seeing you later. Love – then, now and always – from Kate xxx PS How did we EVER manage to get so old?!*

Dear Kate. Cass pictures her friend issuing instructions to the florist (an expensive one on Marylebone High Street, just round the corner from Kate's mansion flat), carefully dictating each word and flourish. '*Capital* letters, all right? Three kisses, and an exclamation mark to follow the question.' Kate is undimmed by age, or at least seems so – especially in the company of Omar, her handsome, wild-haired playwright, fifteen years her junior, and the best lover she has ever had. (Kate had whispered this discreetly into Cass's ear, over the dinner at which they had been introduced.)

Setting aside her disappointment, then, Cass arranges the flowers in a vase. She works carefully, slowly, taking the time to cut an angled length from each stem; separating orchid from freesia, and freesia from rose, with bundles of glossy, full-leaved foliage.

It is the type of activity – mindless, quietly absorbing and yielding a quick, perceptible result – with which she has, in the course of her years without music, her silent years, begun to take a particular, unexpected pleasure.

Cooking: the miraculous alchemy by which a haul of disparate ingredients might be transformed, step by step, into something fragrant, sweet, sour, delicious: something capable of focusing her, if only for the course of one meal, one plate, entirely on the sensory sensations of the moment. Interior decoration: the change of mood, if only transitory, fleeting, that she has begun to experience with the considered selection and purchase of an object – a bowl, a vase, a table – and its positioning in relation to other objects, beside which it might seem to change, to become something greater than itself. Flowers: their colours, their shapes, their scents; their buds gradually expanding, opening, drawing in the light.

She had never cared much for such things before. Flowers were the bouquets that arrived with Alan, or Kim, or some underling dispatched by the label, arranged by unknown hands. Not ignored, exactly – Cass had always taken the time to admire them, to inhale their perfume – but not truly appreciated, either. There were so many of them, and the displays came, over the years, to exist not in and of themselves but as ciphers for the things that were being demanded of her. Hard work (calla lilies, sent by the label to congratulate her on another sell-out tour). Capitulation (orange roses and yellow orchids, to thank her for agreeing, reluctantly, to add another eight European dates). Forgiveness (red roses, bought by Ivor – or, at least, at his request – and placed on the Steinway's closed lid, beside a card in which the florist had written, *For my dearest Cassie, from a husband who is sorrier than words – or songs – can say*).

And of course there had been flowers, too, in the hospital. A course on flower-arranging, of all things: she'd seen the sign on the noticeboard, a few weeks after she was admitted for the second time. (In the weeks after her first admission, she'd been unable to leave her room.)

'What *is* this place?' she'd complained to a passing nurse. 'The fucking Women's Institute? Let's not kid ourselves, shall we?'

The nurse was young, patient, her hair drawn into a low, sleek ponytail. She had offered Cass a white-toothed smile, and said, 'Why don't you go along, Ms Wheeler? Many of our patients find it therapeutic.'

'Never,' she'd snapped back.

And then, at three o'clock on the following Tuesday, Cass had found herself pushing open the door to the activity room, and being enthusiastically ushered over to a table on which stood a vase, a small bunch of yellow sweetheart roses and gypsophila, and a wedge of oasis floral foam.

Afterwards, she'd been allowed to carry the vase back to her room. She had placed it on her dressing-table – if such a name could dignify the hospital-issue bench on which she kept her creams and lotions, her framed photograph of Anna, and the small stack of library books that she was attempting, with limited success, to read (Dickens; Graham Greene; Paulo Coelho's *The Alchemist*, pressed into her hands by the librarian, with her hennaed hair and her infuriating expression of unwearying optimism). The sight of those yellow roses – each one a tiny sunburst of colour, tightly furled, soon to explode into vivid life – had so cheered her that Cass had, despite herself, returned to the next class, and then to the class after that.

And now, all these years later, here is Kate's bouquet, with its silky whites and deep chlorophyll greens, filling the vase she is placing on the kitchen table. Flowers, where before there had been none. Colour, where before there had been only dusty, lifeless monochrome.

The kitchen clock is inching towards half-past one.

Seven-thirty in Chicago, Cass thinks. *Not too early, surely?*

Not for Larry, anyway, who is an early riser. Often she has woken to find her room bathed in a dim, greyish light, and the shadow of him dressing, quietly and deftly, beside the half-opened curtain.

'Go back to sleep,' he would say. 'It's too early for you.'

And he would place a kiss on her lips, and she would close her eyes and fall gratefully back into sleep, because he was right: it was too early for her. She would rise an hour or two later, go upstairs in her dressing-gown and slippers to find him in the art room, a mug of black coffee grown cold beside his right hand. She would try to enter without making a noise, so as not to distract him, but he would always look up (he has extraordinarily sensitive hearing – 'like a bat's,' he joked once) and see her, and his face would crease into a smile.

That smile of his. How broad and true it is: how it employs each muscle and sinew of his face, and creeps up to his eyes, their colour brightening, the small puckers at their corners lifting and tightening. God, how she misses it. How clearly she recalls the sight of him, smiling at her as she approached him outside the gallery in Washington: a spare, lean, white-haired figure, hands thrust into the pockets of a rumpled black leather jacket.

That was the second time they had met. That bright, washed-clean morning in spring when Cass had stepped out from the hotel lobby and walked along Pennsylvania Avenue to the gallery, drawn by . . . What had it been, exactly? Curiosity; vanity; an unfamiliar sense of anticipation, that intoxicating feeling that something might be about to happen, if she could only be brave enough to admit its possibility.

Over breakfast at the hotel, she had informed Kim and Alan that she was taking the morning for herself. She had, she'd said, made an arrangement to meet the sculptor Larry Alderson for coffee at the National Gallery of Art. She would be sure to be at the restaurant in time for lunch with the label; she had noted down the address, and would find herself a taxi on Constitution Avenue. Or Larry, perhaps, would help her find one: she had not, in any case, Cass assured them, entirely lost the ability to perform such a task for herself.

Cass had, as she'd spoken, sensed Kim and Alan weighing this information, digesting it, each making a supreme effort not to meet the other's eye.

'Well, that's wonderful,' Kim had said.

Alan had nodded. 'Take your mobile with you, won't you, in case you need anything?'

Larry had been standing beside the gallery entrance when Cass arrived. She'd remembered his height, of course, but it had struck her again only as she'd come closer: from the other side of the noisy swirl of traffic, he'd appeared tiny, dwarfed by the building's grand classical portico. Between the central columns hung a banner: 'Andrew Wyeth,' announced in white lettering over a twelve-foot-high detail of a painting. A window left open onto a stretch of yellowing grass. 'Looking Out, Looking In.'

'Good morning,' he said, when she was near enough to shake his hand, which she did, feeling, as she did so, that perhaps the greeting was too stiff, too formal. His eyes were bright blue, amused. 'Glad you came.'

She returned his smile, though she was nervous now: she stood a little awkwardly, not quite facing him, as if she might, at any moment, be taken by the desire to turn and run. 'Did you think I might not?'

'Well.' Larry let go of her hand, ran the other through his hair. It occurred to her that he was nervous, too. 'I wasn't sure. It's a short visit, after all. And I'm sure there are plenty of demands on your time.'

'Oh, not so many as there used to be.'

She remembered it then: how easy he had been to talk to, the previous night, at the Library of Congress, under that ornate roofed canopy of blue and gold. They had stood together for a long while, undisturbed, until Kim, with apologies, had interrupted them, saying that there were still a few other guests to whom Cass really ought to be introduced. Larry had nodded, and melted away, leaving Cass with an inexplicable sense of anticlimax. But half an hour or so later, as they were preparing to return to the hotel, he had reappeared, drawn Cass gently to a quiet corner of the room, and asked whether she would consider meeting him the following day. And she, before her courage could fail her, had agreed.

'And anyway,' she said outside the gallery, feeling suddenly emboldened, 'it's my time, isn't it? And I decide what to do with it.'

Again, that twitch of a smile. 'I'd expect nothing less.'

He led her to a café in the belly of the building. White marble-topped tables, black wrought-iron chairs; potted palms, the soft, watery patter of a fountain, everything cool and calm. They refused the buffet; ordered coffee, pastries. He took off his leather jacket, hung it over the back of his chair, and began to sketch out the details of his life, as she imagined he might begin, on paper, to conceive of the design of a new maquette: its shape, its line, seeming at once familiar and strange.

He'd been born, he said, in Chicago, where, since his second divorce, he had recently returned to live, in an enormous loft apartment on the top floor of a building that had, in his child-hood, lain derelict: a handsome old Victorian factory, slowly crumbling to ruin. Two children from his first marriage, another from his second: all of them grown up now, living in Paris, Con-necticut, Vancouver.

'Scattered to the winds,' he said. 'Todd does something to do with economics at the Paris Embassy – damned if I know exactly what. Maddy teaches grade-school and has three kids. And Harper – well, Harper's a free spirit, I guess, but of a particular sort. She's had a ton of jobs, can't seem to work out which one to stick with. In *that*, I suppose, she resembles her father. God knows what I'd have done with myself if I hadn't found art. Or, I should say, if it hadn't found me.'

Cass didn't tell Larry that the architecture of his biography – birth, education, family, exhibitions, awards – was already familiar to her; that she had, in her hotel room last night, spent some time acquainting herself with it on Wikipedia.

She had found, too, the catalogue for Larry's show at Tate Modern, five years before, and for another larger, more recent retrospective at MoMA. She had spent time scrolling through the many reproductions of his work: the graph-paper sketches, hard-angled, precise, more like architectural blueprints than other artists' breathless, impressionistic drafts; the wooden maquettes, works of painstaking craftsmanship in their own right, but just toys, she could see, in comparison with his finished sculptures. She had observed the blocks of clay and bronze and poured concrete of his early years diminishing, over time, into smaller, more delicate pieces – wood and agate and hand-blown glass – as if the emphatic certainty of his youth were being gradually eroded by his growing awareness of the impossibility of ever truly owning a space, a thing, a moment. By the creeping knowledge that the harder you sought ownership of anything, the more slippery and evanescent it would inevitably become.

This, at least, was what Cass had seen in the photographs, though she said nothing of this aloud. She listened – enjoyed listening; slipped into the stream of Larry's monologue. Finished her coffee, her pastry; watched the quick, animated dance of his features. Decided that it was true: he did look a little like Abraham Lincoln. And she didn't mind the resemblance at all.

'I'm talking too much,' he said after a while, noting that their coffee cups were empty. 'I'm boring you. I'm so sorry, Cass. I get like this when I'm nervous. Just drone on and on about myself. When it's *you* I'd like to hear about, really.'

She smiled. 'You're not boring me at all.'

There was time enough, just, for them to slip into the Andrew Wyeth exhibition. Cass admitted, as they entered, that she had never heard of Wyeth, and Larry said, 'Oh, he's the most brilliant painter. A realist of the old school. Hated by the critics, of course, because he was actually popular. Mostly, he painted rural scenes – fields, abandoned houses, wide, louring skies. He didn't seem much interested in people. But then, would you believe, it turned out he'd painted the same woman in secret for years, without his wife or her husband ever knowing.'

'Actually,' Cass said, 'I can believe that.'

The paintings in the exhibition were all of windows, and the views they framed. Grey clouds massing beyond a white clapboard locker room. Four peaches icily mouldering on a cold concrete sill. A tall white house hunkering down into a hillside under the bare, colourless light of evening.

They walked through the gallery quickly, aware of their diminishing portion of time. And the pictures, seen so fleetingly, began to form a narrative in Cass's mind – one of loneliness and silence, of light and life glimpsed only at a distance. Of lives lived elsewhere, viewed through a transparent skin of glass.

Outside, back on Constitution Avenue, Larry hailed her a taxi. As the car idled, waiting, he placed a hand on her arm.

'I'd like to see you again, Cass,' he said. 'I can't think exactly how, or where. But do you think it might be possible?'

She looked up at his long, rough-hewn face, with its pits and craters, its startling eyes framed by thick white brows. There was kindness there, she knew, and intelligence, and something else, too – something she hadn't sensed, in anyone, for such a long, long time. Desire, she supposed it must be; and the presence of it, in that moment, made her afraid.

'I don't know,' she said. And then, as disappointment struck her, and was matched by the deflated expression on his face, she added, 'Yes. I think so. I'd really like that, Larry. Yes, I would.'

Now – in her kitchen, with the flowers that are not from Larry, and the house horribly quiet around her, as if reproaching her for his absence – Cass reaches for the telephone, punches in the number she knows by heart.

There is a moment of silence, as the cables or the satellites or whatever they are these days wait to make their connection. Cass looks out to the garden. The foxes have slunk off again to some undisturbed corner, and Otis is on the patio, sated (he'd followed her into the kitchen earlier, demanding food), washing himself with methodical concentration.

The connection is made: the foreign ringtone – each tuneless note held a beat too long – rises to her ear. She swallows, picturing Larry in his downtown apartment with its high factory windows and expanses of unpainted brick (he has shown her photographs, dark black-and-white studies of plane and shadow), making coffee, or shaking the water from his hair as he steps from the shower. Perhaps he is, right now, drawing the towel around his waist, leaving damp footprints on the parquet as he sprints over to the phone.

Her mouth is dry as she silently prepares what she will say to him.

Larry. It's Cass. I'm sorry. I miss you. Come back to me, won't you? Come back to me so we can continue what we've started. You must know that I didn't mean what I said. You must know that I was afraid. And I am trying so hard not to be afraid any longer.

But the telephone rings on and on. Outside, Otis, aware of being watched, lifts his head and returns her stare with his frank, amber eyes, while on the other side of the Atlantic and beyond, in Chicago, in an apartment she has never visited, a telephone shrills out, unanswered, unrelenting.

'Just Us Two'

By Cass Wheeler
From the album *The State She's In*

There's you in the morning
When I open my eyes
And you in the evening
When we say our goodbyes
It's just us two and that's enough for me
Just us two and that's enough for me
It's just us two and that's enough for me
It's just us two
Just us two

Some are only happy
When they're in a crowd
Others walk alone
In the dead of sound
It's just us two and that's enough for me
Just us two and that's enough for me
It's just us two and that's enough for me
It's just us two
Just us two
One and one is all we need
One and one is all we need

It's just us two and that's enough for me
Just us two and that's enough for me
It's just us two and that's enough for me
It's just us two
Just us two

RELEASED 13 September 1971
RECORDED June 1971 at Union Studios, London NW10
GENRE Folk rock
LABEL Phoenix Records
WRITER(S) Cass Wheeler
PRODUCER(S) Martin Hartford
ENGINEER(S) Sean O'Malley

She knew all their names by now.

There was Serena, a primary-school teacher who was always commandeering the kitchen table for some new craft project: cutting potatoes in half in order to stamp bright patterns onto paper, or fashioning a papier-mâché model of a giraffe, standing clumsily on its sticky, tapered legs.

The house on Savernake Road ran to Serena's rules. On Saturday mornings, she would go round knocking on doors, announcing that it was time to 'clean up this godforsaken pigsty'. Usually, only Cass and Kate would obey – the men remained, for the most part, impervious to Serena's demands, drew the covers over their heads and slept on. And so, under Serena's tutelage, the women would don Marigolds, tie scarves over their hair, and set about emptying the bins, wiping down surfaces, and gathering up the ashtrays and record sleeves and discarded newspapers.

Once, not long after she'd moved in, Cass had set about cleaning the bath with bleach. (It was a Sunday afternoon, Ivor had gone off on a painting job with Hugh, and she was struggling to finish a new song.) She'd become aware, after a moment or two, of Serena standing at the bathroom door, watching her.

'Oh, don't worry about that, Cass,' Serena said. She spoke lightly, but with the firm expectation of being obeyed. 'I usually do the bathroom myself.'

Cass had happily relinquished the task. As she went back across the landing to Ivor's room (her room, too, now: how thrilling that knowledge still was), she had noticed Serena bending low over the bath with the cloth, correcting whatever it was Cass had done wrong.

Serena's boyfriend (though they didn't use the term: he called her his 'old lady', and she referred to him as her 'old man') was Bob, and he was as relaxed as she was uptight. Bob was studying for a master's in medieval English literature, but rarely left the house, for lectures or for anything else. He spent most days smoking grass on his favoured armchair, a hideous, sagging, paisley-patterned thing that had, like most of the furniture in the house, been bequeathed by the landlord, or picked up from skips and flea-markets. There was one particular variety of weed that Bob said made his mind feel pure and cloudless; he acquired it on a weekly basis from his dealer in Swiss Cottage, and then consumed it, slowly and methodically, while listening to *The Piper at the Gates of Dawn*.

Bob's inertia didn't seem to bother Serena: she'd get home from school, say in the good-natured tone of an exasperated parent, 'Oh, Bob, have you not moved from there all day *again?*' And then she would bring him a cup of tea, and set about preparing his dinner.

Serena and Bob occupied the attic room; on the first floor, next to Cass and Ivor, was Paul. He was a sweet, soft-voiced man, a little overweight, with a florid complexion that was unflatteringly enhanced, most nights, by copious amounts of red wine. Paul never grew rowdy, or displayed much other evidence of drunkenness – he just shrank back into himself, inch by inch, until, quite often, they all forgot that he was in the room, and would be surprised to find him still there the next morning on the sofa, his mouth slightly open, emitting the low rumble of a snore.

Paul was, Ivor told her, rumoured to be gay, though none of them had seen any evidence of this, or of sexual activity of any sort; there was, Cass thought, something rather lonely about him, and it seemed fitting to her that he wanted to be a writer, for what lonelier activity could there be than that? He used that very phrase, too – 'I *want* to be a writer' – as if the writing he actually did every day in his room for hours (he had no other job, and nobody knew where he found the money for his rent) were nothing more than practice for the time when he might finally consider himself worthy of the title.

Kate's room was across the landing, beside the bathroom. She was twenty-one, an actress and so beautiful, with her waist-length dark hair and china-doll skin, that Cass had, at first, been a little wary of her – not least because she knew that Ivor and Kate had been 'involved' for a time.

It was Serena who had told her – they were sitting in the garden on deckchairs one warm summer afternoon, drinking the sweet pink wine Serena favoured. 'Of course,' Serena had said, 'you know that Kate was desperately in love with Ivor. Probably still is. But she's hardly the only one.'

Cass had opened her eyes wide behind her sunglasses, looked across at Serena, at the bare skin of her shoulders glistening above her long strapless dress. (They had both smothered themselves in cooking-oil before settling under the sun.) 'No. I didn't know.'

Serena lifted her sunglasses onto her forehead. 'Oh, don't worry about it, Cass. He finished with her ages ago. Didn't want to be tied down. Not one for that, our Ivor. And of course, after Ursula . . .'

Cass, with great effort, let the ellipsis hang. She knew, by now, who Ursula was (or, as she preferred to phrase it to herself, 'had been'): a singer, well regarded on the London circuit, who had been Ivor's 'old lady' for about six months, and had then, quite suddenly, suffered a breakdown and moved to the south of France, where her stepfather kept an apartment.

The south of France was far enough away to permit thoughts of Ursula to slip, mostly, from Cass's mind; Kate, on the other hand, lived just across the hall. From then on, Cass kept her distance from Kate (a challenge, when they shared the same bathroom and their bedrooms were just a few feet apart), and watched her interactions with Ivor with a hawkish eye.

Ivor didn't seem to notice – she was coming to understand that there was a lot Ivor didn't notice – but Kate did. One night, when they were all down at Joe's bar, she leant over to

Cass, and said, 'You don't need to worry about Ivor and me, you know, Cass. It's ancient history. And I'd really like us to be friends.'

Cass, looking back at Kate in the club's murky light – remembering Irene and Linda, missing their closeness, their easy intimacy – decided that she'd like that, too.

And then, finally, there was Hugh McMaster, who had the huge room on the ground floor that had once been the dining-room, and was a law unto himself.

He played the drums: he kept his kit in his room, shaking the whole house with its clash and shudder, and causing the neighbours to issue regular complaints. He rode a motorbike, and had pinned photographs of himself, taken by the girl he brought home most frequently – Suzanne, who was twenty-six, with aggressively short black hair and a thin, sharp-chinned face – all over his walls in an ever-shifting collage.

Hugh had curly hair that framed his face, softening the hard angle of his jaw, and eyes of a quite arresting green. His presence in the house was erratic, unpredictable. Some days, Hugh would head out on a painting job with Ivor, but on others, he'd simply disappear: the space in the front garden usually occupied by his motorbike would suddenly empty, and would remain so until Hugh re-emerged, wild-eyed, his face half obscured by three days' growth of new beard.

Ivor and Hugh had a particular rapport: they jammed for hours in Hugh's room, and got drunk and high together. (Hugh preferred whisky to weed, and amphetamines and cocaine to whisky.) And when Ivor was with Hugh, Cass felt a tightness in her chest, for she could feel Ivor slipping away from her, out of her grasp. Hugh seemed to know it, too, and savour it. With her, Hugh employed an extravagant, exaggerated politeness – he called her 'Lady Cass', or 'our own musical genius' – which made her feel that he was laughing at her.

'Hugh doesn't like me,' she said to Ivor a month or so after she'd arrived at Savernake Road; they were lying in bed, her head on his arm.

'Of course he does,' he replied, but she shifted onto her back, looked up at him fiercely, and said, 'You're just saying that to shut me up. You're not really listening.'

'All right. So what if he doesn't like you? What do you care?'

'So he doesn't, then.'

Ivor reached across to the bedside table for his cigarettes. 'Cass, man, come on. Chill about it, won't you? Why've you got to be so uptight all the time?'

I am not *uptight*, she thought, and said nothing more, in an effort to prove that this was so. But a few days after that, she came back from a walk on Parliament Hill – it was a sweltering afternoon, and she'd been feeling cooped up in the house, with nobody but stoned Bob and silent Paul for company – to find that Ivor hadn't come home, and Hugh's motorbike was still missing from the front garden.

They didn't come back all night. Cass ate Serena's rice and lentil dhal, and then sat with the others in the garden as it grew late, strumming her guitar; but her attention was focused on the road, on listening out for the sound of Hugh's bike, or of Ivor's key turning in the front door.

'I don't know what you're getting in such a state about, Cass,' Serena said. 'Ivor's a free agent, you know. He can do what he likes, and so can you.'

'No.' Cass's voice was rising. 'That's not how it is with us.'

Serena rolled her eyes, and Cass got up and went upstairs. She took her guitar with her, and channelled her anger into song; a song that she had finished, note by note and word by furious word, by the time Ivor and Hugh finally returned the following night. By then, Cass was no longer angry but icily calm, and she turned the lock in their bedroom door and sat on the bed, waiting for him.

She listened to his tread on the stairs, to him moving across the landing, then reaching for the door handle, shaking it, over and over again, as he realised it was locked. She stretched out on the bed, lay her head on the pillow. Behind her closed lids, she saw her father, grey-faced and shrunken in the vicarage; the way the life had come out of him, breath by breath, hour by hour, in the weeks and months after her mother's leaving. Why had he loved her, that plain, unremarkable girl, so many years his junior? Cass didn't know, and yet he had, and her desertion had broken him. But she was not weak, like Francis. She would not tolerate Ivor's absences, his sudden withdrawals, or Serena's sly insinuations. *Ivor's a free agent, you know.* No. That was not how it would be.

'Cassie. What are you doing?' Gradually, Ivor's whisper grew louder, became a shout. Cass kept her eyes closed and drew the pillow up over her head, replaying, in her mind, the chords and cadences of her new song. Her pulse slowed; her breath came steadily: she would not back down.

After a while, she heard Kate's voice join Ivor's on the landing, sleepy, confused – '*Ivor*, keep it down, can't you? Some of us have to get up in the morning.' And then Ivor again, stage-whispering through the door, 'Fine, then, Cassie. Have it your way.' The resentful thump of his feet carrying him back downstairs.

He spent the night on the sofa in the living-room, under one of Serena's crocheted blankets. In the morning, Cass observed him sleeping there from the open doorway, and then went through to the kitchen to make herself a mug of Nescafé. Ivor came through a few minutes later, bleary-eyed, his long hair greasy and unbrushed.

'Cassie,' he said. 'What the hell was all that about?'

She regarded him coolly over the rim of her mug.

'Don't,' she said. 'Don't you ever treat me like I don't matter. I don't care what your *other* girls were like. I'm not a toy you can just pick up when you feel like it and then put down again.

We're either together in this, the two of us, or we're nothing at all.'

He looked back at her, and she saw him wrestle with his response. After a few moments, he put a hand to his face, rubbed his eyes. 'Of course we're in this together, silly girl. Crazy, silly girl. There's nobody else. How could I ever want anybody else but you?'

And then he came over to her, and held her face between his hands, and she allowed herself to be kissed.

One morning towards the middle of July, Cass received a note from Lily.

It was brief, pointed, and written in navy-blue ink on a plain white card. *Will be in north London for a magazine job on Friday. Perhaps you could find time to meet? I should be done by five o'clock. I'll come to you. I'd have called, but you didn't leave a number. Lily.*

This was the first communication Cass had received from her aunt and uncle since leaving Atterley. She had wondered, that first evening at Savernake Road, whether they might come after her: she had slept poorly that night, alive not only to the strangeness of Ivor's room, the room that was now hers – the musty, unwashed scent of his sheets; the warmth of his slumbering body – but also to every sound from the street below. Around one a.m., she had heard a car splutter to a halt, and had rushed to the window, pushed the curtains aside. But below, she had seen only a taxi cab, its engine running, its amber light aglow, and a smart couple in evening wear stepping out onto the kerb. No Lily. No John. Unable to decide whether she was disappointed or relieved, Cass had pulled the curtains into place, and slunk back to bed.

When the next day had passed without their arrival or acknowledgement – and the next day, and the day after that – Cass had come to understand that she had been wrong to expect them. Lily and John had given her freedom – a freedom she had exercised, in leaving them. For a moment, she had felt abandoned once again (her mother, turning her back on the vicarage, sloping off into the grey morning with her suitcase). John and Lily were not going to fight for her; they were going to let her go. But this, after all, was what she had wanted. And so Cass tried not to think of the pain she had caused them, telling herself she would have to learn to live with it; and over time, the burden of her guilt did seem to ease. She wondered if this was how it had been for Margaret, over there in Canada, settling into her new life with Len Steadman, while the scars slowly knitted over the wounds she had left behind.

Lily arrived closer to six o'clock than five. She wore a loose blue shift, her usual red lipstick and brown leather sandals; her toes were painted to match her lips, and the sight of them – the vulnerability of her aunt's bare skin – moved something deep inside Cass, so that for a moment, she was unable to speak. And as Lily said nothing either – stood before her on the doorstep, watching her from behind her round tortoiseshell sunglasses – there was nothing between them but silence, and the heavy weight of things unsaid.

'You're still alive, then.' Lily pushed her sunglasses back onto her head, above the darkly shining canopy of her fringe. 'Well, that's something, isn't it?'

Cass met her gaze. Lily wasn't smiling – not yet – and her eyes were stern, but Cass thought she could detect a faint softening.

'I'm sorry.' She could not raise her voice above a whisper.

Lily nodded. 'Yes. Well. So you should be, you wretch of a girl. I won't come in. There's a pub on the corner, isn't there? Let's get a bloody drink.'

There were few other women in the pub, and nobody at all in the garden, which was more of a scrubby yard, furnished with two wooden benches and a miserable rose bush straggling up an ancient trellis.

'London,' Lily said as she brought out their gin and tonics.

'I don't miss it. But I expect you can't imagine wanting to live anywhere else.'

Cass nodded, took her glass, sipped, and saw, as Lily's face finally admitted the trace of a smile, that she had been forgiven.

They talked, for a while, of other things. John's work on a house in Harrogate. (It was nearing completion, and he was staying up there this weekend.) Francis, whom Lily had been to see in Worthing. Cass's music, Ivor, their friends.

When their glasses were almost empty, Lily said, 'It was me, you know, not John. It was me who didn't want children. I think he'd have had a brood of them, if I'd been willing.'

Cass said nothing, ran a finger over the rough, splintered surface of the table.

'I'd never wanted them. Just didn't have the urge. Couldn't see how it would work, really. I mean, picture editors aren't exactly sympathetic to the needs of a working mother. And then, when I met John, I suppose I just wanted him to myself. I didn't want to share him with anyone – even a child.'

Lily withdrew two cigarettes from her leather purse, lit them both, and handed one to Cass. 'Don't suppose you've given up? No? Well, be my guest, then.'

Drawing deeply on her cigarette, emitting a small circle of smoke, she went on. 'So it was a surprise, really, just how deeply I came to care for you, Cass. To love you. To think of you, in some ways, as my own daughter.'

Lily put her head on one side, watching Cass with an expression that she understood, in that moment, as profoundly, unfathomably sad.

'Silly of me, I suppose. Silly how upset we both were when you just upped and left like that. John, too. I've never seen him like that before. Couldn't settle to anything, for weeks. Neither of us could.'

'Lily . . .'

Her aunt shook her head. 'No, Cass. I'm not saying this to

upset you, or to make you feel guilty – though of course you *should* feel guilty. Neither of us wanted you to stay on sufferance. I just wish you'd talked to us about it, that's all. You've given up everything to follow this man. Your *schooling*, Cass. All your plans. I just wish you'd let us in.'

A sliver of wood had made its way into the soft pad of Cass's index finger. She could feel it there, just below the surface, and she stared down at it, worried uselessly at it with her teeth, before letting it go.

'It's not just about Ivor,' she said softly. 'It's what *I* want, too. Music, I mean. The chance to make something of my songs. I really want it, Lily. It's all I want. What does school matter, really, in comparison to that?'

Lily took a long, last drag on her cigarette, and then stubbed it out. 'You're still so young, Cass. You could have waited. Just a few months – that was all.' After a silence, she added, 'But I know you want it, you stubborn child. By God, I know you do.'

By the end of the summer, Cass and Ivor were out gigging four or five nights a week – at Joe's bar, and at other venues scattered around London's compass points: a riverboat docked at Kingston-upon-Thames; a pub in Hampstead; a candlelit coffee house on the Old Brompton Road.

Their audiences were not large, but they listened, and Cass was beginning to recognise some faces – a woman with shoulder-length blonde hair and a slow, stoned smile, who seemed to follow them wherever they went; an intense-looking young man who sat at the same round table at the front each time they took to the stage at Joe's.

At one gig on the Old Brompton Road in late August, they found themselves, to their great excitement, sharing the bill with Bert Jansch and Sandy Denny. Cass was transfixed by Bert's agile, darting fingers, by Sandy's sweet, breathy, muscular voice, singing the old songs Cass had first heard on Lily's records, and others she had never heard before.

Cass watched Sandy as she sang – her tumble of blonde hair; her voice so simple and easy and *right* – and thought, with sudden, startling clarity, *I want what she has.*

In later years, she would think of that moment often, each time she was asked – and she was asked this many times – when she had known that she wanted to perform. 'When I saw Sandy Denny sing,' she would always say. 'When I saw her hold a room with the power of her voice alone.'

But however deeply Cass was coming to love performing – to feel most at home on those small stages, beside Ivor, with her guitar on her knee, despite the terror that still gripped her before she stepped out under the lights – it wasn't yet paying their way. They were earning no more than a few pounds here, a round of beers there. Why else, Ivor pointed out when Cass first remarked on this, did she think he was having to paint houses to make the rent?

She had known Ivor was hard up, of course – he'd cadged enough tobacco and weed from Lily and John, and she hadn't been ignorant of the fact that he seemed to wear the same three sets of clothes on rotation, and that they were not always clean. But in her eagerness to leave school and Sussex and her childish life behind, she hadn't quite comprehended that, with Ivor in London, she would be hard up, too.

Hard up, yes, but not penniless, and in that she knew she was lucky. She had a small monthly stipend drawn from her father's pension – Francis had made the arrangement with John before moving to Worthing – and, as the weeks wore on, small sums of money began to appear, sporadically, in her bank account.

The first instalment arrived a few days after Lily's visit. Cass went to the bank to withdraw her portion of the rent, and discovered that the balance on her account had, unexpectedly, increased; over the next few months, she found that this happened again and again. The money could only have come from Lily and John, who must have thought carefully about the size of the sums: they were large enough, along with the allowance from Cass's father, to cover absolute necessities – rent, food, petrol for Ivor's car – but no more. And as Ivor had even less money than she did, it became clear that there was nothing for it but for her to find another source of income.

She tried waitressing first – there was a café on South End Road with a sign in the window saying, 'Waitress required.' The owner – Ali, a scrawny, lugubrious Turkish man with a thick, slug-like moustache – took one look at her and said, 'Do you have a black skirt you can wear? Make sure it's short.'

Ali's wife, Azime, ran the kitchen. She was lean and hard-bodied, and seemed, with her deep-etched crow's feet and perpetual scowl, much older than Ali: more like his mother than his wife, Cass thought. All day, Azime aimed a stream of invective at Ali, Cass and the dishwasher, Ali's pimply sixteen-year-old nephew, Ahmed, in a mixture of Turkish and broken English, without seeming to care whether she was understood.

On her fourth shift, when Cass's feet were already hurting more than she'd thought possible, and her hair had begun to reek of sunflower oil and stale smoke (Ali sold strong Turkish cigarettes along with the fried breakfasts), Azime lost her temper completely. She stepped across the kitchen to the serving-hatch, where Cass was preparing to pick up two plates of ham and eggs, and slapped her hard across the face.

A moment of stunned silence: the woman's narrow, snarling face, the colour flaming on Cass's cheek.

'Right,' Cass said, and tore off her apron. 'That's it. You're a bloody maniac. And you can find some other fool to be your slave, because I'm damned if it's going to be me.'

And then she stalked across the linoleum, watched by the silent, wide-eyed customers, forks hovering in mid-air between their plates and their mouths, and slammed the door behind her.

On the walk home, she was filled with righteous rage, but her anger had dissipated, and the red mark on her cheek had already faded, by the time she arrived at the house. When she told the story to Ivor and the others, it was with amusement: Azime, with her wrinkled walnut skin and incomprehensible fury, had already become a figure of fun.

Listening, Kate laughed, and said, 'Barbara's just given in her notice. Why don't you come and work with me?'

Kate had a job in a bridal shop, set a few streets back from Oxford Street. It was a fussy, old-fashioned place – not at all like the boutiques that had sprung up along Carnaby Street and the King's Road, with their lurid patterned dresses and record-players turned up loud. But then, as the manager, Cornelia, said to Cass when Kate took her in to meet her, 'Most women, when it comes to their big day, still want something *traditional*, don't you think, my dear?'

With her cut-glass voice, her tiny, spare figure and her white hair drawn back into a tight bun, Cornelia was like an emissary from another era. A ballet mistress from a Degas painting, issuing stern instructions to her pupils at the barre; or an Edwardian dowager, pouring tea into fine china cups.

'She was a debutante, you know,' Kate said on the bus-ride home. 'From what I can gather, some viscount or other jilted her at the altar.'

'Odd place to work, then, isn't it?' Cass said.

'Yes, I suppose it is,' said Kate, and they both dissolved into laughter.

But Cass, it turned out, rather liked working at the bridal shop. Cornelia could be strict – the dresses were to be presented on their white padded hangers just so; the brides to be treated with the utmost deference, even when they were clearly just shop-girls, whiling away their lunch hours with dreams of white tulle and pintucked satin bodices. But she was also kind. Many of the girls she employed were performers of one sort or another – actresses, dancers, models, musicians – and she allowed them time off to attend auditions and castings, thrilling to their successes and sympathising with their disappointments almost as deeply as they did for each other.

On the day Kate learnt that she'd landed a part in *Hair*, Cornelia produced a bottle of champagne. (She had a particular affection for Kate.) When the last customer had departed, she shut the door firmly behind her, turned the shop sign from 'open' to 'closed', and poured each of them a glass.

'To Kate,' Cornelia said, 'and to all you wonderful, talented girls. May all your dreams come true.'

And Cass, lifting her glass to meet the others', looked from Kate to Cornelia to Daphne, the other assistant, a harpist with a willowy figure and a gentle smile, and saw no reason at all why they would not; for it felt, in that moment, that everything was theirs for the taking, and they need only reach out a hand and pluck it from the tree.

There were parties, and there were dinners, and there was dancing in basement clubs.

There were letters from Lily and John, and the Rolling Stones live in Hyde Park – the crowds, and the scarred grass, and the scent of marijuana hanging heady in the air.

There were the hours Cass spent in Cornelia's shop, quiet and cool, smoothing lace and satin and silk over strangers' bare skin.

There was the week when they all piled into Ivor's Morris Minor and Bob's Ford Escort, and drove to Kate's parents' house in Cornwall, which was even larger than Atterley, and filled with brocade furnishings and flocked wallpaper and oil paintings of stern, anonymous ancestors. Bob had a sheet of acid tabs, and those were lost days, sunlit and magical, pulsing with a strange, intoxicating energy that seemed to them all then, young and stoned as they were, to be something close to the essence of life itself.

But above all, there was music, and there was Ivor, and there was her inability to tell where her love for one spilt over into her love for the other.

She wanted to know everything about him – not only the basic, obvious things, like where he'd grown up, and what his parents' names were, and whether he had any brothers and sisters; but the view he'd looked out on from his bedroom window as a child, and the perfume his mother had worn, and the first song he could remember hearing.

This he could answer – 'Sally' by Gracie Fields, which his mother had hummed under her breath while putting the sheets through the mangle on wash-day, keeping him close by, so that the song, for him, still carried the warm fug of the kitchen and the sharp, clean smell of starch. But on most of her other questions, he would simply not be drawn.

She knew only that he'd been born and raised in Leamington Spa, where his parents, Owain and Susan, still lived; that he was an only child; and that he'd left home as soon as he could, and no longer spoke to any of his family, with the occasional exception of his maternal grandmother, Anna. That, of course, was what she longed to know most of all – *why* he had cut himself off from them, and whether this bore any relation to the scar beside his right eye, the provenance of which was another of his many mysteries. But the first time she had asked him about it, she had watched Ivor's face harden and close, like a shutter drawn down over a darkened window, and she had comprehended that this would be one subject on which, for now, she would not be able to press him further.

She had to admit, too, that although she believed she wished to share everything with Ivor – for there to be no regions of their minds to which they did not allow each other access – in practice, his reticence was something she could understand. For there were things about her own mother that she had not told him, that she had not even quite told herself; and Margaret's letters were still lying, unanswered, in the box that Cass had brought with her from Atterley, and which now lay stowed under their bed at Savernake Road.

Cass spoke often of Francis, however. Of how her father had read to her as a child, and how she could still recall the precise timbre of his voice, so much softer, more intimate, than it had sounded from the pulpit. Of how proud she had been of him, striding cassocked and resolute through the church, secure in the attention of his congregation; and of how painful it had been to see him shrink and dwindle away to the man he was now, pale and stooped, measuring out his days in the little flat in Worthing with only his books, his records and his fading memories.

One day, she took down the copy of *Great Expectations* that Francis had given her on her thirteenth birthday, with its green leather binding, and showed it to Ivor. She realised, with a stab of shame, that it was almost six months since she had last been to visit her father.

'Will you come with me?' she asked Ivor, and after a moment's silence, he nodded, and said, 'Yes, I suppose so. If you're sure you want me to.'

They drove down to Worthing on a Wednesday afternoon – early closing day at the bridal shop, and a rare day when Ivor and Hugh had no house-painting to attend to.

It was a fine, crisp autumn day. The roads were clear, and they reached her father's building just before five. Parking on the drive, Cass saw that the oak tree on the front lawn was ablaze with colour; and it pleased her, in some small way, to know that he woke every morning to such a view.

'Does Reverend Wheeler know you're coming?' the warden said when they announced themselves.

Cass hadn't seen him before: he was a small, narrow-faced man who looked them up and down, in their matching jeans and beads and cheesecloth shirts, with a disapproval he didn't bother to disguise.

She stood a little straighter. 'No. But I hardly think he's going to object to his only daughter and her fiancé coming to tea, is he?'

'Fiancé?' Ivor whispered when the warden had disappeared upstairs.

'Don't you dare say a thing.'

The warden was gone for so long that Cass began to fear that her father had, indeed, gone out, and that she ought to have telephoned ahead. But eventually they were permitted to climb the dim stairwell to her father's door, and there Francis was, in the hallway. Smaller than she remembered – surely he shrank a little more each time she came? – and so much older, too: gaunt, grey-haired, wearing a white shirt and brown knitted tank top and an expression she couldn't quite decipher.

'This is Ivor, Dad,' she said, and Francis looked at Ivor, and nodded, but didn't extend his hand.

She made a pot of tea in the kitchen – so tiny and old-fashioned, but clean, like the rest of the flat; everything tidied and put away. There were labels on the cupboard doors, written in her father's neat, careful hand. *Tea and coffee. Canned goods. Pots and pans.* Over the stove, another note read, *Switch off the gas.* What Lily had told her must be true – her father's confusion was worsening, and these handwritten notes, these small attempts to anchor himself, moved her almost more than she could bear. She leant back against a cupboard, closed her eyes, waiting for the kettle's whistle. Then she poured hot water into the teapot, and carried it through to the living-room on a tray with a plate of Bourbon creams.

The room was uncomfortably silent. Ivor was sitting in the armchair by the window, seeming too large for the small, dark space, his long legs stretched out in front of him. Francis, on the sofa, was staring straight ahead, his expression still blank, inscrutable.

Her father looked up when she offered him a cup of tea, and as he took the cup, he said, as mildly as if he were thanking her, 'So this is your fancy-man, then.'

She stood still, stared. 'Dad . . .'

Francis's gaze was cool now, unyielding. 'Don't think I don't know, Maria.' It was years since he'd used her Christian name. 'Don't think I don't know what sort of woman you are. You and your mother both.'

Around her, the room seemed to buckle and spin. She replaced the teapot on the tray, afraid that it might fall, scattering its hot contents across the carpet in a wide, seeping stain. 'Dad, I—'

'Leaving your aunt and uncle like that, without so much as a by-your-leave, after everything they've done for you. Not even bothering to sit your exams. And all for *him*?' Francis waved a dismissive hand in Ivor's direction. 'For him, and some pipe-dream of being a singer. Well, I'll tell you something, Maria – that's all it's ever going to be. A pipe-dream. You're just like your mother – head in the clouds, always dreaming of something else, something better. Well, I don't want to have anything to do with it. Anything at all.'

Cass put a hand to the sideboard, steadying herself. Across the room, Ivor got to his feet. 'Come on, Cassie. Let's go.'

'No.' Cass gathered herself, stood tall. 'Dad. How can you talk like this? This isn't you.'

Her father's voice was cold. 'Because someone has to tell you the truth, don't they? Someone has to tell you what a fool you're being. Your mother's not here to do it, and my sister's almost as foolish as you are, so who else is there? I might be stuck out here, forgotten, forgetting, but I'm still your father.'

She could feel the tears coming. 'Please, Dad. Please . . .'

Francis shook his head. He wouldn't look at her. Ivor was beside her now, placing a hand on her arm. 'Cassie. Come on.'

'Yes, that's right,' Francis said. 'Run along with your fancy-man now, just like Margaret did. Run along and leave me here alone.'

Cass took Ivor's hand, and he led her out across the landing, held open the front door. She held her nerve until they had passed the warden's desk – 'Leaving already, are you?' – and crossed the lawn, under the oak tree with its brightly burning canopy of leaves, to the car.

There, on the front seat, gathering the soft fur of her Afghan coat against her face, she began to cry. Ivor was silent, and held her, and when she was quiet again, he started the car, and drew it out onto the road that would take them home.

As the last scattered outskirts of the town turned into hedgerows, she said, 'It's just us, now, Ivor, isn't it? It really is just us.'

'That's enough, Cassie,' he said, and reached across for her hand. 'Really. That's all we'll ever need.'

'Road of Shadows'

By Cass Wheeler, Ivor Tait, Hugh McMaster
and Danny Ingleby
Previously unreleased

In the dark
Sodium glows
The white lines come and the white lines go
Under quiet chimney ghosts
We're knocking down miles like dominoes
The old world music is the scenery
The back drop, back line, you don't see me
Engine hums as the feeling grows

We're knocking down miles like dominoes
Knocking down miles like dominoes
Rolling past this town on this road of shadows
Knocking down miles like dominoes
Rolling past this town on this road of shadows

Well listen here, listen there's nothing I need
When I'm on the road just you and me
To feed the song inside that grows
Knocking down miles like dominoes
Above us the moon's so round tonight
Wheels like wings as we take flight
And as the grass beneath, beneath us grows

Knocking down miles like dominoes
Knocking down miles like dominoes
Rolling past this town on this road of shadows
Knocking down miles like dominoes

Rolling past this town on this road of shadows
Knocking down miles
Dominoes
Knocking down miles
Stop. Go. Dominoes
Knocking down miles
Stop. Go. Dominoes
Knocking down miles
Stop. Go. Dominoes
Knocking down miles
Stop

WRITTEN June 1969
RECORDED September 1970, at 45 Savernake Road, London NW3
(previously available only on the bootleg *Cass Wheeler and
Vertical Heights: The Demo Sessions*)

'It's a good crowd,' Angus said. 'Boisterous, but good.'

Cass nodded. She was standing beside the van, smoking a cigarette. It was dark in the car-park now, and the streetlight lent Angus's face a yellow, ghoulish glow. 'Think they'll quieten down?'

Angus shrugged, and offered her one of his enigmatic smiles. His eyes were wide, black-pupilled: she had watched him earlier, on the motorway, taking a pill from Hugh's outstretched palm. Each of the men had accepted one in turn, lifting it to his mouth in one swift, choreographed movement. A religious offering: she had thought of her father at communion, leaning down to place the sacrament on Mrs Harrison's pinkly lolling tongue.

Hugh had extended his hand to her, too, but she'd shaken her head and turned away. The nerves were coming on already, circling and snapping, and they did not respond well to amphetamines; she'd try to banish them later, in the dressing-room, with a large glass of red wine.

'Well, you'll just have to make them, Cass,' Angus said.

She took a last drag on her cigarette, crushed the stub under her foot. 'Where's Ivor?'

'In the dressing-room. It's a cupboard with a mirror, really. But we've got the drinks in.'

'My wine?'

Angus rolled his eyes. 'As if I'd forget.'

She followed him across the car-park, and inside. As they pushed open the door, she felt the weight of the beery, smoke-laden air settle on her skin. The club was a long, wide, breeze-blocked room, awash with noise: from the band on the stage (a local rock group called the Heavy Elements, whose fans were out in force); and from the shouting of the crowd, the young men muscled and sleek in their shirtsleeves, the women creamy-skinned and full-bosomed, spilling out of their low-cut tops.

One woman caught Cass's eye as she crossed the floor; she had a head of dark, bottle-black curls, and a red plastic handbag slung across her chest. She looked Cass up and down – took in her long dress with its tiny mirrors (a gift from Serena, and almost identical to Serena's own), and her loose-flowing blonde hair. The woman turned to her boyfriend, nudged him in the ribs.

'Who does she think she is?' Cass heard her say, just audible over the racket of the band. 'Bloody Marianne Faithfull?'

In the dim corridor backstage, the noise from the bar only just dampened by the double doors, Cass turned to Angus. 'Why the hell did you book us in here? They're going to eat us alive.'

He shook his head. 'Never. You'll win them round. You always do.'

Cass still couldn't quite make up her mind about Angus.

He had approached them at Joe's bar one night, when they'd only just stepped down from the stage: the intense-looking man she'd noticed at their gigs for some time, staring up at them from a lonely table in the front row.

He'd said that he was managing a few bands, and asked if they'd ever thought of expanding their line-up: he loved the songs, but felt they'd suit a bigger sound. Drums, bass, electric guitars. 'Really broaden things out, you know?'

Watching Cass, he'd added, 'Or you could stick with the acoustics, mike them up. I'm not saying you need to go the whole nine yards. But have a think about it, won't you?'

Ivor had been enthusiastic: he'd written Angus's number down on the back of a beer-mat, slipped it into the pocket of his jeans. Back at Savernake Road, as they were getting ready for bed, he'd said, 'We should try this out, Cassie. Hugh on drums . . .'

He'd seen her face change. 'I really don't know what your problem is with Hugh. At least give him a try. Jonah knows a guy, Danny, who plays bass, and has just quit his band. He says Danny likes our stuff. I think this could really work.'

She'd held fast for a while, convinced that the music she could hear in her head was exactly as they played it, and should remain so. Two unamplified guitars, two voices – plain and unadorned as the old oak table that stood in Lily's kitchen at Atterley. The folk sound her aunt had taught her to love, and under whose tutelage she had strummed out her first, faltering chords.

That was not the only music that spoke to her, of course. Her record collection was growing steadily, her long-adored Beatles and Stones records filed alongside carefully chosen albums by the Kinks, the Byrds, the Small Faces, the Who. She now had her own copies, too, of the folk discs Lily had introduced her to, to which she had added others by Simon and Garfunkel, Tom Arnold, Judy Collins, Pentangle, Dave Van Ronk. She liked best the singers who told stories, for whom the words were as important as the music, each element indivisible from the other.

At Savernake Road, where Bob ruled the record-player, they all sat up late into the night listening to Pink Floyd, Jefferson Airplane and the Incredible String Band. Jonah had introduced her to the rough, bluesy acts he knew and depped for, on oc-casion: the Yardbirds, the Bluesbreakers and Fleetwood Mac, whom she, Jonah and Ivor had been to see one night at the Marquee. They'd been unable to take their eyes from the singer, Peter Green, intense and messianic in his long white robe: *he* played an electric, Ivor was at pains to point out.

'It's not enough, Cass,' he said, 'just you and me sitting on stage like that, unamplified. It's been four years since Newport now. It's time to move on.'

Somewhere, deep down, she had begun to sense that Ivor was right – but she would not let him know that just yet. 'You said it was just you and me. You said that would always be enough.'

He nodded. 'It *is* you and me. You, me and the others.'

Still, for weeks, Cass had withstood Ivor's pressure, ignored his pleas to at least let him call Angus back.

And then, one day, on her lunch break from Cornelia's shop, Cass had found herself wandering down Denmark Street, and standing in front of a shop window, staring at a Gibson Les Paul.

The guitar was solid-bodied, its long neck studded with mother-of-pearl, its dark wood polished, shining. In her mind, she'd heard it: full-voiced and resonant, weaving under and over the plucked strings of her acoustic, while their voices merged, and the rhythm section kept a steady pulse, like the heart beating deep inside the body of the animal, pumping blood to brain, and lungs, and coiled, twitching muscle.

The next day, at lunchtime, she'd taken her father's green-tooled edition of *Great Expectations* to a second-hand bookshop on Charing Cross Road and handed it over before she could change her mind. Then she'd quick-marched along to Denmark Street, and exchanged the notes the bookseller had given her – more, in fact, than she'd anticipated – for the Les Paul.

At home that night, she'd presented the guitar, in its black case, to Ivor. 'For you. All right. Let's give this a go.'

Things had moved quickly after that. They'd brought in Danny, who was slight and affable, with an impressive handlebar moustache, and begun rehearsals in Hugh's bedroom, his wild green eyes staring down at them from the walls.

She was still wary of Hugh – there was something rather feral and unpredictable about him, and she hated the way he spoke to her as if she were a child, there only to be petted and patronised. But she couldn't deny that he knew what he was doing: with Hugh and Danny's input, their songs seemed to open out into something fuller, wider, more layered and intense.

And there was something exciting – erotic, even, though she did not quite articulate the thought – about having the three men arranged around her, immersed in the music she had written. Sometimes, at a song's end, they would all stay silent for a few seconds, eyes closed, like lovers unwilling to let the moment go.

After a month or so, Ivor had called Angus and asked him over to Savernake Road to hear them play.

They'd set themselves up in the garden (hang the neighbours – they were all squares anyway), surrounded by candles and flowers stuffed haphazardly into jugs, and played five songs straight through – 'Common Ground', 'Living Free', 'I Wrote You a Love Song' and a couple of new ones – while Serena, Kate, Bob, Paul, Jonah and the rest of their crowd danced barefoot on the grass.

Angus had smiled his sphinx-like smile and said, 'Great stuff. I'm glad you took my advice.'

The next day, in a pub on South End Road, they'd signed a makeshift contract Angus had scribbled on the back of an envelope. *We, the undersigned, agree to the representation of Angus Mackinnon, and only Angus Mackinnon.*

'Now,' Angus had said, pouring each of them a celebratory glass of Blue Nun, 'we just need to get you a name.'

It was Bob who'd come up with it. 'Vertical Heights,' he'd pronounced solemnly one night after watching Hitchcock's *Vertigo* while tripping. None of them particularly liked the name, or even quite understood its significance, but nobody could think of anything better. And anyway, Angus had already found them a van and booked a string of gigs, so 'Vertical Heights' would just have to do for now.

Wakefield, Northampton, Lowestoft, Bury, Spalding: towns that were, to all of them, no more than words on a map, and which quickly began to seem indistinguishable. A shifting series of car-parks and student unions and working men's clubs where they played on tiny stages between the comedian and the bingo-caller, and could never be sure if they'd be greeted with whoops and cheers or booing and cat-calls.

And yet, through it all, Angus remained sanguine, unruffled. He was sanguine the time a crowd of lads in leather jackets turned up and stood at the front, shouting obscenities at Cass until one of the other punters suggested they treat the lady with some respect, and they turned on him, beginning a fight that ended with the tables being overturned, the police being called, and all four members of Vertical Heights running, with Angus, for the safety of the van. He was sanguine the time the student comedian who'd been on before them had got drunk, outstayed his welcome, and walked up and down the front of the stage throughout their set. He was sanguine when people clapped, and called for more; and he was sanguine when people didn't clap, and sat watching them in stony silence. (This was an increasingly rare occurrence, but there had been a night in Mablethorpe that they all preferred to forget.) He booked their gigs, made sure they arrived on time, checked the footfall on the door, and handed over their earnings in cash (less his twenty per cent, of course) once a week.

Angus was the least mutable person Cass had ever met, and this, she'd decided, was the source of her incipient mistrust: she simply couldn't understand a person whose emotional state never seemed to shift out of neutral, no matter the chemicals he pumped into his body. And yet she couldn't help but find Angus's confidence contagious – for they were good, she knew they were, and no matter how unpromising the crowd, they would always find a way to prove it.

In the dressing-room that evening – Angus was right: it was no larger than a wardrobe, and its mint-green paint was flaking from the walls – he handed her the requisite glass of wine, and said, as he always did, 'It'll be great. Just go out there and enjoy yourselves.'

Ivor was perched on a battered metal chair. Cass settled herself on his lap, put her face to his neck, breathed in the smell of him: damp velvet (he was wearing the new green jacket they'd picked up the week before on Petticoat Lane); tobacco; and the faint, alluring tang of sweat.

'All right, babe?' he said, and she looked up at him, pale-faced under the stark, unshaded bulb, and said, 'I will be when I'm up there.'

Hugh, behind them, took a final swig from his bottle of Bell's, and got to his feet.

'Right,' he said. 'Let's go and knock their little northern socks off.'

This is what she remembers.

Hot lights and smoke and faces. Amps like black, gaping mouths, opening and closing, pouring out sound: the screech and howl of guitar; the deep undertow of bass, vibrating underfoot, up through leg to thigh, to chest, to brain. The thud, thud, thud of drums. The beat of the heart, the passage of blood along artery and vein. The measured drip-feed of time, now fast, now slow: unignorable, siren-like, issuing its relentless rhythm.

Her feet stepping, unbidden, in time with the kick. Her hand cradling the neck of the instrument, claw-fingered, moving over string and fret. Her microphone close and intimate as a lover's ear.

Her voice, and his, and theirs. Hips moving, heads moving and the heat of the lights and the rising clouds of cigarette smoke. The crowd staring up, all their many eyes and noses and mouths belonging to the same single, writhing creature. No place but this place, no time but this time, and she is nowhere, and everywhere, diving and swimming in this pool of sound. Waves and eddies and riptides, pulling her under. No air, no space to breathe.

At the song's end, she rises, and catches her breath, and there is a tiny interval of silence and stillness, so brief that she almost misses it, for they are clapping now, and shouting, beating out their own rhythms with the ancient pressure of palm on palm. And there, up on the stage above them, she is smiling, and Ivor is whispering in her ear, 'Count four, then straight into "Living Free".'

It is a dream, and it is not a dream: the grey breeze-block walls, and the high, broad windows with their garlands of dust and cobweb; the psychedelic whorl of the dartboard; and the tattered posters flapping from a sheet of cork: 'Bingo Wednesdays' and 'Friday is Live Music Night!' and 'Book now for the OAP Day Trip to Blackpool.'

When Cass closes her eyes, leans in close to the microphone, she sees her mother, and her father, and the church on the common with its high white dome; and Ivor, and Lily and John, and Cornelia, surrounded by her empty white dresses of lace and tulle.

She has shucked off the skin of the girl she used to be: she is wide-eyed and unafraid, rising weightlessly above the crowd. And there, high above, she thrills to it all, as they do down there on the floor. For it is here, and now, drawn by the ebb and flow of the song, that they know they are alive, and together, and that nothing can take that away from them: not now, not here, not for as long as the music lasts.

Those years with Vertical Heights seem, now, coloured by the greyscale spectrum of night.

Wet black tarmac and white lines, unspooling endlessly beyond the steamed-up windows of the van. The sodium flashes of motorway lights, and the blinking tail-lamps of cars. Shuttered factories, stately and silent; cooling towers exhaling their great out-breaths of steam, and the hulls of gasometers, ribbed with struts and fins of steel.

The sudden, unforgiving glare of service-stations. Improbably jaunty waitresses in tiny skirts, pouring tea into brown china cups. The greasy Formica tables at which they sat up for hours with their own kind – some they already knew, others they recognised by their clothes, their unbrushed hair, the nocturnal energy that pulsed, electric, from them all. Whisky poured over tea dregs; joints rolled over the congealing remnants of double egg, chips and beans. Waitresses drawn giggling outside to the lorry-park, with its long, secretive shadows.

Music on the jukebox, and bikers milling in restive herds, and tired truckers washing down their sausage and chips with mugs of Bovril. Cass standing with Ivor on the forecourt smoking Players cigarettes, while Hugh and Danny and Angus slipped off with whichever girl had caught their eye, and she drew her arm tighter around Ivor's waist.

She was rarely alone, on those nights – not with the five of them crammed into the van alongside their kit; the unending cycle of loading and unloading; the crowds in the clubs, and the bright, strip-lit bustle of those service-station jamborees. And yet when she recalls those early tours, she sees herself as set slightly off-centre, a figure placed almost at the edge of the frame. The men laughing together in the back of the van, sharing a joke she hadn't quite caught. Angus at the wheel, Cass beside him on the front seat, and the other guys tumbled together in the back like exhausted children, stretched out on the thin mattresses they'd thrown down between the drum boxes and guitar cases, and where, she knew, they sometimes brought their women after gigs.

She was not naive about this, even then; she was not a child. Several times, Cass returned to the van or the dressing-room to find Ivor with some new slender, miniskirted girl. Each time, Cass slid her arm around Ivor's back, or laid her head, briefly and emphatically, on his shoulder; and the girl, whoever she was, looked at her, and shrugged, and moved away.

There were arguments, then: snarling, drunken rows that

undercut the joy they shared on stage. Rows that began, most often, with Cass pointing out that Ivor encouraged these women, that he liked the attention; and Ivor throwing back at her the fact that she didn't seem to mind too much when other men came sniffing after her.

And it was true – they did come. Not as consistently as the women, but Cass would, some nights, become aware of the eyes of certain men in the audience watching her with an intensity that she found both unsettling and thrilling. Other men might shout things out: stupid, puerile comments that made her blush. *Show us your tits, love. Got something else you can get your mouth round down here.* Sometimes, Ivor would lose his temper, and turn on the audience with raised fists.

But it was the men who said nothing that she really had to watch out for. The men who might sidle up to her in the hour or so of downtime Angus permitted them between the last song and the loading of the van, and say, as if each of these phrases were newly minted, entirely original, 'Fancy a drink, darlin'?' Or, 'You looked sexy up there.' Or, 'So what's a nice girl like you doing with a rabble like that?'

One night, in Newcastle, an argument that began in the dressing-room (Hugh had brought a couple of girls backstage, and Cass had walked in to find one of them sitting on Ivor's lap) spilt across the gig, and limped on into its aftermath.

Cass was at the bar, finishing her fourth glass of wine and pointedly ignoring Ivor, when a man with a shaggy mane of blond hair and a sallow, fleshy face came up and offered to buy her another drink.

'Bell's,' she said flatly. 'Double. No ice.'

'Whisky-drinker, are you?' the man said. 'Well, if we haven't got ourselves a regular Janis Joplin.'

He wasn't at all her type – stocky and heavy-set, and dull with it; and anyway, she was Ivor's, and he, she reminded herself as the whisky slid down her throat, was hers. But when the stranger asked if she'd like to step outside, she went with him willingly, and allowed him to lead her round the back of the clubhouse, to where the shadows were thickest, and to press his slippery mouth to hers, and to place his hands on her body. And when, just a few moments later, Ivor stepped out from those shadows, furious, his arm drawing back to land a blow on the man's face – she didn't even know his name, and she never would – Cass stood back and watched them with an ugly sense of triumph.

Later, in the van, when the shouting was over, Ivor leant over to her and said, quietly, 'Why did you do that, Cassie? Why did you have to make a fool of me?'

'So you'd know,' she said, 'how it feels when you make one of me.'

One dark, freezing day in late December, Cass and Ivor managed to ignore their alarm clock and sleep on through most of the morning.

'Watch out,' Daphne whispered when Cass finally arrived at Cornelia's shop, 'she's on the warpath.'

Indeed, Cass was shortly called into the back office, where, among bolts of silk, tiaras and glittering paste jewels, Cornelia said, her voice tight, 'I try, as you must know by now, Cassandra, to be as patient as I can with my girls – to support you all, and your ambitions, in every way I can. But there are limits, and you, I'm afraid, have reached yours. So tell me – do you actually wish to keep this job?'

Cass looked at her boss – at her kind, thin, hollow-eyed face. She felt tiredness settle over her; it had been a very late night – a show in Leicester, followed by a particularly boisterous gathering at the Blue Boar. She thought of the envelope that Angus had handed over as the van had finally drawn up on Savernake Road just after five. 'Happy Christmas,' he'd said, as if the money were a gift. It wasn't a lot, but it would, she decided in that moment, be enough.

'No,' she said now: gently, because she liked Cornelia, and knew how ungrateful she must sound. She was, it seemed, becoming fluent in the language of ingratitude. 'I don't think I do.'

'Well.' Cornelia looked down at her desk. 'This will be your last shift, then. And don't think you'll be getting your Christmas bonus, Cassandra, or any sort of reference. I'd expected better of you. I really had.'

It was a frenetic afternoon – brides in for final fittings for their Christmas wedding gowns, slipping on long-sleeved satin and fur wraps. Dusk fell early over Oxford Street, and Cass's tiredness seemed to thicken until it was all she could do to keep from laying her head on the counter.

'Irene Lewis,' Cornelia said at half-past four, as Daphne was laying an ivory silk gown carefully into its pink tissue-lined box. 'First fitting, wedding next August, which hardly leaves us much time, does it?'

'Irene Lewis?' Cass echoed.

Cornelia looked up from her appointments book, and sighed. '*Yes*, Cassandra. Good to know you're actually paying me the courtesy of listening.'

'I'll take that fitting,' Cass said quickly, and Cornelia gave a peremptory nod.

'Well, I suppose we might as well get some use out of you.'

They arrived at a quarter to five: Irene and her mother, twin figures in camel double-breasted coats, hats perched on their neat shampoo-and-sets.

'My goodness! Maria Wheeler!' Irene's mother said at once, beaming, and coming forward to kiss Cass on each cheek. 'Whatever are you doing here?'

Irene hung back, not quite matching her mother's smile.

'Cassandra, now, Mum,' she said. 'She's called *Cassandra* now.'

'Of course.' Irene's mother – her name, Cass remembered then, was Alice – still had a gloved hand on each of Cass's arms. Up close, she smelt of Pond's face-cream and hairspray, and the mingled scents took Cass back to that yellow living-room across the common, with its genteel chaos and its piano and its soft brown rug. She was filled with such a rush of nostalgia that, in her exhausted state, tears gathered in her eyes.

Alice, kind as ever, pretended that she hadn't noticed. 'This really is the most remarkable thing. Will you be doing Irene's fitting?'

'How long have you been working here?' Irene asked in the fitting-room. She was undressing; Cass stood a few feet away, sliding the camel coat onto a hanger, taking Irene's blouse, jumper and skirt. Irene was down to her slip now, and Cass could see that her old friend had filled out: the flesh of her arms and stomach had the soft, malleable quality of unrisen dough, and her breasts were heavy, pendulous. Sensing Cass's eyes on her, Irene drew her arms protectively across her body.

'Just over a year,' Cass said. 'But it's just to pay the rent. I'm a singer. This is my last shift here, actually.'

'A singer?'

'Yes. And I play guitar. We have a band, Ivor and me. Ivor's my boyfriend. We both write the songs.'

'Goodness.' Irene caught Cass's gaze in the mirror, and smiled. 'That's wonderful. I always thought . . . Oh, I don't know. I just always thought you'd do something special, Maria. I mean Cass.'

Cass returned her smile. 'Thanks, Irene. And what are you doing these days?'

She was studying history at University College London; her fiancé, Mike, was in his third year, too, taking medicine. They were to marry the following summer, once Irene had graduated.

'Mike will have a good few years to go,' Irene explained as Cass was busying herself around the dress, pinning and tucking, drawing it out a few inches at the waist, 'but it feels right to marry now. We'd like to start a family straight away.'

She coloured a little, and Cass, to spare her old friend's embarrassment, said, 'You can have a whole brood of them, like you and your brothers. It was always so much fun at your house. There was so much light and noise.'

'Yes.' Irene was silent for a moment; when she spoke again, her voice was deeper, more intimate. 'I cried for weeks, you know, Cass. When you went off with Julia and her crowd. I'd never felt lonelier in my life.'

Cass was grateful for her mouthful of pins. When she'd slid the last one into the hemline, she said, 'I'm sorry, Irene. I really am. I suppose I lost it a bit, after . . . well, after my mother left.'

It was the first time in many years that she'd said these words aloud. She turned away, looking for the tape measure.

'But you were happy with your aunt and uncle, weren't you?' Irene said. 'You seem happy now.'

'Oh yes,' Cass said, turning back to her. 'I loved living at Atterley. Lily and John gave me my first guitar, and, I suppose, the confidence to start writing songs, and . . . well, I can't tell you what that means to me. Just about everything.'

'Good,' Irene said, and she took Cass's hand in hers. 'I'm so glad.'

It was fully dark when the fitting ended, and the Christmas lights blinked above the street, over the milling, hatted heads of shoppers.

At the door, Alice asked whether Cass might like to join them for a glass of mulled wine – they could find a table in the pub on the corner, wait for her to finish up. But Cass, aware of Cornelia and Daphne watching from the counter, said, 'Oh, that would be lovely, but I can't, I'm afraid. Not tonight.'

'What a shame,' Alice said, and she leant in to kiss her again. 'Well, take our number down, at least – surely you two have a lot to catch up on?'

Irene nodded, smiled, and produced a notebook from her neat brown leather handbag. 'We're at home for Christmas. I know Dad would love to see you, too. And the boys.'

Cass nodded. 'Thank you. Happy Christmas.'

She took the folded sheet from Irene, slid it up under the sleeve of her cardigan. But she knew, even as she did so, that she wouldn't call – that she and Irene, after a moment or two of politeness and faintly remembered affection, would find that they had nothing at all to say to one another. And then she thought of Ivor, of that terrible moment outside the Newcastle club, that stranger's hands on her body, and Ivor's face made ugly by rage and incomprehension, and she had the strange, disorientating sense of her life stretching out before her in this way, in a series of shifting alliances – nothing solid, nothing lasting, everything falling away as quickly as it came into being. She felt suddenly dizzy, and put out a hand to the wall.

'Honestly,' she heard Cornelia say, 'you really *must* go home and get some sleep, Cassandra. You look quite done in.'

'Yes, thank you,' she heard her own voice say in turn. 'I will. I'm tired. I really am so very tired.'

'Don't Step On the Cracks'

By Cass Wheeler
From the album *Songs From the Music Hall*

Don't step on the cracks, he said
That sad-eyed old man
With the dirty and tattered blue coat
And the bag in his hand holding everything he owned

I told him I wouldn't
But that was a lie
For I look for danger
His rules are not mine

Don't step on the cracks, you said
You've broken my heart again
It's shattered and splintered apart
And fallen too far to make up from the start

I told you I wouldn't
But that was a lie
For I want my freedom
And rules are not mine

I'll step on the cracks to get there
Although it may seem I don't care
If I have to leave you, it's not fair
But I'll step on the cracks to get there

I told you I wouldn't
But that was a lie
For I want my freedom
And rules are not mine

Ahhhhhh
They're not mine they're not mine they're not mine

RELEASED 10 September 1973
RECORDED July 1973 at Château d'Anjou Studios, France
GENRE Folk rock / soft rock / pop
LABEL Phoenix Records
WRITER(S) Cass Wheeler
PRODUCER(S) Martin Hartford
ENGINEER(S) Luc Giraud

A Wednesday in February, damp and bone-cold, smelling of woodsmoke and mulching earth.

Cass made her way downstairs, wrapped in the oversized cardigan Serena had knitted her for Christmas, and set the kettle to boil. The kitchen was freezing. She stood by the stove, warming her hands beside the flame, debating whether to slip another coin into the gas meter: it ate money in winter, so they were rationing its use.

She could hear Ivor moving around upstairs: the creak and give of the loose floorboard on the landing as he crossed to the bathroom; the sudden gush and gurgle of toilet and basin. A low guttural rattle coming from behind Hugh's closed door (he was a terrible snorer – they often had to poke him awake in the van) and the intermittent bark of the neighbour's Alsatian.

The high-pitched whistle of the kettle; the rush and hiss of boiling water as she poured it into two mugs. And then the telephone, squealing from its perch in the hallway. She let it ring, reaching for the milk, then stepped quickly through with a mug in her hand, placing the receiver to her ear.

'Hello?'

'Hello. Is that Cass Wheeler, by any chance?'

A man's voice, a stranger's: softly spoken, educated, betraying only the faintest trace of flat London vowels.

'Yes. That's me. Who's calling?'

His name was Martin Hartford. He was a producer at a label called Phoenix – a division of Lieberman Records, he explained, which he had established for new artists working, as he put it, 'in the intriguing hinterland between folk, rock and blues'.

An image struck her – a flat, desert landscape, sand and barbed wire – and would lodge itself in her memory for some time.

'Jonah Hills passed me your tape a few weeks ago, before he

went back to the States,' Martin said. 'I liked it – I liked it a *lot*, in fact – but I wanted to see you guys live. I've been busy, so it took me some time to get round to it. But I did see you, last night. And do you know what?' He paused, as if waiting for Cass to supply an answer, but she did not. 'Well, you blew me away. I'd have told you that myself, but I couldn't stay.'

'You saw us last night? At the Avenue?' Cass was buying time: she'd heard Martin perfectly clearly, and with each word she could feel the excitement rising inside her, ready to explode and swallow speech. Beneath it, the certainty, cool and bright and true, that this was the moment she had been waiting for, the moment after which nothing would ever be quite the same.

The creaking complaint of the loose floorboard. She looked up, saw Ivor standing on the stairs, drawing a jumper on over his shirt.

'Who is it?' he mouthed down to her, and she put a finger to her lips.

'I did,' Martin was saying, 'and it was some gig. I mean, the songs are great, but your performance, too . . . Well, I haven't seen anything like that in a long time. Ever, maybe. Not from a . . . well, to put it bluntly, a *woman*. Not on this side of the Atlantic, anyway. There's something about you, Cass, something that makes people stop and listen. So many seek it, I can tell you, but so few truly have it.'

The excitement, now, was loud as the roar of the sea inside a shell; the leap and rush of waves, forming and breaking, forming and breaking.

Martin cleared his throat. 'So I was wondering, Cass, whether you might be interested in coming to meet me. Have a chat.'

Cass leant back against the wall, the mug unsteady in her hand. She glanced up at Ivor, crouching bent-kneed on the stairs. His brown-green eyes, in the half-light, seemed almost black, the irises swallowed by the dark discs of his pupils. It was not only whisky he and the others had celebrated with the previous night: they'd slipped off together backstage to the men's toilets, returned glassy, euphoric, carrying that faint sweet, lingering scent of burnt sugar. They had asked her to join them, but something – a wordless impulse that she couldn't disobey; the instinctive reluctance to lose herself – made her refuse.

'Well, yes,' she said, 'I don't see why we couldn't come in. When were you thinking? I'll get the band together. Ivor lives here, with me. And so does Hugh, the drummer. But I'll need to call Danny. He's the bassist. But of course you must know that already . . .' She faltered, aware that she was babbling.

'Yes, I do know that, and today would be wonderful, if you're free.' There was a brief, pregnant pause. 'But, Cass . . . I wondered, actually, whether you might come in alone. It's you I'd like to speak to first, if that's all right. Just you.'

'Just me?' she repeated dumbly. 'But we're a band. I can't see why . . .'

Ivor, on the stairs, did not lift his gaze from her face. She talked on into the telephone, and he looked away, got to his feet, and went back upstairs.

After the meeting, she emerged, blinking, onto Tottenham Court Road. The day was still dull and cold, and the clouds had gathered, threatening rain; she drew her coat more tightly around her, pulled her scarf up over her chin.

It was a quarter past three. In the blank-faced buildings overhead, office-workers were clattering away at typewriters, or standing up from their desks to boil the kettle for another cup of tea. Shop-girls were dawdling at counters; white-costumed chefs were sitting on fire-escapes, cupping cigarettes between curled palms; neatly dressed women were stepping briskly into taxis. A few paces ahead of Cass, a man in a filthy blue anorak, fastened with a length of string, was making slow, juddering progress towards her, talking softly to himself; and a group of tourists in raincoats were striding purposefully towards Oxford Street, cameras dangling from their necks. As they passed, Cass heard one of the women say something to another – a clipped, brisk language that she thought might be German – and then her friend's incomprehensible reply.

She walked north, towards Goodge Street, with only a vague sense of where she was going, seeking the comforting solidity of the pavement beneath her feet. Outside Whitefield Chapel, she stopped, reached into her pocket for her cigarettes, then stood smoking, stamping her feet against the cold.

'A unique talent,' Martin had said, as the other men – they had all been men, with the exception of the secretary who'd brought in the tea – had nodded. The era of the 'singer-songwriter'. (They said the word so, between invisible quote marks, as if trying it on for size.) Confessional songs: frank, emotive, honest. Carole King. Joni Mitchell. Did she own *Tapestry*? *Ladies of the Canyon*? Yes. And did she like them? Of course she did. Those women were good. They were more than good, in fact – they were *real artists* – and so, these men felt, was she. And she might, just might, be what intelligent British music fans were looking for – women, above all, and more and more of the record-buying public were women. Did she realise that? Not *girls* – not those teenyboppers who'd hoarded their pocket money for 45s, massing outside Beatles concerts, screaming so loudly nobody could catch a damn note. Had she been one of them? Yes, without the screaming: she'd always hated the screaming. Five nodding heads. Well, like her, those girls were women now, with their own money to spend, their own record-players spinning in their bedsits and living-rooms. And they needed an artist who would take their own lives, their own dreams and ambitions and failed love affairs, and reflect them back, help them understand themselves anew.

Five pairs of eyes, boring holes into her skull. What did she think? Surely she could see how much stronger – how much *freer* – she would be up there on her own, her name on the bill, the band there to support her, rather than trying to claim the glory for themselves?

Glory. She didn't like that word. She didn't see her music in those terms.

In what terms, then, did she see it?

Songs. Fragments of time, caught in three, four, six beats to a bar. These melodies that appeared in her mind, tugged at her sleeve, refused to let go. The moments, on the stage, when there no longer seemed to be any distance between herself and the band and the strangers down there on the floor.

More nodding. *That* was how they knew she was the real thing. It was the music that mattered to her. They could see it; they could feel it when she sang. That was what made it *special*. But didn't she want to share that music with as many people as possible? Was she happy playing to dozens of people, when they could put her in front of hundreds, even thousands?

But Ivor. Ivor, Ivor, Ivor.

Yes. Ivor Tait. They wrote well together, and they could see there was chemistry between them. She'd need a lead guitarist, anyway, and he was good. Not *Clapton* good – not yet, anyway – but good enough. Danny and Hugh – if she didn't mind them speaking plainly – well, they were nothing to write home about. There were scores of session drummers and bassists in London. They'd audition some. Get her in the studio. Get her talking to the press. Get her out there.

So. It was a lot to take in, they knew. Did she want some time to think it over?

She did. She had shaken their hands, taken the lift downstairs, and stepped outside.

Now, her cigarette had dwindled to a stub, and her gloveless hands felt stiff. Across the damp pavement, the man in the dirty blue anorak was inching back towards her, staring intently at the ground.

'Cracks, cracks,' he was muttering. 'Mustn't step on the cracks.'

There was something about the man's face – some firm-chinned air of dignity, despite the dirt, the delirium, the un-washed smell rising from his clothes – that reminded her of her father. She saw Francis in her mind, hard-faced in his tidy little flat. The way he had spoken to her, so cruel, so unfamiliar. *Some pipe-dream of being a singer. Don't think I don't know what sort of woman you are.*

She hadn't been back to Worthing since that disastrous afternoon, though Lily said Francis kept asking when she was coming back. She knew she was being stubborn, but something had altered in her; some connection had frayed.

Lily was impatient with her. The doctors, she reminded Cass, were now calling it dementia: Francis, at sixty-six, was still rela-tively young, but they could find no other diagnosis. His mind was clouding, and quickly: all that intelligence, that knowledge of scripture, literature, history, fading away. Lily said that he probably hadn't known what he was saying. Oh, but Cass knew that he *had*: he'd seen her mother in her, and in that moment, as Cass poured his tea, he'd hated them both, and he had wanted her to know it.

'Well, all I can say is that it's a shame,' was Lily's reply, 'when you're all he has left in the world. You'll regret it one day, Cass. I know you will.'

Cass had thought of Margaret, then, over in Canada, still sending her cards and letters twice a year: her birthday, Christ-mas. Last Christmas Day, grown sentimental on the generous measures of brandy Uncle John had poured after pudding, Cass had finally written back: *I'm writing music now. I'm living in Gospel Oak, in a beautiful Victorian house with a big garden filled with long grass. I'm in love with an amazing, talented man named Ivor Tait.*

I don't need you, she had hidden between the lines. *I don't need you now, and I never did.*

Margaret's reply had arrived early in the New Year. *I can't tell you how happy we are to have finally heard from you. Josephine is almost eight now – she's growing up so fast – and she's always asking about her sister in London. Write to us again, won't you, Maria, and tell us more?*

How would it be now, she thought, *to go home and compose another letter back?* She'd write, *Tell Josephine I've signed a record deal. Tell Josephine her big sister is 'the real thing'. Tell Josephine that plain old Maria Wheeler is dead and gone.*

And Ivor, waiting for her at Savernake Road – he'd refused, at first, to let her attend the meeting alone: had insisted on coming with her, until she'd stalked out in a huff, letting the front door slam – what was she to say to him? There were, it seemed, no words; and yet, somehow, she must find them. For she already knew that she would not walk away from this; that inside her, there was steel, and ice, and the unignorable voice of her ambition. *Take this*, that voice was saying. *Take this chance, and hang the consequences. You can do this. You must do this.*

The man in the blue anorak was level with her now. He looked up, met her gaze. His eyes were startling blue pools in the dirt-rimmed crevasses of his face.

'Cracks,' he said gently. 'Mind you don't step on the cracks, now, love.'

'No,' she said. 'Thank you. I won't.'

She was expecting many things of Ivor: coldness, fury, even violence. He had never been violent towards her, but she sensed in him – in the often frenzied rhythm of their love-making; in that moment, behind the Newcastle club, when rage had overcome him, his face seeming transformed, entirely *other* – the capacity to be so. And that knowledge, in some bone-deep way that Cass had not yet fully acknowledged to herself, filled her with an uncomfortable feeling of inevitability. Margaret's hand whipping against her skin. Her own childish brown eyes staring back at herself in the vicarage hallway. The anger that had welled up in Cass then, fervent and hot, and that she knew lay inside Ivor, too, as it had lain inside his father, and his father's father, back up through the shifting generations. He had not had to say much about his childhood for her to understand its pattern, and its legacy.

She was not, however, expecting Ivor's silence.

'I see,' he said. They were sitting at the table in the kitchen, where, just a few hours earlier, she'd made their morning coffee. Already, it seemed transformed, as if all of it – the scuffed, freestanding cabinets, not changed since before the war; the tattered Pink Floyd poster Bob had picked up at Kensington Market; the washing-up stacked in the sink, with its days-old layers of congealed grease – were a stage set designed for other people, living other lives.

She watched his face; he seemed not so much angry, or jealous, or even disappointed, as thoughtful. 'Well? What do you think? What should we do?'

Ivor did not reply. He looked back at her for a long moment, his head on one side, as if taking the measure of her for the first time. And then he leant forward, placed a hand, gently, on her arm, and got to his feet.

'Where are you going?' she said. But he just squeezed her arm, withdrew his hand, and left the room.

She got up to follow him. 'Ivor! You can't just ignore me . . . *Talk* to me. Tell me what you're thinking. I need to let them know . . .' Her voice was a shrill, plaintive whine, and he did not turn back. She pursued him outside, down the garden path, onto the street.

'Ivor!' she called, but still he didn't turn, and a woman passing with a pram looked round to offer her a censorious glare.

'Ivor,' Cass said again, more quietly, but he was a good few yards away now, a hunched figure in a green velvet jacket that was too light for the weather, his hands thrust deep inside his pockets.

She broke her news to the others in the dressing-room that night, just before the show: her offer from Phoenix Records, and her concern for Ivor, who had not come home.

'Right. That's that, then, isn't it?' Danny hissed, his usual affability dissolving. 'You're selling us down the river. No, actually, you're selling *yourself* down the river, and leaving us on the bloody bank.'

'Danny.' She placed a hand on his arm, but he threw it off. 'I haven't made up my mind yet. I'd like to talk to you all about it. Calmly, you know? Make a decision as a band.'

'Well, Lady C.' Hugh was heavy-lidded, dreamily stoned. 'Trouble is, it's not really our decision to make, is it?' He licked his lips, drew his tongue along the shaft of a fresh joint. 'Now, I don't know about anyone else, but I've dragged my arse down here, so I'm bloody well going to do the show. Ivor'll be here. He'll have been off licking his wounds. And personally, I don't blame him.'

Angus, fortunately, wasn't there that night. (She was dreading telling him about Martin and Phoenix almost as much as she'd dreaded telling Ivor.) And Hugh was proved right – in the seconds before they were due on stage, Ivor appeared, wet-haired and stinking of whisky.

'Where've you been?' Cass asked him as they stepped out into the corridor, but he stalked ahead without saying a word.

On stage, Ivor did not turn to her once, and he missed several of his cues – deliberately, Cass suspected, as he was usually precise in his timing. As she sang, she could sense her concern for him – for his hurt pride, for the blow Martin's offer must inevitably deal to his own ambitions – beginning to fade, replaced by a fast-burning, blue-flamed sense of outrage. This was *her* success, *her* opportunity – and one that included him, too; she'd done all she could to ensure that there would still be room for him – yet Ivor wasn't happy for her in the least. He was acting like a spoilt, selfish child, and she was damned if she was going to indulge him.

At the set's end, Cass bowed to the applause, and then strode quickly off stage. By the time the others appeared in the dressing-room, she'd already stowed her guitar in its case, and was buttoning her coat.

'You should really mess with our heads like that before every show, Cass,' Danny said. 'Oh, whoops – there probably won't *be* a next time, will there?'

She gave him a sharp look. 'Danny, I'm sorry. But I argued for you, all right? I did my best.'

He shrugged. 'Wasn't worth much, then, was it?'

Ivor came in then, with Hugh. Turning to him, she said, 'What the *fuck* was that out there?'

Ivor returned her gaze unsteadily, his eyes blinking, unfocused. 'What? I'm just meant to get up there and play for *you*, am I? Be your little backing singer?' His words were slurred, but flung like rocks. 'Well, Cassandra, fuck that. If you want to go out there and try to make it on your own, that's exactly what you'll be. On your own. Because I'm buggered if I'm going to stand there next to you like some bloody session player.'

Her anger was a blaze now, scorching everything in sight. But at the centre of the flame, there was a cool, open space, and she walked into it, closed her eyes.

'Fine.' She was no longer shouting. 'Don't think I need *you*, Ivor Tait. Or any of you. I didn't ask for this, but it's happened. And if it had happened to any of you, you'd have said yes straight away. You *know* you would. Don't even try to pretend you wouldn't.'

And then she stepped past him, out past Hugh and Danny,

down the long corridor, and out through the side entrance into the street.

The air was fresh, icy, the road rain-slicked, swept by the yellow headlamps of passing cars. There, in the shadow of the building, leaning against the brickwork, she felt the heat of her anger fade away. In its place came the knowledge that, whatever its outcome, this day would lie between them for ever, sour in its recollection, carrying the rank aftertaste of smoke and ash and bitter disappointment.

She went to Kate's. Kate had moved out of Savernake Road six months before, and into a flat in Covent Garden that was owned by the merchant banker, Lucian, who had pursued her, charmingly and relentlessly, after seeing her in *Hair*. (They were sleeping together; he was married; the arrangement suited them both.)

The flat was huge, with two enormous bedrooms, each with its own bathroom, and a cavernous split-level living-room with a terrace on which Kate had planted herbs and bay trees and a jasmine that, last summer, had filled the air with its sweet, blowsy perfume. But it was winter now, and the plants were shrunken, folded in on themselves. Cass and Kate sat beside them on the terrace, wrapped in blankets, drinking their way determinedly through a bottle of Lucian's Sauternes.

'I'll tell them I'm not interested,' Cass said. 'I'll tell them it's the whole band or nothing. I mean, it's not as if they're the only label in London, is it? We'll do the rounds again with the tape.'

Kate nodded. They'd made the demo last year, in Hugh's room at Savernake Road, on Angus's Revox reel-to-reel. He'd sent it out to all the labels, all the A&R guys he knew, worked every contact he had. A few had been interested enough to come along to gigs. There'd even been a meeting, of sorts – three rounds of pints in a Charlotte Street boozer with a thirty-something man in a crumpled paisley shirt who'd said they had 'real potential, man. Real potential.' But nothing on the scale of Martin's offer, of those five smartly suited men watching her, weighing her up, offering her a vision of the future that matched so precisely the shape of her ambition.

'But is it selfish,' Cass said, 'to think that what Martin's saying might be true? Am I kidding myself?'

Kate shrugged. 'Maybe. But we all have to be a little bit self-ish, don't we? Ask yourself – ask yourself honestly – what Ivor would be doing in your place. Because I can tell you' – she leant down to the table between them, took up her glass – 'that he wouldn't be round here, wondering if he was doing the right thing. He'd have bitten their hands off, right there in the room. He's the most ambitious man I know. That's why he's so angry. Because it's you, not him.'

'I know.' Cass sipped her wine, let it slip silkily across her tongue. She thought, not for the first time, of Kate and Ivor together, of his pale white face leaning down to meet Kate's with a kiss. 'I've never asked you, have I? I've never really asked what happened between you and Ivor. Serena told me about it, but I didn't really . . . I suppose I didn't want to know.'

'Oh, that's old news now, Cass. Such old news.' Kate waved a hand, but when she saw that Cass was still looking at her, and waiting, she said, 'It's simple. I fell for him – who wouldn't, for God's sake? And he didn't fall for me. And then there was Ursula . . .' Cass's eyes narrowed at the name, and Kate added hastily, 'And then, of course, there was you. I could see it was different between you two. A meeting of equals, if you like. You could play him at his own game.'

'And he hates that, doesn't he?'

'Perhaps. But then, show me a man who doesn't.'

It was late now, very late; the only light was the residual glow of the living-room lamp, and the candle Kate had placed on the table. She was just a few years Cass's senior, but in the shadows, Kate seemed suddenly much older.

'If you want my advice, Cass – and I'm guessing you do, though it sounds to me like your mind is already made up – just go for it. Grasp it with both hands. Danny and Hugh will join other bands, or they won't – that's up to them, isn't it? And Ivor will come round, or he won't, and if he doesn't, at least you've struck out for something for yourself. At least you're not just trailing around after him – the little lady, waiting for *his* dream to come true. And what would you have if it never did? What would be left for you then?'

The question hung for a moment on the cool night air.

'But, Kate,' Cass said, her voice dropping to a whisper, 'what if Ivor doesn't come round? What if he says it's over?'

Kate shrugged. 'Then you have a choice, don't you? And if you choose him, well . . . then you know that you're doing it all for him. That the music – owning it, performing it, knowing that people are there to see *you* – doesn't really matter to you. That you're content to live your life through him.'

Cass closed her eyes, threw back the last drops of wine. When she opened her eyes again, she knew that her decision was already made.

Monday morning on Tottenham Court Road. The blare and hiss of traffic; the grime of unswept pavements; the faint, nauseating stench of unemptied bins. And Cass Wheeler, twenty years old, standing outside a tall limestone office building in her Afghan coat, her guitar case lying on the ground at her feet.

A hand on her shoulder. She turned, and the world spun, blurred, righted itself.

'You're here!'

'I'm here,' Ivor said, and his hand slipped into hers.

3 p.m.

Mid-afternoon: drowsy, numbing, rudderless.

Somewhere over the north Atlantic, Larry Alderson puts down his book, stretches one long leg out as far as it can go beneath the airline chair in front, accepts a refill of scotch from a passing stewardess, and hopes – believes – that he is doing the right thing.

A thousand miles east, high above the jumbled roofs and walls and gardens of Kent, another plane inches slowly up towards a loose drift of cloud.

Out on the Tunbridge Road, a car takes the blind corner a little too quickly, its brakes offering a complaining squeal.

Inside her studio, Cass Wheeler pours herself a glass of water.

The sun has shifted across the garden, leaving the listening-room in shadow: she is chilly in her loose cotton shirt, her mind a cacophonous jumble of sound, image, memory.

She has always been muddle-headed in the middle of the afternoon. 'The death hour,' she used to call it on the tour bus, and worse for her spirits than the darkest moments of the night: a nothing, nowhere time, seeping past so slowly, to be endured for the eventual reward of the fresh, invigorating hours of evening. A new city; a new stage; the thrum of bass, the roar and shiver of guitars, and all those figures moving in the black cavern of the auditorium. The fear, the nausea, the desire to run, so overwhelming that Cass had even, once or twice, stalked alone from her dressing-room to the fire-exit, pushed open the door, taken in a gulp of evening air. And then she had turned back, not knowing whether, afterwards, would follow the euphoria, the rush or the choking sense of her own inadequacy, the paltry summation of her talent, even as the crowd was calling out her name.

Afternoons were different after Anna was born. She'd go down for a nap after lunch, and wake at three, or thereabouts, filled with an infectious, wide-eyed energy. Tiny hands clasping and clutching; mouth open, noiselessly smiling; eyes blue-green, neither Cass's nor Ivor's, but carrying their own spectrum of colour.

'A sunny baby,' everyone said – Alan, who already had a son by then; Kim, who would soon have a daughter; Martin, and Johnny, and Kate, and Lily and John. Nothing original in that observation – so many babies, surely, were smiling, laughing, wriggling creatures, though Anna, like most of them, was certainly not so when she woke hungry and wailing in the night. But Cass took it to heart; she held her daughter to her, felt the warmth coming from her skin, and yes, she saw her as a little sliver of sun, fire-warmed and dazzling, drawing them both into her orbit. *Light in our darkness. Show us another way to be.*

When had it set, that sun; when had the clouds drawn across it so completely? It had happened gradually, step by step, so that they hadn't seen the darkness for what it was until it was too late.

Anna at eight, standing among removal boxes in the naked living-room at Home Farm, when it had, to Cass, all suddenly seemed too much to bear. She had stood silently for a moment, caught in the terrible realisation of her utter, inexpressible loneliness, even as her daughter was standing beside her, saying, 'Don't worry, Mum, I'll help you unpack.'

Anna at fourteen, slender, as she had always been, but still naturally so: athletic, muscles toned by the sports she loved to play. Back from a weekend with Ivor, lifting her face to say – unconvincingly, if Cass had only been paying enough attention to understand – 'Oh, I had a great time, Mum. Really great.'

Anna at twenty, coltish, brittle-limbed: that light already occluded, yes, but still there, still shining. Surely it had still been shining then, even if, just five years later, it would be difficult to believe that it ever had.

Cass draws on her cardigan, steps back out onto the cool, shaded terrace. Kim will be here any moment, and not long after that, the caterers, Callum, Alan, her guests. There is still so much to listen to. There is still so much to recall. But for now, a moment of stillness, and the old, familiar comfort of silence.

'Working hard, then?'

Kim: the tall, narrow outline of her, with her magnificent corona of fine-spun black hair: it is years, now, since she gave up on the relaxers, the dreadlocks, the cascades of tiny plaits. She wears a light beige belted mac and smart navy trousers that taper at the ankle. Kim has always worn her clothes well, with the easy nonchalance of a woman who could make a powder-blue shoulder-padded jumpsuit look attractive – and did so, many times, in those distant, strobe-lit, younger years.

'Just taking a breather.'

Kim leans in to kiss her on both cheeks, and Cass catches the scent of clean linen and her rich, distinctive perfume. Mimosa and cardamom: Kim had bought Cass a bottle one Christmas, but it had seemed wrong to wear it – an affront, somehow, when the scent was so inextricably associated with Kim herself.

Stepping back, her hand still resting on Cass's arm, Kim says, 'How's it going?'

'All right, I suppose. Disorientating. Tiring. I've taken a few breaks.'

Kim smiles, withdraws her hand. Her face is broad, even-featured, unlined, as it has always been. 'Avoidance tactics?'

Cass returns her smile. 'You know me too well. But I got right back on it. A florist came at lunchtime, with a bouquet. From Kate.'

'I saw the flowers in the kitchen. They're stunning.'

Cass nods. 'For a moment, when I saw them, I thought they might have been from . . . But then I realised that wasn't really his style.'

They are silent for a moment. Cass, looking out across the garden towards the house, catches a flash of black and ginger fur amid the undergrowth. Otis, set on some darting feline quest. 'It's getting chilly, isn't it? Come inside for a minute?'

'Just for a minute. I don't want to hold you up.'

They settle together on the sofa, side by side. The room, so neat when Cass had pushed open the door this morning, has slumped into a mess: records strewn across the coffee table and carpet, released from their sleeves; discarded bottles of San Pellegrino; a small regiment of dirty mugs.

'We could turn this into an artwork,' Cass says. 'Recreate it piece by piece. "*Inside the memory of a washed-up old has-been.* Mixed media. 2015."'

Kim doesn't laugh. 'Hardly a has-been.'

'Well. We'll see later, won't we?' Cass doesn't like her own tone – it sounds brittle, forced – but the old fears are circling, seeking purchase. Her songs – the first she has written and re-corded in a decade – are now caught, speared like specimens in a display case, to be held up to the scrutiny of strangers. *But my guests are not strangers*, she tells herself, in the soft, silent voice they had first taught her in the hospital, drawing it out of her gradually, like a language in which she had once been fluent, and had forgotten how to speak: reasonable, measured, compassionate, even – especially – with herself. *They are friends. There is nothing to fear.*

'I can cancel the party, Cass, if you want me to,' Kim says softly. 'Rearrange it for another day. Perhaps it's all too much.'

'No.' She takes Kim's hand, squeezes it, lets it go. 'No, really, I'll be fine.'

'All right. If you're sure.'

Kim takes a record sleeve from the coffee table, holds it up. *The State She's In.* Cass, impossibly young, skin so clear and fresh she could weep at the sight of it, framed against the window of a workman's café on the Old Kent Road. Stark morning light – six a.m.; plumbers and carpenters and scaffolders tucking into egg and chips as Johnny danced around her with his Nikon. Her hair loose, artfully undone. Behind her, on the window, the words 'Breakfast, Lunch, Dinner' in scuffed, white, backwards-marching hieroglyphics.

'True realism,' Johnny had said, explaining the concept to Alan and Cass. 'No artifice. A girl who's been up all night. A girl who's done it all.'

'God, Johnny was good, wasn't he?' Kim says now. 'Still can't believe he's gone.'

Cass remembers the church service. It was autumn: fallen leaves gusting around the graves; mourners in their multi-coloured peacock finery. *No black for Johnny Saunt*, the invitation had decreed, and nobody – not even Johnny's tiny, shrunken mother, wobbling unsteadily on her walking-stick – had dared to disobey this, his final concept, the last image he would offer them.

'I know. I miss Johnny, Kim. I really do.'

There is nothing much to say to that. On the table, in the space the album cover has left, is Larry's card, lying face up: that Henry Moore sculpture, three figures, small-headed, dark-hued. Cass picks it up, and notices, for the first time, that one of the figures is not female but male.

'I've been trying to call Larry,' she says. 'There's no answer at the apartment or the studio. And his mobile's going straight to voicemail.'

'Perhaps he's working. He turns off his phone, doesn't he?'

'He does. But it's been two weeks now, Kim. I've heard noth-ing from him at all, other than this card. I just thought that today . . .' *I thought he might reach out to me*, she thinks. *I thought he might offer me another chance*. 'I've really ruined it, haven't I, Kim? I don't think he's ever coming back . . .'

There is a slow, measured silence. Then Kim says, 'Cass. Let's just try to concentrate on today, all right? The album. The party. The new tracks. I'm sure Larry just needs some time.'

'I only want to talk to him, Kim. I want to tell him I made a mistake.'

Kim rises to her feet. 'Try not to think about it, Cass. Not now. Not today. I'll leave you to it, all right? I'd better go and call the caterers. I'll be in the office if you need me. Alan's coming around five. And Callum, of course.'

'All right.' As Kim is sliding open the door to the terrace, Cass adds, aiming for lightness, 'Just ignore me, Kim, won't you? I know I'm a silly old fool.'

Those dark brown eyes on hers.

'Hey,' Kim says. 'Less of the old.'

And then she is gone: a figure in a belted mac, moving up the garden towards the house, then slipping gradually out of sight.

Johnny Saunt.

Friend, collaborator, confidant, comrade-in-arms. Late-night drinker, visionary, translator of dreams. A man with the build of a boxer and a poet's soul.

Anna had loved him: 'Uncle Johnny', he'd been to her, and 'that bloody queer' to Ivor, in whom Johnny seemed able to plumb a vein of dislike that Ivor denied was homophobic.

'Half our friends are gay, Cass,' Ivor said. 'I just don't like *him*.'

Johnny, for his part, had been circumspect enough to keep his true feelings about Ivor to himself – at least until after he'd deemed it safe to let them be known. It was Johnny Cass had telephoned – not Alan, not Kim, not Kate – from Rothermere that terrible night. Johnny to whom she'd driven with Anna, along the dark country roads, the motorway, through the endless south London suburbs, as her daughter slept in the passenger seat beside her.

He owned a house in Spitalfields: narrow, many-roomed, warren-like, filled with intriguing objects he'd picked up on his travels – a Masai warrior mask; a lump of Icelandic lava; a set of matryoshka dolls from Siberia. The walls were lined with his prints and contact sheets: models, actors, writers and musicians (Cass herself among them, of course), and the work Johnny considered far more interesting. Three gaudy drag queens on a New York subway carriage, caught in a moment of private reverie; a plumed, painted dancer at the Rio Carnival; Johnny's mother and her friends at the Walthamstow Working Men's Club, with their lacquered beehives and Saturday-night smiles.

The night she'd left Rothermere, Johnny had made hot chocolate for Anna in his basement kitchen at two a.m. Cass had put her daughter to bed in the room they would share – drawn the coverlet up over her sleeping body, under the watchful eyes of the Manhattan drag queens. And then, back downstairs, Johnny had poured her a whisky, looked frankly at the cut, the split lip, the purplish bruise, and said, 'Well, this will be the last of it, then.'

It was a statement, not a question. Cass had sipped her drink, looked across the table at him, and said, 'Yes.'

They'd stayed for two months, in the end: two months during which the album launch had had to be postponed, and the tour dates rebooked, and Anna had woken most nights crying, calling for Cass in a way she hadn't done since she was tiny. Asking when they were going home.

'What do I tell her?' Cass asked Johnny, desperate, and he stared at her with his shrewd, brown-black eyes and said, 'Well, the truth, of course. Or as much of it as you think she can stand to hear.'

And so, in the night, Cass had held her daughter close, and

stroked her hair, and said, 'We're not going back to Rothermere, darling. I'm going to find us a new place to live.'

A few months after that, she had. Home Farm; that frizzy-haired estate agent; that hideous brown carpet; those cracked tiles and the flaking paintwork; all of it speaking to her of freedom, of a place that would be theirs, and theirs alone.

Such a kind friend, Johnny. It had been to him, again, that Anna had gone when she'd set her heart on London, on art school: he'd offered her the top floor of the Spitalfields house, promised to let her come and go as she pleased.

Anna had been well, then – healthy, productive, upbeat.

'Talented, too,' Johnny said, and both Cass and Anna had thrilled to the sound of his praise.

But it had also been at Johnny's that Anna had begun to fail, and that her light had begun to dim once more.

'I think it's back, lovey,' he'd told Cass on the telephone. 'She's terribly thin. And she hardly ever leaves her room.'

The next day, Cass had driven up to London and taken Anna out to dinner at an Indian restaurant on Brick Lane. It was true that she was thin – very thin – but she'd emphatically denied that the illness had returned.

'I'm fine, Mum,' she'd said. 'I'm just busy. There's so much to do.'

And as if to prove a point, she'd eaten a great deal that night – cleared the metal tureens of prawn dhansak and aloo gobi and brinjal bhaji, all washed down with several glasses of white wine.

'See?' That face, that unique composite of Cass's and Ivor's, and yet utterly, entirely, Anna's own. 'I'm eating now, aren't I, Mum? Honestly, Uncle Johnny's such a worrier.'

How, when, had Anna developed such an ability to lie? Cass had not believed her capable of it, until she'd been forced to confront the fact that it was so. And then, when it had already

184

been far too late, she'd realised that she herself had given her daughter the tools.

All those days when Cass had woken early, spent half an hour concealing her bruises with the special heavy-coverage foundation Sue, the make-up artist, had procured for her. The tours on which she'd always worn long-sleeved blouses and dresses, even when it was a hundred degrees and more under the unremitting glare of the stage lights. The interviews in which she'd spoken so convincingly of her partnership with Ivor, of how fully he supported her, of how easy, how intuitive their relationship – both musical and personal – had always been. The times she had been held up as the epitome of a strong, independent woman, succeeding on her own terms . . . All of that had been a lie, a fallacy, a construction; a shimmering mirage concealing the ugly truth. In music, she had always been honest; but the rest of her life, it seemed to Cass then, had become an exercise in mendacity, in papering over the cracks. So why would Anna not have believed that she must do the same?

Johnny, dear Johnny, had not seen things in these terms.

'How, darling Cass, can you *possibly* believe you are to blame?' he'd said to her, over and over again, when he came to visit her in the hospital that first time.

She'd looked at him, sitting there beside her bed in his battered leather jacket, and felt nothing other than a distant, remote awareness that her old friend was speaking to her; that he was saying something important, and that she would like to listen to him if only she weren't so very, very tired.

There is something about Larry, Cass thinks now, alone in the listening-room, that reminds her of Johnny.

They had the same strong physical presence; the same playfulness, belying the plain, almost monastic purity of their artistic intention. The same commitment to the bright, uncompromising clarity of a visual composition. A photograph, each element arranged perfectly within the frame. A sculpture, hewn doggedly from stone, its lines clean, emphatic, unapologetically occupying the space in which it stands.

The men had known of each other, but had never met.

'Ah, the *great* Larry Alderson,' Johnny had said with a smile that day last year, not long before the end.

And Larry, before Johnny's funeral, when she had told him of their long friendship. 'I saw his retrospective at the Institute. Amazing work, Cass. A true original.'

She wonders, now, how it would have been if they had met. Would Johnny have flirted gently, playfully, with Larry? Would he have taken her aside, and said in that wise undertone of his, 'Be good to this one, Cass. Don't mess things up. Don't be afraid to let him in.'?

If only, that night two weeks ago, when Larry had put his question to her – when he had turned to her and offered her all that he had – she'd had such advice ringing in her ears. Perhaps, then, she'd have looked back up at Larry, taken his hand in hers, and said, unwavering, 'Yes, Larry. Stay with me always. Yes.'

The sheer, utter uselessness of regret. She looks back at the card on the table: the clean, sweeping lines of the Henry Moore; inside, the elegant loop and curl of Larry's handwriting. *Today, Cass, find a way to forgive her. And then – please – find a way to forgive yourself.*

Such a thing, in that moment, seems beyond her, and she doubts herself – wonders whether there can really be answers to be found here, in the music she has made. These frozen moments; these still-frames, seeking to capture a place, a person, a feeling, before they disappeared, and were lost to time.

Johnny had never understood why she had decided to retire, to pack up her music and close down that part of herself – the best part, really; the part that she had understood, from the moment she'd first laid her hands on Irene mother's piano, as her simplest, clearest, truest self. And so it had continued to seem to Cass, really, until her daughter had withdrawn into herself, moment by moment, hour by hour, day by passing day. Then Cass had seen the world change, its sounds becoming cacophonous, each note jarring, out of place.

She could not bear to listen back to the soundtrack she had once so easily set to a life that had revealed itself as nothing but a long, featureless road, along which she was condemned to walk, alone, at the whim of some cruel, merciless deity. To think that people built churches, mosques, synagogues, temples to such a god. To think that her own father had once believed that He was benign, loving, placatable with prayer. How could Francis have subscribed to such a fairy tale? How could Cass go on making music, hymning an essential symmetry, a harmony, a truth that had revealed itself to be nothing but a mirage?

That, perhaps, had been the worst of it: this new knowledge that at the core of things, under all the bustle and fuss, there was no sense to be made of anything. Just chaos, and mess, and impenetrable silence.

Right to the very end, however, Johnny had seen things differently.

'You can't live without music,' he'd said. 'You can't turn your back on your art, on the very thing that defines you.'

She could still see her friend's pale, hollowed face, asserting the vigour and beauty of life even in the knowledge of its imminent withdrawal. 'Imagine if I'd just decided, on a whim, never to pick up a camera again. It's unthinkable, Cass. Impossible. What, I ask you, would have been left for me then?'

'She Wears a Dress'

By Cass Wheeler
From the album *Huntress*

*She wears a dress
Of silk and feathers
That was her mother's
They sewed it together*

*Needle in the lamplight
Dancing in the gaslight
That hand she held so tight
She'll wear her mother's dress tonight
She'll wear her mother's dress tonight
She'll wear her mother's dress tonight*

*She wears a dress
Of lace and linen
The girl who was chosen
What was she given?*

*Needle in the lamplight
Dancing in the gaslight
That hand she held so tight
She'll wear her mother's dress tonight
She'll wear her mother's dress tonight
She'll wear her mother's dress tonight*

Ooooooooooo

*Needle in the lamplight
Dancing in the gaslight
That hand she held so tight*

She'll wear her mother's dress tonight
She'll wear her mother's dress tonight
She'll wear her mother's dress tonight

RELEASED 10 January 1977
RECORDED October 1976 at Rothermere, Surrey
GENRE Folk rock / soft rock / pop
LABEL Phoenix Records
WRITER(S) Cass Wheeler
PRODUCER(S) Eli Glass
ENGINEER(S) Mike Edwards / Sean O'Malley

His name was Alan Leddie.

He was stocky, square-faced, with dark eyes and shoulder-length, sand-coloured hair. He'd played rugby at Cambridge, where he'd studied history, and run a popular series of Friday music nights in his college bar – British blues; psychedelia; the odd bearded folkie, passing through.

'Knows his music does Alan – I think you'll get on,' Martin had said.

She needed a manager, and Angus, they both agreed, was not up to the job. She'd talked through Vertical Heights's earnings with Vince, Phoenix's laconic, leather-jacketed accountant, and he was pretty sure that Angus had been quietly siphoning off more than his agreed commission.

But from Martin's description of Alan, she'd pictured someone older: a Brian Epstein figure, smartly suited, businesslike – not the disconcertingly boyish-looking man who stood up to greet her when they met in a pub close to Parliament Hill Fields.

'I know what you're thinking,' Alan said, returning to the table with her whisky. '"What does *he* know about anything? He looks like my little brother." Well, I know enough – and the rest I'll learn. But the main thing is, I want this, Cass. I want to work with you – *for* you. Your songs are special. And when you sing . . . well, you're the real thing. Not a poser, you know? A folk singer's honesty and a rock singer's swagger. Martin thinks you could go all the way, and I believe I can help make that happen.'

He placed her glass on the table, slipped back onto his stool, and fixed her with an expression of such exaggerated, wide-eyed sincerity that she couldn't help laughing. 'Steady on, Alan. At least let me get a drink down first.'

His face rearranged itself, embarrassed. 'Sorry. Didn't mean to launch the big sell.'

'It's all right.' She looked across the table at him, and decided that she liked Alan – that she believed him, and could trust in his belief in her.

They talked of many things that evening. The trip Alan had taken through the southern states of America, Washington to New Orleans, after graduation: juke joints and honky-tonks and white-hooded men still moving ghostlike, after dark, through the deserted streets. His preference for Mississippi blues over Chicago. 'You can hear the South in the music, somehow,' he said. 'The empty fields, the cotton gins, the huge, heavy skies.' His love of English folk, New York jazz and good old rock-and-roll.

'Where do I fit into all that, then?' Cass asked. (How quickly, how easily, she had slipped into using 'I' over 'we'.)

'You?' Alan sipped his pint. 'Ah, we'll have to invent a whole new category for you.'

Ivor joined them just after nine: he'd stayed behind in the studio with Martin, tinkering with the lead line to 'Common Ground'. He was stoned (Martin liked his grass, too; said it 'favoured the creative process'), and was easy and placid as a sun-warmed cat, though Cass, alert to the nuances of his mood, could sense him weighing Alan up.

'Private school, eh?' he said, interrupting Alan's description of the house in which he had grown up. (A rambling Victorian villa, close to the river at Barnes; father a solicitor, mother a violinist who had given up her career for her children, but had never made them carry the weight of her sacrifice.) 'Cambridge? Had it pretty easy, then, haven't you, Alan?'

Alan, across the table, stared back at Ivor. He was still smiling, but his eyes were cool. 'If you mean I'm grateful to my parents, then yes, I am. They taught me the value of everything I have.' After an emphatic pause, he added, 'What about you, anyway, Ivor? Where are you from?'

Ivor looked away. 'Here, there, everywhere. A citizen of the world.'

Alan nodded, and the moment passed.

At closing time, as Ivor went off to the gents', Alan said, 'Angus Mackinnon. I hear he's kicking up a bit of a stink.'

'You could say that.' Angus, banging on the door of Savernake Road in the middle of the night: drunk, high, furious. *You signed a contract, Cass. You can't just fuck off and leave us in the lurch.*

The last time, the neighbours had called the police. Angus had slunk off before the squad car arrived, and Cass and Serena had served the officers tea in the kitchen while the others ran around upstairs, ensuring their stashes were out of sight.

The policemen – neither of them older than thirty – had been rather friendly; one of them had flirted with the women quite openly. 'No need for us to go upstairs, is there, love?' With a smirk, 'Not unless you'd *like* to . . .'

But as they'd got up to leave, the other officer had turned serious. 'Mind we're not called back again, all right? We're not as stupid as we look. Next time, we won't be turning a blind eye.'

'Give me Angus's details,' Alan said now. 'Address, phone number. Leave it with me.' He hesitated. 'That is, of course, if you think this could work. If you'd like me to work for you.'

He looked, in that moment, rather sweetly shy. Cass reached out, offered her hand for him to shake.

'I would, Alan,' she said. 'I really would.'

The flat was in Muswell Hill, in a broad Edwardian building of a sort Cass had never noticed in London before. It was fronted by an elegant timber portico, white-painted, with a veranda spanning the full width of the first floor.

'I threw some fantastic parties here,' Harriet said.

The flat belonged to her – Lily's university friend, who worked in publishing, and had once spent a fortnight at Atterley, mourning her errant fiancé. She was newly engaged to an Irish poet; they were to live in Connemara, in a grey stone house with a view of the sea. The poet was almost seventy, Harriet confided, and had been married twice before; she was fifty-six, never married, and as giddy and excitable as a schoolgirl in the first flush of romance.

'Your aunt Lily got so drunk once,' Harriet went on, 'she almost fell off the balcony. I'm not joking. John only just caught her in time.'

Cass smiled, picturing Lily, pink-cheeked and laughing in John's grip. 'Thank God.'

There were two bedrooms – one at the front, next to the living-room, with its own door to the veranda; the other at the back, beside the bathroom, overlooking the rectangle of lush green lawn that belonged to the flat downstairs.

'You can't use the garden, unfortunately,' said Harriet, 'but old Mr Dennis is a sweetie. Deaf as a post. Won't mind a bit if you play music all day and all night – which I suppose you will?'

Cass nodded. She was already furnishing the front bedroom in her mind. That would be their music room, she thought. They'd hang their guitars from wall-hooks, and place the piano beside the veranda doors. (Lily and John had offered to buy her an upright, by way of congratulations.) The desk from their room at Savernake Road, and an old armchair in one corner, for thinking, writing, waiting out the inevitable crises that came when a song refused to conform to its given shape. Harriet was bequeathing them a comfortably sagging sofa, a bed, a wardrobe and a dining-table, and they'd scrabble together the rest of the furniture somehow.

It was a shame to leave Gospel Oak, to see the sturdy old house on Savernake Road dismantled piece by piece – the owners were renovating, preparing to sell. Serena, now four months pregnant, was moving to Harrow with Bob, who had, against all their expectations, found a job teaching English at a girls' grammar school. Paul, his novel still unpublished, was uprooting to Manchester; and Hugh – well, who ever knew what Hugh was doing? And she and Ivor would be here, in this bright, high-ceilinged flat, with its veranda and its white walls and its scrubbed wooden floors.

'It's wonderful,' she said to Harriet in the living-room, which was flooded with late-spring light. Dust swirling in the golden shafts; the faint adenoidal buzz of a lawnmower floating up through the open doors. 'I can't wait for Ivor to see it.'

Harriet beamed. 'You're doing me a favour, really. Couldn't bear the idea of renting to a stranger. And to know that I'm contributing, in some small way, to the creation of wonderful music . . .'

Cass looked at her, and blushed. 'Well. I wouldn't quite put it like that.'

Harriet – voluptuous, green-eyed, her long blonde hair shot through with paler strands of grey – said, 'Why not? Be bold, Cass. Grasp this opportunity with both hands. It's going to be a wild ride.'

She laughed. Harriet's mood was infectious; Cass took a turn around the room, arms spread wide, feeling loose-limbed, feather-light. 'I hope so. It still doesn't feel quite real.'

They moved in a week later. Alan hired a van and two enormous, silent men to carry their belongings. 'I'm here to make your life easier,' he'd explained when she'd protested that they were perfectly capable of handling the move themselves. Ivor seemed quite content to take a back seat, placing their most treasured possessions – their guitars, amps and turntable; their stacks of records and notebooks; the box containing Margaret's letters and photographs – in the back of the Morris Minor, and otherwise letting the removal men get on with it.

A relationship was developing between Ivor and Alan that could not quite be called friendship but which lay somewhere between mutual tolerance and respect. Ivor had been impressed by Alan's handling of Angus – it would be years before they actually found out how Alan had warned him off by threatening to inform a friend in the drug squad about exactly how many varieties of narcotics were passing daily through Angus's flat – and Alan esteemed Ivor's skill as a guitarist. And Cass, for her part, could already see that Alan was living up to the promise he had made her: he was calm and level-headed, mature beyond his years (despite his boyish appearance), standing between her and the messy practicalities of work and life.

That night, among the suitcases and crates, they threw their first party. Tealights on saucers; greasy packages from the chippy on the Broadway; beer and whisky and wine, and records on the turntable – *Tea for the Tillerman*, *After the Gold Rush*, *Led Zeppelin III*, *The Summer Never Ends* – giving way, after nightfall, to an impromptu jam: Ivor on guitar, Cass on the upright piano, the new drummer, Graham, banging away on the side of a crate.

Flickering darkness; glint of beer-bottles and the lit tips of joints. Everyone smiling, clapping, joining in, and above them all, Cass's voice, rising high and pure, as if framing a question they had not, until this moment, known how to ask, but were now waiting, longing, for her to answer.

Cass woke early in those days, even when they'd gone to sleep with the dawn.

Bread and jam in the little kitchen, overlooking Mr Dennis's garden. She watched him sometimes as she drank her coffee, the tonsured globe of his head bobbing up and down among his roses and his dahlias; a trug in his hand, and his low, tuneless murmur drifting up to her open window.

The fine spring was slipping into summer, and she remembers those mornings as always bright, doused with sunshine. The house faced east and the front windows admitted such an abundance of light that she was often dazzled by it. She would sit at her piano, or with her guitar, and close her eyes, watching the fractured afterimages of the sun's brightness dance against her shuttered lids; feeling, in some strange, fanciful way, that those patterns – shifting, glowing, in a perpetual state of frantic re-arrangement – were representations of the chords and melodies that came pouring from her hands.

She was writing with an ease and profligacy that she had never experienced before – not in John's office at Atterley, not in their bedroom at Savernake Road. Ivor would join her after rising from their bed sometime towards the middle of the morning. A whole song could appear, from first chaotic chord to full, measured structure, in the space of an hour; and then they would play it back to each other, over and over again, hardly daring to believe it could be as good, as true, as they instinctively felt it to be.

It was not always so, of course – there were still hours of frayed nerves and short tempers when a song simply refused to reveal itself. But these, back then, were fewer than the moments in which their hands moved in unison over guitar or keys. Then, Cass felt as close to Ivor as she could ever imagine being to anyone. Theirs, she told herself, was an understanding that transcended the petty niceties of domesticity. There, in the music room, was the truth of what they were to each other: a truth beyond jealousy, or fidelity, or any of the strictures imposed by normal society – by all those who didn't know how it was to create, together, something that had never before existed; to dredge a thing up from the brackish depths of the mind, and polish it until it shone. To make music, and with it, flush away the disquieting uncertainties of silence.

After lunch each day, Cass and Ivor threw their things into the Morris Minor, and drove over to the studio. Martin liked to start the sessions at two, and end whenever they were all too tired to stand, which was usually far into the night.

It was a nondescript-looking place on a corner of Willesden High Road: a plate-glass shopfront, obscured by plastic Venetian blinds; two flats above (the building was soundproofed, but still, God knew how the tenants got any sleep), with the studios spread across the ground floor and basement. They were in the smallest, studio three: a gloomy, subterranean chamber, the walls of the live room studded with fabric-covered panels, and the sound in the tiny vocal-booth deadened, echoless.

'It's like a coffin in here,' Cass said the first time Martin showed them around.

Martin threw her a look – half irritated, half amused. 'Well, you'd better get used to it. You'll be spending a lot of time in there.'

There was a green room, too – larger, more comfortable, with sofas that had seen better days, a small fridge and ashtrays that never seemed to be emptied. Here they congregated in the breaks that Martin and Sean, the engineer, permitted them: Ivor and Cass and Alan and Kit, the bassist, and Graham, the drummer, and whichever other bands were in that night. Three long-haired guys from Milton Keynes who had yet to settle on a name for their group but were unfailingly generous with their drugs. Hawkwind, several of whose members lived not far from Martin in Ladbroke Grove. A psychedelic four-piece from Crouch End whose priapic lead singer would, one night towards the end of their sessions, follow Cass into the ladies' toilet, and require considerable force to be disabused of the notion that she was interested in 'travelling to the moon with me, man – to the *moon and back!*'

Sean, the engineer, was shy with Cass at first: he could never quite meet her eye, and blushed like a schoolboy when she spoke to him. But as the weeks passed, he grew more comfortable with her, especially after a joint or three.

It was Sean who, very late one night, came up, unwittingly, with a name for her debut album. Cass, exhausted, was returning from the ladies'. (The Crouch End group were elsewhere that night.) She'd splashed water on her face to revive herself, spreading blackish traces of mascara across her cheeks, and had left the room without looking in the mirror. As she'd pushed open the green-room door, Sean had looked up and said, 'Good God – look at the state she's in.'

She'd laughed, along with everyone else, then returned to the ladies' to dab at her face with a tissue. There, under the stark glare of the strip-light, she'd considered her reflection – unbrushed hair; skin blotchy, sallow; dark shadows deepening the hollows around her eyes. Sean's words slipped back into her mind – *The state she's in* – and she thought, *Yes. That's perfect. That's it.*

Those were long, tiring, windowless afternoons, slipping into long, tiring, windowless nights; but she remembers them now as being cast under the pale, pure light of innocence. They were so young, all of them, even Martin. Play-acting, really; chasing a dream; refusing to be cowed by doubt or inexperience.

In the vocal-booth, under headphones, she was as deaf and self-contained as a deep-sea diver drawn gradually underwater: as she sang, there was nothing but the vibration of her voice, the swelling of ribcage and lung.

The wooden walls of the booth held her, close and intimate, as the microphone drew her secrets from her; and through the glass, the men played on, each of them watching her, the connection between the four of them intense, tangible, stretching out until the final bar of the song.

Back on the road again. Motorway tarmac, lacquered by rain. Sunsets pegging out their colours over road bridges and water towers. Car-parks and dressing-rooms and sound-checks and the rough, bitter tang of Players cigarettes.

Alan had acquired a van: the old one, with its dubious cargo of mattresses, had belonged to Angus. This was a custom Transit with built-in seats, a table and straps to prevent the instruments from toppling over and damaging anyone – or, perhaps even more importantly, sustaining damage.

Cass still preferred to ride up front, beside Alan and Martin, and her memories of those countless journeys are mainly sensory now: the cool lick of the breeze on her face through the open window; the radio's tinny rattle and whine; the chatter of the men drifting through the metal grille that separated front from back.

She began to draw again – to carry a sketchpad, curl up with her shoeless feet tucked neatly under her thighs, and fill pages with scattered images, both observed and imagined: the emphatic set of Alan's profile at the wheel; Martin, rolling a joint; Ivor, looking down at his guitar, hair half covering his face. She was one of them, and yet, through those long hours on the road, she still felt remote, set apart – and on stage, too, there had been a shifting, a minute recalibration of space. Ivor stood to her left, Kit to her right, but the front of the stage – that lonely square-foot – was hers now, and hers was the name announced as they stepped out from the wings.

A new routine was evolving. Alan would draw up in the van outside the Muswell Hill flat around lunchtime, and they'd stop for tea, or something stronger, on the road. (It was Ivor, now, who passed round the pills, or slipped into a back room with a candle and a twist of silver foil, though only Martin, Graham and Kit usually joined him.) These journeys were defined, for Cass, by a growing sense of unease. She was quiet, watching the road, slipping deeper inside herself; the sight of the first sign announcing whichever town was their destination for the night – Ipswich, Bristol, Sheffield, Carlisle – was enough to quicken her pulse and cause her breath to catch in her throat.

One night, before a support slot for Black Sabbath and Freedom at Birmingham Town Hall, the feeling came to a head. Her nerves (she saw them as a group of formless shadows) seemed to loom so large above her that she became convinced she couldn't step out on stage – that if she tried to, the shadows would run after her, and consume her whole.

'Ivor,' she whispered in the dressing-room, drawing him apart from the others. 'I don't think I can do this. I don't think I can go on.'

He looked down at her – those green-brown eyes; the hard angles and planes of his face. He cupped a hand to her chin, as he'd done the first night they'd met, in the hallway at Atterley. His grip was firm – not a caress, but an act of balancing, the grip placed to the tiller of a listing ship.

'Course you can, Cassie,' he said, his eyes fixed firmly on hers. 'You're amazing out there. You know you are. You're born to it. It's as natural to you as breathing.'

She held his gaze, allowed it to steady her. *As natural as breathing.* Gradually, her breath came slower; her heart resumed its regular, metronomic beat. And a few moments later, they were stepping out on stage, hand in hand, carried by the inexorable momentum of the music.

'You need a character,' Kate said one afternoon soon after that.

She was just back from a film shoot in Rome, tanned, grown sleek on pasta and ice cream; they were on her Covent Garden terrace, drinking limoncello out of teacups. 'Someone you become on stage. Someone bigger and braver than you are.'

Cass considered this. 'An alter ego, you mean?'

Kate screwed her eyes up against the light. 'Yes, if you like.'

'How on earth do I do that? I'm no actress, Kate.'

'Costume.' Kate's eyes remained closed; she was easy, relaxed. 'We need to find you a costume.'

An idea slipped into Cass's mind.

'Cornelia,' she said, and Kate opened her eyes.

'Bingo.'

They drove down to Oxford Street in Kate's red bubble car, both a little drunk. Cornelia was framed in the doorway when they arrived – trim pastel-blue suit, string of pearls, neat white hair – turning the shop sign to 'closed'. Daphne and a new girl – blonde, hardly out of her teens – were gathering up their jackets and handbags, preparing to leave. Through the glass, Cornelia stared at them, her mouth widening in surprise.

'Darling girls,' she said, opening the door, her former anger with Cass apparently forgotten. 'To what do I owe the pleasure?'

They stayed in the shop until long after it had grown dark. Cornelia opened another of her special-occasion bottles of champagne, and brought out the trunk she kept in the store-room. Inside were the vintage gowns she'd picked up over the years in flea-markets and house sales, and kept aside for the rare modern bride who preferred not to be married in white. A late-Victorian confection, bodice frothing with pink chiffon; a nineteen twenties bias-cut slip of oyster satin; a neat twin-piece suit from the forties, in lemon-yellow shot silk.

Cass stood in the dressing-room where she had busied herself around so many other women – around Irene, that last afternoon, tucking and pinning – slipping dress after dress over her head. The last she tried was from the thirties: long-skirted, sleeves reaching demurely to her wrists; a dark green lace shift over a chartreuse slip of butter-soft silk.

'Come on, Cass,' Kate said through the drawn curtain. 'Let's see you.'

She stepped out, and the dress moved with her, its fabric shimmering and settling with each step.

'Well, darling,' Cornelia said, lifting her glass. 'You are quite transformed.'

The dressing-room mirror showed a woman, her long blonde hair loose across her shoulders, her brown eyes frank, focused. A woman who might command the attention of three hundred pairs of eyes; a woman in whose presence those ugly, hovering shadows might take fright, and flee.

The woman stared at herself and smiled.

*

The success of *The State She's In* must, Cass can see now, have come as something of a surprise to everyone – even Alan and Martin.

For all their talk, the label must have been expecting to grow her slowly; indeed, they talked in such terms, in meetings, as if she were a plant they had seeded, and must now carefully cultivate. After all, she was more Sandy Denny than Sandie Shaw; more Joni Mitchell than Dusty Springfield. Such artists needed time, care, the gradual accumulation of interest – press, radio, the attention of serious music fans; then, and only then, like ripples spreading across a pond, might come the triumphant slippage into the mainstream. And of course, some artists – Alan was careful to point this out to her – didn't care to swim in that stream; were content to paddle away in a backwater, free to get on with making music in whichever way they chose, without the pressures that commercial success would inevitably bring.

If pressed, Cass would have said that she saw herself in the latter camp: that the money mattered little to her (she knew she was luckier than some, as she had always had enough to get by); that what she really cared about was writing music. But this would not have been entirely true. Her ambition was rooting itself, growing, seeking out the light. The photograph on her bedroom wall at Atterley – the woman with her firm, uptilted chin. Sandy Denny, holding the audience rapt in that candlelit club. The way Cass felt when she stood on stage, before crowds of strangers – feeling their eyes on her, knowing no other moment than this. She wanted it. She craved it. She would make it hers.

'I want to do it all,' she told Martin and the tableful of suited executives in the label's offices on Tottenham Court Road. 'I want to go the whole way.'

She saw surprise flit across Martin's face, and then transform itself, just as quickly, into respect. 'I know you do,' he said. 'And if you're prepared to work hard, we believe you can, and you will. But it might take time, Cass. It might take some time.'

She did work hard. A live session for John Peel; an appearance on *Top of the Pops*, for which Cass wore her green lace dress and a pair of black lace-up boots she'd picked up on Petticoat Lane. 'Biker suffragette chic,' Johnny called it: Lily had suggested him for the album-cover shoot, and he was already becoming a friend. During filming, six dancers wove around the stage between them in miniature fringed waistcoats and shorts. Kit and Graham were barely able to keep their attention on miming to the song: one of the dancers, a strong-featured, red-haired woman named Alison who was studying political science at King's College, would later be persuaded to go home with Kit, and a year or so after that, became his wife.

Interviews with *Melody Maker*, *Sounds*, the *New Musical Express*. One writer was sniffy, calling her 'the phoney British answer to the new crop of full-blooded American female singer-songwriters, like some provincial branch of Marks & Spencer squaring up to Saks Fifth Avenue', but Alan and Martin didn't care. 'Just be happy,' Martin said, 'that he's mentioned you at all.'

A feature in the *Daily Courier*: tea and sticky buns in a Soho café close to the Phoenix offices with a journalist named Eva Taylor. She was a slight, dark-haired woman in her early thirties with whom Cass felt an instant, instinctive affinity – perhaps because she reminded Cass, faintly, of Lily.

'A serious writer,' Alan said. 'Should be a serious piece.'

And it was: a double-page spread, with photograph – Cass sad-eyed and melancholic, stirring her tea with a metal spoon. *The State She's In*, Eva Taylor wrote, was 'full of intelligent, quick-witted and frequently poetic observations about love lost and found; about joy and sadness. If we were waiting for a woman from our own turf to speak to us in the way that Joni Mitchell, Carole King and Carly Simon are speaking to our cousins across the pond (and, of course, to many of us on this side of it, too), well, sisters, we've found her.'

On the day the *Courier* article was published, Cass wrote Eva a note. *I can't tell you what it means to me*, she wrote, *to read a piece like yours – to feel properly understood.*

A few days later, a postcard came back, care of Phoenix Records – Monica Vitti in a strapless black gown, spotlit, shading her face with an outstretched arm. *It struck me after we met that you look a little like her*, Eva's message ran. *Or perhaps I should say that she looks a little like you. I wish you the greatest success with your music, Cass – and may that success always be on your own terms.*

An impromptu party in the Phoenix offices, to celebrate *The State She's In* entering the charts. Crisps and celery sticks and Martin's secretary, Rachel, pouring champagne. The men in suits – Cass was still struggling to remember their names – beamed at her, as if she were a precocious child whose cosseting was beginning to pay dividends. Journalists flirted with her, and grew steadily, determinedly, drunk.

One of them – Don, Cass thought his name was; he had a round, unremarkable face and a thin, downturned mouth – accosted her on the fire-escape, where she had stepped out for a smoke, and a moment alone in the cool London air.

'So,' he said, reaching into his jacket pocket for his cigarettes. 'Ivor Tait – you're together, aren't you? A *couple*, I mean, just to be clear.'

Cass said nothing. He offered her the packet – she'd just extinguished her own cigarette – and she shook her head. The journalist shrugged, and continued as if she'd answered his question in the affirmative.

'How does he feel about all this, then? He was on the folk scene for a while, wasn't he – touring the clubs, looking for a break that never came? And then forming Vertical Heights, which was *his* band, really. Can't be easy for him, now – you stealing the limelight, as it were.'

'I haven't stolen anything.' She spoke sharply, and Don looked pointedly at her, the corners of his mouth dragging upwards into a mirthless smile. She saw, then, that he wanted this, was trying to rile her. She looked back into the office with its silent typewriters and telephones, to where Ivor was standing beside Graham and Martin, sipping champagne, his eyes wide, animated. (He'd taken a pill earlier, at home, and another when they arrived.)

She thought of Ivor as he'd been on the day he'd signed his contract, had seen that he would not be receiving a joint writing credit on every song. His face had changed, stiffened, and then he had got up and stalked from the room, just as he had that morning months before, when Martin had telephoned for the first time.

'Well,' Alan had said, 'you'll need to give him some time. But there's nothing else for it, Cass. I don't think the Lennon-McCartney model is going to work here – you write too many songs on your own. And it isn't as if Ivor's not coming out of the deal pretty well, too.'

She'd nodded, and felt reassured. But later, in the flat, they had shouted at one another for hours, their words blunt, brutal, irretrievable. Towards five a.m., Ivor had thrown a few things into a bag, picked up his guitar, and left; and she had pushed open the doors to the veranda, curled up on a wicker chair, and watched his hunched, angry figure march off up the street.

Now, keeping her voice light, steady, she said, 'That's really not how we see it, Ivor and I. He's proud of me. And I am of him.'

'I see.' The journalist was still wearing his ugly little smirk. 'How very touching.'

Kate appeared in the doorway, then – elegant in a floor-length dress, her bare shoulders glistening under the bright office lights.

'Cass, darling,' she said, 'whatever are you doing out here?' And Cass, relieved, reached for her friend's hand, and strode back into the room, without offering the journalist another word.

One day in late November – they were just back from touring France, and had a few days off in London before setting off on a three-week trip to Holland and Belgium – Cass took a train to Worthing. (She had still, much to the amusement of Alan, the band and the roadies, not learnt to drive.)

In a cotton carrier bag, she carried a copy of *The State She's In*, along with a framed photograph, taken by Johnny, of herself on stage, and a handsome edition of *Great Expectations* that she had picked up a few months before in a second-hand bookshop in Manchester.

Lily met her at the station, in the same old car. And she seemed just the same, too, in a smart navy coat and her trademark red lipstick, the fine grey threads in her hair the only indication that almost a decade had passed since her aunt had appeared at the vicarage on that painful, distant afternoon.

She eyed Cass's carrier bag, with its carefully chosen selection of gifts. 'You mustn't expect too much, you know, Cass darling. Your father hasn't been doing well at all.'

Cass nodded. 'I know.'

But she didn't know, not really. Lily had informed her of Francis's deterioration, of the necessity of moving him from the neat little flat to a residential home where he would have proper access to nursing care. But still, the change in him was a shock. It was like expecting to meet one man and finding another in his place – carrying his name, but bearing only a faint resemblance to the father she had known.

The home was a good one (Lily had reassured her of this): a tall, white stucco building on the promenade, with generous windows admitting the grey glimmer of the sea. Francis's room was on the first floor, at the front, and that view was the first thing Cass saw when she walked in: the jumble of shingle; the green flashes of seaweed clinging to the groynes; and beyond, above acres of wet sand, the slate-coloured layers of water, cloud, sky.

The room was large, and fussily decorated: swagged curtains, swirling patterned carpet, two chintz armchairs placed in front of the window, a low table between them. Her father was installed in one of these chairs, slippered feet just poking out from under a tartan blanket. He wore pyjamas, purple with a thin grey stripe. The two top buttons of his pyjama shirt had been left undone, exposing several inches of pale, crêpe-paper skin, and a small, wiry coil of white hair.

Francis had always been a fastidious dresser – those cassocks hanging in the vestry, perfectly pressed; the clerical collars held just so between the starched edging of his white shirts – and his dishevelment was, to Cass, jarring and faintly obscene. She leant forward to fasten the buttons, saying softly as she did so, 'Hi, Dad. It's me.'

His hands shot up to defend himself, pushed her violently away.

'No, Margaret,' he said fiercely: an echo of the voice that had once boomed out from the pulpit, so confident of being listened to. 'Leave it alone.'

Cass looked up, over the back of the chair, meeting Lily's eye. *I did warn you,* her aunt's expression said, though aloud, Lily said brightly, 'Come on, Francis, you know that's not Margaret. It's your daughter, Cass.'

'I had a daughter,' Francis said. He was quiet now, his tone conversational, but he stared warily at Cass with his watery brown eyes. 'Her name was Maria Cassandra. Where is she? What have you done with her?'

'I am Maria Cassandra,' Cass said, and she reached for his hand. 'Dad. It's me.'

She sat with him for a while, in the armchair next to his, holding his hand. They said little at first – she commented on the loveliness of the view; he told her that he hadn't liked the oxtail soup Margaret had served for lunch. And then, after a while (Lily had discreetly left the room), she began to talk more easily, to sketch out the details of her life. Ivor; the flat in Muswell Hill; the gigs, the album, the reviews.

Francis said nothing – just kept staring out to sea, his head lolling gently to one side – but Cass was sure that he was listening. Time seemed to hold its breath. When Cass became aware of her aunt stepping back into the room, together with a white-uniformed nurse pushing a trolley, she couldn't have said how long she had been sitting there, in front of the window, talking to her father, watching the dark smudge of the sea blur into the horizon.

'Here's the turntable,' Lily said. 'Nurse Brenda's brought it up from the lounge. Isn't that kind?'

The nurse – efficient in her uniform, her grey hair gathered under a starched white cap – was busying herself with wires and cables, arranging the record-player and its twin speakers on the trolley.

'Yes, very kind,' Cass said. 'Thank you.'

Francis twisted round in his chair, snatching his hand from hers. 'What's that? What are you doing over there?'

'Nothing for you to worry about, Reverend Wheeler,' Nurse Brenda said, without looking round. 'Your daughter's going to play you some music. Now, won't that be nice?'

From the canvas bag, Cass drew out the record, handed it to her father. There she was in the café on the Old Kent Road, caught by Johnny in the stark early-morning light.

'Cassandra,' Francis said. 'Isn't that my Cassandra?'

Cass reached across, removed the sleeve, gently, from his clasping fingers.

'Yes, Dad. That's your Cassandra. That's me.'

She took the disc from its sleeve and handed it to the nurse. As the first plucked notes flooded the room – the notes she knew so well, but which here, in her father's room, seemed transformed, as if played by someone else – the nurse retreated, closing the door behind her. Francis whipped round again to face the source of the sound, his eyes wide, staring.

Cass looked at Lily, unsure whether to lift the stylus and usher the room back into silence; but Lily mouthed at her to wait, and indeed, after a minute or two, as the song built and swelled, Francis's anxiety seemed to dissipate. He sat back in his chair, his eyes tugging shut. He maintained that same position, eyes closed, as the record spun on from track to track, transmitting that strange, disembodied echo of Cass's voice – backed by Ivor's, lifted by the layered swell of bass and drum.

She was sure, after a time, that he had fallen asleep; but when she got up to turn the record over, Francis opened his eyes, and she saw that they had pooled with tears.

He met her gaze. One of those tears loosened itself from the others and spilt over, inching down across the gathered skin of his cheek. She reached across, unthinkingly, to absorb it with the wool of her sleeve, and her father did not brush her hand away.

'Lilies'

By Cass Wheeler
From the album *Huntress*

Lilies in the bathroom
Old men in the back room
Talking in low voices the way old men do

The young girl and her mother
Gentle with each other
Eat their dinner
In their finest Sunday clothes

Did you see the flowers, Mama?
I think they're called lilies, Mama
Oh if we could buy some for her
And put them in my room

Lilies in the bathroom
I am in the back room
With the old broom
And all things left behind

The young girl has a mother
They're gentle with each other
While I eat my dinner in this room that was yours

Yes, I saw the flowers, daughter
And yes, I also thought of her
And yes, why don't we buy some for her
And put them in your room

Flowers in the bedroom
Mother's in the back room
You are in the garden and
Autumn is coming soon

RELEASED 10 January 1977
RECORDED October 1976 at Rothermere, Surrey
GENRE Folk rock / soft rock / pop
LABEL Phoenix Records
WRITER(S) Cass Wheeler
PRODUCER(S) Eli Glass
ENGINEER(S) Mike Edwards / Sean O'Malley

Cass was not expecting to love America.

Like many Europeans of her generation, her opinion of that colossal, sprawling landmass had been formed at a distance, refracted by newsreels, music, literature and the overbearing influence of received ideas. It also veered wildly between two poles.

At one end, there was Richard Nixon, with his soft, treacherous jowls and heavy, uncompromising brows; the tongues of fire licking up into the Alabama night; the Vietnamese children running, shoeless, from clouds of smoke. This was the America her peers had railed against in London and Paris: they had tussled with police at the Sorbonne, carried placards outside the US Embassy in Grosvenor Square.

Cass had not joined the protests – she had still been living at Atterley, pretending to show an interest in school, when the first sparks had ignited – but their aftershocks had reached her, as they had reached them all. Bob, Serena and Paul had marched on the embassy with a crowd from Bob's faculty, on the day dozens of students had been injured in the fray. They had scattered to a pub before things turned ugly, but the sign Serena had fashioned out of card and poster-paint requisitioned from the school art cupboard – 'US OUT!' – had occupied a corner of the living-room at Savernake Road until someone, at a party, had spilt red wine over it, and it had to be thrown away.

And then, at the other pole, there was Greenwich Village. Pete Seeger, Judy Collins, Dave Van Ronk, hunched over their guitars in dimly lit cafés. Bob Dylan and Suze Rotolo, thin-jacketed and freezing, as a cool sun rose over black fire-escapes and grey pavements and the voluptuous pale blue curves of a VW camper van. There was California – beaches and bikinis and open-top convertibles sweeping along the oceanfront to the sound of surf guitar and five-part harmony; and John Wayne's arid, sun-bleached West; and half-naked hippies rolling in the Woodstock fields. There was Joni Mitchell, and Buffalo Springfield, and Neil Young, and the old blues masters on their splintered porches, whose plaintive music Cass had first heard relayed by Jonah's deft fingers and gravel voice, and to whom they all owed such a debt of gratitude.

She saw reflected, then, in these tired, well-worn images of an America she had never visited, both the very best the world had to offer and the very worst. And when their first trip across the Atlantic was discussed, she could not imagine how her love for the one might come to outweigh the disgust she felt for the other.

And yet, somehow, it would. In February 1972, they would touch down on the black tarmac at John F. Kennedy Airport, and she would stand at the top of the metal steps, still nauseous from the flight nerves, and breathe it in, the smell of this new country – engine-fuel and hot rubber and the icy savour of winter, and some unfamiliar tug of sweetness that she couldn't identify. And she would feel it seep into her: the strangeness of it, the novelty, the sense that everything here was known to her, and yet she also knew nothing of this place at all.

'We're here,' she said to Ivor – he was behind her, shouldering on his coat. 'We've arrived.'

'We have, Cassie.'

She looked round at him, and saw in the tiny, quickening movements of Ivor's face, its twitching realignment, that he felt it, too – this sudden sense of possibility. He bent down to kiss her, and together they walked down the steps from the plane, and into America.

She remembers the hotel they stayed in, that first night: a grim fleapit on the Lower East Side, above an Asian grocery stocked with packets of dry noodles, inky bottles of soy and boxes of dried foodstuffs labelled with incomprehensible Chinese script.

The walls of each room were as thin as cardboard, the windows narrow and barred. Alan took a furious look around him as they checked in, taking their keys from an elderly woman with her hair tugged into a tight grey bun, and said, 'This is outrageous. I'll have the label move us tomorrow.'

And he did: the next day, they upped sticks to a hotel in Greenwich Village. This place was no larger or more luxurious than the first, but there were no bars on the windows, and their room looked out over the linden trees and apartment buildings of Macdougal Street. Cass would perch on the windowsill in the early morning, watching the city rising and stretching in the street below: wailing fire-trucks and darting yellow taxis and the gruff, pot-bellied owner of the corner deli drawing a striped awning down over his racks of vegetables and flowers. And of course, in her mind, she could hear Dylan and Collins and Simon and Garfunkel.

The American arm of Lieberman Records did not, however, seem especially interested in her own incipient career. A few days into the trip, there was a meeting in a dizzyingly tall building on Sixth Avenue. Suits, head-nodding, the issuing of coffee; typed sheets confirming dates, route, transportation.

'Of course,' one of the suits said, 'you're gorgeous, sweetheart, and we *love* your record, but it takes time to get a new artist set up over here. Especially . . .' He trailed off, offering Cass a meaningful glance whose significance she immediately understood.

'A woman?' she supplied, and the man's eyebrows disappeared behind the wire frames of his glasses.

'Well,' he said, 'you have to admit we do have some pretty top-class female artists of our own. Joni, Carly, Carole, Linda . . . We need to get you out there, see if we can get you sailing in their slipstream.'

Cass stared back at him, and said, quite calmly and reasonably, 'In that case, maybe you should hire us a boat rather than a truck.'

In truth, however, she hadn't really minded any of the privations of that first tour: it had seemed only right that she should have to prove herself, to take her time to map the landscape of this new country.

She remembers the bars and clubs they played, first in New York and then in an unravelling sequence of towns and cities as they traced a zigzagging route from coast to coast. Cass was opening for a psych blues six-piece from Birmingham – much better known than Cass and her band at the time, though it wouldn't be long before their fame dwindled to a faint, cultish memory – called the Puritan Experience. They were nice guys – solid, decent types, under the long hair and waistcoats and wide-eyed stage posturing, aware that all that separated them from the lives they had expected to be theirs – jobs as plumbers, electricians, butchers; marriage at twenty-one, children by twenty-four, and a thirty-year mortgage – was a hair's breadth of luck and hard work.

'To think,' the singer, Ricky, said to Cass before a gig in Syracuse, lifting his tumbler of whisky to chime with her glass of red wine, 'that my mates from school are sat in the boozer right now drinking bitter while I'm out here. Makes your head spin, doesn't it, love?'

Together, they played basements, dingy and dark-walled, lit by table candles and wall sconces. (Cass was comfortable there: they reminded her of Joe's bar.) University campuses: wood panelling and clean white plasterwork and flags flying over manicured lawns. Saloons, with their neon beer signs and bowls of French fries and shimmering foil curtains casting a nacreous glamour over the tiny raised stage.

She remembers the billows of smog over Cleveland, the mirrored sidings of Chicago skyscrapers, the snow clinging to the frozen banks of Lake Michigan. The Puritan Experience had a good-sized bus and a proper crew, but Cass and the boys travelled in an ancient, spluttering Dodge, hardly larger than Alan's van back home. The bank seats served as hard, uncomfortable sofas by day, and converted into bunks by night: just four diminutive slots, when there were six of them trying to snatch an hour or two of sleep when they could.

Tyson, their driver and roadie, was a small, wiry Pittsburgher with a head of cherubic black curls and a full, luxuriant beard. He was taciturn by day – especially when the truck gave out entirely, as it often did – and loquacious by night, especially after distributing the white powder he would acquire, at each stop-off, from some mysterious, unseen source.

Cass tried cocaine herself a handful of times, but then never bothered with it again. (No journalist would ever believe this, later, but it was the truth.) The drug's speed and lucidity held an appeal, especially after another sleepless night crammed in beside Ivor, a tangle of limbs vying for space beneath unwashed nylon sheets. But Cass found the tiredness that inevitably followed – the weight of it, settling over her, making her limbs feel solid, ungainly, and dredging her mind of thought – so intolerable that any hold the drug might have had over her was quickly lost. The men – with the exception of Alan, who eschewed drugs of all kinds, bar alcohol – felt differently, and slipped most of their per diems Tyson's way.

The men liked to stay up into the early hours, singing, playing cards, while Cass pressed her face against the thin pillow and tried to sleep. And there were, as a consequence, many nights when sleep eluded her entirely, and she would climb over to the front seat of the van, beside Alan (he shared the driving with Tyson), and take up her sketchpad.

Their adjacent positions, their easy silence, were familiar to them both, comforting; they might have been in England, back on the M1, were it not for the wide ribbon of the freeway, the exotic place names, the tangle of overhead cables and traffic lights and neon signs stamping their giddy colours on the dark. TEXACO. LIQUORS. MOTEL. At such a sign, perhaps one night in three, the truck would shudder to a halt behind the other band's bus, and they would all slip gratefully into beds with proper mattresses and clean sheets. And alone, finally alone, Ivor and Cass would reach for each other, explore the familiar landscape of their bodies, and then, exhausted, drift off into sleep.

She remembers that their old closeness, their easy intimacy, returned in those weeks. The fractious tensions of the previous few months – Ivor's jealousy, or disappointment, or whatever name she might give to the way he had looked at her as if he hardly knew her at all – seemed to disappear. She recalls no women; no long-haired, large-eyed strangers disappearing with Ivor into some dark back room. The whole trip, in fact, she remembers as rather sweetly chaste. Alan had been seeing Rachel, Martin's secretary, for six months, and already appeared to have no interest in other women. (In just over a year, in fact, Rachel would become Alan's wife, and remain so for the next forty years.)

Kit was fervently in love with his dancer, Alison: each time they landed in a new town, his primary concern was to establish the time difference, and then find a payphone to place a staggeringly expensive call to London.

Only Graham, Tyson and two members of the Puritan Experience were single, and they picked up a woman or two along the way, but even they seemed to be holding back. And so there was, for all the privations – their limited funds; the freezing temperatures; the jostling for space inside that old bone-shaker of a truck – a sense of shared endeavour that she would never quite find again with any other group of musicians, on any other tour.

Before they had left New York City, Cass had also written a letter to her mother in Toronto.

They were not crossing into Canada – not on this tour,

anyway – but they had a date booked in Buffalo, New York, a city that, on the roadmap Alan spread out across their table in a Sixth Avenue diner one afternoon, seemed unignorably close to her mother and to her half-sister, Josephine.

I'm here, Cass wrote. *Well, not in Canada, but America. We'll be in Buffalo on Wednesday 15 February. I thought perhaps you and Josephine might like to come and hear me sing.*

A reply came two days later, care of the Macdougal Street hotel, just as they were packing to leave.

Josephine is still a little young for concerts, Margaret wrote. *But we could certainly drive down to meet you for lunch. Len will be at work, I'm afraid – as I would usually be on a Wednesday afternoon. (You may remember that I'm working now, part-time, as a receptionist for our family doctor – I'm sure I put that in one of my letters.) But I will book a day off, and arrange to take Josephine out of school. She's desperate to meet you. Just tell us where to come.*

Ivor, after reading the letter, fixed Cass with a shrewd look. 'Are you really sure about this?'

She nodded. 'Where shall I tell them to meet?'

'Ask Alan. He has all the answers, doesn't he? But just so you know, Cassie . . .' Ivor placed a hand on her arm; in the pale light of the morning (it had snowed heavily overnight, and the streets were brilliant with it), his face was grey, its shadows deep. 'I think you're making a mistake.'

Ivor and I will meet you outside the Firelight Café on Main Street at one o'clock, Cass wrote back. (They weren't due to sound-check until five, and Alan and Tyson thought they should be able make it there from Syracuse by lunchtime, weather permitting.)

Buffalo was a handsome city of broad avenues and elegant skyscrapers built of red brick and glass. The snowfall, here, had been significant – downtown, grimy drifts were still compacted against lamp-posts and kerbsides, but the roads were passable, and cracks were forming in Lake Erie's frozen skin. The Firelight Café was about halfway along Main Street; it was closed, but Cass and Ivor huddled under its red awning, drawing their scarves up over their ears. The others had gone off in the truck to find a diner, and a phone.

'All right?' Ivor said, his voice muffled by the thick wool of his scarf; and Cass, swaddled in her own, leant in and said, 'I don't know.'

Margaret Steadman did not keep them waiting long. She wore a brown tweed coat with a fur collar, and a cloche hat in a matching shade. From one of her hands, sheathed in brown leather gloves, dangled a tall, large-boned child wrapped in sheepskin, a navy beret perched prettily on her long blonde hair. It was the girl Cass focused on first, not quite ready to acknowledge her mother's sudden presence – the undeniable solidity of her, standing just a few inches away.

'Hello,' she said to the child, who looked back at her with wide, slanted brown eyes that, she could see straight away, were the precise shape and shade of her own. 'I'm your sister, Cass.'

'Hello,' the girl replied, clear-voiced, without a trace of shyness. 'I'm Josephine.'

Behind them, Margaret and Ivor were exchanging a cautious greeting. Cass turned, faced her mother squarely for the first time. She saw a woman in comfortable middle age; a broad, plain face leavened by those same lively dark eyes. She was extravagantly, inexpertly made up – her powder had gathered and clotted, and her pink lipstick had seeped into the tiny fissures around her mouth. Margaret was, Cass understood, more nervous than she was, and the knowledge made her feel distantly sorry for her mother; as she had, a few days before, for a woman she and Ivor had seen on the New York subway, smartly dressed, walking from car to car with a crumpled photograph, asking each person she passed, in a polite, desperate, Southern voice, *Could you tell me, please – have you seen my son?*

'Maria,' Margaret said, and she brought her cool cheek close to Cass's, left the imprint of a kiss. Then, as she moved away, she checked herself, and said, 'No. Of course. You're Cassandra now.'

They chose the first open restaurant they could find. It was an Italian, almost empty, but filled with warm, appetising smells: garlic, rosemary, roasting meat. Accordion music played at a low volume, barely audible. They went about the business of ordering. Cass and Ivor wanted wine; Margaret said she didn't usually drink, but was persuaded to accept a glass of Chianti.

Josephine sucked her Coca-Cola through a straw. Under her sheepskin coat, she was wearing a hand-knitted jumper (white rabbits gambolling on apple-green wool), a blue denim skirt and thick white tights. She talked incessantly, of school and softball and their house in Toronto and where Cass and Ivor lived and whether London was bigger than Toronto and why were they in America and which instruments did they play and how did they write songs and why did they write them and was it very hard to do?

Cass was glad of her half-sister's chatter, and she answered most of her questions while Ivor and Margaret drank the larger part of the wine, her mother's cheeks gradually acquiring a reddish rash that clashed unflatteringly with her rust-coloured cardigan. From time to time, Cass glanced across at her, weighing the woman she carried in her mind – hard, inaccessible, given to sudden, unpredictable bouts of fury – against the woman sitting here at the table, so bland and unthreatening. The two were simply irreconcilable.

After dessert – fat, cream-filled cannoli for Josephine; coffee, hot and strong and served in tiny white china cups, for the adults – Josephine said she needed to go to the bathroom. Margaret offered to go with her, but the child shook her head and set off determinedly on her own. Ivor, looking from Cass to Margaret, slipped on his coat, and said he was stepping outside for some air. And then they were alone, Cass and her mother, for the first time in almost twelve years, sitting at a restaurant table in Buffalo, New York, neither of them quite sure what to say.

A moment passed, then two. Margaret said, 'Lily tells me Francis isn't doing too well.'

Cass looked beyond her mother, through the plate-glass windows to the street, where Ivor was a dark-coated silhouette, black wool against whitish cakes of snow, cupping a cigarette with his hand as he held a lighter to its tip.

'I'm sorry,' Margaret said.

Cass shifted her gaze to her mother's face. The red rash had only partly faded, leaving a livid leopard scatter across her cheeks and nose.

'Rosacea,' Margaret said quietly. 'That's why I don't usually drink. Alcohol brings it on.'

Cass nodded. Still she said nothing. Through the window, she watched a man in a dark grey jacket stop beside Ivor, who then offered him a light. The two men's mouths opening and closing as they exchanged the banal cordialities of strangers.

'I was very unhappy, you know,' Margaret said, in the same small voice. 'Very unhappy, until I met Len. I couldn't go on, Cassandra. It was my only chance.'

'So,' Cass said, 'you decided just to start again, did you? To pretend you didn't already have a husband, or a daughter. To move to the other side of the world and make a new family.'

She met her mother's eyes then. There was so much she had imagined saying to her, in those painful, dislocated months – years – after Margaret had left. And yet she had said none of it – she had ignored her mother's letters; she hadn't given breath to the questions hanging unanswered in her mind. And now, it seemed, it was too late. This woman was not the vicar's wife who had packed her case one Saturday morning more than a decade ago, before the house was stirring, and stolen silently across the common to meet the man she believed would restore her to life, no matter the cost. Margaret was another woman now: a wife; a doctor's receptionist; a mother come up to town for the afternoon with the young daughter for whom she had slowly, painstakingly, knitted white rabbits across the bodice of a green jumper: weaving more love, more tenderness, into each purl and plain-stitch than she had ever offered the daughter she had left behind.

'My girl.' Margaret's eyes were wet; she reached across the table, laid her hand over Cass's, but Cass snatched it away. 'My daughter. My God, it was so hard to leave you. Can't you see that? Can't you imagine? But I was so unwell, back then, don't you see? I wasn't a good mother to you. I thought you'd be better off without me.'

Cass closed her eyes. 'That is true,' she said. 'You weren't, and I was.'

'They have real flowers in the bathroom, Mom,' Josephine said. She had reappeared beside their table without either of them noticing. 'Lilies, I think. Are they the big white flowers, with the orange powder on the sticky-out bits?'

'Yes, darling,' Margaret said, removing her gaze from Cass's face. From her handbag she produced a tissue, and dabbed at the corners of her eyes. 'The stamens. Those are lilies.'

Out on the street, they said their goodbyes: kisses on the cheek for Josephine, brief, polite embraces for Margaret. And then Cass's mother and half-sister were gone, two figures walking hand in hand towards the parking-lot, and the car that would carry them home to Canada.

Ivor threaded his arm around Cass's shoulders, and held her close; then slowly they retraced their steps along the street.

They had to drive a long way south-west to see the snow begin to melt.

It was cold in St Louis, but not the still, glacial cold of Cleveland and Chicago. Waking early in the morning in the fugged, stale heat of the truck, they found the Missouri freeway gilded with a fine layer of frost that by mid-afternoon had melted away.

They played a club called Ace's Cowshed Lounge, with joint support from a local prog-rock band called I Am Your Shadow. Four skinny, denim-jacketed guys just out of high school, who travelled with them on the truck to Kansas City, instigating a complex all-night poker game that culminated with the band's eighteen-year-old bassist, George, requisitioning almost every last cent from Graham, Ivor and Kit.

In Denver, under the ragged, white-capped outline of the Rockies, they played the Coliseum, and came off stage to find a familiar face waiting for them: Jonah Hills, up from Albuquerque in a battered black '58 Chevy Impala. They embraced with the fervour of long-lost friends: neither Cass nor Ivor had heard from Jonah since he'd slipped their demo to Martin Hartford the previous year.

'Only been on the road for seven hours,' he said, offering Ivor a lopsided grin as Cass threw her arms around him. 'No distance for old friends.'

Over steak and mashed potatoes at an all-night café, Jonah told them he'd moved to New Mexico for the sunshine, and a dancer named Sylvie, whom he'd met on a Caribbean cruise. (He'd been playing guitar in the house band.) Not long after the ship had docked in Louisiana, Sylvie had discovered she was pregnant; she'd wanted to move home to Albuquerque to have the baby, and Jonah had agreed to go with her. But just a few weeks after the child was born – they'd called him Todd – Sylvie had left, taking the boy with her.

Now, he suspected that Todd might never have been his; that what Sylvie had been after, really, was a down-payment on an apartment. (She'd also skipped town with the slender envelope of dollars Jonah had been saving for that purpose.) Where she was now, he had no idea: she'd sent a postcard from Las Vegas, with a single word – 'sorry' – and had not been in touch again. Her parents, who had rather taken a shine to Jonah, were none the wiser, either.

'So there I am, stuck in Albuquerque, with no girl, no son and barely a dollar to my name,' Jonah said, another, weaker smile easing the weathered contours of his face. 'But hey – at least I still have the sunshine.'

He was still playing guitar, he said: just local places, for tips and a free meal.

'Nothing like *this*.' He looked from Ivor to Cass. 'Don't forget me, will you? Don't forget who brought the two of you together.'

It seemed so long ago, now, that she had seen Jonah coming up the drive at Atterley, his steel guitar strung across his shoulder. How strange, how inconceivable, that such a moment could lead to this one: the three of them in a Colorado café at midnight, eating, talking, remembering the past. 'How could we ever forget?'

They asked Jonah to come with them to California – they were starting the long drive in the morning – but he declined.

'Got to see a man about a dog,' he said. It was three a.m., and they were standing in the parking-lot outside the café. Jonah was half-cut on bourbon – not to mention the several toots Ivor had slipped him in the men's room – but he insisted on driving straight back to Albuquerque.

'Come and crash at the motel with us, Jonah,' Cass said. 'Drive home tomorrow.' But he shook his head; his expression was glazed, remote. 'I'll drop you guys off, and then get on the road.'

At the motel – a low-slung clutch of red-roofed buildings just off Route 70 – Jonah stopped the Chevy, waited for them to get out, and then sped off, his hand waving through the open driver's window. Ivor and Cass stood together on the tarmac, watching the fading tail-lights of his car.

'Do you think he's all right?' Cass said.

Ivor put his arm around her shoulders. 'I don't know, Cassie. I hope so.'

She drew closer to him. Out on the freeway, Jonah was lost to the neon night, just another faceless driver chasing the miles towards home.

The truck was pulling onto Route 5 outside San Francisco – it was early morning, the sky a lurid, striated wash of pink and orange – when Graham first complained of feeling unwell.

'It's just a cold,' he said, and retired to one of the bunks to sleep it off. But by the time they arrived in Los Angeles, Graham was feverish, his shoulders shuddering to the rhythm of a deep, hacking cough, and the colour leaching from his face.

Tyson and Alan drove him to hospital, where he was diagnosed with pneumonia – an impossibility, they'd have thought, under the azure skies of California. Bed-rest and a hefty dose of antibiotics were prescribed; exhaustion and excessive smoking, the young, blandly handsome doctor informed Alan with not a small hint of disapproval, had worsened Graham's symptoms. There could be no gigs, or work of any kind, for several weeks; Graham would remain under observation until they could be sure he was well enough to fly home.

What to do? The Puritan Experience had flown home to England from Denver, but Cass and the guys had a date booked at the Troubadour in West Hollywood in two days' time, and others scattered across southern California over the coming week.

'I'll sort this,' Alan said, grim-faced. 'Just give me a couple of hours.'

'Sure we can't help?' Cass said, but he shook his head. 'No. Get some rest. This is what you pay me for.'

They checked into another motel: this one tall, flat-fronted, furnished in the bright, geometric style of ten years before, each room boxy and identical. Alan disappeared into his room while Ivor, Kit and Tyson gathered by the pool in the last rays of spring sun. Two pale, ivory-skinned Englishmen, stretched out on sun-loungers in their jeans and jumpers; Tyson darker, barrel-chested, swigging Jack Daniel's straight from the bottle.

Cass stayed up in their room on the third floor, trying, unsuccessfully, to sleep. She had just picked up her acoustic guitar, begun plotting out the arc of a song, when a knock came on the door.

There, framed against the pinkish twilight, was Alan.

'I've found a guy,' he said. 'Jake Larsen. Let's just cross our bloody fingers this works out.'

Jake had played drums for James Taylor, Tom Arnold and Linda Ronstadt, and he lived, Alan said, in Laurel Canyon. So that was where they drove the next day, the old Dodge lurching up narrow, winding roads to a hillside that, with its pines and palms and low, stunted bushes, looked to Cass more like the Mediterranean than America.

Along the road that, they hoped, would lead to Jake's house, the path grew narrower, and the vegetation thickened, the slender, heavy-headed trees bending together as if engaged in whispered conversation. It soon became clear that they would have to abandon the truck and finish the journey on foot.

'Goddammit,' said Tyson. 'Where the *hell* are you taking us?'

But the others were quiet, awed by the sudden bucolic beauty of the place, green-shadowed and rustling and heavy with some rich, resinous scent, after all those miles of concrete and tarmac and steel.

Cass, her guitar case in one hand, the other looped loosely around Ivor's waist, looked around her, and thought that she had never seen anywhere more beautiful.

Jake's house lay in a clearing at the path's end, like a cottage in a storybook. It was built of wood, painted a dark forest green; there was a porch with a swing-seat, and a picnic table constructed from rough-hewn logs. Jake was out on the porch to greet them: a tall, tanned Viking with a shoulder-length mane of blond hair, and a moustache the colour and texture of dry straw. He was barefoot. 'I usually play that way,' he explained as they went inside. 'Helps me feel the beat, you know?'

Jake brewed a pot of tea, then rolled a fat joint, which he passed round as they sat on the floor of his living-room, with its thick Turkish rugs and Indian marquetry tables. A huge Yamaha drum-kit squatted in one corner of the room, its sleek black bodywork and shining metal incongruous among the wood and tapestries.

Cass closed her eyes as she inhaled, let the smoke gather in her throat, glad of something to occupy her attention as their music – *her* music – filled the room from Jake's record-player. Already, she was finding it difficult to listen back to her recordings – those distillations of a time, a place, a feeling, that could inevitably only convey a fraction of the moment's true resonance.

At the record's end, the silence rolled out unbroken; four faces turned to Jake's, whose eyes remained closed, his expression distant. Alan, across the floor, gave a small, impatient cough.

And then, just as Cass was about to speak, Jake opened his eyes. He clambered to his feet, unfolding his long legs in their blue jeans. Behind his drum-kit, he slipped onto his leather stool, started measuring out a beat. Still nobody spoke; they followed his lead, drew their guitars from their cases, and began to play.

Alan looked on, still curled on the rug. And the music layered itself around them, gathered pace and texture, and seeped out through the open windows, and into the whispering trees.

That Wednesday night in March 1972 was a watershed. Cass knew it then – divined it, through some indefinable instinct – and she still knows it now.

In their room in the Los Angeles motel, she had dressed

with care – green lace gown, black boots, the black velvet coat she'd acquired in a Chicago thrift store. (In his write-up of the concert, the critic for the *Los Angeles Times* would, rather feverishly, describe her as looking 'like an ethereal English wraith stepped out from the pages of Charles Dickens: blonde and pale-faced, baring her long neck at the microphone as if for Dracula's fangs'.)

She had pinned up her hair, painted a thick layer of black kohl around her eyes. In the dressing-room, she'd refused Ivor's proffered dose of cocaine, and drunk her customary single glass of red wine.

The nerves were circling, as they always did, but she felt strong enough to banish them. Alone in the dressing-room for a moment (the others were already making their way to the stage), she paused before the mirror, and regarded herself with a level, clear-sighted gaze.

This is it, she thought. *This is the one.*

From the stage, she could see vaulted wood, red lights, smoke-clouds writhing in the darkness. The technician moved among them, performing last-minute checks, and she stood still, looking out, sensing that the crowd was behind them; there was an expectant quietness, a collective stilling of breath, that they had felt only once or twice on their long journey across America.

In the audience, she knew, was Tom Arnold, whose first album, *Long Time Coming*, she had bought on Oxford Street in the summer of 1968. She had played it over and over in the living-room at Savernake Road, until Bob had accused her of trying to torture them by repeat listening. *Even music as good as that, Cass, drives you mad when you hear it for the* twentieth *time.* She and Ivor had spent hours studying the sleeve of Arnold's last record, *The Summer Never Ends*, wondering how he had achieved such an effortless marriage of music and meaning, of poetry and sound.

And now Tom Arnold was here to see *her*. 'Invited a few guys down tonight,' Jake had said as he'd swept in for the sound-check, strings of fine brown beads layered around the open collar of his white shirt. 'Told them about you, Cass. They can't wait to hear you.'

And so the stage. Jake's sure, steady beat. Ivor beside her, meeting her eye, leaning forward as they dived into the song, headfirst, drawn by its swelling, tidal pull. Kit at her other side. An energy, a quickening, that was impossible to define: a shared sense that the room was theirs, that the audience was with them. That the music they were making was the music these strangers wanted to hear.

So rare, that feeling, and so intoxicating. Cass sang, she played, her feet planted firmly on the stage in her black leather boots. Blonde hair haloed by the stage lights, green dress sweeping the floor; mouth open, eyes closed, and around her the three men playing, beating string and cymbal and drum-skin in a blur of muscle and movement and sweat.

At the set's end, the applause ran for one minute, two, three.

She looked from Ivor to Kit to Jake, her hair plastered damply to her face. 'Another?'

Ivor nodded, strummed the first chords of the song she'd begun in their motel room two days ago, and finished the day before, the two of them sitting up late beside the swimming pool, wrapped in blankets. She raised an eyebrow – they'd never played it live, of course; they hadn't yet had the chance – but he stared back at her and nodded again. And so she stretched her left hand to fit the shape of the chord, and joined him, dived back in to the crest of the wave.

Kit and Jake were silent, watching. It was just the two of them then, Ivor and Cass, voices rising and falling, as it had once been in the attic room at Atterley; as it was now, though hers was the voice the crowd was straining to hear, and Ivor's was its complement, the stem from which it grew.

Later, there was an after-party at Jake's house in the Canyon. *The State She's In* on the record-player. Drifts of cocaine littering the coffee table. A woman in a long, patterned skirt passing round a tray of home-baked brownies. '*Hash* brownies, man – you have to try them.'

Cass stood on the porch, beside the swing-seat, looking out into the dark forest, smoking. Beside her, Tom Arnold sipped his drink and said, 'I want you to come out on my next tour. I'll put our managers in touch, make it happen.'

'All right.' Her calmness was a surprise.

He reached out, tucked a stray slip of hair behind her ear. 'You're very beautiful, Cass. But you know that, don't you? I'm sure your old man tells you all the time.'

Cass said nothing, neither agreed nor disagreed. The moment stretched between them, broken only by the sound of her own voice from the stereo. Ivor was somewhere inside, she thought: the last she'd seen of him, he'd been rolling up a twenty-dollar bill, bending down to the hand-mirror where the white trail of coke was waiting. She heard a woman laughing, and a man saying, 'Well, Jerry, if I'd wanted to live like a square, I'd have gone and joined my father's bank.'

Tom Arnold was watching her, voicing a silent question. She knew she ought to thank him, turn away, go back inside; but still she did nothing. She knew what was coming, and what she would do when it came.

It seemed an age, still, before he leant towards her, brought his face down to meet hers. Then and only then did she raise a hand, place it on his chin, and, ever so gently – as a mother might reprimand a child – push it away.

'No,' she said. His face was only inches from hers. 'Not for that.'

Tom smiled, wise enough not to try to disguise his intentions. 'Shame. But I still want you on the tour.'

He stepped back, still watching her, reached into his pocket for his cigarettes, lit two, and handed one of them to her. And then they stood for a while, smoking, staring out into the ripe, sweet-smelling Californian night.

'Brightest Star'

By Cass Wheeler
From the album *Huntress*

Flying through this empty night-time sky
Bridging the distance between your heart and mine
Nothing at the windows but the night
And a tiny yellow quiver looking like some fire

Sirius you are the brightest star
The wishing and the wanting, that will get you so far
So come and share the limelight, honey,
Come and shine your starlight over me

Oh, is it the darkness in your eyes?
The black hole where I fell for all your lies
But space between us only seems to grow
All you want is for the whole world to know

That yes, you are the brightest star
The highest and the brightest I have seen by far
So come share the limelight, honey,
Come and shine your starlight next to me

The brightest star
The brightest star
However far
Oh, you're so far
The brightest star
The brightest star
Oh, you're so far
My brightest star

RELEASED 10 January 1977
RECORDED October 1976 at Rothermere, Surrey
GENRE Folk rock / soft rock / pop
LABEL Phoenix Records
WRITER(S) Cass Wheeler
PRODUCER(S) Eli Glass
ENGINEER(S) Mike Edwards / Sean O'Malley

She remembers a still, golden Sunday in the summer of 1973, drowsy with heat and the basso profondo of bees.

Cass and Kim were stretched out on sun-loungers beside the swimming pool, its smooth surface dark blue, glassy. Behind them, the Château d'Anjou loomed black-roofed and silent. The shutters were still drawn over many of its tall, wood-framed windows, giving the house an unguarded look. It seemed, on this perfect afternoon, less forbidding than it had on other days, and other nights, with its whispers, and its silences, and the coolness of its empty rooms.

'I think it's over,' Kim said, 'between Graham and me.'

Cass shifted onto her front, lifted her sunglasses. Kim didn't move; she was lying on her back, her acres of bare skin (they were both wearing their smallest bikinis) glistening with sun-lotion. She had drawn her hair, with its dozens of tiny plaits, into a bun at the nape of her neck, and a few coils had struggled loose: they had the look, to Cass's tired eyes, of so many tiny black lizards, creeping across the cushion towards her.

'Are you sure?'

Kim nodded. 'He called Terri again last night. He said he was calling his mother, but I knew he wasn't. He hates his mother almost as much as I do. I went and picked up the receiver in the kitchen.'

Cass replaced her glasses. She stretched out an arm, bridging the distance between them. The other woman's skin was warm, slick to her touch. 'Ah, Kim. Graham's an idiot. Doesn't know a good thing, clearly. And the booze doesn't help, does it?'

'No.' Kim's voice was taut. 'Or the rest.'

It was seven weeks, now, since Cass and Kim had met for the first time; eight since Cass had packed two cases for herself and Ivor, and he'd carried them downstairs to the car that would take them to Heathrow. They'd flown with Alan and Martin to

Paris by Concorde, though even that novel luxury hadn't been enough to rid Cass of her nerves: her hatred of flying, it seemed, was unassailable, and so it would remain.

Martin had wanted her there a few days earlier than the others to settle in, and to meet the engineer, Luc. Chopin had once lived at the château, and Van Gogh had committed its fractured, lurid image to canvas. But Cass had hated the place on sight, and, from the very first night, had slept poorly: twice she'd insisted that she and Ivor move bedrooms after waking with the unsettling sense that someone – or some*thing* – was watching them from the shadows. She had, however, warmed immediately to Luc, a quick-witted Parisian whose English was laced with an impressive array of expletives.

Kim had arrived a week later with the keyboard player, a session musician named Frank Smith. She was wearing a short white shift dress, platform sandals and a straw hat with a broad brim. Graham hadn't been able to stop going on about Kim, this woman he'd met at a party, for weeks; but then, Graham hadn't been able to stop going on about Terri, or Lucy, or Saskia, either, so they hadn't paid him a great deal of attention.

Cass might easily, when she saw her, have thought Kim a model rather than a singer: she had that long-limbed looseness, that enviable sense of ease in her own skin. But there, in the château's gloomy hallway, she had also immediately understood that Kim was not the sort of woman who was only truly comfortable in the admiring company of men.

Kim had put down her case, come forward to kiss Cass on each cheek, and said, 'Thank you so much for bringing me in on the sessions. *The State She's In* got me through the worst break-up I've ever had.'

'Welcome,' Cass said. 'I'm glad you're here.'

Cass suspected that Kim had been singled out as a backing singer as much for her looks as for her musical abilities: she was not, it had to be said (and it wouldn't be long before Kim herself would say it), the best vocalist on the circuit. But Cass had discovered, in the course of the sessions, that Kim's voice had an easy, naive warmth that drew out the brighter colours in Cass's own.

'God knows when they'll stir,' Kim said now, beside the pool. 'It must have been five when Graham came up to bed. Even later when I'd finished shouting at him.'

Ivor had come up a good while after Cass, too: he had woken her, stumbling around their room in the darkness, but she had kept her eyes closed and turned her face away.

'Martin and Alan were going to get up early,' Cass replied. 'They wanted another listen to the mixes.'

Kim adjusted her position on the cushion, rearranged her hair under her neck. 'God, the tracks sound great, Cass. *Really* great.'

'Do you think so?' Her doubt was unfeigned: she thought – *hoped* – the songs were good, that Luc and Martin had captured them, imprinted their essence on tape and metal. But always, in the listening, she had the sense that something was missing – that no recording could ever quite measure up to the music she could hear in her mind, and which seemed truest, most authentic, in those moments on stage, unmediated by the tricks and polishes of production.

Still, last night, at the party, everybody had seemed convinced that they had a sure-fire hit on their hands. Alan had opened the champagne, Luc and Frank had distributed the drugs, and the night had passed in a blur of raucous celebration, culminating – as far as Cass could remember – with Graham, Ivor and Frank stripping off all their clothes and jumping into the swimming pool.

'At least,' Johnny had remarked drily to Cass as they'd watched the men's antics from the terrace, 'they can't get a car back here and launch *that* into the pool. There's a bloody great château in the way.'

Cass had been so happy to see Johnny: he'd arrived three days before, with his friend Sue, a make-up artist, in a car packed with lights, costumes and props. Now that the sessions were finished, they were to make use of the château for the cover shoot: Sue and Johnny were transforming the master bedroom into a dressing-room. Here, in the photograph she and Johnny had discussed at length, a man (Ivor) was to be seen in reflection, applying make-up, while Cass, dressed as an Edwardian dandy, looked on.

The picture had been Cass's idea, arriving simultaneously with a name for her second album: *Songs From the Music Hall.*

She'd been at home in Muswell Hill one idle Sunday evening, watching *The Good Old Days* on television, when the image had slipped into her mind: a man powdering his face before a mirror, watched by a woman in a suit and tie, in homage to Vesta Tilley and her like – the female singers who had once caused such a sensation in the London theatres. (Faintly, she recalled plain old Mrs Souter singing 'Jolly Good Luck to the Girl Who Loves a Soldier' as she cleaned. 'What's that song?' the eleven-year-old Cass had asked, and Mrs Souter, seeming suddenly playful, girlish even, had said, 'What, you mean you don't know Vesta Tilley?')

But Cass had not, initially, imagined Ivor in the role of the man at the mirror; that idea had come from Johnny.

'He'll hate it,' she'd warned him, and it had been true.

'That bloody *poof*,' Ivor had hissed, 'is determined to humiliate me.' But eventually, he was won over, perhaps by vanity – Johnny had cannily insisted that the young man in the photograph had to be extremely handsome – and by Alan's more prosaic considerations. (Both he and Martin were convinced that Ivor's presence in the photograph, as both Cass's guitarist and her boyfriend, would boost sales.)

'All right,' he'd said the night before they'd left for France. 'I'll do it. After all, who am I to refuse the great Cass Wheeler anything?'

'Don't be like that,' she'd said, and reached up to kiss him, but he'd pushed her away.

'Why not? That's how it is, isn't it? You calling the shots, and me your bloody puppet on a string.'

And so the shoot would go ahead as planned. Johnny and Sue were up in the master bedroom now, putting the finishing touches to the room – they wanted to begin that evening, after dusk. (Johnny wanted tenebrous darkness, the 'sexy chiaroscuro of candlelight'.)

'What time is it, Kim?' Cass said. 'I forgot to put on my watch.'

Kim lifted a languid arm, opened her eyes just wide enough to examine her wrist. 'Almost five. God, it's still so hot.'

'I'd better go up. Sue wants us to try the costumes.' Cass swung reluctantly upright, wincing as her bare feet met the baked terracotta tiles. 'You'll come and keep me company, won't you? Tell me I don't look *too* ridiculous?'

'Of course. Might just have one last swim before I come up. Unless you want me now?'

'No, it's fine. We'll be a while, anyway.' Cass reached for her silk kimono, slipped it on over her bikini. A quick blur of movement drew her eye to the château's second floor: a shutter thrown open, an arm resting on a windowsill. In the dim maw of the windowpane, Ivor's face was framed, ghostlike, as he looked down and met her gaze.

'Afternoon, darling!' she called up, her voice sounding falsely bright, over-loud. 'Ready for the shoot? I'm coming up now.'

Ivor shrugged. And then, after a moment, he stepped away, drawn back into the unseen shadows of their room.

So this, it seemed, was success.

Mornings waking in a featureless succession of hotel rooms, unsure of where she was, drawing gradually back into the present. The next city; the next town; the day's ever-changing schedule of commitments replacing the free, formless landscapes of her dreams.

Hours in Alan's office (he had rented premises on Berwick Street, recruited two members of staff); or in an upstairs room at the American label's Sixth Avenue HQ, talking to journalists, trying to give an account of herself. It was not, she was learning quickly, acceptable to say that she worked simply by instinct, drawn by a creeping sense of how a song might sound, by her need to snare that quiver of notes before they disappeared. They needed more. They wanted her to explain her intentions. They wanted to know where she fitted in.

These writers were almost always men. Eva Taylor was a rare exception, and a loyal one: in a second, larger interview for the *Courier*, just after *Songs From the Music Hall* went to number one, she wrote that 'no self-respecting feminist should be without a copy of this outstanding record, in which the hopes and dreams of the modern woman – our fascinations and obsessions – are writ large.'

If the men were American, they were obsequious, even flirtatious; if they were British, they were usually chippy, even rude – especially to Ivor, whom some of them (Don Collins, especially) seemed to like to goad.

'Ivor Tait, once a promising singer and guitarist in his own right, is now playing second fiddle – or *guitar* – to his famous girlfriend, and doesn't seem at *all* happy about it,' Collins wrote after one particularly bruising encounter with Ivor, backstage at the Marquee. (Collins had gone up to Ivor to congratulate him, in a voice dripping with sarcasm, on showing such solidarity with the feminist movement; Ivor, in response, had swung a punch at him.)

Afternoons on the bus, caught between ennui and encroaching nerves; evenings at the venue, each hour neatly apportioned to the unchanging sequence of tasks – sound-check, dinner, hair and make-up, show, party, sleep. The new buses were large

239

and well appointed, almost inconceivably luxurious compared with Vertical Heights's old Transit, or Tyson's Dodge; but they were still, after all, buses, with the same stuffy, recycled air, the same lingering odours of air-freshener and tobacco, the same white-noise of the engine lulling her to a broken, insubstantial sleep.

She and Ivor travelled alone, now, while Graham, Kit and the crew piled into a second bus. Alan, when he joined them on tour – he was gradually taking on a handful of other clients, to whom he had to devote a reasonable portion of his time – preferred to travel separately: he didn't like to intrude on Cass's privacy, and disliked the druggy, locker-room atmosphere of the men's vehicle.

Cass had a rule now, too, enforced by Alan: no more than two consecutive nights were to be spent on the road. She still found it difficult to sleep in her bunk, even when Ivor went off to join the men's card game. (Adrian, the new tour manager, was a demon at poker.) Even then, alone under clean white cotton, she would spend most of the night awake, watching the unspooling road (interstate, motorway, autobahn, autostrada: each one different, each one exactly the same), and scribbling scraps of lyrics in her notebook, or painting.

She bought herself a set of oils, with which she began to fashion thickly layered, abstract images, each one no larger than a postcard. (It was difficult to manage a larger sheet of paper amid the unpredictable rolling and shuddering of the bus.) She had no idea if her miniature paintings were any good; indeed, she didn't care at all whether they were or not. They were simply reactions to the mood of the moment, ways to fill the long, fractious, moonlit hours. For her music, when they were travelling, seemed to desert her: even in quiet moments, no sounds found their way into her mind but the low, tinnitus after-buzz of the amplifiers; and the shotgun scatter of applause; and fragments of her setlist, tuning in and out like the radio broadcasts she had once treasured, under her sprigged counterpane at the vicarage, all those years ago.

Already, so quickly, she was falling out of love with touring. Often, on those endless afternoons and sleepless nights, she thought of their little flat in Muswell Hill (and soon, it really *was* theirs – Vince suggested she invest in property, and Harriet, happily settled in Ireland, agreed to sell). Then, Cass's longing for home – for that lovely, light-filled music room, with the veranda on which her plants, uncared for, were surely withering – was so strong it was almost painful.

There was no option, of course, but to tour. And those moments on stage were still what she lived for – those heady, perfect, transcendent moments when there was no past and no future, but only the five of them (Frank, the session keys player, was now a more or less permanent presence in the band), locked together in a groove. It was still there, on stage – gowned, sweat-sheened, exhausted; letting the great urgent sound of her voice swell up from her body and roll out over the heads of the crowd – that she felt most truly alive.

Tom Arnold's tour had been the breakthrough. Those two six-week support stints in America in November 1972 – one on each coast, with a couple of brief forays into the Midwest – had propelled *The State She's In* (much to the surprise of her own American label) to a respectable position on the Billboard chart.

'Deserves to go higher,' Tom had said, and he had done his best to make that happen: lobbied her label; introduced her to other musicians, publicists, critics; talked her up tirelessly in his own interviews. She was grateful to him, of course, and was also aware of how serendipitous their meeting had been in the first place: had Graham not got sick in LA (Graham reminded her of this fact as often as he could), they would probably never have met Jake, and therefore probably never have met Tom, and therefore could conceivably have stayed rattling around the backroads with Tyson for the foreseeable future.

Tom had come to see her in her dressing-room after their first concert together at the Boston Music Hall. Three thousand people in the crowd: a seething mass that, from the stage, her nerves digging their sharp claws into her throat, Cass had only been able to suppress by imagining that she was singing to one face, one person. In fact, she had found herself picturing her mother; had seen her at her tenth birthday party, all those years ago: Mrs Raynsford's piano, *The Well-Tempered Clavier*, Margaret leaning down to smile at her, her face uncommonly soft, even loving. Very *good, Maria. Very good.*

'You did great,' Tom had said in the dressing-room, unconsciously echoing Margaret's words. '*Really* great. You're electric out there. Just don't take any of it for granted, Cass. Remember not to let it go to your head.'

She'd smiled. 'I'll remember.'

He'd squeezed her shoulder, and stepped back out into the corridor. 'See you back at the Sheraton. Martinis on me.'

She had not remembered his advice, of course – not for a long while. She had stared back at her reflection in the dressing-room mirror, and seen herself through others' eyes: the even symmetry of the face that so many now admired; the soulful dark eyes; the long blonde hair. She was twenty-two years old, set on an inviolable course towards achievement. Her ambition was without limit, and she saw no reason why any such limit should be set.

How difficult it was, all these years later, to shift back into the body of the girl she had once been. So young, so single-minded, so *sure*. To see with that girl's eyes, think with her mind, and wish, against all odds, that there were some way to make her understand how easily it could all just slip away.

*

In the spring of 1975, Alan suggested they find her an assistant. There was too much for Alan to do for her alone, and certainly too much for her to do for herself. They should look for a woman, perhaps. Someone easygoing but organised. Someone who might become a friend.

Cass was unsure. 'I do have Ivor.'

'Yes.' Alan's voice was dry. 'You do.'

It occurred to Cass, as she held Alan's idea in her mind over the next few weeks, that he was already coming to know her better than she knew herself: he'd understood that she was lonely, before she'd even acknowledged this possibility. And yet even as the thought struck her, it seemed absurd. She was surrounded by people – she was rarely alone, even when she wasn't on tour; every moment of every day was accounted for, cut to fit the pattern set by the label. Rehearsal, recording, press, radio, gigs.

She wasn't writing so much these days – not with the ease and speed she'd always taken for granted, and rarely, now, with Ivor. The closeness they had reaffirmed on that first American tour was disappearing: a gulf had opened up between them that she didn't know how to bridge. On stage, their affinity was easy, instinctive, but off stage, it had disappeared, lost itself in absences, awkwardness, half-finished sentences. She knew that he disliked Tom – believed, with some reason, that he was making a play for Cass. But his disaffection went further than that: Ivor seemed to simmer with a resentment whose existence, when questioned, he flatly denied.

On tour, he kept more and more to the men's bus, leaving Cass to travel alone; and at home, he was increasingly absent from the flat. He'd taken up with Hugh again, and was spending long stretches of time at Hugh's place in Crouch End. Hugh threw parties there: noisy, rough, scratchy affairs that lasted several days, and were peopled by a crowd Cass didn't know, or care to know: a rackety, ever-changing flock of squatters and bikers and gaunt-faced old hippies, thin and raw-boned and reeking of desperation (or so it seemed to Cass). Powder and pills and brown sugar: she hated all of it, hated the expression she saw on Ivor's face when, eventually, he came home: exhausted, emotionless, numb, wanting only to sleep.

He denied he had a problem, however – insisted that the problem was hers.

'Don't be such a bloody old woman, Cassie,' he said. 'Dope loosens me up, all right? It helps me relax. And I'm still here, aren't I? I'm still here whenever you click your fingers.'

It was true: Ivor wasn't missing sessions, or gigs; he was doing everything that was required of him. And yet something was missing – their old closeness, their sense of a shared life, a shared future. It was her name on the records, the posters, the deeds to the flat; her face in the newspapers and magazines. Ivor was a part of it – essential to it, in fact, and still essential to her. But this was not his dream, not as he'd conceived it, and she couldn't find a way to atone for this; didn't feel, in essence, that she should be required to do so. For she still believed that she would never have asked such a thing of him.

So she said nothing, and carried on, and missed him, and tried not to think about what he was doing at Hugh's, and who he was doing it with; and yes, she admitted to herself as she weighed Alan's words in her mind, she was lonely.

'All right,' she said to Alan finally. 'Let's find someone.'

A few days later, she received a telephone call from Kim. 'Alan says you're looking for an assistant.'

'He thinks it would be a good idea, yes. Why? Might you know someone?'

'Yes.' Kim hesitated. 'Me. I'm tired, you see. Tired of the hustling. I just don't think I've got what it takes – not really. And when Alan told me about this, something clicked in my mind. It just makes sense, don't you think? I so enjoyed those weeks with you in France, and I'd really like to work with you. Would you think about it?'

Cass found herself smiling. 'I don't need to think about it. It's a fantastic idea.'

She could feel Kim returning her smile. 'Great. Well . . . shall I get Alan to sort it all out, then?'

When she hung up the phone, Cass sat for a moment, coiling the cord round her finger. It was late morning, a Wednesday, and Ivor was out somewhere – he hadn't come home last night. The music room was absolutely quiet, no sound coming even from Mr Dennis's flat downstairs.

She thought about how long it had been since she'd last seen Kate – she was so often away filming now, and their schedules rarely seemed to coincide. It was even longer since she'd last seen Serena and Bob, with their house in Harrow and their teaching jobs and their little girl, Sarah, whom Cass had only managed to see twice since the day she was born.

She thought about Irene: she would have been married now for what, five years? She wondered how many children Irene had by now – a boy and a girl, perhaps, and a house that she imagined to be just like Irene's mother's, cosy and comfortable. She thought about how good it would be to have a friend.

The telephone rang again.

'Kim phoned you, then,' Alan said. 'What do you think?'

'I think,' she said, 'that I should really be paying you more than I do.'

One day in late December 1975, Cass received a card.

She can recall the day quite precisely: they were just back from the *My Loving Heart* sessions in Los Angeles, and the icy, steel-skied London winter was a shock after all that brash Californian sunshine. It was late morning, and she was sitting in her armchair in the music room, catching up on the correspondence that Alan's office had passed on. The flat was, as always, chilly: she had curled her legs up under her feet, and drawn a cream lambswool blanket (one of the several luxurious purchases she had allowed herself in recent months) over her lap.

A small white envelope had been slipped into a larger manila one, along with a letter from Alan. *This was delivered to the office a few weeks ago,* Alan had written. *I had Sandra open it, as usual – you'll see why I've passed it on. It's none of my business, of course. But I'm here, as your friend – and as Ivor's friend, too – if either of you want to talk.*

She opened the white envelope. The card showed a red-cheeked, cartoonish Santa, heavy sack slung over one shoulder, framed by a garland of holly. Inside was a letter – black ink on blue Basildon Bond – folded into a neat square. The message in the card read, *To Ivor and Cassandra, Merry Christmas, with love from Susan and Owain Tait (Mum and Dad).*

Cass's breath stilled in her throat. Ivor was out; at Hugh's, she supposed. As she reached for the blue folded paper, she was acutely aware of each small sound in the empty flat. The sudden disembodied burble of Mr Dennis's television downstairs, the hiss and gargle of a pipe.

The letter, unlike the card, was addressed only to her. The handwriting was neat, rounded, the spaces between each word measured and even.

Dear Cassandra Wheeler, it began. *You will, doubtless, be very surprised to hear from me. You may not even know that I exist. Well, you will know, of course, that Ivor has a mother and a father; but how much – or how little – he has told you about us, I can only imagine. In any case, I suspect it is very little.*

Susan Tait's voice – as Cass heard it through her writing – was warm, diffident; she had worked hard, Cass sensed, to keep any excess of emotion at bay. Plainly, deftly, she constructed the framework of Ivor's childhood, of his father's drinking, of the effect it had had on all of them. (Much of this Cass had guessed at, but Ivor had still never offered her more than the barest of facts.)

Goodness knows, Susan wrote, *he saw more than any young boy should, and I should have worked harder to protect him. It took me a long time to learn to respect Ivor's decision to cut us both off so cleanly – to distance himself from me, as well as Owain. But I do respect it, Cassandra.*

That's why I am writing to you, rather than to Ivor; in the hope that you, as the woman who loves him (I can see that you love him: I have watched every one of your performances on television), will be able to decide what is best for the man he is now, not the boy I used to know.

There isn't much time left – a few months, perhaps. But that's time enough if Ivor feels that he would like to say goodbye to his father. You are, I am sure, a thoughtful, sensitive person – I can hear that in your music. I have bought your albums, and I play them often, as a way to feel closer to you both. I am sure that you will know what to do.

In the meantime, I wish you both a very merry Christmas.
With love,
Susan Tait

After reading the letter, Cass sat motionless for a long time.

Then, resolved, she flung off the blanket, stepped out into the hallway, slipped on her coat, and placed the letter in her pocket. Downstairs on the street, the wintry air turned her breath to swirling clouds, and by the time she reached Hugh's flat, she was numb with cold.

Hugh answered the door.

'Lady Cassandra,' he said. 'The Queen of Sheba herself.'

She pushed past him. 'Where is he?'

She found Ivor on the living-room sofa, among scrabbly drifts of detritus: blankets, clothes, plates carrying brownish tidemarks of congealed food. A woman Cass didn't know – long red hair, brown polo neck, blue jeans – was propped on the floor beside him, her head lolling a few inches from his bare feet. Cass ignored her. To Ivor, who wore the same glassy-eyed expression as Hugh, she said, 'I need to talk to you.'

The red-haired woman giggled. 'Ivor, seems like your *mum's* arrived.'

'Fuck off,' Cass said, and the woman rolled her eyes.

'Touchy.'

Ivor barely lifted his head. 'What is it?'

'Just come with me.'

He followed her out to the yard: grimy brick, rickety furniture, a couple of half-frozen geraniums making a valiant bid for survival. He wore no coat and he was shivering, hopping from foot to foot. 'What is it, Cassie? Do you have to follow me everywhere? Can't I even have *one* fucking afternoon to myself?'

Wordlessly, she handed him the letter. He saw the handwriting, and pushed it back at her, his voice deepening to a snarl. 'No. Whatever she's saying, I don't want to know.'

'You do, Ivor. Read it. She says he's dying.'

'No.' He was loud now, almost shouting. 'I don't fucking *care*, all right? He's nothing to me. Neither of them are.'

'Ivor . . .'

He caught her arms with his hands, then; held her a little too tightly. 'Don't, Cassie. This is mine, all right, not yours. This is *one* bloody part of my life where I get to decide, not you.'

They stood still for a moment. His breathing was shallow, laboured. He couldn't hold her gaze.

'All right,' she said. 'All right.' And then, gently, she removed his hands from her arms, and walked back into the filthy living-room, where Hugh was curling up next to the red-headed woman, his head leaning against her bony shoulder.

'Leaving so soon, Lady C?' Hugh said. 'Why don't you stay? I've got some good stuff here. Might loosen you up a bit . . .' But she wasn't listening: she was striding past, away from their cackling laughter; away from the man who wasn't Ivor but a stranger; a man, it seemed to her then, that she barely knew, even after all this time.

She supposes, now, that this could quite easily have been the moment when it ended between them. Ivor might have quit the band – quit her life – and moved in with Hugh; dived down deeper towards the ocean floor, even stayed there. Or found his own way to resurface, and made it all somebody else's problem.

No doubt it would have been better, in some ways, if that was what had happened – but Cass can't bring herself to regret the path they took. Not when it would lead them to their daughter. To Anna. To that bright, smiling child.

She remembers, then, that she and Ivor spent that Christmas apart: Cass at Atterley, with Lily and John; Ivor who knew where. At Hugh's, probably.

He hadn't come home since the day she'd shown him his mother's letter. She'd written back to Susan: a couple of brief paragraphs, letting her know that she'd told Ivor the truth.

I don't think he will come, Mrs Tait, Cass wrote. *But at least we've given him the chance.*

On Christmas Day, she drove down to Worthing with Lily and John, to visit her father in the home.

She'd offered to give a concert for the residents: an acoustic guitar, the old carols and a few songs of her own. 'The Holly and the Ivy', 'The Coventry Carol', 'Brightest Star', a song she'd begun on the flight back from Los Angeles, sketching the arc of it in her notepad: the sky beyond the first-class cabin window black and empty, lit only by the tiny lighthouse flash at the tip of the plane's wing.

Her father sat propped in his chair, blank-faced: a tiny, shrunken, white-haired man, grown old before his time. His eyes half closed as she played, his expression betraying no emotion – but yes, Cass was still sure of it, he was listening.

249

She drove back to London from Atterley on New Year's Eve, in the racing-green MG she had bought herself the previous year (along with driving lessons). Alan and Rachel were giving a party at their new house in Primrose Hill. She would go alone, or she would go with Ivor: she didn't care either way, she told herself as the car broached the empty, white-skied miles between Sussex and London. And yet, as she drew up outside the flat in Muswell Hill, she knew that she was lying to herself. She did care, of course she did.

If Ivor isn't home, she said to herself, *if he still keeps pushing me away, it's over between us. It really is.*

But she found him sitting in the kitchen, nursing a half-drunk mug of coffee. He was just out of the bath, wearing the Victorian gentleman's robe she'd bought him. His hair was still damp, unkempt, giving him a childish, vulnerable look that threatened to break her heart.

'I'm sorry, Cassie,' he said. 'I'm so sorry.'

He stood up, came to her. He began to cry, silently, his shoulders shuddering in sudden, violent spasms. When he was calm, his breath coming steadily, his body still, she made them a pot of mint tea, and they sat at the table, and he began to talk.

The story Ivor told that night did not shock her, or even come as much of a surprise: she had guessed at most of it, in the gaps left by his silence, and in the few details offered in his mother's letter. Not a story of horror, of neglect beyond one's worst imagining, but of a frustrated, unhappy, uneducated man, expressing his anger with his fists. A man who understood nothing of the lives lived beyond the narrow limits of his own experience, who was afraid of such lives, who didn't know what to make of a son not made in his own image. A woman who lacked the courage – or the means – to stand up to him, and whose weakness her adult son could not find it in himself to forgive. A grandmother who had, in the worst times, offered the boy a place of refuge, a single bed in a small, tidy house where silence was just that – the absence of sound, of fear, rather than the noisy, pregnant pause that preceded each new skirmish.

'I loved my grandmother, Cassie,' Ivor said. 'She was the only person who could make me feel safe.'

His face was wet with tears again, and Cass reached up to stroke his cheek, loving him, feeling the knot of anxiety she had carried for him for so long in the pit of her stomach loosen itself, and slip away.

She held Ivor in her arms and whispered, into his hair, 'You're safe with me, baby. You'll always be safe with me.'

New Year's Eve 1975. Champagne, Swiss fondue and fireworks on the roof terrace of Alan and Rachel's house.

Graham in the kitchen, pouring himself another whisky. Ricky from the Puritan Experience trapping Martin in the corner with a copy of the band's new LP. 'We want a new direction, man. The label's got us stuck in a box. Can't you help us get *out*?'

Kim, luminous in a skintight blue jumpsuit, her hair drawn into taut cornrows, dancing to Steely Dan with Kit's wife, Alison, while the eyes of all the men in the room followed the figure-eights of their swaying hips.

Ivor and Cass stood close together all evening, as acutely, thrillingly aware of each other's presence as if they had only just been introduced. He was ignoring the many sorties others were making to the bathroom with their tiny silver vials of cocaine; and the knowing looks of others, their nudges, their whispers. *Why don't you come and try this, man? Come on, it's New Year's Eve!*

He had given it all up, he said. He hated the way it made him feel: blanked out, empty, numb. Cass wasn't sure that she believed him, but she wanted to. She was giddy with the relief of having him close to her, of feeling the breach between them closing over, mending its fissure.

Long after midnight, when the guests were starting to disperse, Ivor took her hand, and drew her out onto the terrace. It was freezing, and her shoulders were bare above her floor-length red velvet dress. (Another of Cornelia's finds: she was saving her best gowns for Cass now as a matter of course, and Cass had come to treasure their regular afternoons together.)

Ivor pulled her to him, placed his jacket over her shoulders. And there, his face just an inch from hers, he said, so quietly that she had to strain to hear him over the music from the living-room (Bowie, now: 'The Man Who Sold the World'), 'Marry me, Cassie. Marry me.'

He buried his face in her neck. His breath was warm on her skin, and the roof-scape was laid out before them in a jagged, hard-edged silhouette: black windows interspersed with other, brightly lighted rooms in which other parties were going on, other couples were embracing, laughing, arguing.

From somewhere out there in the city's blackness came a staccato, gunshot patter, followed by the tiny sharp starbursts of fireworks. Cass heard her own song in her head, then: 'Brightest Star'. She had written it for Ivor, of course. She had written it for both of them, and the hope – dim, in recent months, but still there – that they would find their way back to what they had once shared both on and off stage. That union. That unthinking, unquestioning intimacy, as easy and natural as a major chord, as the song that shatters the silence, that makes us believe, for a time, that we are not alone.

'Yes,' she said. And because she liked the sound the word made – its bright, clear, affirmative tone, chasing away fear, loneliness, doubt – she said it again, and again, and again.

4.45 p.m.

The caterers are arriving.

In the silence that follows the song, she hears them. The deep, guttural thrum of their vans as they draw up the front drive, scattering gravel, then suddenly falling still. Kim's soft, barely audible lilt, floating round the side of the house and across the lawn to the studio, and a woman's unintelligible response. The faint metallic creak of the van doors, and the gravel again crunching and resettling underfoot.

What would she have done, all these years, without Kim? So much more practical than Cass herself; so much more tethered, somehow, to the world as it really is, rather than as she would prefer it to be. But no pushover, either – no martyr. Kim has always had her limits, and not hesitated in letting Cass know when she has crossed them. 'It's too much, Cass,' she had said to her once, not long before she'd gone into the hospital for the first time. 'How can I be there for you if you refuse to be there for yourself?'

She can remember that moment clearly: the shock of it, the set of Kim's face, thin-lipped, resolute. 'I can't take much more of this, Cass,' she'd said. 'I really can't.' And she had not relented: she had turned and left, and in her grief, Cass had allowed herself to believe that Kim, too, was abandoning her, as everyone, eventually, must do.

But that had been false logic, of course; Kim had never abandoned her, even when Cass had given her good reason to do so. She had stood beside her, and held her hand, and continued to direct the smooth running of Cass's life: all those myriad administrative tasks with which Cass could not, by nature and by circumstance, concern herself. And with far more than that, too: with the decisions that Cass was too afraid, or too weak, to take alone.

Sitting alone, silent, while across the lawn the house swings into action, Cass thinks of the decision Kim had helped her to take two years before, when a letter had arrived at Home Farm from Cindy Russo, Ivor's second wife.

Cass already knew more about Cindy than the other woman might have imagined: she'd read about her in a magazine, back when she and Ivor had still not been on speaking terms. A former model (what else?): toned and tanned as an athlete, her skin taut and unblemished, her hair a lioness's mane streaked with shimmering shades of gold and brown.

Cindy's letter had been written on thick white paper that smelt, faintly and unmistakably, of violets. (The perfume had reminded Cass, incongruously, of her mother's, though surely it was impossible to imagine two women less alike.)

I'm coming over to England with Ivor and the kids, Cindy wrote. *I would so like to meet you, given all the history you and Ivor have shared. And I think there are things he needs to say to you, too, and that he can only say in person. Perhaps you might join us for a day in London?*

Kim, reading the letter over, had put her head on one side in the way she always did when weighing a decision, and said, 'Meet them, I think. But meet them here.'

According to the magazine article Cass had read, Ivor Tait and Cindy Russo had met in the California ashram where they had both been spending a period of 'calm and reflection'. Cass had thought such things as ashrams had gone out with the seventies, but in California, she supposed, anything was possible. 'Ivor is open about the years he lost to drug and alcohol abuse,' the piece had gone on. '"Really, I'd thought my life was over," he says, tears springing to his eyes, his hand gripping that of his new love, the woman he calls his "saviour". "Meeting Cindy has given me a reason to get back on track. She has given me something to live for.'"

It had hurt so much more than Cass would have thought possible, even after all this time: the knowledge that Ivor was moving on, that he had allowed himself a second chance. And with a woman like *that*. A fool, no doubt. A vacuous mannequin.

She had wanted to tear the letter into shreds, but Kim's words had stayed with her, as they always did; and so, after a hiatus of a few weeks, Cass had written back to invite them all for lunch. And then, a few weeks later, they had all arrived at the front door of Home Farm: Cindy, the two children and Ivor, tanned in a white shirt and linen trousers, his handsome, familiar face only minimally altered by the passage of time.

How many years had it been since she'd last seen him: seven? Eight? The terrible week before she'd been admitted to the hospital for the first time, when she had gone to see him in London: he was living, then, in an eighteenth-century pile on Hampstead Grove, Rothermere having long been sold.

All the awful things they had said and done to each other: too many to count, too much to recall. And now there Ivor was in her hallway, leaning down to kiss her on the cheek, saying, in that slow, quiet voice of his, now carrying a distinct mid-Atlantic hue, 'Hello, Cassie. It's good to see you.'

Cindy had turned out to be neither a fool nor a mannequin. She was a brisk, sunny woman who ran two charities and a string of Los Angeles boutiques, and had a Harvard MBA. Cass, against all her expectations, had found that she rather liked her. And the children, India and Travis – then five and four – were a delight: not at all the entitled, overprivileged Californian brats Cass had ungenerously imagined them to be.

Kim had ordered catering – 'The last thing you need to worry about, Cass, is cooking' – and laid the table: they'd lunched on poached salmon, beetroot and feta salad, new potatoes in lemon mayonnaise. Cass offered wine, forgetting that Ivor no longer drank; but she and Cindy each had a glass, and the children sipped their lemonade and ate everything on their plates without a word of enquiry or complaint.

As they ate, it was Cindy who stoked the conversation, complimenting Cass on the house ('I was obsessed with England as a kid – dreamt of one day living in a lovely old place like this'), on her clothes ('Green really suits you, doesn't it?') and, above all, on her music, with a sincerity that had taken Cass by surprise.

'I always wished I'd done something creative,' Cindy said as they finished their pudding. (A huge Eton mess, crowned with layers of whipped cream; Cindy, to her credit, had consumed every mouthful of the oversized portion Cass had placed in front of her.) 'Something I could really *own*, you know? Something that was mine, and nobody else's.'

'Did you not see modelling as creative, then?' There was no edge to Cass's tone: she had already warmed to Cindy, who took the question seriously, holding it in her mind for a moment or two, before answering, with a glance at Ivor, 'Oh no. I hated it, really. Hated the whole lifestyle. The superficiality of it. The photographers pretending not to leer at us as we changed. It didn't suit me at all.'

Ivor, sitting across from Cindy – was that really him at Cass's table, leaning back in his chair, seeming so relaxed, so at ease, every inch the happy, healthy, teetotal family man? – smiled at his wife, and said, 'No, it didn't, darling. You're so much happier now. As, of course, am I.'

After coffee, Cindy had taken the children out into the garden, and left the two of them alone.

'Smoke?' Cass reached for the tin she'd brought down from her bedside table earlier, in anticipation of nerves, but Ivor shook his head.

'I forgot,' she said. 'You don't do that either, now, do you?'

He said nothing, and she filled the moment with the business of rolling herself a cigarette: the swift motion of her hands, laying out the papers, drawing a pinch of tobacco from the tin.

'Thank you for this,' he said, when she had drawn in her first, sweet drag. 'For lunch. For having us.'

'You're welcome. It's good to see you happy.' She spoke without malice – she was surprised, in fact, at how calm she felt, how calm she had been from the moment she'd opened the door, and found him there – but he frowned, and cleared his throat.

'Cassie. There are things I'd like to . . .' He trailed off, and she looked at Ivor across the table – at the luminous whiteness of his shirt; at his hair, cut short now, but still dark, only faintly threaded with grey; at the tiny scar still visible beside his right eye, and the fretwork of fine lines stamped across his face like a map she no longer had the ability to read.

'Don't,' she said. 'Please don't say anything at all.'

He had held her gaze, and, after a few moments, nodded his assent. And then they had sat in silence, the silence that was, for her now, familiar, comforting: the element in which she swam. A silence that was not charged, not tense, but companionable – easy, even – until India came running in from the garden for her father, drawing Travis behind her, and breaking its spell.

Now, there are voices coming from the garden once again: not India's high-pitched American twang but an English bass and a Scottish baritone, performing a low, disembodied duet.

'We're thinking of the Union Chapel,' she hears Alan say. 'Somewhere small, you know – intimate. Somewhere with atmosphere.'

'Yes – that'd be perfect,' Callum replies. 'I saw Kathryn Williams there a few years back. Bloody amazing. Maybe we could get them on the same bill?'

She watches their two figures approach, silhouetted through the glass against the sharp late-afternoon light. She waits for Alan to knock: two quick successive raps on the glass. Then she gets up from the sofa, goes over to the door. There they are, the two men, manager and producer. The white-haired elder statesman, with his comfortably protruding belly and billy-goat beard, still improbably boyish. The young pretender, slim and dark-haired, his legs encased in skintight black jeans.

'All right, Cass?' Alan says, as she leans forward to kiss him on each cheek, then does the same with Callum. 'How's it going?'

'All right, I think,' she says. 'I'm facing the demons.'

The two men regard her, each of them aware, in his own particular way, of what this might mean.

Alan places a hand on her arm. 'Come, now, Cass. There isn't a demon brave enough to stand up to you.'

She smiles. 'Oh, Alan, you'd be surprised.' She covers Alan's hand with hers, gently removes it. 'How are the caterers getting on?'

'Fine, as far as I can see. Kim's running around like a bunny on speed. And I hope you're hungry. There's enough smoked salmon blinis in there to feed an army.'

'An army marching on blinis? Now that I'd like to see.' They laugh, and there, in the softening cast of Alan's face, she sees it: relief. She has not gone to pieces; her exploration of the past has not drawn her irretrievably back into that darkness, that void. Irritation flares in her, and then, just as quickly, dissolves: for how, after all that has happened – all that she has put him through – can she blame Alan for watching her so carefully?

To Callum, then, she says, 'Have you got the masters there?'

'Sure do.' He reaches into the pocket of his jacket, withdraws a small block of grey metal. An external hard drive, she knows now, though she will never lose her belief that it was strange – unnatural, surely – that all that work, all those hours and days and weeks, could be contained on such a nondescript-looking object.

'Are you ready?' he says.

She draws a breath. 'As I'll ever be.'

Callum leads the way to the control room, turning on lights, settling himself in the larger of the two leather chairs that are set in front of the mixing-desk, the console, the glass hatch that divides the control room from the live room. Her studio has, over the last few months, become Callum's domain, really, as much as hers: he is at home here, switching on the computers, bringing the blank screens to flickering life.

He had, from the first day of the recording sessions for the new songs, assumed this control gently, discreetly, almost without her noticing. Callum seemed to have sensed, implicitly, how nervous she was, and calibrated the atmosphere accordingly: he'd run the recordings with a politeness and lightness of touch that had only served to emphasise his natural air of authority. The musicians had all respected him – even Kit, whom Cass had drawn – reluctantly, at first – out of his comfortable retirement. Kit, who had always, before, maintained protracted disagreements with their producers as a point of honour.

'He's all right, that Callum,' Kit had said over the dinner they'd shared at the end of that first day, accepting a second glass of his own excellent cognac. (He has reframed himself, in the decade or so since his third divorce, as something of a bon vivant, with a collection of vintage hats, shares in a French vineyard and a penchant for Cuban cigars.) 'Seems to know his way around the desk, Cass. I think we're in safe hands.'

She had been impressed, too, by how instinctively Callum – and Gav, his engineer – had seemed to understand the sound-world in which she wanted the recordings to live: to prepare its palette, shade its particular colours. Her voice was deeper now, and she wanted the arrangements to match that: to carry a certain late-night, torch-song quality, full-bodied and languorous. The drumming would be jazzy, subtle, understated; a cajón – or bongos, maybe – weaving in around the kit. Acoustic guitar on 'When Morning Comes'; an accordion, perhaps, on 'Gethsemane'.

Callum had listened carefully, nodded, taken notes; disagreed with her where necessary. The musicians he had brought in had all, without exception, been a pleasure to work with. She had particularly warmed to Martha – a twenty-five-year-old multi-instrumentalist in leggings and biker boots who had, with her sheet of dark hair and self-deprecating sense of humour, reminded Cass a great deal of Kate – Kate as she had been, anyway, all those years ago in Savernake Road.

The sessions had, in short, probably been the easiest and least fraught of Cass's career. Had they been otherwise, she suspects that she would have lost her confidence entirely, and retreated, a naked creature ducking its head back inside its shell.

And for that, looking at Callum now, fiddling with the computer, biting his lower lip with his teeth as he always does when he is concentrating, she feels a fresh rush of gratitude.

'Thank you, Callum,' she says. 'Thank you for making all this happen.'

He turns, smiles. 'You're welcome.'

He returns his attention to the desk, the screens. And there, after a moment of pregnant, crackling silence, they come: the opening bars of 'Gethsemane', slow and measured; the swoop of the accordion, and the gossamer layers of Hammond organ, piano, guitar.

It is a different kind of listening, this: a meditation, of sorts. A quiet, internal observation of the present moment, of the woman she is now, not the many women she has been, and the past she has sought for so many years to forget – and of which, perhaps, she is beginning to understand that there is no longer any need to be afraid.

Later, when the men have gone back up to the house to prepare for the party – 'I'll be along in an hour or so,' she'd said as they'd closed the door behind them – Cass sits alone in the green room, picks up the phone, and dials Larry's number once more.

Again, no answer: that long foreign tone ringing out, un-heeded. She tries his mobile and it goes straight to voicemail. This time, she leaves a message.

Larry, it's Cass. I've called you a few times today. Ring me back, won't you? I don't know if you got my email, but I . . . I miss you. I really do. I just want to . . .

A long, pregnant pause.

Thank you for the card. It means a lot. You were right, you know. It's not as hard as I thought, the listening. You're right about so many things, aren't you? I know that now. I—

The long beep of the mailbox, cutting her off in mid-flow.

She had called Larry's mobile for the first time from her hotel room in Washington.

He'd handed her a card as she'd climbed into the taxi outside the gallery: creamy-white paper – thick, expensive – his name printed in an elegant, seriffed font. Below it, two numbers: a Chicago landline and a mobile phone.

'I'm in Washington until Tuesday,' he'd said as he closed the door, and the cab drew itself back into the flow of traffic. 'Call the cell if . . . Well, you've got my numbers there.'

She'd placed his card in her wallet, and there it had remained all day, through the label's lunch reception; through the bath she'd taken in the afternoon, her head spinning, unaccus-tomed to the effort of socialising; through the light dinner she'd eaten with Alan and Kim in the hotel restaurant. She'd retired to her room just after eight, citing exhaustion – their flight home was at ten the following morning, so they'd recon-vene early for breakfast. And there, in her twelfth-floor suite, she'd poured herself another glass of Merlot, reached for her wallet, drawn out the card, and found herself dialling Larry's cell.

The arrangement had been made briskly, without ceremony: he was out to dinner with friends in Georgetown, and would come as soon as was polite. The moment she'd replaced the receiver, she'd doubted herself: a great wave of fear had consumed her, and she'd dialled his number again, intending to tell him that she'd changed her mind. But he'd switched off his phone, and at the sound of Larry's voice – careful, measured, Midwestern – on his voicemail message, she'd grown flustered, put the phone down once more.

Then she'd finished her glass of wine, poured herself another, and looked out at the dwindling colours of evening – the layers of sky and cloud and the lurid embers of the sun, and the lights coming on across the city. Her reflection was fractured and ghostly in the glass: an old woman, long past middle age, jowled and pouched, her beauty – such as it had been – long gone. *You're ridiculous*, she'd told herself. *Hideous. A joke. He'll take one look at you and run.*

And then, just as she was finishing her second glass of wine, the telephone had rung. The concierge, informing her politely that she had a guest in reception. Mr Larry Alderson. Would she like him to send Mr Alderson up?

The seemingly endless pause between her answer and Larry's knock at the door. Her fear swallowing all rational thought. She'd regarded herself again, sternly, appraisingly, in the ornate mirror above the dressing-table. Her face was flushed from the wine, the nerves; she'd hardly known the woman looking back at her. She'd powdered her cheeks and nose. She'd reapplied her lipstick with a shaking, uncertain hand. She'd told herself, *Calm down. Do you want him to think you're as silly as a teenager?*

And then: the tap on the door. Crossing the pale beige carpet in her stockinged feet.

Larry Alderson standing there against the gilded wallpaper, wearing his black leather jacket, smiling a smile that – yes, it was true, she couldn't deny it – brought her own answering surge of desire, so long buried, so overwhelming, now, moving up from the very core of her to the flaming colours of her face.

'I can't tell you how glad I am that you called,' he said.

She nodded, swallowed, didn't lift her eyes from his.

'Come in,' she said, and he did.

'In This Garden'

By Cass Wheeler
From the album *Huntress*

They were young when they were married
Two kids of slender means
He was working for the council
She was painting all the scenes

And the house that they moved into
Was dark and old and cramped
Too hot to breathe in summer
And in winter, cold and damp

But outside, there was a garden
They planted beds of flowers
And she took his hand and told him
'This garden here
This garden here
This garden here is ours.'

It's years since they were married
Those kids of slender means
He still works for the council
She painted on their dreams

And the house that they still lived in
No longer dark and cramped
In summer open windows
And the warm light of a lamp

Outside, there was a garden
They lay in beds of flowers

And she took his hand and told him
'This garden here
This garden here
This garden here is ours.'

RELEASED 10 January 1977
RECORDED October 1976 at Rothermere, Surrey
GENRE Folk rock / soft rock / pop
LABEL Phoenix Records
WRITER(S) Cass Wheeler
PRODUCER(S) Eli Glass
ENGINEER(S) Mike Edwards / Sean O'Malley

They were married on a Saturday in August 1976, in Surrey, in the gardens of the house they had recently acquired.

Its name, inscribed by the original owners on the twin stone pillars that flanked its tall wrought-iron gates, was Rothermere.

It was a large, comfortable, two-storey house, constructed in the nineteen twenties on the edge of a copse of tall, broad-leaved oaks and thickly needled conifers. The trees lent a measure of privacy, but also, in Cass's view, made the place feel rather dark and hemmed in. It was Ivor who had fallen in love with it, Ivor who had toured it the first time, alone (Cass had been unable to postpone an interview with the *Sunday Times*), and come home to Muswell Hill absolutely assured that this was the house they should buy.

'It's a palace, Cass,' he'd told her. 'Beams in the kitchen – you'll love them – and a barn we can use for the studio. A bloody *lake* in the garden. Honestly, it's perfect.'

She had looked round it herself, of course – requested a second viewing from the agent. She'd asked her uncle John to come, too, to cast his professional eye; Lily had travelled with him from Atterley, and Cass had driven up with Ivor in the MG. Under the summer sunshine, the house had seemed grand, well proportioned: everything was clean and freshly painted, and John had been confident in the solidity of its construction.

'But do you *love* it, Cass?' Lily had asked her, quietly, when they were alone for a moment in the kitchen. Cass had smiled at her aunt and said, 'I like it, Lily. It's a beautiful house. And it's what Ivor wants.'

Had she sensed, then – in the unconscionable conviction that had unfurled itself inside her as the agent had showed them from room to room (unconscionable, really, because the house *was* beautiful, even if that screen of trees did block much of the light from the upstairs rooms) – that this was not a place in which she and Ivor would be happy? It was impossible to know for sure; impossible to think back to that moment without the treacherous clarity of hindsight.

On their wedding day, Kim and her squadron of builders, caterers and florists worked wonders with the house and garden. A marquee occupied the front lawn, its interior festooned with bolts of silk, and its round tables set with huge, sweet-smelling vases of old English roses, reddish hydrangea leaves and frothy, milk-white cascades of lily of the valley.

A full-sized festival stage was erected beside it, complete with dance floor, and Kim arranged for a flotilla of glass swans to be launched, as night fell, onto the lake, each one carrying a flickering candle between the feathers of its sculpted back.

Cass was dressed by Cornelia, of course, in a gown of ivory silk with a wide sash and delicate lace-capped sleeves. The dress was modelled on a design from the thirties, and made by Cornelia's own hand: she wouldn't trust even her best Hackney Road seamstresses, she said, with such a task.

The week before the wedding, Cornelia had come to Rothermere for the final fitting.

'Dearest Cassandra,' she had said, as Cass stood in her new dressing-room – a sizeable, thickly carpeted room off the master bedroom, one of its walls hung entirely with floor-to-ceiling mirrors – 'I'm so proud of you, do you know that? I'm proud of all my girls, of course – but you most of all.'

Cass had embraced Cornelia – her old boss, now the most unlikely and dearest of friends – and thought how peculiar it was, how uncanny, that she should feel more for this woman than she did for her own mother.

Margaret arrived at Rothermere the evening before the wedding, with Len Steadman and their daughter, Josephine – now a tall, rather awkward thirteen-year-old, still a little bloated with puppy fat.

This was the first time Cass had seen her mother and half-sister in four years. Not long after their meeting in Buffalo, Margaret had written Cass a letter. She had listened to *The State She's In* – to 'Common Ground', in particular – for the first time. She said she found it difficult to believe that Cass could take something so personal – Margaret's own letter to Francis; a letter that had never even been meant for Cass's eyes – and air her feelings about it so publicly. She couldn't see, Margaret concluded, how they might begin to rebuild their relationship if Cass continued to hold such resentment towards her.

Cass can remember quite clearly where she was when she read her mother's letter – in the back of a bus with Ivor and the band, on their way to the Great Western Express Festival.

'What is it?' Ivor had said, seeing her face. 'What does she say?'

Wordlessly, she'd handed him the letter. After he'd read it, he'd taken another swig from his can of beer and said, 'Fuck her, Cassie. What do you need her for, anyway? She's never done a bloody thing for you.'

Much later that night, after their set, they had performed a drunken ritual amid the wet grass: taken a lighter to the letter, and watched it shrivel, burn, then disappear. And that, Cass had decided, was enough: she would not write back.

But over time – during the long hours she spent in buses, taxis, planes – she had found herself thinking more and more about her half-sister, Josephine. The girl with the hand-knitted jumper, and Cass's own oval brown eyes. And she had started to send her postcards from Hamburg, Rome, Sydney, Tokyo. Josephine had replied with breathless excitement – *I can't believe how amazing it is that you're FAMOUS, Cass! Everyone at high school thinks it's just the COOLEST THING EVER!!!* And gradually, Margaret had begun to include her own letters with Josephine's. A truce, it seemed, had been called. And so, despite her misgivings, Cass had found herself asking Kim to issue them with an invitation to the wedding.

Len Steadman, of course, she had never met. What struck Cass most about him, as she opened the door, ushered them into the living-room with its enormous white marble fireplace, the new Steinway piano occupying its allocated space in the bay window, was his absolute ordinariness. He was a mild, colourless man in a cheap-looking navy pinstripe suit, looking around him with an awe he didn't bother to disguise.

'Goodness, this is some place,' he said to Ivor. 'Must have set you back a fair bit.'

It was impossible, Cass thought as she handed Len a glass of champagne, to imagine such a man tearing a jagged rip in the weft of her young life; of bringing about such a stirring of romantic feeling in Margaret that she'd decided she had no choice but to leave her daughter, and her husband, and start a new life five thousand miles away.

They did not talk of Francis, who could not attend the wedding – he was too frail, now, to leave the home other than for brief, blanket-wrapped excursions along the seafront in his wheelchair. Ivor's mother, Susan, would not be coming either. Ivor had still not responded to her letters, even the one that had arrived, a few weeks after the first, letting them both know that Owain Tait had died the previous Tuesday in Warwick Hospital.

Cass had asked Kim to send flowers to the funeral (Ivor had been reluctant to do even that), and had written to tell Susan that she and Ivor were engaged, and that she hoped, in time, that they might have the opportunity to meet.

She wondered, afterwards, if it had been wrong to offer Ivor's mother false hope – it certainly didn't seem that Ivor was prepared to go back on the decision he had made when he'd left home. But she did not, in truth, think often of Susan Tait; not when there was My Loving Heart to promote, and the wedding to prepare for, and another American tour that would begin, with relentless efficiency, two days after their return from honeymoon.

*

Their wedding day. Ivor in his dark blue velvet suit, a button-hole of blush-pink roses and lily of the valley pinned to his broad lapel. Kim and Kate in pink silk, lilies glowing white against their dark, gathered hair. Hugh McMaster as best man (Cass had not been happy about that, but Ivor had insisted): clean now, but putting away the booze with an enthusiasm that implied to all that he had simply swapped one addiction for another.

There were no speeches, but each member of the wedding party had been asked, after sunset, to take to the stage and perform a song. Ivor sang 'Just Us Two'; Cass 'In This Garden', which she had written for the occasion on the new Steinway. Kate and Kim duetted (rather presciently, it would occur to Cass later) on a version of 'Will You Still Love Me Tomorrow?'; and Hugh stumbled his way through an exuberant, drunken rendition of 'Jumpin' Jack Flash'. Then the band – Graham, Kit, Frank and various friends guesting on guitar and vocals – played on until the early hours as the house watched with benign interest, a dowager duchess observing primly from the sidelines.

Sometime towards dawn, Cass found herself standing on the lawn with Serena and Kate, arms woozily entwined. (Serena, since putting her daughter, Sarah, to bed in a spare room, had been dedicating herself to the consumption of champagne.)

'You know, Cassie,' Serena said. 'I was wrong. I'll admit it. I didn't think you and Ivor would go the distance. I didn't think he could ever be tied down.'

Cass's eyes travelled to her new husband, dancing unsteadily under the lightening sky. His eyes were closed, and he was smiling, waving his arms above his head. It had been a long time, she thought then, since she had seen Ivor so childishly, unquestioningly happy, and she felt a rush of love for him; of optimism for the future that would be theirs. She thought of the moment he had stood before her, in the hallway at Atterley, placed his hand to the curve of her chin; of the times – so many times – that she had stood beside him on stage, the warm chords of her guitar merging with his, their voices blending and soaring.

'I don't *want* to tie him down,' she said, and led her friends off by the hand to dance.

'What are you doing?' Ivor said.

She lifted her hand to her mouth, placed the small white tablet on her tongue. Took a sip of water, let it slip coolly down her throat. 'Taking my pill, of course.'

They had been on honeymoon for almost a week. Ibiza: a white-walled *finca*, tucked into the gently angled slope of a hillside. The interiors decorated in the latest style – mint-green paintwork; giddying op-art wallpaper; deep-pile rugs softening the polished wooden floors. But they were spending little time indoors (except in the bedroom): the gardens were heady with lavender and scrub-rose, and the pool terrace, shaded by palms, overlooked the glistening dark blue expanse of the sea.

A housekeeper, Inés, came up twice a day from a neighbouring farm to prepare breakfast and lunch, clean the rooms, and ask, in halting English, if they would be dining at home or in a restaurant. On the second day, Ivor had tried to explain, as tactfully as he could, that they would far rather be left alone, but she had stared at him, uncomprehending, and had returned as usual at eight the following morning.

Inés was there now, as Cass followed Ivor out onto the terrace: she was serving breakfast under the vine-covered pergola. Plates of melon and Serrano ham; sweet sponge cakes that Inés called *magdalenas*; bowls of milky coffee. Ivor and Cass were silent until the housekeeper had retired to the kitchen. Then Ivor said, 'Are you sure you want to keep taking the pill? Couldn't we let it go, and see what happens?'

Cass looked at him, tanned and relaxed in his swim-shorts, his loose white shirt unbuttoned. 'You know what would happen, Ivor.'

He speared a slice of melon with his fork. 'So you don't want kids.'

Cass was silenced for a moment. She took a sip of coffee, buying time. It wasn't that she didn't *want* children; well, she had no idea whether she did or not – the subject had never come up between them. They had always been so busy with the music, the recording, the touring. *She* had been so busy, and Ivor not much less so, though it was true that, even since giving up the dope, he still hadn't returned to writing with the intensity the act had once demanded of him.

'What's the point, Cassie?' he'd said when questioned; without resentment, but with a clear-sighted honesty that she couldn't find it in herself to dispute. 'You'll end up putting your songs on the next album, anyway. I might as well just play my parts and leave the songwriting to you.'

Still, they were busy, both of them: where on earth did he think a child would come into that? What would *she* do – place a screaming baby in a Moses basket and leave her in a corner of the tour bus? Give her to Kim to hold while she went out on stage? No: it was absurd; there was no way for her to tour, record and be a mother to a child. Not the kind of mother she would like to be, anyway. A mother who was there for her daughter, her son. A mother who did not, unquestioningly, always put her own needs first, and hang the consequences out to dry.

All this Cass said to herself, sitting there beneath the pergola, sheltered by the vines from the fierce Spanish sun; but she knew, even in the moment it arrived, that her anxiety was also rooted in something far deeper than mere logistics. The fear that she, like Margaret, might lack some key element of the maternal instinct. The fear that in creating new life, she would destroy the one she had built for herself. And what of her music? What if those sounds inside her head – those pure, shimmering, otherworldly sounds, for which the music she actually produced could only ever stand as poor, flawed facsimiles – were drowned out by the deafening, prosaic, earth-dwelling noises of a child? What if, in short, she found herself unable to write ever again?

She drew a breath, took another gulp of coffee. 'I don't know,' she said. 'Maybe someday. Not at the moment, Ivor. Not when everything's going so well.'

He laid down his fork. 'For you, you mean.'

'No.' She reached across the table for his hand. 'For *us*. What's brought this on, anyway? You've never even mentioned children before.'

He let go of her hand, drew his sunglasses down from his forehead. The mirrored lenses reflected Cass back at herself, her face distorted, fractured. 'I don't know, Cassie. It's the wedding, I suppose. It's got me thinking. Even when things were terrible at home – when my dad was on the warpath – I'd always thought I'd have kids. Do it better than he did, maybe. Than them both.'

She closed her eyes; saw, behind her lids, the small, frightened boy, drawing his pillow over his head to muffle the sounds rising up from below. She knew the provenance of his scar, now: his father, Owain, had swung a punch at him, and Ivor's face, in falling, had collided with the sharp corner of a skirting-board. He was ten years old; he had needed stitches. The doctor, examining him, had said, 'How did you get this nasty cut, then, lad?' And Susan, sitting beside her son, had said, 'Oh, he fell over, would you believe? He's ever so clumsy.'

'We'll talk about it, all right?' Cass said now. 'Someday, we'll talk about it. But not here, Ivor. Not today.'

He nodded, and they ate, drained their coffee mugs, left the dishes for Inés to clear. The pool water was cool, inviting, dappled with shade from the tall palms. They swam, floated, embraced in the shallows; and that moment slid off into the distance, and was, for a time, forgotten.

She would say, in interviews at the time, and subsequently, that *Huntress* was the album she was proudest of, if not her favourite.

'It's impossible to choose a favourite,' she always said. 'It's like asking a mother to say which child she loves the most.'

The cover artwork, famously, she painted herself: a self-portrait in thickly layered oils, wild-eyed, staring, open-mouthed. She looked less beautiful than unhinged, and that, frankly, was the point: a woman's wild inner self, freed from its shackles.

Few knew – or still know – that the model for the portrait was a photograph taken by Johnny in the grounds of Rothermere, for which he asked Cass to perform a primal scream that drew the security guard recently posted at the front gate running to find her, and confronting Johnny with a brandished truncheon. Johnny, once his terror had subsided, would dine out on this story for months, if not years.

The US label hated the picture. The record would always, in America, carry a different cover: a photograph – by Johnny again – of Cass dressed as Diana, preparing to launch an arrow from her drawn bow. For the more observant fans, the photograph was imbued with a degree of knowing irony: Cass's prey, a murky portion of its face just visible between the massed trunks of the trees, was Cass herself, added by Johnny by combining the two negatives in his darkroom.

They recorded the album in the new studio she and Ivor had installed at Rothermere, with Eli Glass, the young American producer who had masterminded Tom Arnold's last record. Cass never quite took to Eli – there was an arrogance about him that she instinctively disliked, and they would not work together again. But she could see, from the very first day of recording, that he knew what he was doing: transforming her songs – twelve of them, with 'Brightest Star' as the first single, and 'Follow Me' as the second – into something truly arresting.

Poppier, perhaps, than her first three albums, the rougher,

folkier edges of her sound smoothed and planed, in keeping with the changing aesthetic of the era. *Huntress* would always, given the quirk of timing of its release (her record in January, the other a month later), be spoken of in the same breath as Fleetwood Mac's *Rumours*, and be rather eclipsed by the latter's success. Not, of course, that *Huntress* didn't do very well in its own right; but Cass's own pride in the record would be less for its critical acclaim and more for the sense she had then, and has retained, that this was the album with which she had really found her creative stride.

There, caught like prized specimens inside a display case, were the songs she had wished to write, expressed exactly as she had wished them to be, and elevated beyond the limits of her own experience into something universal: not highbrow or impenetrable, but accessible to ordinary women (and men, of course: she would always be admired by men, though often not in the way she might have preferred).

She had been receiving letters from women for some time – women who'd seen something of their own lives reflected in *The State She's In*, *Songs From the Music Hall* or *My Loving Heart*. But with *Huntress*, the letters increased tenfold; Kim employed a fan-club manager (Pauline, a twenty-six-year-old secretary from Coventry who'd been coming to Cass's gigs for years) to read, sort and reply to them, and pass on only the sparest few to Cass herself.

Cass has kept several of these letters in the drawer of her desk at Home Farm. One of them is from a young woman named Annabel Macdonald, from Aberdeen. *I've never written to a musician before – I'm not some kind of crazy fan – but I just had to tell you how much I love* Huntress. *We're the same age, and yet you seem so much stronger than I am, so sure of who you are and what you want. I wish I had even an ounce of your strength.*

Cass had first read Annabel's letter in a hotel room in Singapore. It was evening, the island's skyscrapers gaudily lit against the night sky; Ivor was in the top-floor bar, drinking Singapore slings with Frank and Kit. She never usually wrote back to her fans – where, if she began, might it end? But in this case, she had felt suddenly compelled to offer Annabel Macdonald something more than Pauline's standard-issue fan-club reply.

Thanks so much for writing to me, Annabel, Cass wrote. *I'm so glad my music means so much to you – it certainly means a lot to me. But I have to tell you that I'm not as strong as you think. No stronger than you are, anyway. Each new day, each concert, each city holds more fears than I can express. And loving, too. Loving is terrifying. But there's no alternative, I think, than to face it – for what else is there, in the end?*

She'd given the letter to Pauline to post, and forgotten all about it. But later – years later – the words she had written to Annabel would return to her with sudden clarity, and she would wish, more than anything, that she could find again that young woman, that long-faded replica of herself, who had been strong enough to look fear in the face, and go on living.

She remembers, somewhere in the chaos of those years, a week of stillness in Switzerland with Kate and her banker, Lucian. They were a more or less established couple by then: he had left his first wife, Marian, and was angling to make Kate his second.

He had rented a grand, white-pillared mansion on the upper shores of Lake Geneva: an absurdly beautiful place, looking out over the serene, mirrored surface of the lake, and the red-roofed village houses clustering at the water's edge.

Lucian – a looming, mutable man, with a dangerous, irresistible charm – had also chartered a boat, which he liked to sail out onto the lake each morning after breakfast. This was an activity for which Ivor turned out to have a surprising natural ability: he had never, he joked the first time they took the boat out on the lake, had much of an opportunity to learn to sail in his parents' semi in Leamington Spa.

'No,' Lucian said. (He, being half-American and wholly privileged, had grown up dividing his time between boarding-school winters in Edinburgh and long summers on Cape Cod.) 'I can quite imagine not.'

They had all nodded and laughed, while Cass stared at Ivor across the stern. She had noticed, since his father's death, that he was talking more openly about his childhood. She had not yet decided whether this filled her with anxiety or relief.

For the first couple of days of the holiday, Cass and Kate joined the men on the boat, sunning themselves on the deck, enjoying the postcard view of the high white mountains and the freshness of the wind on their skin. But on the third day, they decided to stay behind – 'have some girl time', as Kate put it. (She adopted, in Lucian's presence, a coquettish, almost baby-ish manner that Cass found faintly distasteful, although she did not, of course, air her feelings aloud.)

And so, as the men set off down the path to the landing-stage, the women remained together on the broad veranda, with a fresh pot of coffee, and blankets wrapped around their laps to ward off the morning's slight chill.

'It's a far cry from Savernake Road, isn't it?' Kate said, and Cass agreed. And it was then, quite suddenly, that Kate began to cry – quietly at first, and then with greater intensity, until her shoulders were shaking, and the tears were running in quick succession down her carefully made-up face.

Cass said nothing for a while – just held her friend's hand, then moved from her chair and wrapped Kate in her arms. *Bloody Lucian*, she thought. Aloud, she said, 'What is it, darling? Have you had a row?'

Kate shook her head. As her breathing steadied, Cass returned to her chair.

'He's not having an affair, if that's what you think. No – it's my fault, really. Well, in a way. You see, I've had two miscarriages.'

Cass reached for Kate's hand again across the table. 'God, Kate, I'm so sorry. When?'

'The first was a year ago . . .' Seeing Cass's expression, she nodded. 'And yes, I know I should have told you, but we haven't seen much of each other, have we? And it's not exactly the kind of thing you put in a letter.'

'You could have called . . .'

'Yes, I could have. But who knows where you are, these days? And to be honest, I just wanted to forget about it and try again. So we did, and then it happened again, Cass. Seven weeks in. That was a month ago.'

'God. Kate. You poor thing.' Cass moved her thumb across the soft pulse-point of her friend's wrist: a small, rhythmic gesture of reassurance. 'And how are you feeling now?'

Kate wiped her face with her other hand. 'All right. Pretty washed out. That's why Lucian wanted us to come here for the month – for me to rest. Where better to recuperate than Switzerland?'

'Well, that's true. It's very peaceful. All this clean mountain air.'

They were silent for a while, watching the lake. The boat was a fair distance from the shore now, Lucian and Ivor two crouching figures in yellow rain-slickers. Beyond them, grey clouds were massing against the white peak of Mont Blanc.

Kate let go of Cass's hand. 'I'm all right, Cass. Physically, anyway. It's just that I can't seem to shift the feeling that Lucian's somehow relieved about it. He hasn't said so, of course, but he has his two kids with Marian – he hardly ever sees them as it is – and I don't think he really wants another. So what I can't decide is where that leaves me. Where it leaves us.'

'Because you definitely want children?'

Kate looked at Cass then, her brown eyes still damp with tears. 'Of course. Don't you?'

Cass swallowed. Out on the lake, the boat was growing

smaller and smaller, drawing a widening vector in its wake. 'I don't know. I think Ivor does. He's suggested I come off the pill. He's . . . straightened himself out, I suppose, and I guess he's ready. I think he wants the chance to do things over again. To undo the mistakes his parents made, if that makes any sense. I think I understand how he feels.'

'And you? Are you ready?'

'No. I . . .' She hesitated, aware that it might not be tactful to say more. 'Well, I don't know. Not yet, anyway. I just can't see how we would make it work.'

'Well,' Kate said. 'It will either happen, Cass, or it won't. There's no more comfort than that for any of us, is there?'

'No,' Cass said. 'I don't suppose there is.'

The women sat together in the wicker chairs, talking of other things – the latest film role Kate had been offered, and was unsure whether to accept (the script insisted on her being nude throughout several scenes, while her male co-star would remain fully clothed); Cass's incipient ideas for her next record. The men returned exuberant, hungry, their hair sculpted into boyish tufts by the spray. Lucian suggested they go out for lunch, and as he was not the sort of man accustomed to being disobeyed, that was what they did.

He chose a smart restaurant – stiff white tablecloths and heavy glassware and elaborate plaster cornicing – for which they were all, in their jeans and jumpers, underdressed. But the maître d' didn't seem to mind.

'Mr Hillier,' he breathed at Lucian as he showed them to a table by the window, with its inevitable view of the lake. 'Please. Your usual table.'

Lucian ordered the food, to be shared between them on heavy white china plates: *escargots*, prawns swimming in garlic, an enormous platter of *côte de boeuf*, exuding a sticky trail of blood. The sommelier kept their glasses brimming with pinot noir, and soon they were all pleasantly drunk. Cass's earlier conversation with Kate – her friend's tears, the soft pressure of her hand – acquired the murky quality of a dream. She looked from Kate – restored, now, to equanimity – to Lucian, whose arm was thrown proprietorially around the back of her chair. She thought, not for the first time, of how utterly impossible it was to understand the inner workings of another's relationship; of how every couple must carry its hidden places, its secrets, its taboos.

Under the table, she reached for Ivor's hand.

She would never, in the years after leaving it so abruptly, miss Rothermere.

The house would remain, in Cass's memory, a dark and shadowed place – unfairly, no doubt, as they did have their measure of ease and contentment there. (It was, after all, the house in which Anna was born, and lived out her early years.)

But the gardens she would miss. The lake, with its reeds and lily pads and sudden, mysterious stirrings; as a Valentine's gift to her two years into their marriage, Ivor had it filled with a shoal of koi carp. The walled rose garden, with its sundial, and the bench where, on sunny days, she liked to sit with her old Martin guitar. It was there that she had composed the lyrics for 'In This Garden', scribbling them in her notebook; and where, for as long as she performed the song, she would always picture herself and Ivor, sitting side by side into old age, like a pair of film actors ageing in rapid, cross-cut montage.

It was there, too, in the summer of 1979, that Cass first learnt that Jonah had died.

Kim delivered the news, having learnt it via a circuitous route: Jonah's sister, Mary (Cass and Ivor hadn't even known he had a sister), had telephoned Lily and John at Atterley, after finding their telephone number in one of Jonah's notebooks.

The story was a terrible one – almost unbelievable at first. Jonah had been sleeping rough in Detroit. (Even his sister didn't know what had drawn him there from Albuquerque: she, like all of them, hadn't heard from him in years.) He'd been using again: this, thinking back to his strange, unsettled mood the night Jonah had come to see them play in Denver, had not come as a surprise to Cass. The family was choosing to believe that he'd taken a dubious hit, rather than deliberately misjudged his limits. He had, in any case, been found dead in the street one morning by a young nurse named Kayla Dwight, who was on her way to an early shift at the Henry Ford Hospital. The funeral was in three days' time, at the family's Baptist church in Clarksdale, Mississippi.

'My God,' Cass said. Kim held her hand tightly. 'Where's Ivor?'

'In the studio,' Kim said. 'He was there when I took the call.'

Cass let go of Kim's hand, ran across the garden to the studio. Inside, she found Ivor sitting blank-eyed on the sofa, holding an empty whisky glass.

'Pour me one,' she said. 'We'll raise a toast to Jonah.'

And they did. And then, after their glasses were drained, they held each other, and remembered the friend they had loved and lost, and who had never offered them, or anyone else, a chance to save him; who had perhaps, in the end, simply not wanted to be saved.

They flew over for the funeral: first-class tickets from Heathrow to Chicago, bought at the last minute for an astronomical sum, and then a driver charting the miles down through the deserted flatlands of the Mississippi Delta.

The crowd at the church was large: family, local worshippers, musicians from all over America and Europe. At the wake, an ancient bluesman in a three-piece suit took to the stage. He had been something of a mentor to the boy he recalled as all skinny legs and arms, trying desperately to fit his tiny hand-span to the strings of the old man's guitar.

'Jonah Hills was born with the music in him,' the musician said, his voice cracking a little as he settled that same guitar on his knee. 'I knew it from the moment he started to play.'

Cass listened, and remembered the man she had first seen walking up the driveway at Atterley, and assumed was homeless: the very thing he would eventually become.

She looked around her, and realised that even music hadn't given Jonah enough to live for – or any of these people who, here and now, spoke only of what a wonderful musician he had been. It was true – he'd been the real thing, with no interest in chasing money or fame. But now his music had died with him, however sincerely that kind old man claimed it would live on.

They stayed a few nights in New Orleans – would have stayed longer, were it not for the series of London live dates scheduled for the following week, which Alan had been unable to postpone.

Kim had booked them into the Hotel Monteleone. From there, Cass and Ivor walked the streets of the French Quarter, looking for the seedier, darker alleys where the real music was played. Warm tropical air and brass bands on every corner. Sweat pouring from the faces of the jazz musicians in the Preservation Hall.

Was there something truer, Cass asked herself as they sat in that tiny, tumbledown room with its bare wooden floors and roughly plastered walls, in the efforts of these men – and the occasional woman – playing for little more than tips and beer, than in the cavalcade her own career was becoming?

The pomp and pageantry, the peacock-strutting and the preening. The driving force of her ambition, her desire to be . . . what? Listened to? Recognised. Acclaimed. *Cass Wheeler* – a name to be shouted, whispered, caught in newsprint, each new utterance erasing the last traces of the girl she had once been. The girl lifting a hand to her cheek, still feeling the sharp sting of her mother's blow. The girl lying awake in the dark, wondering where her mother had gone, and if she would ever be coming back.

And yet, Cass thought, as the New Orleans jazz band played on, what did her success really mean? What did any of it mean if a life could end, without ceremony, on a side street in downtown Detroit? A mother, a father and a sister, crying in the church where Jonah had been baptised. A group of so-called friends who hadn't heard from him in years. A child that Jonah had, for a short time, believed was his, and whose loss, perhaps, had proved impossible to bear.

A child. She closed her eyes, and there, on her lap, Cass felt her imaginary weight. A girl. A daughter. Their love made flesh: the answer to their mistakes, and to the mistakes of the parents who had borne them.

She knew the child: she recognised her as clearly and certainly as she would an old, old friend. Irene. Linda. Kate. Serena. Alan. Johnny. Kim. None of her friends' faces was as sharply defined, in that moment, as that of the daughter Cass was holding in her arms.

Hello, little one, she said to the child silently, as the trumpeter lifted the gleaming bell of the instrument high into the solid, stifling air.

'Queen of the Snow'

By Cass Wheeler
From the album *Fairy Tale*
(Demo version)

New York was silent
With fresh fallen snow
The glass and the concrete
The hard neon glow

On the fifty-fifth floor
On the Lower East Side
A woman stood and watched
Her newborn child

Oh daughter, my daughter
Your mother is here
The queen of the snow
The empress of tears

The mirror, it shattered
The shard's in my eyes
Ice and shadows
In this great kingdom of mine

One day, it will be yours
This freezing cold land
My face in your mirror
My hand in your hand

Oh daughter, my daughter
Your mother is here
The queen of the snow
The empress of tears

May you grow taller
Than I ever was
May you bring sunlight
To this nation of ice

Oh daughter, my daughter
Your mother is here
The queen of the snow
The empress of tears
O daughter, my daughter
Your mother is here
The queen of the snow
The empress of tears

RELEASED Album released 7 January 1983;
this demo version previously unreleased
RECORDED November 1982 at Rothermere, Surrey
GENRE Folk rock / pop
LABEL Lieberman Records
WRITER(S) Cass Wheeler

A sunny child. A daughter. Brown eyes too large for her face, and a luxuriant cap of sandy-blonde hair: so much of it, arriving slick and reddish in the fierce, exhausting, long-anticipated moment she was born.

A mouth that sought to smile even when the nurses insisted that she didn't yet know how. A small, hot baby body, bird-boned, fragile, yet also strong, determined, firm: gripping, grasping, reaching. Warm night-breath, odours of cotton and talcum and sour milk, and that piercing, rasping, expertly modulated cry, cutting through sleep and dream and the cotton-wadded delirium that was neither sleep nor dream, but a waiting-room between one desperate summons and the next.

Not sunny, then: a moon baby, pale mother-of-pearl skin; eyes narrowed, heralding the squall. But calm once more with the daylight: smiling, moving her tiny fists in tandem with the music that surrounded her – that was, in those early months, the natural soundtrack of her days.

They named her Anna Lily Joan Wheeler Tait. Lily for Cass's aunt, of course; Joan for Jonah; and Anna for Ivor's grandmother, whom he had loved.

Lily and John came to visit with flowers, and a crib mobile John had fashioned from balsa wood and paint: a flock of seagulls, caught on the rise of the wind.

Alan and Rachel brought white roses (Rothermere was gaudy with bouquets, each room headily perfumed), and their own small son, Jerome. He was just a few months older than Anna, with his father's eyes and his mother's halo of curls.

Kim brought expensive French bath oil for Cass; and for Anna, an enormous stuffed polar bear.

Kate came alone, with a tub of chest-firming lotion, and a

special-edition set of children's fairy tales, each book exquisitely hand-bound.

'I know she's far too young for them yet,' she said, drawing *The Snow Queen* from its box, 'but I couldn't resist.'

'They're perfect,' Cass said. She didn't ask if Kate had any good news of her own; she already knew the answer from her friend's face – stoical, resigned, her own sadness deliberately overlaid with her happiness for Cass.

Johnny brought his camera. 'Only *you*, darling Cassandra, could possibly turn me into a bloody baby photographer.'

He took a whole film's worth of portraits of Anna, and had six of them framed. Cass hung them in the attic room they'd had redecorated as a nursery. Sitting alone with her daughter in the blackest hours of the night, watching the baby's tiny, fierce mouth as it puckered and sucked, she would look across at the photographs and think of Johnny, and smile.

Margaret sent a card. The expense of flying over from Canada, she wrote, was too great, unless Cass wished to make the necessary arrangements? She hoped, in any case, that Cass and Ivor would soon bring Anna to Toronto.

Reading her mother's words, and withdrawing from the air-mail package a small teddy bear with soft, oversized ears and a crest of bright-white hair, Cass was overcome with long-buried fury: a feeling that perhaps she could only fully articulate now that she was a mother herself.

The fear that had lain coiled inside Cass for so long – the fear that she was her mother's daughter, that Margaret's rejection had, inevitably, cut the pattern for her relationship with her own child – had disappeared with Anna's birth, leaving Cass giddy with relief. The love she felt for her daughter was full, profound, unquestionable. Cass could no more imagine leaving Anna – or even shutting the door on the child's wretched night-crying – than she could imagine shifting out of her own body, out of all that ripe maternal flesh, and assuming another form.

A few days later, she sent her mother back a brief note that did not, perhaps, betray the full force of her anger (she found, as she began to write, that she was just too tired for that), but certainly offered her no promises.

We have no plans to visit America, or Canada, anytime soon, Cass wrote, not expecting a reply. And, indeed, none came.

Francis, in his room overlooking the sea, held his granddaughter in his arms, looked down at her, and smiled.

Cass had arranged for him to be moved to the top floor of the home – the largest, best-appointed suite, with broad windows that the nurse, that day, had left open, admitting the dry, saline freshness of the morning.

'This is your granddaughter, Dad,' Cass said, and leant down to tickle the baby's chin. 'This is Anna.'

Francis looked up at Cass. His eyes were filmy, their whites yellowing, pink-seamed. She watched his expression change; she could almost see the fog of his illness as it rolled in. He cried out: an inarticulate, voiceless sound that brought back to her that night more than twenty years ago: his closed door, the church ladies in the kitchen, those terrible animal cries. How cruel the elasticity of time, collapsing the distance between that moment and this.

Gently, she reached forward, released Anna from her grandfather's grip. It was broken, now, but that small moment of connection between them – conscious or unconscious – was enough for Cass. She would carry the image of it in her mind for years, long after Francis was gone, and such images – together with his books, his papers and a small, inadequate cache of photographs – were all that she had left of him.

Susan Tait also sent a card, and an extravagant gift she had delivered to Rothermere from Hamleys: a rocking horse, pale grey, with a long white mane and a soft leather saddle.

Ivor unpacked the rocking horse in the hallway. He stood looking at it for a moment, Cass standing beside him, Anna asleep in her arms.

That evening, over dinner (one of Kim's lasagnes: she had filled the fridge with foil-wrapped dishes in anticipation of Cass's tiredness), he said, 'I think I'll write to my mother, Cassie. Invite her to meet the baby. I think perhaps it's time.'

Susan Tait came to Rothermere one afternoon in May: a petite, slender woman in a yellow skirt and white jacket, her hair newly permed and set.

In her mind, Cass had pictured someone mousy, cowed – overweight, perhaps, the prettiness of her youth (she assumed it was Susan who had bequeathed Ivor his good looks) lost. But the Susan Tait who offered her a smile at the door, and then sat at her kitchen table drinking tea, cooing over the baby in her Moses basket, was not such a woman.

There was, perhaps, a shyness about her, a slight diffidence, but nothing else that might fit with the role that Cass had assigned Susan in her imagination. Helpless, weak. A shadowy, indeterminate figure, straining to read the shifting patterns of her husband's moods.

Ivor was restless in his mother's presence: he got up several times, left the room, and then returned not to sit with them at the table but to stand a few feet away. His anger with Susan had not entirely disappeared; but it seemed, at least, to have dwindled to a low heat. One that was tolerable; one that might allow their daughter, Anna, to know at least one of her grandparents first-hand.

Her own mother; Ivor's mother; Cass now a mother herself. How complicated it all was, and yet how simple it seemed now that Anna had come into the world: how sure Cass was that the mistakes their parents had made would never be repeated.

Impossible, now, not to see herself as absurdly naive: still a child, really, for all her outward-facing confidence and success. So sure, then, that she was in charge of her future, as she was of the music she could bend to her will.

Anna was just over a year old – full-fleshed and strong-limbed; tall for her age, and given to emitting babbling streams of noise that Alan said reminded him of the music of John Cage – when Cass became aware that Ivor was making plans for a solo album.

Hugh had been coming to Rothermere for some time, sequestering himself away in the studio with Ivor and a motley group of musicians whom Cass privately dismissed as bootlickers: hangers-on, more interested in mainlining Ivor's steady supply of malt whisky than in writing anything approaching proper music.

She had been expecting that all this would stop with Anna's birth. And it did, for a time: those first weeks after Anna was born Cass recalls as being fully inhabited by all three of them. The baby cradled to her chest, Ivor staring at her, wide-eyed, lost in admiration (or so it seemed to Cass then) as their daughter locked her toothless, suckling mouth to each breast in turn.

And then, gradually, there came a falling away – the slow erasure of Ivor's presence from their little band of three. Cass climbing from their bed, roused by Anna, as Ivor turned over, drew the pillow over his head, and dived back into a resentful sleep. Ivor disappearing to the studio for long afternoons that turned into evenings, and then into nights. And then, one day, Hugh's return, without a present for the baby, followed, day by day, week by week, by the other men.

They were all men, at first, and the presence of them – standing smoking on the terrace outside the studio, moving to the living-room at three a.m. to eat cheese on toast and drink, drink, drink – was at first only dimly visible to Cass, absorbed as she was in the wondrous, tedious, all-encompassing minutiae of motherhood.

But soon, she was being woken in the small hours not by Anna, who had begun (thank goodness) to sleep soundly through the night, but by Bruce Springsteen or Blondie playing at full volume on the living-room hi-fi. And in the mornings, she would come down from the nursery to find the cleaner, Lorraine, methodically putting to rights a house that looked as if a hurricane had blown through it, scattering all their possessions in its wake.

It was not long before Cass learnt that Ivor and the musicians – he was already calling them 'my band' – were working on a set of new songs that he was intending to release under his own name.

'What's the problem?' he demanded, late one blustery Sunday afternoon after Lily and John had come to lunch, and Ivor had informed them of his plans – easily, casually, as if it were a decision they had taken together, after a sensible, mature discussion, like any sensible, mature married couple.

His face was hard, closed. Across the room, in her playpen, Anna sent a stack of building-blocks tumbling, and gurgled in delight as they fell.

'For God's sake, Ivor,' Cass said, her attention caught between her daughter and her husband, and not, she knew, fully attuned to either. 'Why didn't you talk to me first? It will mean releasing you from your contract, won't it, at least for a while? And what happens when we're ready to make the next record?'

'When *you're* ready, you mean.' His tone was crisp, each word clipped. Anna was stacking the blocks again, her lips taut with concentration; she looked up every so often to ensure that her mother was watching. And so, in watching her, Cass missed the expression that passed across Ivor's face as he said, 'God forbid that you should have to release your husband from his fucking contract.'

That, Cass would decide, had been the stray note, sending a shiver through the harmonic progression of the song.

She had always instinctively recognised the power of a misplaced sound: flattened or sharpened, anti-chromatic, an interloper in the smooth, sequential pattern of the scale. She was, after all, famous for her idiosyncratic tunings.

Perhaps, then, it had always been there between them – that sharpened note, that jarring semi-quaver – and Cass had simply not wanted to hear it. She had trusted in – what? In the rare, astringent beauty of it; in the crack in everything; in the small sliver of a scar marring an otherwise symmetrical face. Perfection was impossible, its pursuit banal: in art, in life, in love, it was the flaws, the mistakes, the disharmonies, that spoke the loudest, that drew us closest to the stuff of real experience.

But what, she asks herself now, is to be done when that small, hairline fissure begins to undermine the whole? No sudden shift and crack, no crash and fall, but a slow and gradual process of subsidence, of beauty turning to ugliness, and the light slipping finally into the dark.

As it happened, Alan foresaw no problem with Ivor going solo.

In the last month of Cass's pregnancy, Alan had arranged for Graham, Kit and Frank to have nine months off on full pay, in the expectation that Cass would not immediately wish to return to the studio. And Kim, then four months pregnant herself (her own daughter, Tasha, would be born on a blazingly colourful day in September), was happy to reduce her working hours. Her husband, Bill, a Californian sound engineer whom she had met on the My Loving Heart sessions in Los Angeles, was already being offered more work than he could handle.

Even now, a year after Anna's birth, Cass was still determined not to employ a nanny; she couldn't bear to think of her daughter's cries being answered by anyone other than herself.

And although an idea for a new album was beginning to take shape – she had in mind a series of contemporary reworkings of Kate's fairy stories – it was still not much more than that. She couldn't expect her band to wait for ever: Frank had already had an offer of session work, and Graham was thinking about taking a year off, and moving to Nashville with his new American wife.

'Ivor needs to get this out of his system,' Alan said. 'And if he is ever going to do that, now is probably the right time, while you're busy with Anna. While you're not in the studio yourself. And besides' – he shifted his gaze – 'there's an appetite for it, Cass. Ivor's record could sell very well.'

She didn't like it. She didn't like it at all.

'Alan doesn't understand,' Cass said to Kim. 'Jerome's fifteen months old, and Rachel's pregnant again. It doesn't make any difference to Alan – Rachel will always be the one at home, doing everything. But what am I meant to do, Kim, if Ivor goes off and does his own thing? How am I meant to manage?'

Cass could sense her friend weighing her words carefully. 'Well, you could think about getting someone in to help with Anna, so you can spend some time writing. Maybe even get back into the studio?'

Cass's response was swift and strong. 'It's Ivor who should be helping. He's her bloody father.'

Kim turned her attention back to her paperwork. 'In my experience,' she said quietly, 'the more you tell a guy he can't do something, the more he digs in his heels.'

She was right, of course. Ivor was set on making the album, and he was damned if Cass, or anyone else, was going to dissuade him.

'We'll get a nanny,' he said. 'We can afford one, for God's sake. It's just stubbornness that makes you think you have to do everything yourself. Stubbornness and your need to be in control. Well, I've had enough of it, Cassie. I'm going to make this record, and there's fuck all you can do about it.'

She stared at him, his eyes narrowed in the half-light: they were standing on the attic landing, outside the nursery. It was after midnight – Anna had woken, crying, and Cass had only just managed to get her back to sleep. She didn't want to wake her, and yet she couldn't stop herself from shouting: she hardly knew what she was saying until the words emerged, ugly and blunt-edged, impossible to withdraw.

'You wouldn't have any of this, Ivor, if it wasn't for me. Who bought this house? Me. Who pays for your fucking whisky? Me. So fine – go off and do your vanity project, if you have to. But don't forget who's made it possible.'

It came so quickly, then – the hard, sharp sting of his hand, drawn lightning-fast across her cheek.

She staggered back, closed her eyes. She couldn't see Ivor as he said, his voice sounding nothing like the voice she knew (the voice that, on stage, in the studio, wove so sweetly around her own), 'You will not control me, Cassie. You will *not*.'

She said nothing, didn't trust herself to speak. She kept her eyes closed, heard his footsteps move off across the landing, and down the stairs. Her cheek felt raw, exposed; she moved her hand across it, feeling its heat beneath her palm, as behind the door to the nursery, Anna began to cry.

It wasn't long before Ivor's plans were set in place.

He was insisting on a fresh sound, something that would be entirely his own. A producer was found; the musicians contracted; a gap in the schedule allocated for the release on Lieberman's new electronic division, Apex.

At the behest of the producer, a twenty-eight-year-old synthesiser obsessive named James Lyons, Ivor bought a dizzyingly expensive machine called a Fairlight CMI, whose dark-faced monitor presided over the live room in a way Cass found vaguely sinister. But she couldn't deny that it was capable of magic: the machine could reproduce a sound – any sound at all – and transfer that sound to its keyboard.

'Here,' Ivor whispered to her, late one night, when Anna, miserable with a cold, was struggling again to sleep. 'Come with me.'

She looked up at him from her nursing chair. That night a month before – the sudden whip-crack of his palm across her face – already seemed surreal, nightmarish. She had lain sleepless in their empty room – she didn't know where Ivor had gone, and she didn't care – her sore cheek pressed against the pillow. In the morning, she'd told herself, she would call Kim, ask her to help her pack her things. She and Anna would go to stay with Kim and Bill, or with Johnny (she couldn't quite bear the idea of going to Lily and John: her aunt's words, her warning, now echoed in her ears), until she had found them a place of their own. The marriage was over: it had to be. She could see no other way.

All this Cass had said to herself, and then she had dropped gratefully into sleep, and woken to the bright, transformative light of a summer's morning.

Ivor was curled against her, his arms around her waist, and his voice – his own voice again, now, the voice she knew – was saying softly in her ear, 'I'm sorry, my love. I'm so sorry. Forgive me.'

She had allowed him to hold her, allowed the previous night to slip off into the distance – an aberration, a misstep. She had got up, dressed, and seen to Anna. She had not called Kim, and she had not packed her case.

Now, in the nursery, Ivor took Cass's hand, and led her, still carrying Anna, downstairs, through the living-room, and across the damp, cool garden. In the studio – which was quiet, for once, Hugh and the men disbanded – Ivor switched on the Fairlight machine.

Smiling, still holding Cass's gaze, he said, 'Listen to this.'

He fiddled with the machine, and then Cass heard Anna's voice, played back with pin-sharp clarity. *Sing. Sing. Sing.* It was the first comprehensible word they had ever heard her say: she'd uttered it clearly and brightly a few weeks before, imperious as a miniature duchess. Ivor must have brought Anna out to the studio one day, persuaded her to speak into the machine.

Anna, drawn by the light and noise, opened her eyes, and smiled for the first time in hours. Across her, Ivor and Cass looked at each other, hardly daring to breathe.

Ivor would start *Inside the Machine* with this sample of his daughter's voice, repeated ten times, blurring gradually into the drum-machine intro of the opening track.

And, twenty-four years later, alone in Home Farm, Cass would find herself playing those ten bars, over and over again, until she could no longer bear the sound, and the memory of that moment of pure, unadulterated happiness: so intense, so deeply felt and so impossible, it would seem, to hold on to.

The Reverend Francis Wheeler died on a Tuesday morning in July 1982, after a brief struggle with a chest infection.

England was in the clammy, relentless grip of a heatwave, Anna was only just over a nasty outbreak of measles, and two IRA bombs had exploded in London's parks. Driving down to Worthing from Rothermere with Kim, Anna and Tasha engrossed in each other in their twin car seats, Cass turned off the radio, unable to bear any more gloom.

Ivor was in Bangkok, on the south-east Asian leg of his *Inside the Machine* tour: the album had charted high in almost every territory, and its lead single, 'I Need Your Love', was on radio playlists in both the UK and the US. He had been touring, more or less continuously, for three months. The rare week or two he had at home at Rothermere he spent in the studio with James and Hugh, laying down demos for a second album.

'Come and hang out with us,' he'd say to Cass. 'Let Anna see her daddy making music.'

So Cass took Anna out there most afternoons – sat with her in the control room, beside James; held her daughter's fascinated face up to the glass to watch her father at work. But Anna would soon begin to tire and fret, and Cass would have to leave them, trudge back up to the house with Anna crying in her arms. And yes, as she did so, she hated Ivor a little; as she hated him, too, on the nights when he was on the other side of the world, standing on stage, losing himself in his music, while she was at home, lost in motherhood's relentless tedium and unfathomable joys.

On the day her father died, then – that hot, humid, terrible day – she telephoned Ivor's hotel in Bangkok from her own hotel in Worthing.

There was no answer from his room.

'Would madam like to leave a message?' the Thai concierge asked.

Cass put a hand to her forehead, wiped away a fine layer of sweat. Outside, the grey-green sea was shimmering under a haze of heat, and Kim was drawing Anna and Tasha, one toddler dangling from each hand, down from the promenade onto the beach.

'Please tell him that my father has passed away,' she said. 'His funeral is on Friday at St Saviour's Church in Worthing. I'm staying at the Chatsworth Hotel. Could you please ask him to call me here as soon as possible?'

'Of course, madam,' the concierge replied. 'I'll make sure Mr Tait gets the message.'

She tried the Apex press officer, Zoë, next, and managed to reach her. The musicians and crew had a week's break between gigs, Zoë said. A group of them had made off for the beaches at Phuket, but Ivor was not among them. Nobody – not Zoë; not the tour manager, Andy; not Alec, Alan's assistant, who had been sent out on the tour – knew where he was.

Cass liked Zoë: she was clever, funny, unflappable, with platinum-blonde hair and a filthy northern laugh. She was also, Cass observed, a terrible liar.

'Zoë,' she said, 'my father has just died, and I'm really not in the mood for any crap. I think you know exactly where Ivor is. Am I right?'

There was a long pause at the other end of the line. 'I'm sorry, Cass, I really am, but I can't say. I work for Ivor, after all. Please understand.'

Cass took a breath. 'You work for Apex, and Apex is owned by Lieberman Records. And I, as you may be aware, am the biggest-selling British female artist on Lieberman's roster. So if you know where Ivor is, Zoë, I believe it might be in your interest to tell me.'

Another long pause. A sigh, and then, 'He's gone off on his own somewhere. Well, not on his own. I don't know her name, I'm afraid . . .' A cough, another sigh. 'Look, Cass, you don't need me to tell you what it's like on tour. Bitches on heat, throwing themselves at the guys everywhere they go. I'm sure it's just one of those groupie flings, you know? Nothing serious.'

'Right.' On the beach, Kim and the girls were turning from the sea, high-stepping over the pebbles in their jelly shoes. Watching her daughter – the tiny, plump-armed shape of her in her white sunhat, her blue striped OshKosh pinafore – Cass felt nausea rise up from her stomach, and settle in her throat. 'Thanks, Zoë.'

'I really am sorry, Cass. And about your father, too.'

It was Thursday morning when Ivor finally reached her. He sounded breathless, cross, as if he were the one who'd been trying to find *her*.

'I had no idea where you were,' he said. 'The staff here are fucking useless. Now Zoë tells me you've checked into some bloody hotel in Worthing.'

'Well, we did need somewhere to stay for the funeral, Ivor.' Cass hated how bitter she sounded, how easily she had slipped into the role of shrewish wife. She thought of the voices – low and tender, or urgent, hot, fast-flowing – in which they had once spoken to each other as they made love. She thought of Ivor's hands running across another woman's body, through another woman's hair.

'So where have you been?'

'I went off by myself for a bit. I just needed some space, you know?' She heard him swallow, draw breath. 'I'm sorry about your dad, Cassie. About Francis. I really am.'

She closed her eyes. She hadn't cried, yet, but she knew that the time would come.

'Not sorry enough,' she said, 'to give your tart a kiss goodbye and fly home.'

He issued no denial, no retort. He was silent for a long time. When he spoke, his voice was calm and cool. 'How can I fly back? We've got a show tomorrow. I can't cancel now. We'd have to issue refunds.'

'But you could have cancelled two days ago.'

A silence. Then, 'Would you have done that for me, Cass? *Would* you, really?'

'I can tell you right now, you bastard,' she said, her anger rising, 'that I have *never* done what you're doing to me. And how could I, Ivor, when I'm so busy changing our daughter's fucking nappies?'

And then she slammed the receiver down.

Ivor flew home two weeks later. It was eight o'clock when his car drew onto the drive: Cass was in the kitchen with Anna, spooning cornflakes into her reluctant mouth.

'Daddy?' Anna said, as she had over and over again since

her father's departure, each time she'd heard the growl of an approaching car.

'Daddy,' Cass confirmed.

He was red-eyed, the hard angles of his face seeming bloated, softened by booze and whatever else they'd all had far too much of on the tour. He didn't meet Cass's eye, offered her only a peremptory hello as he drew Anna up into his arms, kissed her, lifted her top and blew raspberries on her bare stomach as she giggled and writhed.

Cass stood on the other side of the room, drinking her coffee, finishing her toast.

'I'm going for a bath,' he said after a while, handing Anna back to Cass, ignoring his daughter's indignant screams as he closed the door behind him.

At twelve, after she'd put Anna down for her nap, Cass pushed open the door to their bedroom and found Ivor dozing, wrapped in his damp towel.

She watched him, took in the pale skin of his chest, with its scattering of dark hair. She loved him, and she hated him, and she didn't know where one feeling ended and the other began.

'What's her name, Ivor?' she said.

He didn't open his eyes. 'Whose name?'

'You know whose name.'

He opened his eyes now. He lifted his gaze to meet hers, and the moment stretched out between them, taut and resonant.

'Cassie,' he said. 'Please. It doesn't matter. *She* doesn't matter. I'm not going to tell you her name.'

Inside her, the spring snapped, and unfurled: she rushed over to the bed, climbed astride him, pounded his chest with her fists. Her words were empty, banal, even to her own ears. *How could you? What's wrong with you? Off with some woman on the day I find out my father's dead, for fuck's sake. After everything I've done for us, looking after our house, our daughter. I've given it all up for you, haven't I? Every single thing I had. Every single thing that made me happy. And I hate you for it, Ivor. I really do.*

He held her arms, pushed her away: gently at first, then employing his full strength. She lay beside him, her breath coming in short, fast gasps.

'I don't want this, Ivor,' she said. 'I don't want it to be like this.'

He reached for her hand. 'I'm sorry, Cassie. I really am. I'm a stupid bastard. I'm weak and I'm foolish. But I love you, Cassie. I love you both. And I didn't know about Francis then, did I? How could I have known?'

She moved their joined hands to his chest, released her palm from his grip. His skin was warm, still clammy from his bath. She drew her fingers gently across his stomach, to the hem of his towel; his lips met hers, and the love they made was angry, and tender, and forgiving, and filled with grief. And afterwards, they lay together, Ivor's breath deepening as he fell asleep, and Cass lying with her eyes open, watching the ceiling, waiting for their daughter to wake up.

Anna was two and a half when Cass and Ivor finally employed a nanny. Her name was Alberte; she was a small, blonde, strong-limbed woman from Copenhagen whose fiancé, Mark, was a pilot for British Airways.

Cass liked Alberte, and enjoyed her company; she often found herself, on the many nights when both Ivor and Mark were away, sitting up with her in the living-room, playing records, drinking red wine.

'I know Mark sleeps with other women when he's away,' Alberte said one night, when they'd had one glass too many. 'But I don't care. I know he loves me.'

'Aren't you jealous?' Cass said.

Alberte shrugged. 'A bit. Not so much. It means I can have my freedom, too.'

Freedom. Cass had thought about the word a lot while recording *Fairy Tale* at Rothermere in November 1982: her fifth album, and her first in six years. Ten songs; ten modern fables. Her favourite, and the lead single, would be 'Queen of the Snow': the Snow Queen recast as a single mother in wintry New York, wondering how many of her own mistakes would eventually be repeated by her baby daughter.

She heard the song, the whole album, as cool, stripped back, standing in opposition to the prevailing fashion for electronic sounds: just Cass, her guitar and her Steinway alongside a cello, or perhaps a violin.

'The trouble,' Alan said, 'is that the label doesn't agree, Cass. They hear you with a bigger sound. Poppier. More contemporary.'

'Then please tell them,' she said, 'that's not what *I* hear.'

It had been a couple of years now since Martin had been tempted out to Los Angeles by a rival company: in his absence, Phoenix had been disbanded, unseated by the rising gods of post-punk and new wave. Many of its artists had been let go, but Cass had been absorbed onto the mainstream Lieberman list, under the personal supervision of the managing director, Roger O'Brien – who telephoned a few days after Alan had conveyed her message about the new record.

'I hear you're not too happy about the musical direction we'd like you to take,' Roger said. He was an old Etonian – no longer, in Thatcher's brash, money-driven age, something to be ashamed of, it seemed – with a loud, nasal voice and a florid drinker's complexion.

'No,' Cass said.

'Cass, you know how much we value and respect you as an artist. You're unique. There's nobody like you, and your fans are desperate to hear from you. But . . .' He lowered his voice, softened it. She didn't like him, and she didn't believe a word he said. 'We've waited a very long time for this album, and this is the way we'd like you to go. So I'd be very grateful indeed if you would at least give Ed Riccione a try. He's very bright, very fresh. He's been working with Culture Club. We think he's just what you need.'

She gave in: she simply didn't have the fight left in her. Not when she was having to acknowledge just what a fool she had been; what an absurd cavalcade her marriage was becoming. To think that she'd allowed herself to dismiss Ivor's dalliance in Bangkok as just that: a momentary lapse, an insignificant fling. To think that, two nights before, she'd been woken at one a.m. by music from downstairs – 'Computer Love' by Kraftwerk, those disembodied voices and unearthly blips climbing the stairs to her bedroom. She'd gone down and found Ivor and Hugh in the living-room, incoherent with drink and who knew what else, and two women in short skirts and thigh-high boots.

As Cass came in, one of the women had looked up from the line of coke she was cutting on the coffee table and said, 'Hey! Want to try some of this?'

In the kitchen, behind the closed door, Cass had screamed at Ivor, reached for the closest thing to hand – Anna's china mug, with its pictures of Jemima Puddleduck and Peter Rabbit – and thrown it at his head. Her aim had been more accurate than she'd expected – the mug had smashed against Ivor's temple, sent a trickle of blood running down towards the bridge of his nose. The blood was dark red against his skin. So absorbed had she been in the shock of having actually struck him – in watching the viscous ooze of the blood – that he'd been upon her almost before she'd noticed.

He'd put a hand to her throat, pushed her back against the kitchen counter. She'd realised, then, her breath caught in his grip, that she was actually afraid of him, and that she was also afraid of herself.

And so she could not find the strength to oppose Roger O'Brien. And so the next month, in the studio, she worked with Ed Riccione to lay down the tracks, let him layer them with brass, strings, electronic beats.

'It's going to sound awesome,' Ed assured her. 'Just awesome.'

When, at the sessions' conclusion, she listened back to Ed's mixes, she hardly recognised the songs as her own.

'I hate it,' she told Alan. 'It's awful. It's some godforsaken disco party. Tell Roger they can't release it. Tell him I'm not putting my name to that.'

But her contractual obligations, as Roger reminded her during a tense meeting at the Lieberman offices, implied otherwise.

'We've spent a lot of money on this record, Cass,' he said, as lightly and sociably as if he were offering her a fresh glass of champagne, 'and we need a decent return. So this, Cass, is the album we'll be releasing next January. And I think you'll find that there's not much you can do to stop us.'

It had bombed, of course. The fans were nonplussed, the critics merciless.

'If we needed any reminder at all of just how completely irrelevant the singer-songwriters of the last decade have become,' ran one review, 'it's all there in Cass Wheeler's new album, *Fairy Tale*. It's a ten-pound Christmas turkey, wrapped in bacon, stuffed with Paxo. It's your mum putting on a glittery dress and going out on the town. It's your aunty wearing a low-cut top and bending just a little too low over her fifth pina colada. It's a wife trying desperately to match her husband's grasp of today's new sounds, and failing miserably. Well, Ivor Tait, this is it: your time has come. Time to step out from your wife's shadow and take the stage.'

'Don't read them, Cass,' Alan said. 'It'll pass. They're baying for blood, but they'll soon move on. Take some time at home with Anna. Write. Rest up. We'll tell Roger where he can stick his bloody contract. I'm already setting up meetings.'

'It's all right, Alan,' she told him. 'It's my own fault. I let this happen.'

And it was true, she thought – she had. Everything was slipping from her grasp. Her music, her marriage. Ivor's affairs, which he was now making no attempt to conceal – as their growing contempt for each other was also unconcealed, leaving its mark in bruises, scratches, the sudden impact of fist on skin. But none of this, it seemed to Cass, was as damaging or destructive as the words they hurled at each other like missiles. Words that Anna overheard, of course; words that fired off in all directions, and couldn't fail to hit their daughter.

'She's started wetting the bed,' Alberte told her one morning. She didn't meet Cass's eye as she added, 'She wakes up in the night. She comes into my room. She says she's afraid.'

Three-year-old Anna: a bundle of warm flesh; strawberry toothpaste and Johnson's bubble bath; that smile still there, still reaching across her face, but already, it seemed to Cass, becoming rarer, and dissolving quickly into tears.

Sometimes, holding Anna, Cass still felt a love so strong it was almost physical – the desire to become one, again, with her daughter, to merge their flesh, to carry her inside the protective casing of her own skin. But at other times – so private she could hardly admit them to herself – she held Anna and felt only the weight of all that she had given up. Her music. The freedom to tour, to stand before a crowd of strangers on a stage, and think only of herself, and Ivor, and the sound that stilled the moment, and held it.

That freedom was only Ivor's, now, it seemed. For he was writing, shutting himself away in the studio for weeks on end; and when he wasn't writing, he was touring; and when he wasn't touring, he was with his women; and when he wasn't with his women, he was here, hating his wife and loving his daughter – loving Anna, yes, but not allowing that love to swallow him whole.

One day that July – the July of 1983, when Ivor was on tour in the US – Cass found, in the pocket of an old cardigan, a slip of paper, folded in half.

A telephone number.

Irene. Irene's mother. Their matching camel coats and darkly shining hair.

Cass looked at the number, written in Irene's careful handwriting on the sheet she had torn from her notepad all those years ago in Cornelia's shop. And before she could quite acknowledge the impulse, Cass went downstairs to her office, picked up the phone, and dialled the number.

'Yes, this is Alice Lewis. Who's calling?'

Goodness, Alice said, how lovely it was to hear from Cass. How proud they all were of her success. And married, with a daughter! Well, that was just the icing on the cake, wasn't it? Oh yes, Irene and Mike were very well. They were living in Kingston-upon-Thames. Three children – two boys and a girl – aged twelve, ten and seven. Well, she was sure Irene would be very happy to see Cass. Alice would call her right away and let her know.

A week or so later, then, Cass strapped Anna into her car-seat in the MG, and drove the ten short miles that separated her from her oldest friend.

She still hardly knew what she was doing, or why: she was aware only of an overwhelming desire to see Irene, to roll back the years, somehow, to the time before everything changed. The two of them, six, seven, eight years old, playing in the back garden of the little house on the other side of the common. The yellow-painted living-room, and the thick brown rug, and Alice Lewis's piano, polished and gleaming and calling Cass's name.

The woman who answered the door of the whitewashed cottage was taller than Cass remembered, and her girlish heaviness had settled into fat. She was wearing a loose pale blue dress with a broad white collar. Her dark hair was shorter, her curls permed into a tighter hold; her lipstick was pink, and she had daubed her eyes with a brownish sheen.

'My daughter, Katherine,' Irene said, kneeling down to greet Anna, 'is just dying to show you the paddling-pool. Would you like that?'

Anna nodded shyly. Cass, on the doorstep beside her, still holding the huge bunch of irises she had brought, said, 'I'm afraid we don't have her costume with us.'

Irene straightened up, and placed a kiss on each of Cass's cheeks. 'I'm sure I've got an old one of Katherine's somewhere. It really is good to see you, Cass. It's been so long, hasn't it?'

They sat in the back garden to eat, on plastic chairs that had seen better days.

'The kids have already eaten,' Irene explained. 'I thought I'd get them out from under our feet. But will Anna be hungry?'

Cass shook her head. 'I gave her lunch before we left. Well, the nanny did.'

Irene regarded her, her head on one side. It was strange, Cass thought, returning her gaze. She seemed older than their thirty-three years, every inch the busy stay-at-home mother (for this, she had gleaned from Alice, was what Irene was). But Irene's face was remarkably youthful – free of the creases and furrows that marred Cass's own, and that she had begun to examine, obsessively, in the bathroom mirror. *Perhaps this is what contentment looks like*, Cass thought. *Perhaps this is what it looks like to live an ordinary, happy life.* And she looked around her – took in the narrow garden, with its comfortable muddle of lawn, flowerbeds, discarded children's toys – and envied Irene, then. Envied her the fact that she had found a way to make all this be enough.

'A nanny,' Irene said. 'Of course. It just wouldn't be possible otherwise, would it?'

They ate baked potatoes with coleslaw and grated cheese,

and a salad of lettuce and tomatoes from Mike's allotment. 'He spends most Sunday afternoons over there,' Irene said. 'Enjoys the solitude, I think.'

She poured each of them a glass of Aqua Libra, and apologised for not having bought in wine. 'Mike and I don't tend to drink much. But I can run round the corner for a bottle, Cass. I'm sorry. I should have thought.'

'No, honestly, it's fine,' Cass said, sipping her drink, although she was indeed thinking, wistfully, that a cool glass of Chardonnay or two would take the edge off. She knew she was drinking too much – the bottle just seemed to empty itself, most evenings, as she sat in the living-room after dinner, Anna asleep upstairs. Sometimes, Alberte joined her; but on the nights when she was alone, Cass surprised herself by how quickly and suddenly she would find that she had finished the bottle. But she was not drinking as much as Ivor was, and that thought offered her some meagre comfort.

There, in the garden, Irene and Cass sat in the sunshine on their plastic chairs, watching the children splashing in the paddling-pool. Harry, a lithe, narrow-chested twelve-year-old; Sam, who was ten, and had a crop of deep auburn curls that Cass assumed he'd inherited from his father; and seven-year-old Katherine, a brisk, motherly little girl who had taken Anna under her wing, and was carefully helping the smaller child step in and out of the water.

It was easier between them, perhaps, than Cass could have imagined. Each woman sketched in the spare outline of the last decade. Mike's promotion to partner in his GP surgery. Alice's breast cancer scare. Sam's struggles at school, which Irene and Mike were working to have diagnosed as dyslexia. Cass's music, and her tours. Francis's slow decline. Her decision to become a mother.

'And Ivor?' Irene said. It was mid-afternoon now, and still warm; her chest was pink from the sun, and she was shielding her eyes with her hand. 'You haven't said much about him. Goodness, he is handsome, isn't he? Mike and I actually saw him on *Top of the Pops* the other night. I called the kids to come and watch. They haven't been able to stop going on about "Mummy's famous pop-star friend and her famous pop-star husband". They're not usually so shy. I think they're a bit in awe of you.'

Cass looked down at the table. 'Less of the star, I think. In my case, anyway. Not now. Not after they crucified my last record. And God, they were right to. It was dreadful. The label was . . .' She ran her finger up and down the curve of her glass. 'No. I can't blame anyone else. It was my own fault.'

'There'll be other albums, Cass.' Irene spoke quietly, and Cass was reminded of their last meeting, in the changing-room in Cornelia's shop. Irene's embarrassment; her admission of how deeply and carelessly Cass had once wounded her. It seemed to her, then, that she couldn't lie to Irene, not to the woman who had known the girl Cass had once been. Maria Wheeler, bare-kneed, her hair in plaits, her mother lost to her, her father fading day by day.

And so she began to talk, as she had talked to no one else. Not to Alan, or Kim, or Lily, or Kate or Johnny or Serena. She told the truth, and understood it as that only in the moment it was uttered. Ivor's infidelity. His violence, and her own. Her anger with her mother, and her grief over her father's death. Her ambivalence about motherhood. Her suspicion – no, her fear – that it might have cost her her career: that all the urgency she had once channelled into her music had rerouted itself into her daughter. That the songs she had once heard in her mind were still there, but almost inaudible, and she was afraid that, even if she turned to listen to them, they would turn out to be no good at all.

Irene listened – distracted only, from time to time, by the arrival of one of the children asking for juice, or ice cream, or her adjudication in some minor dispute.

'It's not easy, is it,' Irene said when Cass, at last, fell quiet. 'The path you've chosen. If I'm honest, I've always envied you – I just saw the glamour, the money, the excitement. I didn't understand that it would all come at such a cost. Most people don't realise that, I suppose.'

Cass shook her head. Irene reached across the table for her hand.

'I'm not going to tell you what to do,' she said. 'I don't know you well enough for that any more, do I? And even if I did, I know you'd still make up your own mind. So if I can say anything, it's just that I know you will come through this, Cass. You'll be all right. You're strong. You've always been strong.'

Cass's voice, when she spoke, was halting, threatening to break. 'I don't *feel* strong any more.'

From the bottom of the garden, then, Anna called out to her. 'Mummy! *Mummy!*'

Cass squeezed Irene's hand, and then let go, and went to find out what her daughter needed.

Was it weakness, then, that had made her stay?

Weakness, she would decide, and love (for yes, she did love Ivor then, even as the feeling slowly ebbed away) and stubbornness; and her determination that her daughter would not grow up wondering why one of her parents had abandoned her.

Anna. Four years old, then six, seven, eight: home-educated, with Kim's daughter Tasha and Alan's children Jerome and Katie, by a Steiner-trained tutor who believed in self-expression, creativity, unguided play.

She was still, was she not, a sweet-natured, enthusiastic, happy child? And yet there were moments – how could there not be? – when the high wattage of Anna's expression dimmed, like the sun slipping behind a stretch of cloud. Too many nights when she wet the bed, or went looking for Alberte, or asked her why Mummy and Daddy were so angry with each other; whether it was something she had done. Cass could see that Anna was becoming more serious, more withdrawn, more comfortable in her own company, or with Alberte, than with her parents. Cass knew it, because she had once known it in herself.

There were rumours of what was happening, beyond the restricted confines of her loyal circle. Ivor spotted entering and leaving Annabel's nightclub in the company of a string of 'attractive blondes'. A large bruise on Cass's arm, revealed unwittingly by a long sleeve as she gripped the microphone, caught by photographers at a gig in Bristol. Speculation in the papers that these two observations were connected.

Lily arrived at Rothermere the day after the first rumours appeared in the press.

'Cass,' she said, 'if even one word of this is true, you're to pack your things right away and come with me.'

Cass couldn't deny that it was true – she could not look her aunt in the face and issue such a denial. And yet, for all Lily's insistence, she refused to go. Each time Ivor went away, she convinced herself that things would be different on his return; and then, when he did return, they would be exactly the same. The brief, tantalising sweetness of reunion; and then, too quickly, the same old cycle of anger and blame.

'You're just like your father, you know,' she said to Ivor one night.

He turned then, his face contorted into a snarl, and said, 'Then why can't you be more like your bloody mother and leave?'

And then, finally, she did leave. That night in April 1988, when Anna was eight years old: a night that would imprint itself on each of them for ever.

Cass remembers, above all, the banality of it, like something from a low-rent bedroom farce. Drawing back the covers of her bed – *their* bed, though Ivor now slept so often in a spare room

311

on the second floor that even Alberte had taken to calling it 'Ivor's room'. Finding the underwear that wasn't hers. Black lace, cut high on the thigh.

She would struggle to make sense of this later: if Ivor was going to bring a woman home, why take her to their shared bedroom, the room he hardly ever used? It would strike her that he had *wanted* to be found out: that Ivor had already made the decision to end the marriage but wanted to confer on her the act of parting. It was this, among so many other things, that Cass would find it so difficult to forgive.

And so the inevitable confrontation. The shouting. The whistle and smash of glass (his whisky tumbler, lobbed at Cass's head. Perhaps he hadn't meant for it to hit her. Perhaps). Anna drawn whimpering from her bed by the noises downstairs: not unfamiliar, by now, but louder, worse, that night, than they had ever been.

She had found her mother crouching like an animal on the living-room floor, scattered shards of glass at her feet, the cut above her right eye already spouting a livid stream of blood. Her father pacing, silent now, but still wound into a tight coil of fury.

Cass had turned, half-blind, at the sound of her daughter's footstep on the stairs. She would never erase the sight of Anna then: pale, her skin bluish, her long hair hanging, Medusa-like, in matted cords. Her expression was not so much one of fear as of bewilderment, tempered by a perceptible, too-adult shade of disgust.

For a long moment, none of them spoke. And then Cass said, 'Darling, please go upstairs and get dressed. We're going to take a little trip.'

Anna's mouth hung open. She looked from her father to her mother. 'Now? Where? Is Daddy coming? And Alberte?'

Ivor had stopped pacing; Cass wouldn't look at him, but she knew that he had stopped beside the Steinway, placed his hand on its lid. A few inches from his fingers, across that black

312

polished wood, the last roses he had bought her – the card he'd asked the florist to write (or, more likely, had had Zoë ask the florist to write) – were silently bowing, preparing to shed their velvety bloom.

'No, darling,' Cass said. 'Please go and get dressed.'

She would deal with the where in a moment, upstairs in her study; placing the call to Johnny in his safe, quiet, beautiful warren of a house in Spitalfields. *I'm sorry it's so late, Johnny. Can we come to you, Anna and I?* His cautious, careful reply, in the rough-hewn East End accent he had never lost. *Of course, darling Cass. Of course you can.*

And then, after that, she would deal with the how, and the why. But for now, there was only the necessity of escape, and her resolution never to return.

'Home'

By Cass Wheeler
Released in aid of homelessness charities

Home is a house
Where the windows are open
Music is playing
And soft words are spoken
All these presents
We just keep on opening
Look at what we call a home

Home is a place
Where the kids play outdoors
Trees in the garden
And rugs on the floors
We've done all our shopping
We're out to get more
Look at what we call a home

Home is a flat
On the rough side of town
With a sheet for a curtain
A patch of hard ground
Look at the Christmas tree
That we found
Sometimes you just need a home

Home is a roof
That lets in the rain
Mould on the walls
An ugly black stain

Carols they're singing
Are always the same
Sometimes you just need a home

Home is a bridge
A tunnel, a yard
A cold rush of air
A mattress of card
Sit round the TV as if it's a fire
And feed all the need and the greed and desire
(Shoo wap a doo we doo wop wop wop sha doobie do wap)
At Christmas
For home
At Christmas
Home
At Christmas
Home
At Christmas
Home

RELEASED 6 December 1993
RECORDED August 1993 at Home Farm, Kent
GENRE Rock/pop
LABEL Lieberman Records
WRITER(S) Cass Wheeler
PRODUCER(S) Steve Linetti
ENGINEER(S) Jim Wright

315

Home Farm.

It was the name, perhaps, that had decided her: that and the warm red brick, with its familiar resonances of Atterley. A gentle, welcoming, easy house, despite its faded decor, its brown carpets, mildewed bathrooms and thirty-year-old kitchen. Wide, generous rooms; high ceilings; casement windows that might be thrown open to admit the fresh, cleansing Kentish air, with its faint bitter tang of earth and hops.

Four attic rooms, one of which, tucked comfortably under the eaves, Anna had immediately claimed as her own. Eleven acres of land on which a new studio might, eventually, be constructed. A barn she could consider turning into garages, with a self-contained apartment for Alberte. (The nanny was staying in Mark's flat in Weybridge, but had promised to join them as soon as Cass had secured a house.) A kitchen garden, and a stringy copse of trees the estate agent had called an 'arboretum', with a brittle optimism that seemed to irritate Kim to distraction, but which, despite herself, Cass found rather cheering.

It was years, the agent said, since the house had been attached to a working farm. An aristocratic couple – some scion of a once-grand local family – had owned it, raised five children here, and lived all their lives between its walls. She was too discreet to say whether the couple had died here, too – but if they had, bequeathing in that act some spectral trace of their long occupation, then it was, Cass decided, benign.

Yes, Cass told the agent there and then, the three women standing together in the garden, watching Anna chase a skinny black-and-white cat across the lawn. A farm cat, probably, the agent had observed with a disapproving frown (she was a dog person, herself): there was a big dairy place, Dearlove Farm, just up the road.

Yes, Cass said again, she would take the house.

Beneath her frizzy perm, the woman's face broke into a smile. 'Well, then,' she said. 'If you'd like to accompany me back to the office . . .'

'Are you really sure about this?' Kim asked on the drive back to Sussex. (Cass and Anna were staying at Atterley, with Lily, Cass having grown concerned at exhausting Johnny's reserves of hospitality.) She kept her voice low, so as not to permit Anna, sketching in her notepad on the back seat, to overhear.

'Yes, Kim.' Cass laid a hand on her friend's arm. 'Thank you, but I really am sure.'

Kim and Alan had arranged everything, as always: she'd had only to sign the papers.

Alan was also taking care of the divorce. He had engaged the fiercest solicitor he could find, and was hopeful, given the potential negative impact on Anna, that they might be able to obtain an injunction to prevent reporting by the press.

He had arranged to delay indefinitely the recording sessions for Cass's sixth album, *Snapshots*. Cass was not, they all agreed, in any state to return to the studio. (Roger O'Brien had, in the wake of the disaster that *Fairy Tale* had proved to be, moved on; the new boss, Iain Urquhart, was far more sympathetic). But the press officer, Simon, couldn't resist pointing out that if Cass were to return to work sooner rather than later, the media attention could be successfully channelled into album sales.

Hearing this, Alan had been firm. 'Think about what you're saying, Simon, for God's sake. What Cass needs now is rest. Rest and time.'

He ensured that she would have it, too: rented a place for her on the Isle of Mull, in the Hebrides, while the renovations to Home Farm were taking place.

Alan had taken Rachel and the kids there, last summer, and had fallen in love with the island: it was, he said, impossible to imagine a more peaceful spot. She could take a guitar, rest, write, walk. Anna would have her sketchpad, her books, the boundless freedom of sea and sky.

It was July when they travelled north, the sun high and golden over the west coast, the tall stone buildings set in a graceful arc round Oban Harbour.

They sat on the top deck of the ferry, huddled together against the wind. A lonely lighthouse, marooned on a steep stack of rocks, gave way to the island's first promontory: a castle, grey-walled and turreted, set on a shaggy outcrop of ancient lava, backed by a wide sweep of pines; and then, opening to greet them, the small landing at Craignure.

A long drive along a pitted strip of single-track road, swerving at intervals to permit the passing of the few cars they met. The sudden shock of open moorland, vast and empty – rock and peat and scrubby thickets of grass presided over by the glowering summit of Ben Mor. Above them, the broad wingspan of what must surely be an eagle, hanging motionless on a pocket of air. A loch; a village, eerily still in the early evening; a series of tight hairpin bends. And then, at the farthest edge of land, a cluster of houses, facing an inlet from which the Atlantic had retreated, revealing a muddy stretch of beach, gaudy with bladderwrack and discarded stones. Gulls circling overhead, and small, long-beaked birds high-stepping in the shallows.

Anna had fallen asleep: Cass, bringing the rented car to a halt there before the beach, leant across, and gently woke her. Blinking, only half awake, Anna considered the vista stretching out before them.

'Is that the Atlantic?' she said. She had researched the west of Scotland before they set out, poring over her picture atlas.

Cass, beside her, nodded, and felt a loosening inside her, a wave of relief that was physical in its intensity; in the knowledge that here, for six weeks – and then, after that, perhaps for ever, at Home Farm – they would be safe. The two of them, holed up together, battened down against the world, and whatever it might throw at them.

There would be no unravelling: not yet. There was Home Farm to furnish, an album to record, a new school to find for Anna: Cass had resolved to find her a place in the local primary for the new term. She feared that Anna was too isolated, too unused to the company of children beyond their small circle.

Gigs. Small at first – acoustic sets in old Victorian theatres, those forlorn victims of an indifferent age. Then, gradually, growing in size and confidence – a seven-piece band, horns and trumpets swelling her sound. Graham and Kit back from the old crowd. A new young guitarist, Pete Roscoe, occupying the place to stage-right where Ivor had once stood.

If Cass was no longer able, with her music, to reach the heights to which she had once flown, then she was grateful, at least, to be working and to be enjoying that work. *Snapshots* entered the UK charts at a respectable number thirty, but climbed no higher; her American tour manager arranged concerts on each coast, but did not bother to plot her old route across the Midwest. But the critics were kind, the fans – those that she had retained – relieved that she had returned to the sound they loved. For Cass, it all seemed to be in the natural order of things. She was thirty-eight years old, and music, as the saying went, was a young man's game. Or woman's.

Her records still sold. Touts still loitered outside the doors of the concert halls. The shiny young things cited her as an influence: in the summer of 1988, she was invited to lend guest vocals to the debut single by a twenty-two-year-old singer-songwriter from Long Island named Dinah McCombs.

Standing in the vocal-booth in the New York studio, she looked across at the younger woman – so lithe and smooth-skinned, so filled with the expectation of imminent success – and felt a maternal stirring of fear for her, and the hope that she would not make the same mistakes Cass had made. But of course, she reminded herself, Dinah would make them – or she would find others of her own.

She missed Ivor, sometimes, in those early years of separation: yes, that Cass couldn't deny.

There was a film she played, sent spooling across the blank screen of her closed eyes, when she was sleepless in the night, and the house was creaking and shifting around her. The man she had seen for the first time in the garden at Atterley, his hair falling across his face as he sang. The sudden touch of his hand on her chin; the memory of that, and of all the other ways he had touched her – tenderly, hungrily, awakening in her reserves of sensation, of pure feeling, to which she had never before had access. The sure, solid, beloved presence of him, beside her in the van on all those endless motorway journeys; and on stage, carrying, with her, the weight of their music: its layers and rhythms, its restless ebb and flow. There had been all this between them, and so much more, for so long: and she cried for it, those nights, and cried for how quickly, how irrevocably, it had all slipped away.

But by day, she knew that Ivor was lost to her, to both of them. His drinking had worsened since she had left: she knew it, because he telephoned Home Farm, woozily issuing his bitter recriminations; and because, many times over the months it had taken to settle the divorce, he had driven over to the house to stand shrieking, blind-drunk, at the gates.

How Cass hated him then: how she hated seeing Anna turn to her, furious not with her father but with *her*, saying, 'Why won't you just let Dad *in*?'

And then that dreadful encounter in the Royal Oak. Ivor had waited for Cass and Anna outside the pub in his Mercedes, and driven slowly beside them along the High Street, alternating between abuse and assurances that he missed them, that there would be no more women, that Cass should throw over this whole divorce idea and come home.

By the time they had reached Home Farm, and her father had finally slunk away, Anna had been shaking. 'Why *can't* we go home with Dad, Mum? I want to go home.'

Cass, drawing her arm around her daughter's shoulders, had been unable to keep the frustration from her voice. 'This is your home, Anna. For God's sake, can't you see I'm doing the best I can?'

Her solicitor, eventually, had put a stop to it, obtaining an injunction from the county court to prevent Ivor from harassing Cass, or coming within a mile of Home Farm until the terms of the divorce had been settled. Ivor was to maintain contact with Anna, but on the understanding that he limit his consumption of alcohol and illicit substances.

Rothermere was sold as part of the divorce settlement. Ivor bought a house on Hampstead Grove, close to the heath, and it was to London that Cass had to dispatch her daughter every other weekend, buttoning her into her coat with a bright, 'Have fun, darling,' and then watching the chauffeured car slink out along the drive, then disappear.

She always quizzed Anna carefully on her return, but her daughter would say little of the visits other than, 'Dad's house is *massive*, Mum.' Or, 'We got a puppy! He's called Ziggy. Dad says he's my dog, really, and I can look after him whenever I'm there.' And then, after a few months, 'There's a woman living at Dad's house now. She's called Jenna. She's all right, I guess.'

Yes, Cass watched her daughter for signs of damage, and believed – hoped – that those she could see went no deeper than the surface. There were still those moments of occlusion, of withdrawal, when Anna seemed to turn in on herself – but that was natural, wasn't it, in an only child, and one who had seen what she had seen?

*

321

Anna no longer accompanied Cass on tour. It was important, they all agreed, that she should have consistency in her schooling, and come to know Home Farm as just that: home.

In December 1988, Alberte returned to Denmark, having broken off her engagement to Mark. So Kim and Cass employed a new nanny, Juana – a good-natured twenty-five-year-old from Toledo, with a twin passion for Real Madrid and the Cocteau Twins. Juana would look after Anna when Cass was away, and Alan and the booking agent would ensure that each tour lasted no longer than two weeks.

Cass was aware, each time she returned home – exhausted, thinking only of her daughter, of how desperate she was to hold her in her arms – of a slight awkwardness between them. Anna would greet her a little stiffly, not quite returning her embrace; and she'd give only brief, curt responses to Cass's enquiries about school, homework, Juana, the weekends with Ivor and his latest girlfriend.

It would be a couple of hours, at least, before Anna relaxed, and Cass could feel their old intimacy returning. The two of them, curled up together on the sofa, Anna's head lolling back against the curve of her mother's arm. Cass reading aloud to her – *The L-Shaped Room*; *A Stitch in Time*; the Chalet School novels – as Francis had once, all those years ago, read to her. It was as if, each time she left, Anna wasn't fully assured of the fact that her mother would be coming back. But Cass did come back. She was not Margaret. She would always come back.

Anna was not at all musical, despite those early indications to the contrary: that babbling soundtrack she had maintained, almost without respite, through her early years; that first word – *sing!* – uttered into the Fairlight CMI. And she did not, as she grew older, display a great deal of interest in her parents' music. She seemed to take it for granted, as a thing that would always be there, regular and predictable as the rising and setting of the sun.

Her fascination lay, instead, with art. Drawing, at first – she filled sketchbook after sketchbook – and then, as soon as she was old enough to manipulate a brush with sufficient skill, creating abstract images in splashes and daubs of acrylic paint.

In the autumn of 1989, Cass had the attic room adjacent to Anna's bedroom turned into an art room, the small window replaced with a sheet of glass that, in the mornings, admitted shimmering shafts of sun. At weekends, when Cass was home, they would spend hours there together, lost in concentration, Cass's larger easel placed next to Anna's smaller one; the radio playing the Happy Mondays and Sinéad O'Connor and 'Love Shack' by the B-52s, to which they both loved to dance, whirling and laughing until they collapsed on the floor in an exhausted muddle of limbs.

In the early months of 1990, Cass began planning her music studio. Anna was fascinated by the drawings she made, carefully measured on graph paper, as precise and meticulous as the blueprints that had once hung on the walls of John's study at Atterley.

John had died, with dreadful suddenness, from a heart attack the year before, and Cass thought of her uncle – his kindness; his absolute devotion to Lily, and to Cass herself – as she produced her plans.

The architect Cass employed was the new partner in John's practice, and about her own age. (Forty! Incredible, really, that she had reached it.) His name was Luke Bennett: a serious-minded man in a black polo neck and jeans, and heavy square-framed glasses that would once have been disdained as unfashionable, but were now, Cass understood, the mark of a certain kind of intellectual.

He looked, she thought, rather like Elvis Costello, though Luke was a jazz fan, and one – she could tell, though he was polite enough to conceal it – who knew little of her music, but a good deal of how much she had meant to John, and how much he had meant to her.

As the building project was nearing completion – the glass-roofed studio looming above the garden like some sleek, space-age machine – Luke Bennett asked her out to dinner. He did so diffidently, casually, so that Cass needed a few seconds to understand his meaning.

'Of course,' Luke added quickly, his clear blue eyes shifting behind his glasses, 'it's no problem at all if you'd rather not.'

'It's not that I wouldn't like to.' He squared his shoulders, anticipating her rejection. 'I really have enjoyed working with you. But I . . .'

What was she to say? How was she to explain that it was as if that part of her life, that whole section of herself, had shut down the night she had packed Anna and their suitcases into the MG and left Rothermere, left Ivor, behind? It was just Cass and Anna, now, and the few intimates with whom she had surrounded them; and that, for now, was how it must remain.

But Luke made it easy for her, in the end.

'So sorry. It was presumptuous of me. I really shouldn't have asked.'

'No,' she said. 'I'm glad you did.'

Those weekend afternoons in the attic art room, before their neighbouring easels, music playing from the radio and the soft patter of rain falling on the roof.

Weekday evenings, exultant in their mundanity. Anna home from school, or wet-haired and aching after an away-match with her hockey team. (She was athletic in a way Cass had never been.) Drinking warm Ribena at the kitchen counter while Juana taught her rudimentary scraps of Spanish, and Cass moved around them, stove to worktop, preparing some new recipe from the cookbook Kim had given her, and through which she was, slowly and methodically, working her amateurish way.

The nights when Anna couldn't sleep, and would appear, wrapped in her towelling dressing-gown, her feet comically over-sized in her fleece-lined Snoopy slippers, at the control-room door, while Cass and Kit and Graham and whichever producer they were working with crowded around the console, smoking, listening back to the day's new mix. Cass would open the door to her daughter, draw her in, and hold her close; her breath lifting loose strands of Anna's long hair as they sat together on the sofa, the girl's eyes gradually drawing shut, undisturbed by the music pouring out from the monitors.

Those annual holidays on Mull, beached at the very limit of the land. Ocean before them, moorland behind them; Cass, Kim, Bill, Alan and Rachel perched on deckchairs with glasses of wine as the children wheeled and screeched and ran, matching the stuttering trajectory of the gulls.

And yes, reaching further back, to the music room in the Muswell Hill flat, where Cass and Ivor (Cass could almost allow herself now to think of things as they had once been, rather than as they had become) had lost whole mornings to the pains-taking elaboration of a new melody, a rhythm, a teasing, elusive skein of song.

Those summer parties at Atterley: Cass drawn from her bed by the drifting strains of jazz rising up to her open window, and the people laughing and chattering on the lawn below.

And, back beyond those memories, to the afternoons at Irene's house across the common, with its comfortable familial chaos, and the boyish clamour of Irene's brothers, and Alice gently guiding Cass's hands to the keys of the piano, black on white, smooth as the iridescent undersides of shells: their attraction, as yet, unfathomable to Cass, but calling her, calling, calling.

All this Cass was thinking of with the song that she would, eventually, give the title 'Home'. She had intended, at first, to keep it for herself, and for Anna. It would be a gift (among others, of course) for Anna's twelfth birthday: a celebration of the safe berth that Cass had, despite it all, managed to find for them.

But Iain Urquhart and the label had bigger ideas. A Christmas single, the proceeds going to homelessness charities. Guest spots from other stars.

Cass was unsure at first. She had never been part of such a thing before; she and Ivor had lent their financial support, quietly, to Live Aid, but had preferred not to join the throng on stage at Wembley. But Alan, as always, was pragmatic.

'What if,' he said, 'we ensured we kept ultimate control – chose the producer, held the sessions here? It would raise your profile for the next album, and' – he looked a little sheepish – 'raise a lot of money for charity, of course.'

And so the recording went ahead, at Home Farm – five shiny cars parked on the gravel drive, the studio crowded, swarming with publicists and managers and personal assistants and, beyond the gates, the inevitable paparazzi. The project was meant to be kept under wraps, but someone along the chain had let something slip; a tabloid newspaper chartered a helicopter that flew low over the studio at regular intervals, requiring several of the early sessions to be scrapped.

At the end of it all, a party: a marquee on the back lawn; champagne and canapés. (The papers would have a field day with that – 'Stars sip champagne while lecturing the rest of us about homelessness.')

Anna and Tasha standing together in vintage prom gowns and denim jackets: tall and long-necked, awkward as cygnets still carrying the downy plumage of babyhood. Blushing deeply as a pair of boys – somebody's sons, Cass presumed – approached them with that brave, vulnerable adolescent swagger.

How clear that moment is in Cass's memory now. She'd been standing in the lee of the studio, smoking a cigarette, taking a moment alone. Her daughter's face had been lit by the kitchen's electric glow, and by the flickering torches Kim had placed around the garden.

Looking up at the boys as they came closer – Anna's expression shy, embarrassed; not coquettish, but intrigued, and wishing to intrigue. Nudging Tasha (already so like her mother, with those slender, coltish looks that had already invited the attention of three modelling agencies). Meeting the eyes of the taller boy – the one Cass could see was the better-looking – for a brief second, and then gazing down at the ground, a small smile lifting the corners of her lips.

Anna had seemed so alive, in that moment – so full of youth, and happiness, and health – that it seemed impossible that it would not always be so; that Cass, in the space of just a few years, would be forced to watch her daughter shrink before her eyes, inch by inch, pound by pound, as all that vivacity, that lightness, was gradually worn away.

It had been so good, during the 'Home' sessions, to see Tom Arnold again.

Fifty years old – a short, tanned, gym-toned man with a platinum Rolex and a flawless set of too-bright teeth. But still the man who had, all those years ago outside Jake's cabin in Laurel Canyon, leant down to kiss her, and had never blamed her for gently turning her face away.

Tom was recently divorced, and Cass sensed the renewal of his interest in her from the moment he arrived at Home Farm – an interest that ran deeper than the platonic friendship that they had maintained over the years. She had kept her distance, offered him no encouragement, though she had, it was true, found herself drawn to him, and returned, in the days after his departure, to thinking of him, picturing the outline of his face.

And then, a week or so after the party, he had telephoned, asked whether he might take her out to dinner.

'I'm not sure, Tom,' she said quickly. 'I don't know if that's a good idea.'

He was gentle, amused. 'Take my number at the Dorchester,' he said. 'Call me back. But I'm flying home tomorrow. Just so you know.'

'Go,' Kim said when Cass went through to find her in the office. 'Juana can stay with Anna, and I'll look in on her in the morning. Just go.'

So she went. She showered, dressed carefully in cropped black trousers, a loose shirt in dark green silk that contrasted flatteringly with her eyes. From the drawer of her dressing-table, she took out a bottle of Chanel No. 5 and sprayed a little scent onto her neck, wrists and in the narrow cleft between her breasts.

'Where are you going, Mum?' Anna asked when she went in to kiss her goodbye. 'Why are you all dressed up?'

'Just out for dinner with Tom,' Cass said. 'You don't mind, do you?'

Anna shrugged. Looking down at her – her lovely thirteen-year-old girl, sprawled on her bed in jogging bottoms and an oversized T-shirt – Cass had almost changed her mind. And then she thought of Tom, dining alone in the hotel restaurant, and of how long it had been since she had felt the touch of a man's hand. A man with whom there was no fractious history, no simmering resentment. It wasn't wrong, was it, to crave the warmth of another's body?

'I won't be late, darling,' she said.

'Whatever,' Anna said, and turned away.

It was different between Tom and her that night, as Cass had known it would be.

She had been alone with him plenty of times: on their first American tour; during the sessions at Home Farm. But they had never been alone like this, with a long evening stretching before them, and neither of them bothering to hide their under-standing of where it might lead.

They ate, they talked, they drank two very good bottles of Château Margaux. Cass talked about Anna, and a concert she'd been asked to play at the Festival Hall, and her concerns for Lily, growing increasingly frail since John's death. Tom talked about his next album, and (briefly and without bitterness) his ex-wife, and their decision not to have children.

'I do admire you, Cass, you know,' he said over coffee. 'I do admire how you've managed to raise such a gorgeous girl and still keep the music going.'

She brushed the compliment away. 'Don't admire me,' she said. 'I've made enough mistakes to last a lifetime. It was . . . bad, with Ivor, when Anna was younger. About as bad as it could get.'

'But it's over now. Long over.'

'Yes,' she said. 'It's over.'

Cass had thought, since having Anna, that it would be impossible ever to forget her existence, even for a second; but she did that night, upstairs in Tom Arnold's room at the Dorchester. There was only his body, and hers, and the rhythm they made together: slow at first, controlled; then faster, looser, hungrier.

When, at last, they lay still – sated, sweat-soaked, breathing hard and deep – she laughed, and said, 'My God, Tom. My God.'

'Nope,' he said, and drew a finger along the length of her arm. 'Just a regular middle-aged man.'

They made no promises, no plans to meet again, but she would carry the memory of that night with her for a long time. The shape of Tom's body under the thick white hotel sheets. The taste of his mouth. The sounds she had made as she came – unconscious, primitive, atonal. The blur of movement and breath and noise and then, finally, stillness.

*

329

Cass would see both her mother and her aunt Lily for the last time at Home Farm.

In the years since Cass had left Rothermere, walked out on the sorry mess her marriage had become, her mother had actually managed to surprise her. In those first raw days after Cass had left Rothermere with Anna, Margaret had obtained Johnny's number, telephoned, and insisted that she fly to London at once.

'Len and I have enough saved up for the flight,' she said. 'Let me do this for you, Cass. I know I've made mistakes. I know I haven't always been there for you. Let me be there for you now.'

Cass had felt her eyes fill with tears, and realised in that moment that she had forgiven Margaret: that she simply had no more use for all that anger.

'Thank you, Mum. I appreciate the offer. I really do. But we're all right. We will be, anyway. It's the right thing to do. We're staying with my friend Johnny for now. But we will find a place of our own.'

And so Margaret hadn't flown over – but Cass had taken Anna to visit her in Toronto, and since then there had been regular phone calls, letters, gifts. And then, one day early in the autumn of 1993, Cass had resolved to call her mother – to invite her, Len and Josephine to spend Christmas at Home Farm. She would invite Lily, too. She would ask them all to forget their differences. She would present it as a chance for Anna to have her family, such as it was, around her – albeit without her father, of course. But surely this was something worth doing. Something to remind Anna that it was possible to repair even those relationships that had been fractured for so long.

Josephine hadn't been able to make the trip – she was married now, with two children aged five and three – but the others had agreed to come.

That Christmas hadn't quite turned out as Cass had imagined it. Margaret and Lily had been frosty with one another – Lily, at seventy-seven, had become a thin, restless chain-smoker with a sharp tongue, all of her old energy and lightness occluded by her grief. Anna had had an argument with Tasha on Christmas Eve – some sort of altercation about a boy, from what Cass could gather – and Len Steadman had spent most of the visit asking Cass, exhaustively, how much everything in the house had cost. But for Christmas dinner – the dinner Kim had helped Cass prepare in advance, leaving her extensive notes about how to bring it all to the table on the day – they had all been together, raising their glasses, filling the Home Farm dining-room with light and noise. And Cass had looked around them, from face to face, and raised a toast to absent friends.

And then, just three weeks after she and Len had flown home, Margaret had telephoned. Breast cancer, she said, diagnosed at a late stage, with a rapid deterioration. Yes, she'd known for a while, but she hadn't said anything because she didn't want to spoil Christmas; and she, too, had wished to escape the shadow of her diagnosis, if only for a few weeks.

A short time later, Cass had flown over with Anna to Toronto to see her mother, and found that, instead, they were attending her funeral: a hundred or so people in a suburban church. A finger buffet afterwards at the house with the white veranda. Embracing Josephine in the garden; hearing the whispered voices of the other mourners. *That's Cass Wheeler, you know, the singer, the girl Margaret left behind in London. And that must be her daughter.*

And then, Lily, just four weeks later. A stroke sustained quite suddenly in her bedroom that had caused her to fall and hit her head. She had not been found until the morning.

Why, Cass asked herself so many times, had she gone along with Lily's insistence on staying on alone at Atterley, instead of bringing her to live with them at Home Farm?

She was haunted by the idea that, had she only telephoned that day – gone to see Lily, even – she might have been able to raise the alarm. Something, surely, might have been done for her.

Instead, again, she had failed; and the knowledge of that failure settled over her, and would not shift.

She remembers an afternoon in 1994 – a weekday, it must have been, in spring. The headmistress's office at Anna's school: beige paint, heavy curtains, an insipid watercolour of the school buildings above the fireplace.

'Ms Wheeler. May I ask whether I have your full attention?'

What was her name again? Mrs Baker. Mary. A plain name for a plain woman: stout, thick-waisted, grey hair cut unflatteringly short, a small silver chain nestled beneath the high neckline of her blouse. A cross on that chain, perhaps: this was a Church of England school, after all. Or half a silver heart, the other half kept by Mr Baker in an embossed leather box. Was he the sort of man to give his wife such a gift? Cass had met him only once, at the school founders' day charity raffle. A short, moleish man, with a grating, nasal voice.

'Ms *Wheeler*.' Impatient now, and not bothering to conceal it. Was it Cass the woman so disliked – her fame; her residual glamour; the fact that she had never, to Mary Baker's mind, played by the rules – or did she dislike all the parents equally?

No, there must be some she liked. Claire Harris, perhaps – the mother of that girl in Anna's form group whom Anna dismissed as a 'dweeb'. Even Cass could see she was irritating, with her perfectly ironed uniform and matching pair of red-scrunchied plaits – plaits! At fourteen! What was her mother thinking of? Claire Harris had baked cakes for the raffle, as Cass recalled. A Victoria sponge and a chocolate cake, their icing slowly curling inside Tupperware.

Reluctantly, Cass lifted her eyes from the carpet and returned them to Mary Baker's round, fleshy face. She was nothing like her own headmistress, Mrs Di Angelis, had been, with her glamorous red beehive and green silk shoes. What had become of her? Cass wondered fleetingly. She would be, what, eighty now, if she were still alive?

'Of course you have my attention, Mrs Baker,' Cass said finally.

The headmistress gave a small cough. 'Good. Thank you. So, as I was saying, we are really rather worried about Anna.'

Anna. Cass forced her attention back to the matter at hand. There had been a school trip to Paris. Several members of the class had, apparently, run wild, disappearing from the hotel after hours, when their teachers had specified that their lights must be turned out. They had got *drunk* – had been unable to conceal it from the teachers – and had then repeated the whole sorry affair each night they were away. Anna, it appeared, had been the ringleader, with Tasha following on behind.

And what was worse – here Mary Baker fixed her with a basilisk stare – there had been a most unpleasant incident. A girl, Polly O'Reilly – a quiet, studious, religious girl – had been *peer-pressured* into consuming half a bottle of vodka. She had been violently sick, later, in the basin of the hotel room she was sharing with Anna. And Anna, rather than helping her, had grabbed her by the shoulders and slapped Polly's face.

('She just wouldn't stop, Mum,' Anna had said at home, offering her own account. 'It was all over the floor. I mean, what was I meant to *do*?')

'I understand, Ms Wheeler, that there have been difficulties at home,' Mary Baker said.

'Difficulties?'

The headmistress's lips tightened. 'Yes. Your divorce. The . . . *tricky* relationship she has with Mr Tait. The death of her grandmother.'

'And her great-aunt,' Cass said.

'Indeed.' A pause. 'Well, that's a great deal for a young girl to cope with, isn't it?'

Yes. There had been *difficulties*. A fog had seemed to roll in over Cass, between her mother's funeral and Lily's. A blunting of perception, a distancing; a sense that nothing that was happening to her was quite real. She had been unable to write; hadn't written anything new at all, come to think of it, for the last three months. She was spending a lot of time just sitting, quietly, in the small, comfortable room in her studio that she had come to call the listening-room. It was equipped with a fridge, a kettle and a cafetière, and a state-of-the-art audio system with CD-player, cassette deck, turntable. She would sit there, drinking coffee, and somehow the time just seemed to slip by.

Even Anna seemed unable to reach her. Since the two funerals, Cass had been observing her daughter remotely, as if through a thick pane of opaque glass. No wonder, then, that Anna felt free to do whatever she liked. And as for Ivor – well, *tricky* was the least of it. He had stopped drinking, it was true, but his other habits were proving harder to break: there was a different woman at the house every weekend, from what she could make out.

Aloud, she said, 'I appreciate your raising this with me, Mrs Baker. I'll talk to Anna, set some boundaries. You're right – there has been a lot going on at home.'

The headmistress sat back in her chair. 'Well,' she said, 'I suggest you talk to your daughter sooner rather than later. I've seriously considered suspending her, but in the circumstances, I am going to give her the benefit of the doubt. Should anything like this happen again' – a meaningful flash of flinty, grey-blue eyes – 'I shall not be so lenient, Ms Wheeler.'

At home that evening, Cass found Anna, still in her uniform – her shirt untucked, her skirt hoisted up in a familiar way that, despite herself, made Cass smile – sprawled on the sofa before the television.

Looking up at her mother, Anna didn't return the smile, but she moved her feet a few inches to the right, to make room for her, and together they watched the remaining minutes of *Neighbours*: white-toothed Australians shouting at each other across manicured suburban lawns. Cass knew better than to interrupt. But as the credits rolled, she placed an arm around her daughter, drew her closer, and Anna, still pliable, still affectionate, did not resist.

'You are all right, aren't you, darling?' Cass said into her daughter's hair. 'You would tell me if you weren't?'

'Of course I would, Mum,' Anna said, as the final credits were replaced by the sombre bell-toll of the *Six O'Clock News*. Cass said no more, then, than, 'I love you,' and went through to the kitchen to see what she might make for dinner.

Why had she not done more, asked more, forced Anna to talk? Cowardice, she thinks now. Cowardice, and that peculiar, deadening feeling of remoteness. That belief – instilled in childhood, and so difficult to shift – that if a thing was not talked about, then it did not, could not, truly exist.

Cass had never wanted Anna to go on Ivor's tour.

She had been categorical, in fact, in her refusal. An argument had inevitably ensued – the worst she and her daughter had ever had – followed by a terrible silence, Anna steadfast in her decision to ignore her mother for as long as it took to persuade her to change her mind. She was stubborn, after all: she was her mother's daughter.

Fifteen years old: long blonde hair hanging to just below her shoulder blades; her mother's brown eyes, her father's sharply angled face. A wardrobe filled with blush-coloured, lace-edged under-slips that she wore tucked into short woollen skirts. (Cornelia, long since departed this earth, would have been appalled.) Men's plaid work shirts, thick black tights and purple Doc Martens threaded with multicoloured laces.

'Grunge,' they called it, this artfully dishevelled style. When its high priest, Kurt Cobain, had been found dead the year before, Anna and Tasha had mounted a candlelit vigil in the living-room at Home Farm: all the lamps turned out, and night-lights guttering in jars, and Nirvana's scratchy, restless music playing on repeat into the small hours.

Cass, too, had been saddened, as she was each time one of her own kind fell: Hendrix, Morrison, Moon, Joplin, Denny, Mercury. It seemed to her, in her more melancholy moods, that her greatest achievement lay not in the music she had written but in simply managing to remain alive to write it – though not, admittedly, with the same ease with which she had once done so. It would be another three years before she would release her next album, *Silver and Gold*.

Ivor, however, had made a new record, a collection of jazz standards reconfigured with a smoky, porch-blues feel. He was to tour America: Brooklyn, Nashville, Seattle, San Francisco. No buses: first-class flights between each city, and bookings in good hotels. Five weeks from late July, coinciding, as it happened, with Anna's summer holiday.

'*Kim* said Tasha can go,' Anna told her mother.

This was soon proved to be incorrect. Tasha had been offered her first modelling assignment, in New York; the girls might fly over together, Kim had said, but Tasha would not be able to join Anna on the tour.

'Anyway,' Kim said, 'I'm not sure I'd let Tasha go, even if she were free. Not without one of us there to keep an eye on her.'

'No,' Cass agreed. 'But hell hath no fury like a fifteen-year-old girl scorned.'

Anna's silence lasted two weeks: two weeks during which she said not a single word to her mother, but regarded her, each time she spoke, with a sullen, dark-eyed glare.

Cass knew she ought to hold firm, but she could not bear it: instead she found herself, one bright May morning when Anna

336

was at school, stepping into her MG and driving to Hampstead. She parked on a side street not far from Ivor's house; at his gates, she announced herself at the intercom, then walked up the pristine sweep of weedless drive.

It was not the first time she had seen the house: there had been a party here, six months before, to celebrate the first anniversary of Ivor's sobriety. Everybody had been invited – Alan, Kim, Graham and Kit, and all the old crew: Kate, Serena, Bob. Not Hugh: he was not yet on the wagon, and Ivor, resolved to keep his distance, had replaced him with another drummer.

'I think it's a good idea,' he'd told Cass over the telephone, 'to get everyone together and ask forgiveness of you all. Step nine: make direct amends to the people you have harmed.'

'I'm not sure,' Cass had replied after a moment, 'that you're meant to do that to everyone at once.'

But she'd gone to the party, all the same. As Ivor had made his speech – his hair longer, his beard newly trimmed, his face still hatefully free of wrinkles – she had felt a wave of shame wash through her; for if Ivor was asking forgiveness, she thought, then surely she ought to be doing the same.

Now, on that fresh, summery morning, it was Leah who answered the door. Leah, Ivor's latest live-in girlfriend – twenty-two years old (half Cass's age, she acknowledged with a shiver), with a fine, elfin face, and endless legs bare beneath her cut-off denim shorts. The dog, Ziggy – long since grown beyond a puppy – wheeled and growled at her heels. Leah leant down, petted him, said, 'Oh, hi, Cass. Well, I guess you'll want to come in.'

They drank coffee together, she and Ivor (Leah did, at least, have the tact to make herself scarce) in his spotless white kitchen, with its glass pendant lights and leather barstools and cavernous American fridge.

'I'll look after Anna, Cassie,' Ivor said. 'I'd never let anything happen to her. You know that. She means everything to me.'

Did she? Cass had had enough cause to doubt it. His drinking – one party, one year of sobriety, was not enough to erase those ugly years. Those women – an endless stream of them, models and dancers and waitresses and yoga instructors – moving into his home in quick succession, Ivor not thinking of the impact this would have on Anna. His daughter, believing herself replaced in her father's heart by a shifting series of women, most of them only a few years older than Anna herself. Any fool could see that she longed for her father's attention, for his love. Any fool, it would seem, apart from Ivor.

But looking at him now, clean-shirted, barefoot, drinking cappuccino in his expensive kitchen, Cass realised that she had no choice but to believe him. Anna would not forgive her if Cass didn't let her go. She would make her mother the villain, as she had done so many times, even when it was Ivor – drunk, forgetful, wrapped up in a new girlfriend – who had let her down.

'All right,' she said. 'I can see I've got no option. But you're to make sure she calls me every day. And we'll get someone along to watch her – a chaperone. You'll be busy, after all.'

Anna was too excited about her mother's change of heart to put up a fight about the chaperone.

Kim found a girl called Rosie: twenty-one, in her final year studying French at Bristol University. She was the daughter of a sound engineer who'd once worked with Bill at Abbey Road; there wasn't time to meet her, but Cass conducted a brief interview over the phone, and Rosie seemed sensible enough. She worked part-time in the university library, and was planning to train as a teacher after graduation.

'How cool to be a chaperone,' Rosie said. 'It's like something out of Jane Austen.'

'Yes,' Cass replied drily. 'But a major US tour is hardly a restorative excursion to Bath.'

'No.' Rosie coughed, turning serious. 'Of course not. Please don't worry, Ms Wheeler. I won't let Anna out of my sight.'

And so, soon after the school broke up, Anna was off – packing and repacking her things, spending hours on the phone with Tasha, poring over her new Lonely Planet guide to the USA.

'Thanks, Mum,' she said as Cass embraced her, fiercely, at the door. 'Thanks for letting me go.'

It was a warm summer, that year. Cass remembers long, easy days on the terrace at Home Farm, windows thrown open, reading *Captain Corelli's Mandolin*. She had resolved to take some time off to rest, to see if she could throw off that enervating feeling of remoteness, and maybe even find the energy to paint or write.

An evening at the theatre with Kate and her new boyfriend – a set designer, much younger than Kate, named Troy McCabe. Lunch in Kingston with Irene. (They had managed, if only sporadically, to keep in touch.) A barbecue at Kim and Bill's new place in Oxted. An enquiry from a publisher, conveyed by Alan, as to whether Cass had ever considered writing a memoir: it was not the first such enquiry she had received, but had been the first to root itself in her mind and set her wondering.

And then, the phone call, rousing her from sleep. The private line, known only by a few. 'Hello?'

A small, strained whimper of a voice. 'Mum. I want to come home.' Breaking, swallowed by a sob. 'Can you book me a flight, please? I want to come home *now*.'

She sprang immediately into action, had the flight booked within the hour. Called Ivor but was unable to reach him – found herself talking to his manager, Charlie, instead.

There had been an incident, Charlie said. Ivor and Anna had had some sort of row after the concert in San Francisco. Anna had run off somewhere with Rosie. They'd had the whole crew out looking for them for hours, and when they'd finally tracked down the girls at a club in Haight-Ashbury, Anna had been almost hysterical, incoherent. Neither she nor Ivor would be drawn on what had gone on between them.

'Well, bloody well *make* them tell you,' Cass snapped down the line.

After a second's crackle and hiss, Charlie's reply came back, 'I hate to tell you this, Cass, but I can't really make them do anything right now. To be frank, I think Anna and Rosie might have taken something. And Ivor's pissed as a newt. He's in a bad way again, Cass. I can't get anything out of him.'

Late that night, Anna's flight landed at Heathrow: Cass drove to meet her, not caring whether she was observed. Shuffling through the arrivals gate, her daughter seemed so small, so thin: a child, really, her skin carrying a sickly, greenish hue. She was wearing a hooded sweatshirt Cass didn't recognise (NYC, NY, read the white letters emblazoned across her chest) and tracksuit bottoms. Her hair, tugged into a low ponytail, looked greasy and unwashed.

There in the arrivals hall, they embraced.

'Anna darling,' Cass said into Anna's neck – breathing in that particular smell that was her daughter's, and hers alone. 'What on earth happened?'

But Anna shook her head; in the car on the way home, she was silent, too, her eyes closing, diving immediately into sleep. On the gravelled drive at Home Farm, she woke suddenly, confused. Cass, sitting beside her, said, 'Anna. Really. Please tell me what happened, before we go inside. What is this all about?'

A long silence followed. It was very late now, and the darkness absolute.

'Dad's drinking again,' Anna said eventually, her voice curiously blank, emotionless. 'It started in New York – he had a crap review and he went off on one. Nobody could find him. I kept telling him he should stop drinking – reminding him about AA, and his sponsor and everything, and what he'd told us at that party. That he was sorry.'

She drew a breath. Cass, beside her, resisted the desire to take her daughter in her arms. 'And yesterday in San Francisco, he just lost it with me. He started saying all these crazy things.'

'What things?'

'That I was a mistake. That you never wanted me. That you always cared more about your music than about him, or me. That you thought having a child would destroy your career.'

A lead weight, falling with a thud. Cass reached across for Anna's hand, but her daughter snatched it away.

'Well?' she said, turning to her mother, her brown eyes fierce. 'Is it true?'

'Of *course* not, Anna. You know how it is when your dad's been drinking. He says things he doesn't mean, just to hurt people.'

Anna shook her head. 'No. I've been thinking about it all the way back, on the plane. I did destroy things for you, didn't I? For both of you. You were fine together until I came along. And *you* were . . . well, so successful. Famous. *Everyone* knew your name. And what are you now?'

'A mother,' Cass said. '*Your* mother. And a musician. Both. And we were *not* fine until you came along. We were always wrong together, Ivor and me. Your great-aunt Lily always knew it, and I know it now. But I don't regret a single moment of that relationship, because it brought me you.'

But Anna wasn't listening; her face, staring out through the windscreen, wore the stricken expression of a frightened child.

'You used to hit him. I remember. I saw you hit him, and I was afraid that one day you'd hit me, too.'

A gasp, welling up from deep within Cass's throat. A small, pitiful voice – surely not her own? – saying, 'It wasn't just me, Anna, was it, remember? Your dad used to hit me, too.'

'You think that makes it better?' Snarling, Anna's face contorted, strange. 'You think that makes it all right? For fuck's sake, Mum. I hate him. And I hate you, too. I wish you'd never

341

had me. You should have had me aborted, like you must have wanted to.'

Anna opened the car door, marched across the gravel to the front porch. The security light snapped on, and Cass stayed where she was, watching the heavy black door slam behind her daughter as she went inside. She closed her eyes; she was dizzy, her breath coming in fast, tight gasps.

The girl was exhausted, overwrought: she'd let her go upstairs to bed, leave her to sleep it off. With this, Cass reassured herself, steadied her breathing. But she knew then, even as she thought it, that this would not be enough; that something, somewhere along the way, had been broken, and she might never find a way to put it back together.

6.15 p.m.

There are some songs, Cass thinks, sitting silently for a moment on the sofa in the listening-room, that are not so much written as transcribed; that obey no will but their own, and refuse to conform to any shape other than the form in which they arrive.

This is what she has struggled, over the years, to explain to those who have asked her why she is so committed to cataloguing her own life in song, to weaving music from the raw stuff of her own experience. She has often sensed, in this question, an implicit criticism, as if this makes her a lower kind of artist: a hack, grubbing in the dirt, unable to fully inhabit the vivid landscape of the imagination.

Don Collins, for one, had been good at making her feel that way.

'Isn't it all a bit . . . well, obvious?' he'd asked her once, in the early years. 'We've got Bowie coming up with Ziggy Stardust – bringing performance art to music, turning pop into something really substantial. And there you are, writing about babies and break-ups. It's just whimsy, isn't it? Self-indulgent whimsy?'

She had smiled at him: already she was learning, with Collins, to conceal her anger beneath a smile. 'You're probably right, Don. Perhaps it is. But I don't have a choice, you see. I don't *decide* what my songs will be about. They arrive with that decision already made.'

He had looked at her, head on one side, a smirk drawing his mouth into a narrow arc. It had been clear that he'd had no idea what she was talking about: 'airy-fairy hippy-dippy nonsense' he'd called it in the article. And she has wondered, over the years, whether Ivor also felt the same way. His own lyrics have

343

always had a remote, emotionless quality to them, as if he were observing life from a safe distance.

But Larry understood it immediately. Larry knows what it is to lose oneself for hours – days, even – in the act of creation; and to only understand, when the mind and body are finally calm once more, what it is that has been created. What, in that act, the artist is trying to make sense of, even though no sense can ever truly be made of this dizzying, maddening, impossible, beautiful life; and, of course, of its culmination, its crescendo and its inevitable loss.

Cass stands, moves over to the door. There is Otis, again, sitting on the terrace, facing her, his tail tucked around his front paws.

She slides open the door, and the cat draws himself up onto his feet, steps unhurriedly into the room; traces a sinuous circle around her legs, the tip of his tail curling into a question mark. The low vibrato of a purr, rising up from his throat. Hungry not for food but for company. She picks him up, buries her face, for a moment, in his fur. He smells of grass and earth and, faintly, of the ripe musk of fox: he must have found their den, somewhere in the deeper recesses of the garden.

The house, she observes through the open door, is quiet now. Faintly, she hears Kim's laugh floating across the garden, and Alan's deep, answering bass.

They'll be standing together in the kitchen: assistant and manager, friends, long-time colleagues. Alan will be admiring Kim's handiwork with the food – her deft marshalling of the caterers, her expert arrangement of drinks, glasses, buckets of ice. Kim will be asking Alan how the masters sound.

In a moment, Kim will excuse herself and go upstairs to the spare room, where her dress (a silken sheath, splashed with a bright, painterly pattern of flowers) is laid out on the bed. She will run the shower in the en suite, dress, apply make-up, spritz

344

herself with mimosa and cardamom, and then sit for a moment in silent meditation before the first of the guests arrive.

Alan, in the meantime, will pour himself a drink – a gin and tonic; thin slice of lemon, three chunks of ice – and offer the same to Callum. And together, in the living-room, the men will sit, waiting for the evening to begin.

Cass, too, must get ready. She is running late, has spent too long chasing the shadows of the past. Her own outfit is waiting for her in her bedroom: a black-and-white printed shirt, a pair of wide-legged black trousers. She must change, arrange her hair, try to make something acceptable of her face.

But there is still one more song to listen to, one more strand of her past she must try to weave into some kind of sense. And it is the most important part: the keystone; the vortex around which everything has whirled for so long. A song that she did not wish to write but which came to her, fully formed, one black endless night, as some songs – the best ones, usually – tend to do.

Yes, she thinks, still holding Otis in her arms, this is probably her best song. And yet it is one that only two people have heard. Herself, of course. And then, just a few months ago – ten years since she had recorded it, sitting alone in her studio in the middle of the night, unable to sleep, finding some kind of solace in the pressure of her hands on the piano keys – Larry.

She had invited him into the listening-room. Had sat with him on this sofa, slid this same cassette into the player, the tape that is sitting on the coffee table now, waiting for her, beneath the discarded sleeves of the other albums she has played over the course of this long, cathartic, necessary day.

Larry had listened carefully, his attention finely attuned to each cadence, each smooth sequence of notes. And then he had turned to her, taken her hand in his, and said, 'Thank you, Cass. Thank you for sharing that with me. I think I can understand it, now. I think I can understand something of what it must have been like.'

She had nodded, and held his hand. It was only when he'd reached out the other hand to meet her face – drawn his long, calloused fingers across her skin with such lightness, such tenderness – that she had realised that her cheeks were damp with tears.

It strikes her now, as she wished it might have struck her in that moment, that she can allow herself to feel that sorrow – the sorrow from which she had shied away for so long, afraid of its power, of its ability to swallow her whole – and no longer feel that it is threatening to break her.

She can, perhaps, miss Anna, mourn her, and still sit with Larry, holding his hand, waiting for whatever might come next.

'Edge of the World'

By Cass Wheeler
Previously unreleased

On the beach
Threw your arms out wide
Closed your eyes against the sun
Turned your face up to the sky
If I could find a way to stay there
One moment in time
Stay behind each other's closed eyes

'This feels like the edge of the world,'
You said,
'The land bleeds into the sea
And the wind blows free.
This feels like the edge of the world,'
You said,
'I am the body of the sea
And my mind is free.'

On the beach
No one but us
Nothing but the wind in its rush
If I could find a way for us back there
One moment in time
Behind each other's closed eyes

'This feels like the edge of the world,'
You said,
'The land bleeds into the sea
And the wind blows free.

This feels like the edge of the world,'
You said.
'My body is the sea
And my mind is free
And my mind is free.'
Oh the sea, the sea, the sea, the sea, the sea, the sea

WRITTEN January 2005
RECORDED January 2005 at Home Farm, Kent

The house was silent, still; the digits on her alarm clock glowed 4:00.

The worst hour, neither night nor morning. A threshold. A blank, featureless place, where not even the birds were singing.

There was music, however, in her mind. A piano picking out a loose series of arpeggios. Bare, unadorned, as the music she and Ivor had made together had once been, all those years ago in the folk clubs, the basements and riverboats. Beer-mats and sticky floors and bearded men nodding sagely into pints of ale. Joe's bar, and Angus Mackinnon staring up at them from his round table at the front. Bob and Serena, and Kate, and poor, sad Paul, who had never, as far as Cass knew, found the courage to call himself a writer. And standing behind them, the faint, spectral outline of Ursula, and all Ivor's other women: shadowy, nameless, indistinct.

But Ivor was not singing with Cass now. It was her own voice she could hear, high and pure as it had been back then: its pitch, by now, in her fifty-fourth year, had commenced its gradual descent towards a lower register.

The lyric was complete, crystalline. Lying sleepless, Cass doubted herself, and wondered whether it belonged to a song she had heard before. These words had the ageless simplicity of the old tunes – 'Scarborough Fair'; 'Mary Hamilton'; 'The Trees They Do Grow High'. And yet she knew that they were hers and Anna's. This song couldn't possibly belong to anyone else, couldn't reflect another's suffering. It was new. It was theirs. It was demanding to be heard.

4:15. Cass rose from her bed, drew her woollen dressing-gown on over her pyjamas, pulled on her slippers. The air was icy, sharp: it had been a long, brutal winter. Downstairs, in the dark hallway, she wrapped herself in her warmest coat. In the kitchen, she turned on the lights, tapped the alarm code into

349

the keypad beside the back door, and stepped out into the night.

Grey shapes loomed freakishly in the darkness, assuming their familiar forms only as she drew closer: the wrought-iron table and chairs, the mahonia bush, the twin olive trees standing sentry in their terracotta pots. The crisp grass crunching underfoot, frost soaking through the soles of her slippers. She hastened her pace to the studio, entered the door-code, and slid her key into the lock.

Through all this, she could still hear the song. Moving around the control room, turning on lamps, flicking switches on the console, the computers, the monitors. She left the live room in darkness, and sat down at the piano.

The black leather stool; the Neumann microphone. The keyboard solid and true beneath her fingers. The pop-shield cocked conspiratorially towards her mouth like the whorl of a lover's ear.

The song, played from beginning to end, as it had asked to be played: no hesitation, no stumbling, no delay.

When the last note died away, Cass sat on silently with her eyes closed, waiting. It wasn't long – fifteen minutes, perhaps, or twenty – before the telephone rang. And then, walking through to the control room to answer it – not rushing or running; her feet steady, sure, as they would not be again for a very long time – she realised that she knew, now, what she had been waiting for.

'Hello?'

A brief, pregnant, endless pause.

'Cass Wheeler?'

Shani. The kind, Kenyan nurse, about Cass's age, who had always, over the last few terrible months, spoken to Cass frankly, neither intimidated by her nor patronisingly dismissive. No apology for calling at this hour: for such an apology, of course, would be obsolete. There was now only one possible apology to make.

Cass said nothing. She didn't trust herself to speak.

'I'm so sorry, Cass,' Shani said.

And then, with a simplicity, a directness, for which Cass would always, in some small way, be grateful, she said, 'It's bad news, I'm afraid. The very worst.'

How to trace back to the beginning, follow the trail back to its source?

That wriggling, perfect baby, opening and closing the tiny buds of her fists. That toddler, with her mop of sandy-blonde curls, and that wordless, tuneless song always on her lips. Propped on the lid of the Steinway as Cass's hands moved over the keys; eyes following those hands, legs swinging, tapping out an ungainly, juddering rhythm on the piano's polished hull. That child, watching wide-eyed from the wings, noise-cancelling headphones pulled down over her ears. Kim beside her, with Tasha, and Cass looking over at them every so often between songs: meeting her daughter's eyes with her own, and smiling, then turning her attention back to her audience.

That eight-year-old, drawn from her bed in the middle of the night to find her mother bleeding, her father white with anger. Bundled sleepily into her mother's car, tucked up in bed in a dim, shadowy house in Spitalfields, a house filled with treasures and secrets. Choosing an attic room in a new house a hundred miles away, not understanding, yet, that her father would not be joining them.

That twelve-year-old, back from a weekend at her father's. *There's a woman living at Dad's house now. She's called Jenna. She's all right, I guess.* Not meeting Cass's eye; chewing at a loose strand on the sleeve of her cardigan. So desperate, of course, for her father to love her; as Ivor did, in his own damaged, distracted and fractured way. That shifting sequence of women – Jenna, Natalie, Kristin, Amy, Leah and who knew how many others. Each one young, showily beautiful, hungry for Ivor's

351

attention, uninterested in the daughter left behind by his failed marriage. How had those weekends in London, in the house on Hampstead Grove, really been for Anna? How hard had Ivor tried to make her see that there was still a place in his life for her? Not hard enough. Not hard enough at all.

That fourteen-year-old, directing her anger outwards. Too easy a victim: Polly O'Reilly, meek-mannered, cowed. Lace-edged under-slips and short skirts; smudged make-up and bottles of Hooch. Kurt Cobain and Courtney Love. Club nights in Soho, Anna and Tasha slipping off to London, each employing the excuse of staying at the other's house: photos in the newspapers, blowing their cover. The calls that came in after that, for Tasha: those modelling agencies, renewing their careful, calculated assaults. Name-calling by the other girls at school. *Show-off. Pisshead. Think you're so great, don't you? Well, you're not. You're a freak. You're a weirdo.* The knowledge of this coming to Cass piecemeal, refracted by a concerned teacher. (Not Mrs Baker this time, thank goodness, but Anna's form tutor, meaning well.)

Are you all right, Anna?

Of course I'm all right, Mum. Why wouldn't I be all right?

That fifteen-year-old, back from her father's American tour, carrying the intolerable burden of his illness – for that, Cass was beginning to force herself to admit, was what they must understand it to be. The terrible things Ivor had said to her resounding in her head, drowning out all other sound. Watching him fall apart, from a distance. A drunken rage caught by cameras in the Holly Bush pub. Police called to Hampstead Grove in the middle of the night. Leah pictured with bruises, cuts. Charges pressed. Their separation. His disgrace.

Ivor's entry, finally, into rehab, splashed again across the tabloid press, laid out, as always, by Sally Jarvis in the village shop. The neighbours' eyes unsubtly averted whenever Anna or Cass passed by. Kind Sheila and Roy, in the Royal Oak, defending them from unquiet tongues. *If you're going to talk like that in here, Sally Jarvis, then I suggest you take yourself off for a drink elsewhere.*

Yes, it was easy to say that it had begun then. Anna's lies; her deceit; her obsession with exercise. Twice-weekly matches with the school hockey team, practices three times a week, and each morning, before school, a run around the Home Farm grounds. The weight falling from her, gradually, until her skin was stretched taut over rib and bone.

Anna had never been overweight, and yet she behaved as if she were, as if she were determined to punish herself for some perceived failing; turned on her mother whenever Cass asked what she'd had to eat that day at school.

Why are you always nagging me, Mum? Why don't you trust me? I'm just being careful, all right. Tasha does the same, and look how skinny she is – why aren't you having a go at her?

Tasha had come to Home Farm with Kim, one afternoon while Anna was at hockey practice, and had asked to speak to Cass privately.

Cass had taken Tasha into her office – slender, beautiful, celebrated Tasha, whose face was now splashed across the covers of magazines. And there, sitting before her, Cass had seen for the first time how different Anna had begun to look from her friend: how unhealthy, how gaunt and hollow-cheeked.

'She's really unwell, Cass,' Tasha had said. 'She'll hate me for telling you this – she might never speak to me again. But she's my best friend. I can't let Anna do this to herself.'

A hard-won visit to a Harley Street clinic; Anna furious, disbelieving. But there, finally, in that wood-panelled room, with tasteful modernist sculptures lining the bookshelves and an original Hockney staring down at them from the wall behind Dr Eleanor Lichtenstein's desk, she had broken down, lowered her defences. Her sudden surrender seemed to take them both – Cass and the doctor – by surprise.

'It's all slipping away from me, Mum,' Anna had said, between fits of sobs. 'I feel like it's all slipping away.' And Cass had held her, and cried with her, and whispered into her hair, 'I'm sorry, my darling. I'm so sorry.'

Tea at Johnny's afterwards – Uncle Johnny, whom Anna loved, and who had taken her in his arms and said, 'Now, now, little thing – whatever have you been doing to yourself?'

A long, damp summer: Cass and Anna, alone at Home Farm, pushing the world away, secure behind those high stone walls. Talking as they had never talked before: not properly, not truly. Talking about Ivor, and his father, Owain, and how deeply Ivor and Cass had once loved each other. Talking about Margaret, and Francis, and Lily and John, and how profoundly they were missed. Talking about music and art, and Cass's old fear – confessed honestly to Anna, for the first time – that she would not have the capacity to be both an artist and a mother.

'But I *am* both, darling, I am,' Cass told her. 'And I wouldn't have missed having you for the world.'

Stroking her daughter's hair; holding her meagre weight as they lay together on the sofa, Anna's head on her mother's lap.

'I know, Mum,' Anna said, and closed her eyes.

A trip to Mull, to the cottage by the sea. Fresh air and small, protein-rich meals, following Dr Lichtenstein's instructions. Anna's recovery coming slowly, inch by inch, pound by pound.

'She's doing very well, Cass,' the doctor said in September, back in her clinic on Harley Street. 'You should be proud of her.'

Looking at her daughter – the sheer, unadulterated beauty of her, the bloom already returning to her face.

'I am so proud of her,' Cass said.

There had been, they all agreed, a slippage, a loss of footing. It happened to so many young women these days (some young men too), and it could have been so much worse. Anna had not missed too much of school: she would sit her GCSEs, study for A-levels in art, English, French (and actually take her examinations, as her mother never had).

'How do you think she's doing now, Cassie?' Ivor asked over the phone. 'Do you think she's all right?'

Cass, sitting in the office in Home Farm, put a hand to her forehead, and sighed. So much to say; so much that could not be said.

'I think so. But we need to be there for her now, Ivor. Both of us. We need to be careful.'

'Careful,' he repeated, as if testing the word.

She pictured him, sitting alone in his big, empty house, and said, 'Yes, Ivor. Careful. We've both made our mistakes. Let's just be careful with her, please.'

Eighteen years old. Still slimmer than she had been before it all began – still cutting her food into small pieces, still running six times a week – but healthy now, the worst of the danger passed.

A boyfriend: Ollie Patterson, who was at the boys' school in Tunbridge Wells and wanted to apply to art college, too.

A tricky moment – Ollie rejected from Central Saint Martin's, where Anna had been offered a place; Anna considering rejecting her own offer, and following him to Sheffield. Anna deciding, finally, that her heart was set on London, and that she and Ollie would make their relationship work at a distance. Johnny offering Anna his attic room, with the tacit understanding, comprehended by them all, that he would keep an eye on her.

How clearly Cass can picture Anna as she'd been the day she left for London: wrapped in Cass's old Afghan coat, packing her CDs, her books, her art materials into boxes. Kim had hired a van: the Polish driver, a man of about their own age, was drinking tea with them in the Home Farm kitchen.

'My wife love your music, when we are young,' he told Cass,

beaming, adding, as if surprised that this should be so, 'You seem very ordinary for famous person.'

Tasha and Anna coming down the stairs together, their differences set aside. Embracing in the hallway: Kim and Cass standing together, a few feet apart, watching them, unable to believe that these young women before them were once their babies, their toddlers, their grinning, screaming children.

Cass stepped forward to embrace her daughter. 'Good luck, darling. Enjoy every moment of it.'

Anna laughed. Such youth, such vivacity in that laugh: the sound of it flooding Cass with relief.

'Mum, I'm only going to London. And I'll be living with Uncle Johnny. You'll probably see me every other weekend.'

'Good,' Cass had said.

Then the driver had come through from the kitchen, and asked whether he should start loading the van. And too soon after that, Anna had climbed into the passenger seat beside him, waved as he turned the key in the ignition; and then the van had spun on its wheels, spitting gravel, and sped off up the drive.

Ivor had been sober again for just over a year.

'No anniversary party, this time,' he said, offering Cass a wry smile. 'That was probably too much. I can see that, now. I was setting myself up for a fall.'

Anna's graduation show. High, bare concrete walls. Chilly electronica thrumming from invisible speakers: the disconcerting realisation that Cass couldn't identify the music, or its author. Angular, bored-looking young men and women dressed in a uniform spectrum of black, white and grey.

Nobody, it seemed, painted any more, including Anna: her own exhibit was a large, wooden-sided cube, swathed in black fabric, inside which a video and sound installation was playing on repeat. There was space inside for only two people at a time,

356

so Cass and Ivor were standing close to the entrance, awaiting their turn.

'Well,' Cass said, 'that's probably sensible, Ivor.'

Ivor Tait at fifty-seven. A tall, lean, loose-knit man, with a thick crop of greyish hair. Face still enviably unlined, his age evident only in a certain loosening of the flesh around the chin and neck. A light sweater of grey merino wool; discreet charcoal jeans; a well-cut black jacket that would, in a more formal age, only ever have been worn with a suit. He fitted in here, might easily have been taken for a lecturer or a mature student, or a critic for one of the more fashionable magazines. But Ivor would never, of course, be taken for anyone other than himself.

'So,' he said. 'How's the album coming along?'

It was not, in all honesty, coming along at all. It wasn't that Cass *couldn't* write, but that what she was writing didn't much interest her. Her new songs seemed insubstantial, somehow: unfinished sketches, lacking the potent urgency that she believed her best work had always contained.

So often, when she sat down at the piano, or placed her guitar on her knee, she found her thoughts wandering to Anna. It was almost a year now, since they'd shared that curry in the Indian restaurant on Brick Lane: Anna had seemed all right – had *insisted* she was all right, and had done all she could to prove it. But it was clear that Johnny's intervention, well intentioned as it had been, had offended her. Anna had spent that summer in London, staying with friends – she hadn't come back to Home Farm once. And then, in late August, she'd informed Johnny that she was moving out, that she'd found a room in a house with friends in Turnpike Lane.

'I can't relax, Uncle Johnny,' she'd told him, 'with you breathing down my neck all the time. You and Mum shouldn't worry about me, you know. I'm fine. I just need to be left alone.'

Now, Cass took a breath, and said, 'Oh, it's going all right, I suppose. Yours?'

Ivor shrugged. 'Much the same. I've been thinking of spending some time in the States – Charlie wants me to meet some of these hotshot young producers. And when I say *young* . . .'

She nodded, smiled. 'They're all far younger than they have any right to be.'

They were next in line now. From the gap below the closed door of the cube, Cass could make out a series of twisted, disembodied sounds; a strangulated, altered music, yet one that seemed, despite its strangeness, faintly familiar. Her eyes met Ivor's, and his eyebrows lifted, quizzical.

'Odd,' he said. 'That sounds like the opening bars of "Just Us Two".'

'Yes,' she said, 'it does.'

The couple inside the cube emerged, blinking as their eyes adjusted to the light; the young woman seemed startled to find her gaze alighting on Cass.

'So brave of Anna,' she said, placing a hand on Cass's arm. 'So truthful.'

Cass and Ivor stepped inside, blinking now too as the darkness enveloped them. The soundtrack had briefly fallen silent, but now recommenced its loop. A layered, clamorous din: fragmented scraps of voices, disembodied, not quite audible, and seeming, for that reason, not quite human. Sections of music, played backwards, or distorted, overlaid with thickets of white noise. Cass heard her own voice, or something like it; then Ivor's, too. Heard, yes, the opening chords of 'Just Us Two', but reversed, muffled by what sounded like the crashing and breaking of waves; heard herself saying, just audibly in the ensuing moment of stillness, 'Anna, darling, it's me. How are you?'

Where had Anna drawn the voices from? Her mobile phone? Her answering machine? It occurred to Cass then that perhaps Anna had been recording both her parents' voices for years; storing up their most banal conversations – and their arguments. But that was ludicrous. This was an artwork: as layered and artificial as any recording Cass or Ivor had ever produced; and just as true to Anna's own experience, of course. This was the realisation that drew the breath from Cass's throat.

After what seemed an age, a screen on one wall of the cube came to sudden, startling life. An empty, white-walled room; Anna standing expressionless before the camera in a white T-shirt and blue denim dungarees. She did seem thin, Cass thought, almost as a reflexive action: she had grown used, by now, to this strange new reality, to measuring her daughter's body against the image Cass carried with her in her mind. Anna's clavicles were visible through the thin cotton of her high-necked T-shirt; her upper arms carried only the barest quilting of flesh, but they were muscular, too, and had lost that brittle quality they'd had in the worst months of Anna's illness.

Her daughter's image stood before them, staring directly at the camera, unsmiling, inscrutable. Then she reached into her pocket, took out a marker pen, and began to draw it, slowly, back and forth, in front of her face, aiming the coloured tip towards the camera. With each stroke, a broadening black line began to obscure the shot. Line by line, Anna's face disappeared from view; then her neck, her shoulders, her arms, her chest. Cass was reminded of those narrow black bands, placed across the faces of those who didn't wish to be filmed, obscuring, however flimsily, their identity. But this was obscurity taken to its limit: a body slowly, painstakingly erased.

When the whole screen had turned to black, and Anna was no longer visible, the soundtrack wound to the end of its cycle, and the end-credits were briefly displayed. *Birth, in Reverse*, announced in white Helvetica. *A graduation film by Anna Tait. Filming by Chris Polarski. Soundtrack and post-production by Anna Tait and Chris Polarski.*

Cass and Ivor stepped from the cube. She looked down, and saw, to her surprise, that she was holding Ivor's hand. Gently, she let it go.

'My God,' he said, running a hand through his hair. He had turned pale, and his face had a haunted quality. 'What the hell was that?'

'I don't know, Ivor. I really don't.'

There, across the room, was Anna, wearing a loose black sack of a dress, and surrounded by a small knot of people: a woman and two men, one of whom Cass recognised. Chris Polarski: one of the four other students with whom Anna shared the house in Turnpike Lane. Her boyfriend, Cass suspected (Ollie and Anna had not survived the distance between London and Sheffield), though Anna hadn't told her so. *My friend Chris. He's a brilliant artist, you know. The best in our year. A visionary. He's not afraid of anyone, or anything.*

Chris was a short, humourless man who reminded Cass of Kate's ex, the banker, Lucian: they had something of the same zealot's conviction, the same brutal, uncompromising confidence. Cass had met Chris only twice, and disliked him, but had known better than to betray a trace of that to Anna. And she had found herself, too, thinking of Lily; of that warm summer's evening on the terrace at Atterley, Lily offering the cautious warning that Cass had refused to hear. *I suppose I'm just trying to tell you, because I care for you very much, to be careful with him.*

Anna turned towards her parents, preparing to cross the distance between them; and as she did so, her eyes fell upon her mother's face. She did not smile: her expression, in that moment, was as hard and ungiving as it had been on the screen inside the cube.

So now you know, it seemed to say. *Now, perhaps, you understand.*

And Cass, watching her, felt herself weaken; faced by the knowledge that she could offer her daughter only a silent, voiceless response.

I'm sorry, Anna. I'm so very sorry. Forgive me. Forgive us both.

*

Was that the moment, then?

The second beginning; a song played on repeat, a looped recording spooling back to its start.

White noise and fractured sound. Discordance, distortion, dissonance. The shriek and wail of feedback. Hiss, spit, pulse. The slowing of a heartbeat. The blank-eyed stare of machines; the fractious blur of electromagnetic waves. A cymbal crash, a drum and then, finally, silence.

Another meeting with Eleanor Lichtenstein.

The painting behind her desk was of a man, black-suited, turned slightly away from the frame; his hair neatly parted, his tie tightly looped, his fingers resting on his knee.

'A portrait of Hockney's father,' the doctor said, following Cass's gaze. 'My own, incidentally, gave it to me. Picked it up for a song in Whitechapel. I'll never part with it, however much it's worth.'

She was about Cass's age, or a few years older: an attractive, well-dressed woman who took care of herself. An appreciator of art, literature and music, who had discreetly let it be known that she owned several of Cass's albums, and had even seen her in concert. The Hammersmith Apollo, 1976; Eleanor and her friends sitting spellbound in the upper circle.

'It was the first time,' Eleanor Lichtenstein had told her, 'that I'd ever felt a singer was speaking directly to me. To my own experience. Uncanny, really. But I suppose you've heard that a thousand times.'

Cass had absorbed the compliment, and smiled.

Now, after a polite moment, she said, 'I really am very worried about Anna. I think it's back – and worse, this time, than before.'

A stave of furrowed lines marred the smooth expanse of the doctor's forehead. She pushed an errant sheaf of black curls back behind one ear, and said, 'I'm so sorry, Cass. But there's very little I can do, especially as Anna's living abroad. In order to intervene, I'd need to be convinced that she presented a real danger to herself. And to establish that I would need, of course, to see her for myself. And even *then*' – her eyes lingered on Cass's face – 'the decision to intervene against her will could not be taken by me alone. Or by you.'

A silence. The tactfully averted gaze of Hockney's father. Looking at the painting again, Cass fancied she saw an awkwardness in the man's pose: a stiffness of the shoulders, a rigidity in the set of his features. What had he been thinking, as his son had moved behind his easel, committing his image to canvas? Had the older man understood the younger? Had he looked back over his life, his decision to have a child, and felt it had all been for the good, that it could have led to no moment other than this?

'If I can offer you any advice,' the doctor said, 'it's to respect Anna's desire for distance. Don't push her. Give her the time and space she is asking for, and then, gently, try to talk to her. If she responds, try to make her understand that she's not alone, that you're here for her, whenever she needs you. And, of course, encourage her to seek psychiatric help as soon as possible, in Germany – I can ask around for recommendations – or here. I am still of the view, as you know, that the anorexia is a symptom of Anna's broader spectrum of psychiatric issues, rather than a diagnosis in itself.'

Dr Lichtenstein paused, and poured herself a glass of water. Then she met Cass's eye and said, 'If you can bring her here to see me, well, I'll do all I can for her. On that, Cass, you have my word.'

The time and space she is asking for. How could Cass offer Anna those, when every instinct, every sinew, every muscle, ached to run to her daughter and bring her home?

Some six hundred miles separated them; six hundred miles of

sea, farmland, forest and motorway. Anna had moved to Berlin a few months after graduation, with Chris Polarski, and a few other friends from Saint Martin's whose names and faces Cass could never quite keep straight in her mind. The rent, Anna said, was cheaper there, and the scene looser, more authentic, less focused on the grubby compromises of the marketplace.

Cass liked Berlin, and had been there many times, though her experience of the city had, she was forced to acknowledge when she flew out to visit Anna, grown closer to that of a pampered tourist. Cass's Berlin, now, was a discreet, elegant hotel in Charlottenburg; cocktails before dinner; the Brandenburg Gate scrubbed, cleansed of history, and the ashes of Potsdamer Platz rising as a soaring, glass-walled shopping centre. Anna was chasing the Berlin of Lou Reed and David Bowie; graffitied squats and damp pavements, huddling for warmth in freezing, uncurtained rooms stalked by the ghosts of the city's past.

Anna had not wanted her mother to see her flat. It was a scruffy old place, she said, in a former Soviet block on the Karl-Marx-Allee: not a squat, exactly, but uninhabited for a long time; the landlord couldn't decide what to do with it, and had let them have it for a peppercorn rent. Four of them lived there permanently, with others passing through; the living-room served as a shared studio, though Chris had a lead on a derelict warehouse in Kreuzberg that they might be able to occupy for free.

They had met for drinks in Cass's hotel bar: a mistake, she had understood immediately. She was an artist like them – or had once been – and now here she was, ordering cocktails, wearing the green designer trouser-suit Kim had picked out for her, her hair neatly blow-dried that morning in a salon on Savignyplatz.

Chris had come with Anna, wearing a khaki military jacket over a black T-shirt that was far from clean; black jeans; army boots. Anna was dressed similarly, her clothes baggy, oversized in a way that set alarm-bells ringing in Cass's mind.

'Darling,' she'd said as they embraced, Anna stiff in her arms, as she had been as a child, those times when Cass had just returned from a tour. 'You're very thin.'

Anna stepped back, shook her head. 'Mum, we've only just got here. Please don't start.'

She had not been sullen, exactly, but withdrawn: Anna had, Cass noted, watching the two of them carefully, adopted some of Chris's attitude: cynical, world-weary, arrogant. Over dinner, Anna had eaten very little (cutting everything, again, into small pieces, leaving most of those on her plate), and had allowed Chris to do much of the talking.

His conversational style was adversarial, each statement issued as a challenge. He made it clear, very quickly, that he disapproved of the association of art with money, in any and every respect.

'Take *your* music, Cass,' he said. 'I mean, no offence, but wouldn't you have felt freer to make the kind of music you wanted to make if you hadn't signed a big corporate record deal? Weren't you just selling yourself to the highest bidder?'

Cass sipped her wine, and settled herself more firmly on her chair. She wanted to take Anna by the shoulders, shake her, shout at her, *Don't you understand how deeply you are loved?* But she could not, of course. Instead she closed her eyes, opened them again, and said, as mildly and evenly as she could, 'No, Chris, to be honest, I didn't. I was just grateful that I wasn't going to have to work in a shop for the rest of my life.'

After dessert (skipped by Anna, enthusiastically consumed by Chris), Anna went off to the ladies'. Cass, watching her as she crossed the dining-room, turned to Chris. 'You do know about her illness, don't you?'

He sat back. His dark brown eyes, fixed on hers, seemed not so much affronted as amused. How much he reminded her of Ivor, in that moment. Ivor as a young man. Ivor as a man who'd had the world at his feet. 'Yeah, I know about it.'

He was not going to make it easy, then. Cass drained her glass, returned it to the starched white tablecloth.

'Please just tell me,' she said, 'that you're looking after her.'

'Oh yes.' Chris reached for the bottle, refilled his glass, and hers. 'I'm looking after her. But then, that's not something you'd know much about, is it, Cass?'

That, surely, was too much. Her fist met the table with a thud; a few diners, startled, turned to look at them. 'Just who do you think you are? You don't know the first thing about me, or about what Anna and I have been through.'

Chris was cool, unperturbed. Sipping his wine, he said calmly, 'That may be so. But I think I know a lot more now.'

When Anna came back to the table, Chris turned to her and said, 'I think we're done here.'

Anna looked from her mother to Chris. 'What's happened? Mum, what have you done?'

'Darling. Please.' Cass reached out, placed a hand on Anna's arm. 'I'm worried about you, and so is your dad. We don't think you're well. We'd really like you to come home.'

'Mum.' Anna placed her own hand on top of her mother's, and gently, kindly, said, 'Please. You have to stop this. I'm fine. Really. And the only place I want to be is here.'

Cass didn't want to leave, but she couldn't see that she had any other choice.

She boarded her flight; stared, unseeing, over thin wisps of cloud. Kim collected her from Gatwick, and Cass unwound the story as they went.

'In a sense,' Kim said, 'Anna may be right. You can't live her life for her, can you? Hard as it is, I think you might have to take a step back. Trust her. Just let her know that you're there for her when she needs you.'

The email arrived a few days later. A Saturday in early autumn: leaves turning on the trees, Cass's office window thrown open, admitting the smells of sap, damp earth and the drifting traces of manure from Dearlove Farm.

Mum, Chris and I think it's better if we don't speak for a while. There are some things I need to get straight in my head. I don't mean to hurt you. I hope you understand that. I'm not going to be talking to Dad, either, if that makes it any better.

God, the pain of it: Cass had placed her head in her hands, and heard a low, keening sound coming from her own throat. Her father. That closed door. That rising, modal melody of loss.

What else was there to do, then, but to beat a reluctant retreat? What choice did she have but to return her attention to her music, to lose herself in that, as she had always done? A new album, *The Eagle and the Hawk*. A small-scale tour, with orchestra, proposed by Alan and the new booking agent, Mike.

She looked there – behind the closed door of her office; at her piano, her guitar; between the velvet drapes, looking out on rows of expectant faces – for answers, as she had always done. But she found, for the first time, none, nothing, nobody at all.

It was Tasha who brought Anna home.

She had flown to Berlin for a fashion shoot; had emailed her old friend suggesting they meet for a drink, but had received no reply.

She had no phone number for Anna, but Kim had passed on the address of the flat on Karl-Marx-Allee. And so, one freezing morning – it was November, and Tasha had spent the last three days shivering on the Reichstag lawn in a series of flimsy dresses – she had gone to the flat to see for herself.

Out on the street, before the noisy blur of traffic, she'd pressed the buzzer and waited. No response. Pressed it again, and then, finally, heard a foreign voice. A woman, not German: Turkish, perhaps.

'Anna Tait?' Tasha had said, over and over again, into the intercom, but the woman had issued an incomprehensible stream of words, then fallen silent, and the door had remained closed.

A man in a black bomber jacket had been standing a few feet away, smoking, watching. Just as Tasha turned to go, he'd said in precise, barely accented English, 'They moved to Kreuzberg. A warehouse, I think. Somewhere by the canal.'

A needle in a haystack, surely. Impossible – but still, Tasha would try. She'd returned to her hotel, emailed Anna again, given her mobile number. Then she'd taken the U-Bahn to Hallesches Tor and walked the banks of the Landwehr canal, not knowing quite where to begin. She was sitting in a café, drinking *Milchkaffee*, when her mobile rang.

Anna sounded breathless. 'It's me, Tasha. I only just saw your emails. Where are you? Tell me where you are.'

Cass didn't know what Tasha said, or did, to convince Anna to come home. Perhaps she had required no convincing, but had simply surrendered, as she had, so suddenly and unexpectedly, in Eleanor Lichtenstein's office all those years before. Perhaps it had just been easier, in the end, for her to submit than to keep on fighting.

Neither of the women would say much about the situation in which Anna had found herself, either. Anna would say only that she and Chris had broken up months before, that she'd moved out of the warehouse and into a squat in Friedrichshain.

She'd been unwell for a while – could feel the illness return-ing, moment by moment, week by week – and the break-up had only tightened its grip. By the time Tasha had got in touch (it was sheer chance that Anna had seen Tasha's emails – she had no phone or computer, and had only popped into an internet café for a moment to warm herself up), she'd known she was in a bad way, but couldn't bring herself to reach out. Hadn't *wanted* to reach out, really; had felt that this – her isolation, her illness – was her lot, and was nothing more than she deserved.

'I don't expect you to understand, Mum,' Anna said. 'I don't understand it myself. But I know it's bad this time. The voice – that voice we talked about with Dr Lichtenstein before. It's back. It's so loud in my head now. I can't drown it out.'

They were sitting in the living-room of the house on Mull, before the wood-burning stove. Outside, an icy Atlantic wind was whipping the gorse and the heather and the testy, winter sea, but in here, with all the radiators turned to full and the fire burning, it was hot enough to raise beads of sweat on Cass's skin. But still Anna was cold: she sat wrapped in jumpers, blankets, feet curled under her, her hands laced around her mug. So thin that Cass had forced herself not to gasp when she'd arrived at Home Farm that night with Tasha; had forced herself not to betray the horror that had surely been written on her face, and that Anna must have seen there as she allowed herself to sink into her mother's arms.

She would go to Dr Lichtenstein, but before that, Anna wondered if they might take a week on the island. She'd thought of it so often over the last few months, in Berlin: that rocky strip of land, at the very edge of the world; that inlet, where she and Tasha and Jerome and Katie had played as children, stalking seabirds, chasing the black-faced sheep across tussock and cairn.

'Just you and me, Mum,' Anna had said. 'You and me, and the island. Can we go?'

They'd gone. Cass had called Dr Lichtenstein, discreetly, from her office the next day, and made an appointment for Anna for the following week.

'Have her eat little and often,' Eleanor had advised. 'Soup, if she'll have it. Hot water with a squeeze of lemon, and a teaspoon of cayenne pepper. Nothing too heavy. Her body won't be able to cope. And, Cass, promise me something, all right? Please don't expect too much.'

It would seem to Cass, later, that this was where Anna had wanted to say goodbye: here, on the island, between the thick whitewashed walls of the cottage, with the tide drawing in and out a few metres from the front door, in its endless, rhythmic cycle.

She had not said as much, of course – she had said very little, in fact; had been too weak to do much more than sleep, or rest under her blankets before the fire.

But one day, they had driven to a beach they both loved on the island's south-western tip: a wide arc of wet sand backed by the native *machair*, with its fine, friable layers of soil and scree and tough grass. The ocean that day was broad, silvery, calm: the wind had dropped, and the sun, breaking through the layers of cloud, had been suddenly dazzling. The horizon had cleared, and there, at its blurred limit, they had made out the shimmering outline of Jura, its peaks rising grey and blunt above the reaches of the open sea.

Cass would try so hard, in the coming years, to think of Anna as she had been in that moment: closing her eyes, tilting her face towards the sun. Her long hair streaming out across her shoulders, and her arms spread wide, as if offering a welcome to something, someone, only she could see.

Better, of course, to think of Anna there, on that beach, holding her face to the light, than as she was a few months later, in the hospital: drip-fed and wired to machines; her pale, hollow face painfully pressed into a stack of starched white pillows.

Hiss, spit, pulse. The slowing of a heartbeat. A cymbal crash, a drum.

A phone call in the night, and that song – that beautiful song; the last Cass would write in almost a decade – already playing on repeat in Cass's mind. Demanding to be heard, and committed to memory, before Cass could allow herself to stop and rest her hands on the keys. To sit motionless on the leather piano stool in her studio; listening, as if for the first time, to the many-layered textures of silence, and following its call.

7 p.m.

The party is almost under way.

Kim has put on the music. They are playing Cass's back catalogue in consecutive order, album by album: Alan's idea, a way to get people in the right frame of mind, and to work up to the new songs. 'Common Ground', then, is wafting up the stairwell and across the landing to Cass's room, where she is standing at her dressing-table, watching her reflection.

Her own face stares back at her. Straight, greyish fringe; faded brown eyes shaded with a thick ring of kohl; the worst of her under-eye wrinkles blurred with a pot of magical concealer. A sixty-five-year-old woman – and not, Cass hopes, one who is trying to pretend to be anything other than who she is.

How long is it since she last held a party at Home Farm? Only Anna's wake, of course, and that bears no comparison, though its echoes are with her, as they will always be. Her daughter's illness, drawn to its terrible conclusion; the result of her decision to withdraw, moment by moment, from this beautiful, broken world.

The flowers, lining the front lawn, and the grass verges on either side of the drive. Returning from the crematorium in the mourners' car – Kim beside Cass, gripping her hand; Ivor on her other side – they had found the flashes of cameras, and the reporters' disembodied shouts, and the crowds staring in, pressing their faces to the glass as the chauffeur made slow, painstaking progress towards the house.

All those flowers, Cass had thought, *whatever will we do with them?* She had imagined them all wilting and decaying in their cellophane wrappers there on the grass – withering away to dust and soiled plastic – and had closed her eyes to ease the dizziness that washed over her; that had come over her in waves since she had first heard the words *Anna is dead*, and had experienced the disorientating sense that the world had tilted, shifted on its axis, and would never again offer her a level footing.

The sandwiches, the wine, the hushed voices. Cass's inability to look directly at Ivor, as one might avoid staring directly at the sun. Anna walking quickly and vividly through her mind – the warm, breathing solidity of her; impossible to believe, really, that she was gone. Everything detached, formless, shifting. The wintry light stark, cool. Kim's arm threaded through hers. The baying reporters outside, beyond the gates, with their lenses, their microphones, their relentless demands.

Alan had suggested they drown out the noise with readings and music. Tasha, sallow and pinch-cheeked in a fur-collared coat, reciting an E. E. Cummings poem. Jerome, Alan's son, playing 'Jesus Don't Want Me for a Sunbeam' on acoustic guitar, while his sister, Katie, sang.

Many other young people Cass didn't know, milling around, crying in corners. Chris Polarski hadn't dared to show his face. But Ollie Patterson had come, and Cass had understood, from his stricken expression, how deeply he had loved Anna, even if they had both been too young to recognise that feeling for what it was. Rare. Precious. True.

That was ten years ago, now. Ten years in which no stream of cars has gathered on the driveway at Home Farm; no music has thrummed from the living-room stereo. No friends and relatives have congregated in this house to drink and eat and talk.

Ten years since Cass stood before this mirror, in this bedroom, in her black woollen dress, and heard herself cry out – a deep, guttural cry that she did not recognise as her own. Kim had rushed upstairs, held her tightly, and still that cry had welled up from inside her, unbidden, unstoppable.

They had stood together like drowning women, until the cry had finally died away; and then Cass had put on her shoes, walked downstairs, Kim following behind. She had opened the front door, stepped outside, and climbed into the back seat of the car that would carry them to the crematorium, to the summing-up, to the obscene brightness of those flowers piled up inside their cellophane.

Ten long, silent, empty years, of which, after her two internments in the hospital, she had made what she could. Her books, her painting. Black-and-white films in the afternoon, soothing voices on the radio, and long drives with no set destination, just the creep of the road beneath the tyres, and the wide, pale English sky.

She had found a kind of solace in those excursions, and in the small, quiet pleasures of home. Flowers; food; objects found in junk shops and antique stores, bought not for their value but for their ability to invoke in her some feeling, some fractured memory.

A Nikon camera, thirty years old, its shutter broken: Lily, on the pier at Brighton, red-lipped, her dark hair shining under the sun. A terracotta flour jar, musty with ancient, unidentifiable smells: John, moving around the kitchen, and the cat, Louis, licking his paws.

A sepia print, age-spotted, its frame sticky with dirt: she and Ivor, stepping up onto the stage in that Lewes pub, back when everything had seemed so easy, and simple, and theirs for the taking.

A copy of *The L-Shaped Room*, its pages yellowed, its spine cracked: Anna, hair spread across the pillow, brown eyes following the movement of her mother's lips as she read. Oh, Cass had stood for such a long time in that dark little shop in Canterbury with that book in her hand, and not known, until she'd stepped out into the sudden shock of the afternoon, that she was weeping.

'Gethsemane'

By Cass Wheeler
New and exclusive

I pawned a golden evening
The sign said
'Please wait for me'
I called it a resting place
You are the shadow of the trees

Because we always follow
Up the hill, Gethsemane
Up the hill in fear
And dropping to my knees

Oh save me father
Save me
Call me Gethsemane
I am lonely
Call me Gethsemane

I stood with them and watched him
Garden of Gethsemane
He held me so tightly
Evening of Gethsemane

You are the shadow of the trees
Eyes burn so brightly
Told me you'd set me free
Oh please believe me

Oh save me father
Save me

Save me Gethsemane
I am lonely
Call me Gethsemane

He told me he would set me free
Set me free Gethsemane
Love would set me free
Love would set me free
Love would set me free
Love would set me free
Love would set me free
Ahhhhhhhhhhhhhhh

RELEASED 18 May 2015
RECORDED February 2015 at Home Farm, Kent
GENRE Folk rock / blues / pop
LABEL Lieberman Records
WRITER(S) Cass Wheeler
PRODUCER(S) Callum Sutherland
ENGINEER(S) Gavin Bryant

There were gardens at the hospital.

A maze, laid out in concentric circles of thorn-sharp yew: this was out of bounds to patients, though several could usually be found there after hours. A walled garden, planted with twenty-five varieties of rose, as the head gardener – a cheerful, ruddy-cheeked man named Dave Yarrow – liked to inform anyone interested enough to listen. And Cass's favourite: a terraced Mediterranean plot, filled with rosemary and French lavender and fragrant oregano, and bordered by a row of tall cypresses that many said they found inappropriately mournful, but which filled Cass with a sense of . . . What? She wasn't sure, exactly; she was no longer sure about anything much at all. But she liked to sit on a bench and look at those trees, and breathe in the garden's heady, scented air.

It was a handsome place, the hospital, as such institutions went. Private, expensive, beyond the reach of most: for this, Cass knew, she must be grateful.

A rambling old manor, its central portion Jacobean, its other wings added haphazardly through the centuries, and its interiors recently redecorated in a neutral, blandly calming scheme. Only the entrance hall had retained its original grandeur: a wide staircase of polished wood, portraits of long-forgotten aristocrats staring glumly down from the panelled walls.

There had been a fracas, not long after Cass's first admission – a young schizophrenic, becoming agitated as she passed the huge oil painting that presided over the first-floor landing. She had, so the story went, been convinced that this armour-clad, moustachioed viscount had crept out from his ornate gold frame during the night, stolen along the corridor to her room, and interfered with her.

But Cass had only been dimly aware of this event, as she had been only dimly aware, during the early weeks of her first incarceration, of everything: of her room – large, magnolia-painted, facing the front drive; of the cool sensation of her pillows, pressed against her face; of the doctors who came and went; of the slow passage of the sun across the sand-coloured linoleum.

'Incarceration', perhaps, was too strong a word. She was free to leave if she wished, as she had been free to come. It was Cass herself who chose to keep to her room; to speak as little, as infrequently, as possible. How precious that silence seemed to her: how new, how rare, how special. It had closed over her like an ocean: she was swimming in its depths, down in the darkness, where no light could penetrate. The doctors wanted her to talk, of course – they spoke of group therapy, individual therapy, therapy, therapy, therapy – but she would not talk, not yet.

And then, one warm afternoon – who knew how long she had been here – she had risen from her bed, dressed, and stepped out along the corridor, down the back staircase and out into the gardens.

Nobody had stopped her, though she had assumed her movements were observed. Past other patients – not seeing them; not wishing them to see her – and along a gravel path. Past the walled rose garden, across a stretch of lurid green grass. How bright the colours seemed, after the pale whites and creams of her room; how vivid the syrupy shafts of sun. And there, silhouetted against the pale blue sky, the feathered plumes of trees: *cypresses*, she thought. Tall, slender cylinders, casting their tapered shadows across the close-clipped lawn.

She followed those shadows, and found, beyond them, a garden. Raised beds chaotic with plants and flowers; a sundial; a bench. She sat on the bench, looked across at the cypresses. She closed her eyes, and tasted the pungent flavours of herbs on her tongue.

In her mind, she saw the garden at Rothermere. She saw Jonah at Atterley, lit by the flickering glow of candles. It seemed

376

like years since she had thought of Jonah. It *had* been years. Where had Jonah gone? Where had everybody gone?

Her mother, Margaret, lying alone on her bed in the vicarage, diving to the farthest depths of her unhappiness. Her father, holding her in his arms, reading to her in the low, soft voice that, in her childish imagination, had seemed like the voice of God Himself.

Irene, whom she had loved, and Irene's mother, Alice, whom she had, perhaps, loved even more.

Stephen Lomax, the sad-eyed scientist, who had once loved her.

Kind, clever, handsome Uncle John, with his drawings and his unruly blond quiff; and Lily, drawing a fine skein of smoke in through her red-painted lips, arm resting lightly on the open window of her car. *If you're going to smoke, you might as well do it properly.*

Ivor at twenty-two – the Ivor with whom she had sat for hours in John's attic office, absorbed in the discovery of music; and with it, the discovery of each other.

Anna. Their child. Their baby, whom Cass had not truly known that she desired, loved, until she had held her in her arms. Just as she had not known, until they had stood together on that Scottish beach, that she must somehow find a way to say goodbye to her; that her own love, her own longing, would not be enough to keep her in this world.

All of them – gone. And yet here she still was, still breathing, alone under this same sun, before this row of slender trees.

After a time, Cass had got to her feet and walked slowly back to her room. There, she had drawn the covers over her head, and fallen into a deep, dreamless sleep.

The next day, she had risen earlier than usual, showered and dressed before breakfast, so that she was already sitting quietly in her chair, waiting, when the doctor came.

*

A breakdown.

Nobody – not her doctors; not Alan; not Kim – ever used this word, but it was the one that Cass preferred. For something, it truly seemed, had been broken. Her sense of self had shattered into fragments. She grasped for them, and cut herself on the shards. She was untethered, falling. She was floating loose in a cloudless sky.

There had been an evening, a month or so after the funeral, when she had driven to Ivor's house on Hampstead Grove.

She would not remember the drive: she might have flown there; might have killed someone, herself included, though at the time, that would have seemed a blessing.

Ivor's high black security gates had remained resolutely closed. She had screamed into the intercom so loudly that lights had blinked on in the grand, solemn houses on either side, and a man passing with a dog had approached to ask her, none too politely, to quieten down. She had turned on the man – God knows what she had said, or how Alan, later, had persuaded him not to go to the police, or – even worse – the papers. But eventually, the gates had opened, and there had been Ivor, barefoot in his grey jeans.

She would remember nothing, either, of what had been said: only the white noise of her own voice, screaming, screaming, and the blows she had landed on him, on his face, his arms, his chest. But she could imagine her words: the desperation of them, their rage, their utter uselessness. *It should have been you, Ivor. Or me. Not her. Not our daughter. Not Anna. Why couldn't we save her? Why couldn't we keep her safe? How are we meant to go on living?*

Ivor had not hit her back. He had cried, and held her, and when she was spent, whimpering like a child on his kitchen floor, he had called Alan, and Alan had called Kim, and together they had come to get her.

Voices whispering in the darkness, beyond her closed eyes, beyond the cool comfort of the floor-tiles pressed against her face. *The hospital. Yes, the hospital. Just take me somewhere quiet, please. Take me somewhere I no longer have to hear this dreadful music. This music, this music. No more of this music, please.*

She hadn't cared at all, in that moment, who knew – hadn't cared about anything but diving down to that quiet, empty place on the ocean floor. But Alan and Kim – and yes, Ivor too – had cared. Together, she would understand later, they had forged a plan.

The hospital they chose was famed for its discretion, its seclusion. A number of very well-known people had been patients there, and they were used to handling such matters. Ivor would not say anything about it; he was selling the house in Hampstead and moving to California. A new country, a new start. His neighbour – whoever he was – would be persuaded to say nothing.

It would be announced, publicly, that Cass Wheeler was taking some time off, to grieve for her late daughter. Her need for privacy at this difficult time would be respected. Those who did not respect it would be pursued to the farthest limits of the law.

She would come to see, eventually, that they had all believed her withdrawal – her breakdown – would be temporary; that she would, with time, and the best psychiatric care her money could obtain, be restored to full health, and continue to do what she had always done. To write. To sing. To play. To live her life under the glare of those hot stage lights.

And she, perhaps, had believed this, too. For it was true that when she left the hospital for the first time, on a warm May afternoon, sinking into the passenger seat of Kim's car, she *had* felt restored, almost whole. Almost herself.

And yet, reinstalled at Home Farm, she began to realise that what she loved most, now, was silence, not sound. She would not write another song, or listen again to those she had written; she could not bear to comb over all those endless attempts to make sense of a life that did not, in the end, seem to offer any sort of sense at all.

And so, then, she had called Alan over, told him that she wanted to call off the plans for the next album, pay Hunter and the musicians what they were owed, and close the studio. That face, looking at her with such love, such tenderness. *I will make it happen, Cass. I will set you free.*

To Kim, she said, 'You'll stay close by, won't you? You'll still look after everything for me?' Adding, embarrassed, not meeting Kim's eye, 'Alan will sort it all out, of course. There's enough money. At least, I think there is.'

Kim had taken Cass's hand, and said, 'Please. We don't need to talk about that. Of course I'll stay on. How could I not?'

After a long moment, she added, 'You don't need to do this, Cass. I know it might feel, on some level, like some kind of penance. But it won't bring Anna back. Nothing will.'

Cass had looked down at her plate, at the last, congealing remnants of the lasagne Kim had brought over with her. She remembered, now, the glass dish she had taken from the fridge a few months before – the day she had later driven up to London to confront Ivor with her raging grief – and had smashed on the flagstones. Shame welled up inside her.

It was a shame, she knew, that she would have to learn to live with, along with the other greater, impossible shame: the shame of not having managed to save her daughter. Or, even worse, of having brought Anna into this world in the first place, and then forced her to endure her parents' unhappiness. That artwork Anna had made: her face on the video screen, eyes impassive, implacable. *Birth: In Reverse.* The slow erasure of her body, head to toe.

No. Cass's silence, her withdrawal from the intolerable mess she had made, wouldn't bring Anna back. But it was, she told Kim – she told herself – the only way that she could think of to go on without her.

And so on she went.

Day followed day, week followed week, year turned upon year. She was fifty-six. Fifty-seven. Milestones passing more or less unnoticed along a road that was not empty, exactly, but quiet, unremarkable. A freeway spooling across endless prairie: she remembered such a road, in America. Iowa, perhaps, or Kansas. Fields of waving golden corn, and a wide, blank white sky; miles of bare tarmac between each homestead and the next.

She was not entirely alone, of course. *No man is an island.* No woman, either. Who had said that: was it Keats or Donne? And Paul Simon, later, had asserted its reverse.

There was Kim, who came three mornings a week to spend a few hours in the office, answering mail, catching up on what little correspondence Cass still received. Many evenings, she returned with a meal and a bottle of wine: alone, or with Bill, with Tasha, with Alan and Rachel.

There was Simone, the new cleaner, whom Kim had found through Sally Jarvis in the shop, and who lived out on the new estate on the farthest fringes of the village. A small, trim, attractive woman in her middle thirties, with a neat black bob, and sharp varnished fingernails that she protected under yellow Marigolds. Three children, and no husband – well, there had been one once, but she'd been glad to see the back of him.

Simone liked to talk. Sometimes, when her shift was finished, they would sit together at the kitchen table, drinking coffee, Simone unburdening herself of the issues of the day – her son was eleven, and troublesome; her twin daughters were eight, and horse-obsessed. Cass listening, offering a response only when one was required.

'You're such a good listener, Cass,' Simone told her. 'Most

people aren't, you know. With most people, it feels like they're just waiting until you shut up, so that they can talk.'

Cass nodded.

'It's taken me a long time,' she said, 'to learn to listen.'

There was Johnny, who telephoned often, and visited whenever he could – he was so often away, working, travelling. And then, in the year Cass turned fifty-seven, Johnny fifty-nine, he had fallen in love.

'It's the real thing, this time, Cass,' he said. And she could see that it was. The man, Alastair, was Johnny's own age – a hedgefund manager, recently retired. A sensitive, mild-mannered man: a lover of opera, theatre, Stravinsky, and a collector of art. It was this that had brought them together: Alastair had wished to purchase an extensive set of Johnny's photographs, and Johnny's galleries had, given the size of the acquisition, agreed to allow him to meet the artist in his studio.

'I was bloody annoyed about it,' Johnny said: he had come to Home Farm with Alastair for lunch. 'I had a deadline – a *Vogue* cover, for God's sake – and there I was, having to stop what I was doing in order to meet some bloody banker.'

'And then I opened the door,' Alastair said, 'and swept him off his feet.'

Johnny beamed. 'You did, my love. You absolutely did.'

It was a warm, soft afternoon. Alastair and Johnny had brought a hamper from Fortnum's – 'A *treat*, darling,' Johnny said as he presented it to her – and they had feasted on smoked salmon, venison salami, dried figs. They sat outside on the terrace, and Johnny poured them each a glass of Chablis, and as Cass toasted the men's newfound happiness, she felt almost . . . How to describe it? Not happy, no. That she could not imagine. But easier. Lighter. Less afraid.

None of them spoke of what had happened – of the hospital, or of what Cass had lost, and what she had given away. Her marriage, her music, her daughter: everything that had once offered meaning and structure to her life. There was just that moment, that transient ration of time: the three of them together, the sun on their faces and the low singing of the bees in the flowerbeds. And that, she had felt then, was enough; was more, surely, than she deserved.

And then, a few months after that, she'd found the magazine, carelessly deposited by Simone in the downstairs bathroom.

Simone had not read it, perhaps; or if she had, she had simply forgotten to gather it up with her other belongings. Cass did not often use the downstairs bathroom, but she did that day; and there, trapped between those glossy pages, she found him. Ivor. Tanned and white-toothed and smiling, hand in hand with the former model Cindy Russo. *Meeting Cindy has given me a reason to get back on track. She has given me something to live for.* Throwing the magazine out through the open door, onto the hallway's polished parquet. Hearing its resounding thwack as the pages buckled and splayed.

Perhaps it was that – the knowledge that Ivor was happy, that he had permitted himself the privilege of starting over – that drew her back to the edge of the darkness. Or perhaps she would always have found herself back there, staring down into its mirrored depths. The water seemed so cool, so inviting; its silence so absolute. She stood there, watching her reflection, edging a toe towards the water. Then, at the last moment, she drew back, and telephoned Kim.

'I need to go back to the hospital, I think. Could you come and collect me?'

Another room, this time; this one at the back of the building, overlooking the terrace where patients were invited to sit in the mornings. The gravel path, and the walled outline of the rose garden. And, beyond that, the terraced beds of Mediterranean herbs, and the sundial, and the tall cypresses, waving their slender branches in the breeze.

It was different the second time. Cass wasn't numb but angry: a wave of rage seemed to well up in her from some previously untapped source. Restless, too: no more long hours in bed, watching the sun shift across the floor.

She slept poorly: the rage wouldn't permit her the oblivion of sleep. She rose early, went out into the garden, walked up and down the gravel paths. She stalked from floor to floor, snarled at those who came near. The nurses, especially, annoyed her, with their clear youthful skin, their neat uniforms, their studied patience. *Please, Ms Wheeler, you're disturbing the other patients. Come now, this is no good at all. Please calm down, Ms Wheeler, or we'll need to take you back to your room.*

Talking, this time, was what she longed for: she couldn't stop talking, unleashing a babbling stream of rage. Her therapist was a woman of about her own age – a sad, defeated-looking, slump-shouldered woman who wore a series of baggy cardigans. Cass hated her. She was furious with her. She was furious with everyone. Her mother. (How could she never have properly confronted her, never made her understand the consequences of what she had done?) Her father. Ivor. Anna. And, most of all, herself.

The therapist closed her eyes as Cass talked – shouted, often – and said, 'Good. *Good.* It's good that you're finally letting it all out.'

And perhaps it *was* good, for after a few weeks of this, Cass felt the rage begin to subside, dimming to a persistent, low-level irritability.

Bored, one day, of the moronic monotony of the television in the shared lounge, she found herself wandering towards the library, and signing out a stack of paperbacks. *David Copperfield, Our Man in Havana, The Alchemist,* pressed upon her by the librarian, a young, softly spoken woman with a tumble of reddish, hennaed hair.

'Many of our patients enjoy reading Paulo Coelho, Ms Wheeler,' she said. 'He's a spiritual writer, in the broadest sense of the word.'

Undeterred by Cass's unfriendly stare, she added, 'I know I shouldn't say this, but I really am the most enormous fan. *Huntress* has to be my favourite album of all time. I found my mum's copy in her record collection when I was a teenager. It just blew me away.'

Cass tried to read, but found that she could not. At the end of a paragraph – a sentence, even – she found that her attention had wandered, and she would have to go back and start again. After several attempts at this, she gave up. She placed the books on the bench she was using as a dressing-table, beside the framed photograph of Anna she had brought from Home Farm, and the lotions and creams Kim had stowed in her case, and that seemed to her the incomprehensible ephemera of another person, living entirely another life.

And then, a few days later, that sign on the noticeboard: a course on flower-arranging, of all things. Cass snapping at the nurse with the sleek ponytail, and then, quite to her own surprise, finding the room, slipping inside and standing behind a bench laid with gypsophila, roses, floral foam. That vase of yellow flowers on her dressing-table, their colour shockingly bright against the bland neutrality of the walls.

The following week, it was white carnations – never her favourite flower. The week after that, she asked the course leader if she might gather her own materials from the Mediterranean garden. Permission was sought and granted, and Cass brought back to her room a glass jug filled with a fragrant bouquet of lavender and herbs. The smell flooded the room for days, lifting her spirits each time she opened the door.

Her anger, she realised gradually, was evaporating. Cass bent her head low over that vase, and drew in a scent that seemed to speak of warmth, and ease, and limitless freedom.

She asked for visitors, that second time, and they came.

Alan, Rachel, Katie and Jerome, bearing a huge basket of fruit, and a bouquet of calla lilies that Cass placed on her dressing-table beside her own smaller display.

Kim, Bill and Tasha – the young woman so vivid, so alive, walking beside her in the hospital garden in her short striped dress. Cass held her hand and said, 'I'm glad Anna had you, Tasha. I'm so glad that you were there for her.'

Kate, hair expensively highlighted, skin glowing, looking around her with a horror she made no attempt to conceal. 'Jesus Christ, Cass. We need to get you *out* of here.'

'It's all right,' Cass said. 'I think this is where I need to be.'

Serena and Bob, exactly as they had always been: Serena in a long dip-dyed dress and Birkenstocks, Bob's shirt untucked, his collar unbuttoned, his expression serene.

'I'm still on the good stuff,' he admitted over tea in Cass's room. 'Sundays and school holidays, anyway. Pure *sativa*. Grow it in the back garden. Neighbours haven't noticed – they're far too square.'

Serena rolled her eyes. 'Ignore him, Cass. Sarah had her twins last month. Lucy and Nancy. They're a handful, of course, but goodness me, if they aren't the most wonderful babies.' She reached into the pocket of her cardigan, withdrew a sheaf of photographs in a plastic folder. 'I brought some photos to show you. Unless . . .' She stopped herself, bit her lip. 'Well. I didn't think, Cass, to be honest. You know what I'm like. Bull in a china shop. Perhaps you'd rather not.'

Cass put down her mug of tea. 'No. Please, Serena. Show me.'

She was aware of these visits as the mirror-image of those she and Ivor had received at Rothermere when Anna had just been born. And yet Anna was absent, now: not only physically but emotionally, too – referred to only obliquely, in allusions and silences and glances held a moment too long. They were all, her old friends, too concerned that saying Anna's name aloud might upset Cass's fragile equilibrium.

Cass didn't blame them for that; but she was grateful, so grateful, for Irene, who came one dull, overcast Saturday in September, with *Harry Potter and the Deathly Hallows* on CD – 'It's brilliantly escapist, Cass' – and a mango gift-set from the Body Shop.

They went out that day: Cass was desperate for a change of scene. Irene drove the short distance to Ascot, the fields and roads and houses seeming surreal, flooded with colour and sound, after the silence and seclusion of the hospital.

They parked, found a café; ordered coffee and two indecently large slabs of cake.

'Let's talk about her,' Irene said when they were settled. 'Let's talk about Anna. All the best things you remember about her. The woman she was before her illness. The woman she would have become.'

Cass looked at Irene across the table. She was wearing a long blue denim skirt and a white short-sleeved blouse that exposed the soft flesh of her upper arms. Her dark shoulder-length curls were shot through with grey streaks. Irene was who she was – who she had always been, since they were children – and she had never made any attempt to disguise herself.

Cass opened her mouth to speak, but no sound came out. After a moment, she tried again. 'Thank you, Irene,' she said. 'Thank you.'

On their way back to the car, Irene said, 'It's not so bad, you know, Cass. Ordinary life. You'll miss her, of course – you'll always miss her – but you might find some peace there, I think. Away from all the craziness and the attention. People recognising you in the street, having opinions about your life. I've never understood how you managed to cope with it, really.'

'No.' Cass looked around her – took in the pharmacy, the newsagent, the bank, the pub, with its freshly painted woodwork, and the ladies' clothes shop with its mannequins posed with hands on hips. The passers-by seemed calm, unhurried; she watched a pair of women stop in front of the clothes shop, nudge each other, smile, and step inside.

'I don't know how I coped with it, either. And I don't want it any more, Irene. I just want some quiet. I want to be left alone.'

It wasn't long after Irene's visit that Cass began making arrangements to leave the hospital.

There were tablets she would take, and a therapist she would agree to see, once a week, at Home Farm. The humiliating exit interview – the pretty young doctor, a size six at the most, solemnly informing her that she had gained two stone in weight. *Healthy diet, plenty of exercise.*

And then, it seemed, she was free to go.

She drove herself home this time – Alan had sent Jerome over the previous day, with the MG. It was a cool, blustery day; the roads were clear, and Cass took her time, reacquainting herself with the unfamiliar mechanisms of the car. At the turning to the M25, she made a sudden, unexpected decision, and pulled not onto the eastbound carriageway, towards Kent, but onto the M3, following the signs for London. Twickenham, Richmond, Putney, Battersea. These once-familiar places slipped past, and then, all at once, there she was, broaching the common, the white cupola of the church standing tall and bright where it had always been.

She parked a few streets back from the common, on the road where she had once taken her piano lessons, in Mrs Dewson's sour-smelling front room. That was the house, wasn't it – the one with the green front door, and the black-and-white mosaic tiles leading up from the street? She stood before the house for a moment, considered ringing the bell, then thought better of it: Mrs Dewson was long gone, of course, as they all were.

Before the vicarage, she stopped once more. It was all exactly as she remembered it: the high gables, the sooty London brick. The apple tree, heavy once again with blossom. Looking more closely, she saw minor changes: the front door had been repainted in primrose-yellow – the new vicar, perhaps, was a moderniser – and the old sash windows had been discreetly replaced. A child's muddy wellington boots stood in the porch, and beside them, a red plastic ball, scarred by the tooth-marks of a dog. This family, whoever they might be, was happy here, it seemed.

She crossed the road, and took the gravel path leading to the church. She wasn't expecting to find the door unlocked – churches never were, these days – but she tried it, and found that it swung open.

Inside, at the opposite end of the nave, before the cloth-covered altar (the place where she had once, incomprehensibly, kissed Kevin Dowd), a woman in a black shirt and trousers was deep in conversation with a man wearing a grey anorak. The woman turned at the sound of Cass's entrance, and Cass saw the white flash of the clerical collar at her throat. She looked away, embarrassed, making for the door; but the vicar called out to her across the cool, echoing interior. 'Don't worry. Please. Do come in, if you would like. We'll be here for a few more minutes.'

Cass nodded and took a pew. The ancient wood was hard and solid beneath her, as it had always been; but the hassocks were new, embroidered in bright primary colours. A white and gold banner hung from the pulpit, and twin displays of flowers (lilies, hydrangeas, white orchids) had been placed on either side of the altar. The smell was as familiar as her own skin: dust, pollen, incense, beeswax. She closed her eyes, breathed it in, and allowed her forehead to meet the cool wood of the pew in front.

In her mind, she saw a garden: cypresses, rosemary, lavender. *Gethsemane*, she thought, and from somewhere deep in the recesses of her memory emerged a passage from the Bible – studied, no doubt, in Mrs Harrison's Sunday school, so many years ago. The Gospel of Matthew. Jesus in the garden with Peter, and the two sons of Zebedee. Turning to them, saying, 'My soul is overwhelmed with sorrow,' and then falling to the ground, praying to the Father to take his cup away.

Cass sat like this for some time, in silence. And then, after a while, aware that the voices from the other end of the church had fallen quiet, she stood up, thanked the vicar, then walked out of the church and drove home.

7.45 p.m.

Late evening, gathering its shadows, inching slowly towards dusk.

In his narrow airline seat, Larry Alderson wakes from a fitful sleep, lifts the plastic window blind beside him, and stares out at a broad vista of cloud: plump, white, cottony, like a child's painting of heaven. On the horizon, a narrow band of diffuse, yellowish light, and above it, the sky deeply, inkily blue.

They are flying too high for him to be able to see the ocean, but he knows that it is there: its fathomless drop, its tall, deep-water waves. It seems, in that formless, elastic plane-time, marked by the passage of drinks trolleys and meals and the flickering of two hundred tiny screens, that they have been crossing the Atlantic for ever; but of course they have not. It is five hours since the plane took off from O'Hare, launching off into a crisp, windswept Chicago morning; there are roughly three hours still to go until it will land at Heathrow, where it will be night-time, red lights marking the runway and no stars visible beneath the velvet canopy of sky.

And here, above the cloud: what time is it here? Who knows? No time. All time. Yesterday, tomorrow and today.

Larry draws down the blind, stretches his legs a little further out beneath the chair in front. A few rows behind him, a child stirs, and he hears its mother say, in a low English voice, 'It's all right, Alfie. Go back to sleep.'

He smiles to himself, and closes his eyes, and sees Cass's face projected on his closed lids. Its fine lines and puckers. The firm sweep of her nose, and the shy, tentative arc of her lips.

He had been surprised to find that shyness, the first time they

391

had met in Washington, in the Library of Congress. And yet he had, instinctively, understood it: he knew, after all, what it was to have been alone for so long – or to have *felt* alone, even in the context of a long marriage.

He had loved her from that moment, he supposed – the moment he had first seen Cass moving across the room towards him, as if in response to a question he hadn't yet voiced. The moment he had turned to her, said something unbelievably banal – 'Gaudy, isn't it?' – and seen that shyness stalk across her face.

Absurd, probably, to feel such a thing at his age, but he didn't care. Cass was shining, luminous; the air around her seemed thicker, denser, more potently charged. He'd grown dizzy on it, high; he'd smiled at her, cracked some silly joke, and willed her not to walk away.

To love a woman so suddenly and with such intensity at this time of life was a surprise, of course. A surprise to them both. And yet it was undeniable: he had loved her then, on that first meeting; he had loved her the next day, at the gallery, walking from room to room, looking at the Andrew Wyeth paintings, but seeing only her deep brown eyes, the quizzical tilt of her chin; drinking coffee, but thinking only of her. Had loved her in the hotel room, that night: loved her sudden boldness, her voice on the telephone; her body, opening up to him, shaking off, he felt – he had *hoped* – all those years of loneliness, grief and fear.

He had loved her on his first visit to her little corner of England, to that big old farmhouse where she had locked herself away for so long, like a character from some old fairy tale; and on his second visit there, his third, his fourth.

He had loved her in the mornings, when he usually woke before her, stole quietly from her bedroom, made coffee in her kitchen downstairs. Then went up to her top-floor art room to attempt a few desultory sketches (his work was suffering, and he didn't care) until she rose and came to join him, her fine, grey-blonde hair unkempt, and all the lovelier for being so.

He had loved her on the night he had asked her the question he'd been carrying inside his mind for months. He had loved her even as she'd pushed him away, and he'd had no choice but to call a taxi and drive away.

He still loves her now. He will love her even if she opens the door to him at Home Farm, in a few hours' time, and then closes it again in his face. He will love her even if he has to drive back to the airport, board another plane, trace his lonely route back across the Atlantic, to another night, another continent. He will love her even if she affirms, despite the pain she knows it must cause him, that she doesn't love him; that it has all been an illusion, a mistake.

For at least then, Larry tells himself for the twentieth time, settling his head against the window, he will know that he has done everything in his power to make Cass understand that, whatever she has lost, whatever the messes she feels she has made of the past, there is still a future to be had. And to show her that he, Larry Alderson, wants nothing more than to share that future with her, and to make of it, together, what they can.

Oh, Larry.

Cass has checked her mobile. No messages. She will not call him again – not now, not today. She is wearing her new black-and-white shirt, her good black trousers, her black velvet shoes with the low heel. Her make-up is done; her hair is as sleek as she can make it.

Downstairs, the guests are arriving; and finally, now, after so long, she is ready.

Such noise. Music – *her* music – overlaid by the xylophonic chiming of glassware and a chorus of voices.

Cass stands for a moment in the living-room doorway, unseen. And then Kim turns, meets her eye, and cuts her way towards her through the crowd (for yes, already the living-room is thronged with people), singing out a greeting. 'She's here!'

The crowd falls quiet. Faces turn towards her, smiling; glasses are lifted against the light. Someone – Alan? – begins to clap, and then they are all clapping, palm on palm.

Cass can feel her cheeks flushing, the blood pounding in her ears. Kim takes her arm. 'All right, all right – that's enough, everyone. Let's get our woman a drink.'

A glass of champagne, pressed into her hand. Bill: a broad, large-featured man, turned jowly in late middle age. She has always liked him, with his affable, guileless face. How deeply he had fallen for Kim, on those sessions in Los Angeles. Cass remembers Bill turning to her in the green room, late one night, during a break in recording, and saying, 'Do you think there's *any* chance for me, Cass? Do you think she might give me a second glance?'

And Cass, looking over at him – a good man, a true man, a man worthy of Kim – had said, 'Yes, Bill. I really think she will.'

Now, he leans down to kiss her on both cheeks. 'You're looking really great, Cass.'

'Thank you, Bill, you old charmer.'

Beside him, his daughter, Tasha, smoothes a hand over her long, straightened hair, and then offers Cass her own embrace. She smells delicious – hairspray, vanilla and some light, floral scent Cass can't identify. Orange blossom, she will think later, remembering that Ibiza terrace where she and Ivor had sat late into the evenings on their honeymoon, drinking Rioja, believing themselves to be so deeply, so inextricably, in love.

'I'm so happy to be here,' Tasha says, and Cass nods. 'I'm happy you're here, too, Tasha.' Placing a hand on her arm, she adds, with emphasis, 'Lovely, special girl.'

'Thank you,' Tasha says, and they stand together for a moment, forehead on forehead.

Sipping her champagne, Cass takes in the people arranged around the room, the groups forming and re-forming as if to the steps of some quick, instinctive dance.

Alan is here, of course, standing with Rachel, Callum and Andrea. Jerome and Katie are talking to Gav, as the engineer's quick, deft fingers roll out a cigarette. Kate is elegant in teal silk, hand tightly clasped in that of a handsome, wild-haired man wearing a green velvet three-piece suit: Omar. Irene and Mike are standing together in a corner; Cass meets Irene's eye, and her old friend lifts her glass and smiles.

Bob and Serena are just coming through from the hallway, talking to a waitress who is offering to take their coats. Serena smiles at the young woman, shrugs off her bright pink mac. Then her eye falls on Cass, and she moves towards her, Bob (who has preferred to keep his denim jacket on) following in Serena's wake.

'You're looking amazing, Cass. God, I should really get out running, shouldn't I?'

Cass laughs. 'Oh, Serena, thank you, but I know I'm still a fat old lady.' And then Serena, shaking her head, looks at her again, and asks, more seriously, 'So. How did it go today?'

The others fall quiet, listening. Kim, Bill, Tasha, Bob, Serena: five pairs of eyes, watching her with kindness, with the wordless understanding afforded by only the oldest and best of friends.

Cass sips her drink, allows herself a moment before answering. 'Quite well, I think. It wasn't as hard as I thought it would be. I mean, it was . . . strange, of course. Painful. But also, in many ways, a relief.' She smiles. Brightly, she adds, 'You know, some of those old songs of mine really aren't too bad.'

'I should bloody say so.' This from Alan, approaching their circle, brandishing an empty glass. He greets Bob and Serena, places an avuncular kiss on Tasha's cheeks – 'Go and find Jerome and Katie, won't you? They're desperate to see you' – and then he draws Cass aside.

'We're mostly here, I think,' he says in a low voice. 'Shall we get started? I'll say a few words, and Callum wants to talk about the production. Do you want to speak?'

Cass is silent for a moment, watching Alan's face: those soft, dark eyes, that neatly trimmed beard, superimposed over all the other images she has of him. The boyish twenty-five-year-old in elbow-patched tweed. The slim, worldly thirty-four-year-old, sporting a narrow handlebar moustache, informing some slippery American promoter that there was *no way, absolutely no way*, Cass Wheeler would play under such terms (an argument Alan almost always won). The stout, comfortable fifty-year-old, long married, father to two children, master of his own empire.

She remembers Alan's face on the night, ten years before, when she had told him she was retiring – that she could no longer stand to hear her music, any music.

He had composed himself carefully, setting aside the weight of his own disappointment, and had turned to her with an expression that spoke far more of his own love for Anna, for both of them – and his grief – than of any professional anxiety. That American producer, Hunter Forbes; the musicians, their bookings already confirmed; all of that would need to be dissolved. And yet, in that moment, none of it had seemed to matter.

'My first duty, Cass,' Alan had said, 'is always to you, and to what you need and want. And if this is what you need and want, then of course I will respect that, and make it happen. I will set you free.'

Those eyes, untouched by age, watching her again now, without expectation, without prejudice, but with the cautious, informed concern of a man who, by now, must surely know her better than she knows herself, despite the fact – or perhaps *because* of it – that they have never been anything more to each other than the most intimate of friends.

Cass has prepared nothing, failed to think ahead to this moment; but now, in her living-room, before all these people, she reaches a decision that surprises her, even as it presents itself.

'Yes, Alan,' she says. 'I think I will say a few words after all.'

And so another kind of silence. Busy, expectant. A rustling, a cough. The clank of ovenware from the kitchen; a muffled burst of laughter from the garden. Rows of faces turned towards her, not to hear her sing but to hear her speak.

She has never been comfortable talking on stage: between songs, she would smile out at the audience, accept a retuned guitar from a technician, perhaps offer some small, banal observation about whichever city she was in. *Hello, Birmingham! Some weather we're having, isn't it?*

Cassandra, in her vintage gowns, her feathers and her pearls, was a woman who preferred to preserve a certain mystery; she had surely given enough away in the songs, and did not need to maintain a showman's patter in the spaces in between. So Cass had told herself, but really, she knew it had been her shyness, her fear, that had prevented her from speaking, from building the rapport that seemed to come so easily to other performers. To Tom Arnold, for one – he was so natural on stage, telling stories, offering jokes, as if to a crowd of friends in a small-town bar. Ivor, too, could be relied on to fill any unnatural silence. And yet it had seemed to Cass that with one wrong word, one burst of unkind laughter from the audience, it might all come toppling down – the edifice she had built for herself. The character she had inhabited, in order to be able to step out from the wings and play.

That feeling, the therapist had told her in the hospital, was not uncommon in performing artists. The perception of a

397

distance between one's true self and the self one must assume on stage.

'It only really becomes problematic,' she had said, 'when you start to lose sight of the person you really are.'

Cass had stared at her, trying hard to focus on the woman's face. 'Yes. That's it. I really have no idea who I am. I'm not sure I ever did.'

And now, here she is: standing not on stage but in a corner of her own living-room, among friends, musicians, fellow survivors. Alan and Callum beside her; Kim standing a few feet away. Irene and Mike, examining the framed photographs arranged on the Steinway's closed lid. Kit and Graham, clutching glasses of brandy. Martin Hartford over from Los Angeles with his Chilean wife, Anaís.

Martha, the young musician who still reminds Cass of Kate, back in their years in Savernake Road. Dark-eyed Javier, from Granada, whom Callum had brought in on percussion; Will, the twenty-four-year-old pianist from Cornwall who had played so beautifully.

Pauline, her old fan-club secretary, now a grandmother living in Tunbridge Wells with her white-haired husband, Jeff. Simon, of course, and his partner, Nick. And huddled around them, a small cabal of carefully selected journalists. Don Collins, a full-bellied, balding sixty-six-year-old, mellowed in his old age, who is now given – against all possible expectations – to writing lengthy appreciation pieces about Cass's music; of even spearheading a campaign, five years before, to persuade her back into the studio. It was not Don, of course, who had finally drawn her back there; but still, it had been good to know that there were people who cared one way or the other. Even such a man as Don.

Now, across the room, she catches the eye of her old adversary, and he offers her a twitch of a smile. What was it he had said to her in that pub all those years ago, while Ivor had shifted uncomfortably across the table? *Do we really need to hear your nice little middle-class songs, when there's a much bigger world out there, calling for our attention?*

Well, perhaps the world hadn't needed to hear them; but she had. And she had needed, above all, to hear them today.

In a second, she will open her mouth to speak; not as Cassandra, the kohl-eyed singer in velvet and silk, but as herself. Cass Wheeler. Ex-musician. Ex-mother. Ex-daughter. Ex-wife.

What remained of her, through all those years when she defined herself only by the people she had lost, and the absences that they had left? A dried-out husk; an empty, silent room. How to explain, now, the way in which music had returned to her, note by note, chord by chord; how she had found herself, ever so slowly, drawn back to her guitars, her microphones, to the old ways she had relied upon to frame this impossible, incomprehensible world? And how, eventually, that music had settled, layered itself, formed the new songs that she will play to them tonight. 'Edge of the World': Anna standing on that Hebridean beach, arms outstretched, stepping off into a place where her mother could not follow. 'Gethsemane': Cass's guilt, her fear, her loss of faith. 'When Morning Comes': Cass's hope, however small, however tentative, that there, beyond the limit of the horizon, is a rising arc of light.

Impossible to explain it, but she will try.

And at the centre of it, underpinning every syllable, she will see a face – the face around which it all spins. And it will be to that face – the face of Larry Alderson, the man she knows, now, that she loves – that she will speak, in the nonsensical belief that perhaps, through some crack in time and space, he will be able to hear her, and understand.

'When Morning Comes'

By Cass Wheeler
New and exclusive

I have spent so many nights, love
Restless and alone
Sleepless in my own bed
Weary for the dawn
Well tonight I am awake, love
Like all those nights before
But nothing is the same
I've found a cure

When morning comes I will reach for you
When morning comes I call you
When morning comes
I can throw off the darkness
I have lived in for too long
And I will listen listen listen
To the song
To your song

I knew that nothing
Could turn me around
Nothing of my own doing
Could help me be found
When you came around to me
You opened something closed
And when you let the light in
Love grows

When morning comes I will reach for you
When morning comes I call you
When morning comes
I can throw off the darkness
I have lived with for too long
And I will listen listen listen
To your song
To your song

RELEASED 18 May 2015
RECORDED January 2015 at Home Farm, Kent
GENRE Folk rock / blues / pop
LABEL Lieberman Records
WRITER(S) Cass Wheeler
PRODUCER(S) Callum Sutherland
ENGINEER(S) Gavin Bryant

Sunrise over Washington, DC.

Below, the pale stone colonnades, pillared porticos and red-roofed domes of Pennsylvania Avenue; above, the pink and orange wash of the dawn. Slashes of cloud, silhouetted against the fiery glow; and to the right, screened by the broad, still-dark crowns of trees, the White House, with its whispers and scurries, its urgent early-morning stirrings.

Cass had not slept: she had closed her eyes, settled herself into the warm space offered by Larry's crooked arm, and remained alive to each moment as it passed. She was too wired to sleep, too attuned to these new sounds (he snored – a steady nasal rattle, bellying up from the base of his throat), and to the unfamiliar weight of his arm on her shoulder. His body, stretched out next to her in the king-size hotel bed; the grey-white sweep of his hair. The pits and craters of his craggy, closed, sleeping face: mouth half open, the extraordinary brightness of his blue eyes concealed behind shuttered lids.

The way that mouth had covered hers; the way those hands, now lying motionless beneath white sheets, had moved across her body, drawn shivers from it, brought it back to sudden, vibrant life. How long had it been sleeping, her body, before such a delirious reawakening? She could not think how long. And now, her body would not sleep. Every inch of her seemed to pulse with the memory of his touch.

Towards five, she had gently pushed back the covers and climbed from the bed. Larry had not woken: he had shifted slightly, turned his face towards her vacant pillow, and slept on. She had pulled on her towelling robe, returned to the chair before the window where, just a few hours ago, she had sat waiting for him, watching her reflection in the darkly mirrored pane.

Her glass was still on the table, with its shallow meniscus of red wine. Larry's, beside it, was still half full. She had poured the wine for him, but he had hardly touched it; he had sat watching her, his legs stretched out before him. They had talked, and the talking had been easy. She had shed her shyness; had raised her eyes to meet his. And Larry had laid down his glass, stood up, come over to her chair and bent until their faces were level, and their lips met in a kiss.

The first kiss: the giddy fixation of a teenager, a giggling ingénue. Not these two almost-strangers in late middle age, their reflections conjoining in the uncurtained window. And yet a first kiss was what it had been. And then, drawing the blind down across the glass, Larry had lifted Cass to her feet, and encircled her in his arms.

Now, it was almost six, and there, before the raised blind, was the Washington dawn. Still he slept, but Cass, sleepless as she was, did not yet feel the tiredness that would come.

It would be only very rarely like this between them, though of course she could not know that yet: soon, very soon, sooner than she could imagine, she would learn to sleep next to him, grow used to his muttering, to his rattling snore. (Love such things, even, if she could not dismiss such a thought as absurdly sentimental.) And then it would be Larry who would wake before her, and she who would shift and resettle in the bed, and allow herself to tumble back into sleep as he moved off downstairs.

It would be that first morning she would think of six months later, in her studio at Home Farm – newly reopened, cleaned and painted, brought lurching into the digital age under Alan's careful supervision – as she committed to guitar the first tentative outline of a song.

That pink and orange dawn; those pale grey offices of governance. Larry sleeping soundly, and she awake, restless, flooded with an exhilaration that was as true, as undeniable, as it was unexpected; waiting, before that wide plate-glass window, for the coming of morning, and whatever the day might bring.

403

He wanted to see her again: he would not, he said, play games with her and pretend otherwise. He was planning a trip to England: to London and Yorkshire.

'And Kent, of course, if you'll have me.'

'Of course I'll have you,' she replied.

In the intervening months, Larry telephoned her often from Chicago, from his vast loft apartment with its parquet floors, its bare brick walls hung with the art he had painstakingly acquired over many years. (None of it his own, bar a discreet series of studies for some of his most famous works.)

He emailed photographs of the apartment, and of his studio: a similarly cavernous, echoing space, filled with workbenches and lathes and mysterious bundles of discarded materials – wood, glass, chicken-wire, misshapen lumps of clay.

In winter, the cold in here could freeze a man to death, he wrote. *But we have to suffer for our art, don't we? Even we who are old enough to know better.*

Larry sent photos of his children, too. Todd, as tall as his father, serious in a well-cut charcoal suit, his arm cast loosely around the stylish shoulders of his wife, Lisette. Maddy, long-haired and smiling, at the centre of a happy trio of laughing, sticky-faced boys. Harper, the third child, complex, uncertain: a thin, white-blonde woman with Larry's cornflower eyes, pictured against the Vancouver skyline. Cass thought she saw Anna in Harper, though she did not say so; as she did not, yet, send Larry photos of her own daughter.

The facts of Anna's death, Cass's grief, Cass's breakdown, hovered at the edges of their conversations; not ominously, as storm-clouds threatening to mar their sunny passage towards intimacy, but as elements of her past that Larry seemed to understand, instinctively, without her needing to explain.

It was this, perhaps, that made Cass feel – on the phone with him, reading his emails, reconstructing in her mind the precise composition of his face – a sense of ease, of safety, that she had not felt for decades.

Larry seemed to ask of her to be nothing more, or less, than who she was; and for that, Cass was more grateful than she knew how to express.

His visit was set for July. He would spend a week in London and Wakefield, with his gallerist, Diana (plans were afoot for an exhibition at the Yorkshire Sculpture Park), making a round of the London shows and studios, and catching up with friends.

He asked her to join him in London – a dinner at Diana's Shoreditch gallery; a party at the home of friends in Dalston – but Cass demurred.

'I think I'd rather see you on home ground,' she said, 'if that's all right with you.'

Across the miles of sea and earth that separated them, she sensed him smile.

'Home Farm,' he said. 'Home ground indeed.'

Johnny, however, was furious when he heard that she'd refused Larry's invitation.

'Go, for God's sake,' he said – echoing, unwittingly, Kim, all those years ago, urging Cass to join Tom Arnold in his Dorchester suite. 'You've spent far too long cooped up out here like a bloody nun. Men like Larry Alderson don't come around often – you and I both know that. So what in Christ's name, Cassandra, are you playing at?'

Discreetly, Cass met Alastair's eye. Johnny, it was plain to see, was not himself: irritable, deflated, his thick-limbed build slackening to fat.

'Prostate cancer,' Alastair said in a low voice when Johnny was out of the room. 'He starts chemotherapy on Monday. He doesn't want anyone to know.'

The living-room shifted, blurred. 'Even me?'

'Well.' Alastair looked down at his hands. 'I've told you now. I had to. So he'll just have to accept it, won't he?'

This was two weeks before Larry's scheduled visit. Not wishing to betray Johnny's confidence, she told Larry that a close friend of hers was ill, and they both wondered whether to postpone their plans. But Johnny, hearing this, insisted that they did not.

'If there's one thing that's all too clear to me now, Cass,' he said, 'it's that we don't have that much time. None of us do. So don't waste any more of yours, all right? Please, do that for me.'

Larry arrived on a Friday afternoon in a rented Audi convertible, wearing a pair of mirrored Ray-Bans and a short-sleeved shirt that displayed his tanned, sinewed arms, with their light scattering of still-dark hair.

'I have a weakness for nice cars,' he said as he stepped out. 'European ones, especially. You're not disgusted with me, are you?'

She shook her head. 'There's a racing-green MG parked in my garage.'

He moved forward, placed a hand on each of her shoulders, and regarded her squarely. His blue eyes were brighter than she remembered; but his lived-in, contoured face was exactly as she recalled.

'Now,' he said, 'you're talking my language,' and then he leant down to kiss her.

These were warm, golden days: the sky untroubled by cloud, the garden heady with flowers and the Weald hazy with reflected heat. Afternoons in bed, learning the rhythms of each other's bodies. Evenings on the terrace, drinking her best wine, cooking, eating and talking, talking, talking.

She loved the cadences of Larry's voice; the emphatic dance of his hands that accompanied the points on which he was most passionate. There was nothing in Larry's life, it seemed, that he was not prepared to discuss. His two divorces (one amicable, one less so; both, by his own estimation, entirely his fault). The years he had lost to drugs and the all-consuming power of his own ego. His anxieties for Harper, so restless, so unable to settle; his concern that Todd, who remembered his parents' tricky years, had never quite forgiven his father his mistakes.

But of Cass, Larry demanded nothing other than her company, her opinion, the warmth of her body and the cool precision of her mind. And it was because of this, perhaps, that she found herself reciprocating, talking to Larry with an honesty and clarity that she had only ever achieved before with her therapist; and perhaps in the earliest of her days with Ivor, before their relationship had soured, become so broken and confused.

It was after one of these conversations – a monologue, really; Cass talking and Larry listening, his eyes fixed on her face – that she led him upstairs to the second floor, pushed open the door to the art room where she and Anna had spent so many happy hours.

It was years – two, maybe three – since Cass had been up there: she had resolved, before her second admission to the hospital, that she would close the door to that room, as she had to so many other things, and leave it alone. When she had wished to paint, she had done so in her office downstairs. Simone, she assumed, would keep the room clean and tidy, and it was true, she had – the easels were neatly folded, the boards carefully stacked, the skylight free of dust.

Cass stood with Larry in the centre of the room, where she had used to stand with Anna, before their twin easels, music playing on the old stereo. She drew a deep breath, and let it go.

'It's just a room, Cass,' Larry said softly. 'Nothing to be afraid of.'

Across the inches that separated them, she reached for his hand.

'I know,' she said. 'I know.'

*

'Don't you miss it?' he said.

It was the day before he was due to fly home to Chicago, and he had taken her to lunch in Canterbury. A heavenly day, cloudless and fine; finishing his breakfast, Larry had said, 'We'll go out today, I think. I've never seen Canterbury.' And she, sitting across from him, had put down her mug, and nodded her assent.

Now, in the restaurant a few hours later, she said, 'I don't know, Larry. I'd always thought that music was a part of me. That I had no choice but to write. But I *did* have a choice. And now I've chosen to leave it behind.' After a moment, she added, 'So no, I don't miss it. Not any more.'

Did her voice falter a little as she spoke? She did wonder at the truth of her words, as soon as she said them; and Larry, finishing his last mouthful of steak, narrowed his eyes a little, and said nothing. But later, after the bill was paid, the table cleared, he said, as if the thread of their earlier conversation had not been severed, 'It's still a part of you, Cass. It will always be a part of you.'

The cobbled streets of Canterbury were cool and shadowed; tourists in shorts and T-shirts wandered with cameras, and gaggles of half-naked teenagers posed and preened on the banks of the river. Larry and Cass walked slowly, arm in arm, like a long-married couple out for an afternoon stroll. Nobody stared; nobody watched. If the eyes of some of the older passers-by did flick over them, they did so discreetly, drawn only by the fleeting sense that they had seen this woman's face somewhere before, but could not, in that moment, quite remember where.

Before the cathedral gates, Larry paused. 'I'd like to go in, if that's OK.'

'Of course,' she said.

The astonishing grandeur of that buttressed stone, the ribbed pillars, soaring up as if to infinity, and the afternoon sun throwing kaleidoscope patterns through the stained glass. A crowd had gathered in the quire, was filing into the high wooden stalls. A white-haired woman, holding printed service sheets, asked if they were here for evensong.

'Yes,' Larry replied, and from the woman's hand, he took a sheet, and led Cass off after the crowd.

'Larry,' she whispered, 'shouldn't we be getting back?'

And he, squeezing her hand, said, 'Not yet, Cass. Let's just stay for this.'

Later, it would occur to her that he had planned it all: the outing; the innocently phrased question over lunch; the apparently casual coincidence of their entering the cathedral just as the choir was coming in. If this was so, she thought, Larry had known exactly what he was doing, and what its effect would be.

The choristers in their long robes, standing at the bidding of the choirmaster; the cushions scarlet-bright against the dark polished wood, and the master lifting his billowing white sleeve. The singers' voices, rising, soaring, offering their music to the rafters and beyond: the high clarity of the boy sopranos, and the answering bass and baritones of the men. A great flock of open mouths issuing that sublime plainsong chant, building and swelling, riding a wave of glorious tonal harmony.

Cass was lost to it, her ears ringing with its music. A swimmer, backstroking in a cool, calm sea; the waves carrying her with them, refusing to let her go.

Was it there that it returned to her, under that ancient canopy of stone? With that chanting ebb and flow: the psalms, the responses, the hymns? The music she had first heard as a child, in that other church, under her father's commanding eye: an indifferent choir, theirs, but one to whose song she had first become attuned; melodies she had tried, as a toddler, to draw from her own small throat. Replaced, over time, by another kind of music: the weight of a guitar on her knee, the pressure of her fingers on its taut strings. The hot urgent rhythms of bass and drum, and the ancient communal responses of the crowd. How she had loved that music. How she loved it still.

That night, in bed with Larry, sleepless, dreading the morning's parting, she heard it: the singing of the choir, that layered music, that sacred offering. And some time towards the morning, her own response: the small, fragmented quickening of a song.

It was Alan who suggested she open up the studio again.

They were standing together in the back garden of Johnny's mother's terraced house in Walthamstow, sharing a cigarette. (She was supposed to have given up – Larry hated smoking, and so, it had occurred to Cass, did she – but this seemed an appropriate occasion to allow herself a small indulgence.)

Around them, a flock of other mourners dressed, in accordance with Johnny's wishes, in a rainbow spectrum of colours. At the crematorium, his mother – eighty-two years old, heartbroken in fuchsia pink – had stared bravely at the wicker coffin from under eyelids daubed in garish ultramarine. She was now installed in her living-room, attended by her daughters – Johnny's four sisters, as quick and slight as he had been broad and strong-limbed – and a gaggle of grandchildren.

'Why don't you let me take a look?' Alan said. 'Dust off the cobwebs. We'll need to replace that reel-to-reel. Technology's moved on a bit, of course.'

Cass drew deeply on the cigarette, watched the smoke hang for a moment in the air and then disperse. 'I'm not sure, Alan. I don't know if I'm ready.'

He looked not at her but through the window to the kitchen, where one of Johnny's sisters was opening another bottle of champagne. *Drink champagne all day*, Johnny had written in the note he'd left for Alastair. *And then drink champagne all night. As you know, my darling, the cellar's overflowing with the stuff. No black, please. Dress up. Dress brightly. Dress for a party. Laugh, and be happy. For I was happy with you, my sweetest love – as deeply, and as truly, as I knew how to be.*

'But you are writing again?' Alan's voice was light, studiedly casual. She watched the side of his face – that slope-nosed face, with its tufted silver-grey goatee. How generous he had always been to her, how good, even when it had all fallen away.

'I am,' she said. 'One song so far, anyway. 'Gethsemane', I'm calling it. It's good, I think. It feels good, anyway.'

He smiled. She handed him the cigarette. 'And Larry?'

She returned his smile; she could not help it. 'Oh, Larry's *really* good. He's coming over again next week.'

Alan nodded, his grin broadening. He took a drag, and then said, 'Well. That's great, Cass. That's really great.'

It *was* great. It was more than great: it was a gift.

She missed him. The days, in Larry's absence, seemed dull, lonelier than they had ever felt in the years in which she had been, by choice, so often alone.

She spent her time listening to music – not her own, not yet (the Washington concert had been enough, for now), but a selection of the new records she had been sent. Kim had, for many years, replied to all such missives with a brief, polite *I'm afraid Cass is not available at the moment*, but Cass had asked Kim to start passing the best of these albums on to her.

A pair of sisters from Oregon, pictured long-legged and tousle-haired, their layered, fluid harmonies betraying their love of Fleetwood Mac, the Beach Boys and, yes, Cass herself, in her *Huntress* era.

A young singer-songwriter from south London, her clever, uncompromising songs swelling to full, Wall of Sound-style choruses inspired (so the woman's accompanying letter said) by the call-and-response hymns that she had sung, throughout her childhood, in her parents' church.

To these albums, and others, Cass listened, stretched out on the sofa in her living-room, drinking in the music; thinking of Larry, thinking of Anna, thinking of all the years that had, with such incomprehensible swiftness, rolled by and disappeared.

And thinking, too, of the music she might make now, of the future it might offer her. Her own music, made by and for nobody but herself – just as those earliest tunes had emerged, making their own stuttering journey from her mind, to her hands, to the guitar she hadn't yet known how to play.

Larry had returned to Home Farm in October, and stayed six weeks.

A routine evolved. In the mornings, he took himself up to the top-floor art room to draw, and every other evening, he prepared dinner. He was an excellent cook – far better than Cass – addressing himself to each recipe with a skill and enthusiasm that reminded Cass of her uncle John.

He suggested outings to London (gradually, he introduced her to Diana, and to a carefully curated selection of his friends), to Brighton, to Oxford. He joined her on the morning runs that she was, under Kim's tutelage, beginning to enjoy. Usually, on their sorties across the Weald, he ran a few steps ahead of her, surprising her with his easy, long-limbed grace.

He walked with her through the village, down the High Street, into Sally Jarvis's shop – he charmed even Sally, who had begun to order in a special selection of his favourite American foodstuffs (Oreos; Big Red chewing gum; Buffalo Trace bourbon) – and past a large thatched house on the green, a 'For sale' sign standing to attention at the white picket fence.

'This,' Larry said as they passed, 'is exactly what Americans think of when they think of England.' And from there, he'd drawn her on to the Royal Oak, where Cass had not set foot in years.

She had, she realised, never made any real attempt to be a part of village life, even when Anna had attended the local school. She had kept her distance from her neighbours not only because her fame, at one time, had required it, but because she had believed that distance to be necessary for Anna; that in sequestering her away at Home Farm, down that long drive, behind those high stone walls, she might keep her daughter safe. And yet she had not kept her safe; and so she wondered, now – aloud to Larry, too – whether she ought never to have tried to hide them both away. Ought not to have allowed her music to stand for her in the world, while she edged further and further into isolation.

Larry sipped his beer, then said, 'You do know that it's not your fault, what happened to Anna, don't you?'

'Larry,' she said quietly. 'Please don't. Not yet. I'm not ready.'

He opened his mouth to say more, but closed it again, and the conversation slipped away.

All through his visit, then, the idea began to form: tentative at first, and then gradually asserting itself, until she knew that she would have to give voice to it. And so, that night in October, after dinner, the night stealing across the room, she had told him.

She would record the new songs here at Home Farm, and release them along with a very particular kind of retrospective. Her life, reflected in the songs she had written; in the songs that she, and only she, could choose.

Larry asked her to Chicago for Christmas, but Cass did not feel up to the flight, or to the meeting with his children and grand-children that would inevitably ensue.

But he returned again in the new year, stayed a month with her at Home Farm. In February, he flew back across the Atlantic to Vancouver and Connecticut for a fortnight, to see Harper and Maddy; then spent a week in Yorkshire preparing for his show; and from there travelled to London, and by Eurostar to Paris to see Todd and Lisette. Then he came, again, to Kent, where the sessions for the new tracks were almost complete.

He continued to spend his mornings sketching in the art room, and asked if she would mind if he brought in a work-bench, materials, something with which he might begin to work on a new series of maquettes. Cass didn't mind. She liked knowing, even as she sat out in the studio for long hours with Callum, Gav and the musicians, lost in this new music they were making, that Larry was there, across the lawn, behind the house's red-brown, wisteria-clad façade.

Larry was working on a new piece, fashioning tiny boxes out of stiff white card. He made one, two, three and then another, and another, until gradually, his workbench was occupied by a miniature cuboid city, held inside an enormous, open-sided crate.

'Worlds within worlds,' he said. 'Memory within memory.'

'Yes,' she said, and put her arm around him. 'I see. I understand.'

Soon, too soon, it was March, and still they made no plans for Larry to return to Chicago.

April, then: the new tracks almost ready for mastering; Kim planning the catering for the party.

Simon, the publicist, came to visit (Larry was in London that day, with Diana), and described – quite to her surprise – the interest Cass's return to music was inspiring. The label were wondering, too, whether she might have any ideas in mind for the cover.

That night, Larry suggested, over dinner, that they photograph his boxes. Black and white: a study of depth and line, and of time and memory; of the many selves, the many closed-off spaces, we all carry inside.

Cass looked at the small city of white-sided cubes, and remembered a biblical passage of which she had not thought in many years. Reverend Francis Wheeler, standing at the pulpit in his neatly pressed robes. Cass at the back of the church, with the Sunday school, staring up at the father whom she had always believed, back then, to be addressing only her.

Do not let your hearts be troubled. You believe in God; believe also in me. In my father's house, there are many mansions: if it were not so, I would have told you. I go to prepare a place for you.

'That's a wonderful idea, Larry,' she said.

Her birthday. Sixty-five years old. Ancient: older, even, than the couple in the Beatles song. And Larry would be seventy at his next birthday – a fact undeniable, for all his youthful vigour, for all his particular allure.

Was it this – the natural jitters of the day, with its unwelcome reminder of her mortality, of the unstoppable quick-march of time – that caused Cass to behave as she did? That and the fears that had been circling ever since she had made the decision to draw herself out from retirement and dive back into the slipstream of her music.

Larry had roused her – on that she was clear; he had shaken her out of her stupor. And perhaps a part of her resented him, a little, for that, even as the far larger part of her loved him with all that she still had left to offer. For there had been comfort in silence. There had been reassurance in not having to produce work – to frame it, present it, offer it for judgement. To live an ordinary life; the life she had once envied Irene, and to whose slow, steady rhythms she had, over the last decade, set the beat of her days.

Or perhaps it was only (this was what Kim, later, would suggest) that she still believed she had no right to happiness in a world in which Anna did not exist; a world in which she and Ivor had failed to keep her safe.

For still, Cass asked herself what sort of mother she had been, what sort of wife, what sort of woman. Selfish, troubled, angry, flawed. A woman unworthy of love. A woman who was surely

415

better off alone. A woman who should not allow this man –
this good man, this man who was so generous, so honest, so
incapable of dissembling – to make the mistake of offering her
his heart, and his future.

And so. She could ignore it no longer. That day.

Her birthday. Fine, sunny, though the wind carried a slight
chill.

They spent the day separately – Callum wanted Cass to go
over his latest mix of 'When Morning Comes'; Larry had a slew
of emails to answer – and then, in the evening, ate the dinner
Larry had prepared.

A bottle of Dom Pérignon. Coquilles St Jacques, and a
spring-pea risotto, delicately flavoured with lemon and mint. A
salad of rocket and parmesan, and then – his showman's flourish
– twin chocolate soufflés, only slightly under-risen.

After coffee, Larry refilled their glasses, and led her through
to the living-room.

She sensed, in his expression, in his slow, deliberate movements, what was coming, and she grew dizzy, sick; wanted to
hear it – longed for it – and yet feared her own response.

Sitting beside her on the sofa, then, Larry declared his hand.
He loved her, and he believed that she loved him. It had come
as a great surprise to him, as he knew it had to her. He had
known her music for years – had loved it, as so many had.
Even so, watching her across the gilded room in Washington
in her long navy dress, he had not expected to feel for her as he
had. During the hours they had spent together at the gallery,
he had sensed her hesitance, her reserve, and guessed its source:
he had not, in short, expected her to call. The fact that she had,
Larry said, had made him, in that instant, childishly happy, in
a way he couldn't remember having felt since his very earliest
days with his first wife; and that feeling had only grown since
then, assumed colour and form.

He wasn't asking her to marry him – they were both too old, he assumed, for all that. And he wasn't asking her, either, to move to America – he knew it was not what she wanted. But he didn't wish to relinquish his life there. Maddy and his grandsons were in Connecticut; Harper was in Vancouver; his studio, of course, was in Chicago. He did not wish to put so many miles between himself and the life he had built.

But what he *was* asking – and at this, Larry seemed so bashful, so nakedly vulnerable, that Cass was forced to look away – was that she agree to share her life with him. That they formalise – if only between, and for, themselves – this precious, late-flourishing love that they had found. That they agree to try to spend as much time together as possible (perhaps he could convert her art room more fully into a studio, stay here for a portion of the year; or she could come out to Chicago for a few months at a time), and to enjoy every moment that the future still had to offer them. That she meet his children, his grandsons. That she promise, here and now, to be the partner with whom he would spend the rest of his life, as he would promise to be for her.

Cass kept her eyes closed as he spoke. That dizziness, that roll and whirl, that ugly, snaking hiss of fear. Ivor, white-faced and snarling; blood seeping from her face as she bundled Anna into the car. The dreadful incandescence of her own rage, of their circular, unending rows. Anna withdrawing, step by step, into a place where they might not follow her. All this, Cass had learnt to live with, and yet now the full weight of it returned, threatening to squeeze the last gasp of breath from her lungs.

Surely Larry did not know her. Not really. He didn't know all the ways she had failed; how difficult she was to love. What did she have to offer him but the totality of her mistakes? He deserved better, deserved more. She could not bear to see his opinion of her change, over time, as it must surely do: as this beautiful new thing they had found became tarnished. She could not bear to see Larry look at her as Ivor once had.

'No,' she said aloud. The word landed in the space between them with a thud. 'No, Larry. No. I can't promise you that.'

She saw his hurt, his disappointment. Larry was a soft, tender, large-hearted man, but a man, too, who knew the limits of his own pride; who did not, she knew, always find it easy to forgive. That, she respected. That, she could understand.

'What are you saying, Cass?' Even in his confusion, he reached for her hand; but she drew it away, left him grasping at empty air.

'I can't promise you anything, Larry. You don't know me. You don't know who I am, what I'm capable of. I'll disappoint you. It'll go sour, and we'll end up hating each other. I can't bear that, Larry. Not again. I just can't.'

He stood up. His face was reddening, his mouth setting into a firm line. He paced to the fireplace, his back to her, running a hand across his forehead; then, as if reaching a new resolve, he stepped back towards her, and said, 'For Christ's sake, Cass. What are you talking about? Of course I know you. Of course I know what you've been through. But do you think you're the only fucking person who's ever suffered, who's ever made a mistake? Jesus Christ, give yourself a break. You're a fucking *legend*. A real artist. You've given up everything that you're good at, that makes you happy – that makes so many other people happy – to sit around doing nothing, out of some ridiculous notion that you have to atone for your shitty marriage, and for how your daughter chose to deal with it, or whatever else made her hurt herself. Well, let me tell you this, Cass: people make mistakes. Marriages go wrong. Children get ill and die. It's bloody tragic, but it happens. So don't give me that bullshit about disappointing me. Don't you fucking dare bail out on me now.'

He was almost shouting, his breath coming shallow and fast.

'No,' she said again. 'No, Larry. I can't. I'm sorry.'

He didn't argue. He packed his case and called for a taxi. He'd spend the night with Diana in London, he said, and fly home to Chicago in the morning.

Cass lay on the sofa, head buried in her hands, listening to the sounds of his leave-taking; wishing, with so much of herself, that she could ask him to stay – and yet motionless, weighted down.

When Larry came through to the living-room to say goodbye, he was calm once more.

'I guess,' he said, 'I had a different idea of where things were going, Cass. I might be an old man, but I can't say it doesn't hurt.'

'I'm sorry,' she said.

He stepped away, went out into the hall. Then, after the briefest of silences, he closed the front door behind him, and was gone.

9 p.m.

Cass is climbing the stairs to her room again, drawn by the silent pull of her mobile phone. There it is, on her dressing-table, where she left it. She enters her passcode, illuminates the screen. No missed calls. No texts. She checks her email, just in case. Nothing.

She was right, it seems: Larry is not a man who finds it easy to forgive. And yet – that postcard he had sent. The Henry Moore. *Today, Cass, find a way to forgive her. And then – please – find a way to forgive yourself.*

She had emailed him the week after he'd left; had tried, carefully and honestly, to lay out the terms of her apology. To explain herself. To explain that she had allowed her fear, at the last moment, to overcome her. That she missed him. That she would try as hard as she could to make room for him in her life – to trust in the power of what they had found together; in his ability to accept her for who she was, and who she had been.

He had not replied to her email, or her voicemail messages. There had been nothing at all from him, until that card this morning. But that card, surely, was enough to allow her to hope. *I'll call him again tomorrow*, she tells herself. *I'll keep trying, and I won't give up.*

She replaces the mobile phone on the table. In the mirror, she repairs her make-up: reapplies her eyeliner, her lipstick, dusts powder across the bridge of her nose.

Her cheeks are flushed: the champagne. The faces watching her as she gave her speech, offering the best account she could for the appearance of this music, these new songs. Afterwards, she had watched her guests, as the songs had poured out from the speakers. Some of them – Kate; Serena; Tasha; Kim – had closed their eyes. Others had nodded in time to the slow rhythm of Javier's percussion; had looked back at her with a searching gaze as her voice floated out across the room. How she had missed it, that communal experience of listening. How she had thrilled to the applause that had risen, spontaneously, when the last note had died away.

Examining her reflection now, she finds herself thinking of her mother. Cass has never thought they looked much alike. But in that moment, in the half-light of her room, there are traces of Margaret in the composition of her features: the angle of her nose, the slight downward tug of her mouth. Her mother's restlessness, her complexity, are hers also. And hers that tendency towards self-destruction; though in her mother's case, she can see that it became a kind of liberation. Throwing off the shackles of an unhappy marriage, of a life that had seemed to promise nothing more than a chain of identical days.

There had been courage, yes, in Margaret's decision to release herself, in her acknowledgement of her need to strike out for what she wanted, whatever the cost. Margaret had made her peace with that. She had reached out, and taken hold of it, and not allowed herself to be daunted by fear. And in that, Cass thinks, there had been a strength of the sort that she, now, must find.

'Cass? Are you in here? Are you all right?'

Kim, stepping in from the landing in her brightly patterned dress.

'Yes,' Cass says, and turns away from the mirror. 'I'm fine.'

Kim, who misses nothing, looks from Cass to the dressing-table, and the phone.

'Still nothing,' Cass says, 'other than that card.'

'Listen.' Kim moves across the room towards Cass, her heels

leaving small, round stiletto-prints in the carpet's high pile. 'I think you should . . .' She hesitates; her tone shifts. 'Come on, Cass. Let's go back downstairs.'

'No. What is it, Kim? What were you going to say?'

Those dark brown eyes, fixed on Cass's face for one moment, two, three. But Kim's voice, when she speaks again, is firm, unyielding. 'Nothing. Honestly. Come back downstairs, won't you? Everyone's wondering where you are.'

Her friend's slender frame, shifting back out to the landing. The set of Kim's narrow, silken back is resolute, and Cass knows she has no choice but to follow. And so she does: drawn back to the light, the sound, the guests all gathered downstairs.

The party is reaching its apex. Its volume has swelled, its soundtrack shifted. Cass's voice – or the ghostly impression of it – is no longer rising from the speakers, but has been replaced by her antecedents, her contemporaries and those who have followed in her wake.

The Beatles and the Stones, whom she had loved equally, and Joan Baez, whom Lily had taught her to love. Sandy Denny, with her red wine and her deep, infectious laugh. Tom Arnold, with whom she had stood on the porch in Laurel Canyon, among the whispering trees; and in whose arms she had, so many years later, sought solace.

The Portland sisters, with their sound that is both timeless and absolutely new; and the young singer-songwriter from south London, with her rousing call-and-response choruses. All this music, playing on rotation through the evening, laying its own particular trail of meaning as her guests talk and drink and dance.

In the living-room, she finds Simon, with his glass of iced San Pellegrino, his impish smile.

'Well.' He takes her hand, leans in close to half whisper in her ear. 'I don't think that could have gone any better, Cass.

You're trending on Twitter, and Don's already promising a five-star review.'

She laughs, looks over, once more, at Don Collins, who is well on his way to full-blown drunkenness, talking intently to Tasha, who, Cass can sense, is preparing an excuse to slip away.

'It's funny,' she says, 'how much friendlier Don is these days. Age, I suppose. Long past the brattish arrogance of youth.'

'He always liked you, I think. He was just staking his reputation on going against the grain. Now there's nothing left for him to prove, is there?'

She shifts her gaze back to Simon, returns his smile.

'No,' she says. 'I suppose there isn't.'

On and on the music plays, as the party sways to its own unpredictable, juddering rhythm. Guests leave – Pauline and Jeff, who have an early start; Mike and Irene, who have a long drive; all the journalists bar Don, who must catch the London train from Tunbridge Wells. Those who are left behind smooth over these absences, allow their glasses to be refilled, consume the last of the caterers' excellent canapés.

Serena, rather giddy on champagne, begins to dance, and Kate dances with her: two women, long past the first bloom of youth, swaying their hips with the sexy, sinuous abandon of the twenty-year-olds they once were.

Cass smiles, and talks, and moves from group to group. And through it all, behind every face, in the shadow of every smile, Cass sees her daughter, as she knows she will always see her, always glimpse her from the corner of her eye.

Anna's long blonde hair, forever falling in front of her eyes; her teenage uniform of under-slips and Doc Marten boots; her ragged, emaciated frame, folded beneath the table in that Berlin restaurant.

Anna standing on that Scottish beach, arms spread wide under the wintry sun. Her eyes shut, her face tilted up towards the light; absorbed in some private music, some silent, pealing melody.

And then, as her mother watches, Anna opens her eyes, turns to her and says – Cass can see it; she can hear it; clear as the freshly formed outline of a song – that she is all right, now; that it is peaceful here, and quiet, and there is no need for her mother to worry for her any more.

11 p.m.

Over this small corner of England, the evening has blackened into night.

Deep inside the belly of Heathrow's terminal three, Larry Alderson stands beside a baggage carousel, watching a string of cases inch by like booby prizes in a game show. *A television, a set of steak knives and a battered black Samsonite suitcase previously owned by an insurance salesman from Oswego, Illinois!*

Here, finally, is his own bag: brown leather, pocked and scarred, bearing the incongruous fluorescent-green tag (a gift from his daughter Maddy, who is nothing if not practical) with which he can always, as she'd pointed out, be sure that the case is his.

It isn't heavy – he hasn't packed for a long trip, wary of tempting fate – so he doesn't bother with a trolley. He draws the case behind him by its handle, through customs and out into the arrivals hall, with its aggressive strip-lighting, its shuttered shops and its rows of strangers' faces turned expectantly towards the gate. One of them – a smiling, dark-skinned man, in a neat black suit and tie – is holding a board with his name inscribed in fat red marker pen.

'You landed early,' the driver says cheerfully in a light, musical accent, taking Larry's case. 'It is lucky I arrived early myself.'

'Sure,' Larry offers. 'Thanks for that. Doesn't happen often, I can tell you.'

The driver smiles, revealing a set of perfectly white teeth. 'Good flight?'

'Fine, thank you. Absolutely fine.'

On the back seat of the Mercedes, Larry settles himself, draws his cell phone from his pocket. It was kind of Kim to arrange the taxi service: kind of her to arrange it all. She had telephoned last week: had explained that Cass would skin her alive if she knew what she was up to, but she couldn't stand by and let her ruin what she knew for a fact was the best thing that had happened to her in such a long time. Ever, probably. No, not probably. *Definitely*.

Larry had been a little affronted, at first – surely, he had told Kim rather curtly, this was none of her business. But his mood had quickly eased, as his anger with Cass – or, more precisely, his disappointment, his wounded pride – had already burnt itself out. He already regretted having left so abruptly – it seemed like the act of a spoilt, impetuous child. If he truly loved her (and he knew that he did, that his feelings were real), he should have offered her time. He should have understood that such a promise would not come easily.

He had been wanting to call her back. She had left him so many messages, written him an email that had, in its simplicity, its brave candour – *I have lived for too long in the shadow of the past, and I don't want to live there any longer* – made him wish to hear her voice, to tell her that he understood, that it was not too late. And so he'd found himself telling Kim that he would fly across to England, come back to Kent: that he couldn't bear to stay away.

'Yes,' Kim had said, 'come for the party. You can't imagine how much that will mean to her.'

But he hadn't been able to make the timings work – there'd been a breakfast meeting at his Chicago gallery that morning that he could not rearrange. And so Larry had resolved to arrive at the party's end; and to do so unannounced, in the hope – the belief – that the surprise would be a happy one.

The postcard, however, he had been unable to resist; he'd posted it to Kim, and asked her to leave it out for Cass to find in her listening-room that morning. A Henry Moore – one of his favourites. A man, a woman and a child. A mother, a father and a daughter – that essential trinity, each of them trying their hardest, each of them carrying their own unfathomable fears.

Now, watching the small, bright screen of his cell phone, he taps out a text to Kim. *Landed early. On my way. Driver says it should take about an hour.*

After a moment or two, he receives Kim's reply. *Great. Clearing up here. All went well. Been really hard not to tell her, but I've managed it – just! I'll head off in a minute, make sure she's alone when you arrive. Good luck – but I know you won't need it, Larry.*

He leans back against the headrest, slips the phone into his pocket.

Outside the car window, the M25 slips by in a blur of tail-lights and tarmac and ghostly signs for places he doesn't know, or wish to know. For what allure do any of these places hold if they are not the place where she is? This, then, is the truth of it, and there is nothing simpler, or more complicated.

He is too tired, now, to feel excitement, or fear. He closes his eyes, but does not sleep; he sits silently, waiting for time to pass, for the slow, methodical erasure of the miles that lie between him and the house where he will find her.

In the kitchen at Home Farm, Cass stands with Kim, watching the caterers load the last of the glasses into the dishwasher. Before them, the surfaces are miraculously clean, emptied of platters, dirty napkins, scraps of uneaten food. Kate's flowers, on the island, form an Impressionist painting of hazy whites, blues and greens, glossily vivid against the white marble countertop.

'Are you sure I can't do anything?' Cass says for the third time, and Kim, beside her, shakes her head. 'They're nearly done, anyway. And I'll have to head off soon.'

'Really?' She dislikes the wheedling note she can hear in her voice, but she had not expected to be left alone so soon. 'Why don't you stay? There's so much wine left . . .'

The catering manager – a blonde, capable woman in her early forties, neat in her apron and white cap – emerges from the hallway. 'That's the van packed, then, Kim. If you're happy with everything, we'll make a move.'

Kim, distracted, offers Cass no answer. Cass feels for the tobacco tin she has slipped into the pocket of her trousers, takes up her half-finished glass of wine, and slips out onto the terrace.

The night air is shockingly cool after the clotted warmth of the house. She ought to have put on a jacket, but the effort, now, seems too much for her. She draws out her tin, lays it on the wrought-iron table, sinks down onto a chair. Begins the meticulous business of rolling a cigarette: a sequence of movements that do not come as naturally to her as they once did. She smokes so rarely, now, that the act carries a freighted, ritualistic quality. A way, it seems to her, to mark the end of something, or the beginning of something else.

The garden is thick with secretive shadows. She has not seen the pair of foxes since the morning; and Otis, discomfited by the party's noise and clamour, is curled asleep on her bed upstairs. Before her, the studio throws up its stark angles against the indigo sky. The place she had, for such a long time, dreaded has now become her home once more: a place to lay down these strange symphonies of sound; to acknowledge them for what they have always been. A part of her. A part of Anna, too. A way to draw order from the chaos that is the stuff of everything. That is something Larry understands; and that Ivor, too, had understood, and had shared with her, beneath the strata of their unhappiness. He had known what it was for meaning to truly exist only for as long as the music played.

She has formed, from the papers, the tobacco, the filter tip, a slender cigarette. She lights it, draws in the first, delicious curl of smoke.

'Caught you,' Kim says, and Cass turns, sees her assistant, her

428

friend, her comrade-in-arms, silhouetted against the back door, her coat belted over her dress.

'Don't tell,' Cass says, and Kim smiles. 'Oh, I think we can allow you just one, Cass. Today, of all days.'

They embrace: Cass closes her eyes in Kim's arms, inhales her sweet, mingled scents.

'Thank you,' she says softly. 'Thank you for everything.'

And Kim, knowing that she is speaking of far more than the party, holds her, and says, 'You're welcome, Cass. You know you are.'

Stepping away, then, Kim adds, 'Call me tomorrow, won't you? Let me know how you are.' If there is a particular significance to her words – an implication that there might be more to happen, more to come – then it is something that Cass doesn't catch.

'I will,' she says.

Then Kim is turning, and leaving; and Cass is alone, with her cigarette, and with the faint, rustling night-sounds that are not any kind of silence, but their own particular, endlessly repeating song.

Half-past eleven. The day is almost done.

Larry shifts in his seat; the driver, drawn by the movement, catches his eye in the rear-view mirror.

'Almost there now, Mr Alderson. Another ten minutes, maybe.'

Larry nods. Now he feels it: the stirring of anxiety. The desire to see her, tempered by his hope that she will wish to see him. That the day, and the evening, have led her back towards him, not further away.

'Good,' he says. 'Thank you.'

Eleven forty-five. Cass is in her bedroom, stepping from her clothes, reaching for her slip. On the bed, Otis sleeps in a tight

429

circle, head on paws, tail tucked neatly under the curve of his small body.

A sudden, unanticipated, jarring noise: the crunch of gravel under car tyres. Her pulse quickens: Kim, retrieving something she has left behind? Anything else could only, surely, mean bad news. And did Kim reactivate the security alarm before she left?

Cass moves across to the window in her bare feet, drawing her dressing-gown tightly across her chest, and tugs open the curtain. Stares down at the deep, dark mouth of the driveway, from which, now, a black Mercedes is emerging, its headlights casting long beams of light across the scattered gravel.

The car slows, stops, is quiet for a moment, its engine emitting a soft purr.

And then, from the back seat, he appears: a tall, white-haired figure, unfolding his long legs, withdrawing a brown leather suitcase from the boot.

Looking up, then, and seeing her, framed against her bedroom window; throwing wide his arms, as if to say, *It's all right. I am here. I have come.*

Three minutes to midnight.

From behind the shed, the bolder of the pair of foxes emerges, moving swiftly on light black feet. At the centre of the lawn, it stops, sniffs the air, then stands motionless for a moment, as if unsure which way to turn.

A stirring in the bushes, a breeze lifting the leaves of the trees. The low, disembodied hum of a car, wheeling off down the Tunbridge Road. The call of a sleepless bird, and the fox, sloping towards the flowerbed, melting back into the darkness from which it came.

The faint sound of a woman's voice from the house, and a man speaking in counterpoint, bass and alto, and then the sweet, staccato peal of shared laughter.

With these noises, this strange, fragmented music that is the sound of the world as it turns, the minutes pass, and are gone.

And here, then, is the moment where the night slips into morning, and a new day will begin: pure and unsullied as the still, anticipated, weightless moment in which a woman opens her mouth, and prepares to sing.

Cass Wheeler: Discography

With Vertical Heights
Demo, recorded 1970; released 1978 by Angus Mackinnon and Hugh McMaster as the bootleg album *Cass Wheeler and Vertical Heights: The Demo Sessions*

As a solo artist
The State She's In, 1971
Songs From the Music Hall, 1973
My Loving Heart, 1976
Huntress, 1977
Fairy Tale, 1983
Snapshots, 1988
The Best of Cass Wheeler, 1990
Silver and Gold, 1997
The Eagle and the Hawk, 2003
Greatest Hits, 2015

Miscellanea
Backing vocalist on Dinah McCombs's single 'Don't Make Me Scream Out Loud', August 1988

Writer and lead vocalist on the charity single 'Home', December 1993

Demos for several abandoned album projects – including 2005's *On This Island*, under US producer Hunter Forbes – scheduled for reissue during 2017

Rumoured to be working on a new album, featuring at least fourteen original tracks, under Scottish producer Callum Sutherland, with a slated release date of 2018. Working title believed to be *Feel No Fear*

Original paintings to be exhibited alongside sculptures by the American artist Larry Alderson at the Cargo Gallery, London E1, in spring 2017

Acknowledgements

Nobody – at least in my experience – writes a novel in complete isolation. Yes, we shut ourselves away for long hours to get the words on the page. But the ideas, characters and themes that can – with time, hard work and a good deal of revising and rethinking – become a novel are inspired by the world around us. Our friends, partner, family. The art we look at, the plays we see, the books we read and – particularly in the case of this novel, of course – the music we hear.

I'll start, then, by thanking the women – and men – whose music has so inspired and moved me for as long as I can remember. There are too many to list in full here, but among them are Joni Mitchell, Sandy Denny, Carole King, Paul Simon, Nick Drake, Peter Gabriel, Kate Bush and all the members of Fleetwood Mac. In preparing to write *Greatest Hits*, I read many books by, or about, these artists, and I am grateful to all those authors for giving me an invaluable sense of the architecture of a musician's career.

To Kathryn Williams – a songwriter who can spin magic out of thin air – thank you for stepping off the cliff with me. To Romeo Stodart, thank you for joining us. And to Derek, Sue, PJ, Tones and everyone at One Little Indian, thank you for providing us with a safety net.

To Indigo, aka Tallulah, aka Mumra, aka Bus Pass (!) – Liv, May, Morgann, Alis, Suzannah and Pob – thanks for the years of 'raw musical energy', and, I suspect, for sowing the seed.

To the bassist and absolute gentleman Dave Markee, thank you for your time, generosity and fascinating recollections.

To Andy Prevezer, surely the nicest music publicist in the

business, thank you, also, for your time and insights into the industry.

To James Radice, senior vice-president of Business Affairs at Warner Music UK, and Sandra Davis, head of Family at Mishcon de Reya LLP, thank you so much for your advice on legal matters. Any resulting errors of understanding are entirely my own.

To Simon Armson, thank you for offering your expertise in the fields of mental health, eating disorders and psychiatric care. And to my other first readers – Colin MacIntyre, Ian Barnett, Jan and Peter Bild – thank you for your honest and invaluable feedback.

To Judith Murray – agent, friend, possessor of an enviably stylish collection of acid-bright accessories – what can I say other than thank you? You are without equal. Thanks also to Kate Rizzo and everyone at Greene & Heaton.

To my editor, Kirsty Dunseath – I am so lucky to have you. And to Rebecca Gray, Jo Carpenter, Jess Htay, Jennifer Kerslake, Craig Lye, Katie Espiner, David Shelley and everyone at Weidenfeld & Nicolson and Orion – well, what a marvellous bunch you are. Thank you for everything – not least your willingness to let me sail into uncharted waters.

And finally, to Andy: 'thank you' doesn't feel like enough, really, but it's all I've got. So I'll say it again. Thank you. I couldn't have written this novel without you.

LB

A note on Kathryn Williams,

and the songs from *Greatest Hits*

This novel is founded on my belief that there is no art form more evocative than music. A song has the power to transport you, in an instant, back to the moment you first heard it: to the person you were then, to the sounds and colours and feelings that shaped the contours of your world at that time.

When I hear Kathryn Williams's Mercury-nominated 2000 album *Little Black Numbers*, I am eighteen again, on my first day at university. Autumn light shining through wood-framed windows. My room spartan and empty, but for the hifi I've just unpacked. And me standing among boxes, hugging my mum goodbye, wondering whether I'll be able to avoid crying (I won't), and whether the girl in the room next door might become a friend (she will).

I've loved Kathryn's music ever since. So when, in 2015, I heard her on BBC Radio 6 Music talking about her latest album *Hypoxia*, inspired by Sylvia Plath's novel *The Bell Jar*, I stopped what I was doing and took note.

I was halfway through an early draft of *Greatest Hits* – and I knew, as I had from the moment I'd first had the idea for the novel – that I wanted the songs of my character, Cass Wheeler, to have a life beyond the page. To exist as an album, interpreted by a real-life singer-songwriter who could bring her own creativity to a unique collaboration, blurring the lines between music and literature, between the experiences of reading and listening.

Here, then, was a musician who seemed to be thinking along the same lines. The next day, I sent off a tentative email to

Kathryn's label, One Little Indian. The day after that, Kathryn herself called, and – to my amazement and delight – agreed to take on the project. As far as either of us knew, nothing like this had ever been attempted before. 'Let's jump off the cliff,' Kathryn said, and I had a vision of us doing just that, hand in hand, hoping we might just land safely.

Together, then, we have created an album of songs that exists both in its own right, as part of Kathryn's incredible, diverse output – this is her fourteenth album, and she's worked with everyone from John Martyn and Ed Harcourt to Chris Difford of Squeeze – and as a companion piece to my novel.

Kathryn has taken my own embryonic lyrics, composed in response to Cass's feelings and experiences – her attempts to make some sort of sense of her life, as all artists, in their various ways, try to do – and turned them into songs. We've cried together, drunk wine together, and laughed a *lot*. And, bit by bit, we've come up with a body of music that sits somewhere between the songs that Cass Wheeler, in my imagination, actually produced, and Kathryn's own interpretation of them: for Kathryn's own experiences as a musician, as an artist, and as a mother, wife and daughter, have of course also been brought to bear.

In October 2016, Kathryn and I spent several days holed up together in a house in Durham with a group of other novelists, poets and musicians: a retreat, organised by the Durham Book Festival, aimed at sparking more of the crossover collaborations Kathryn and I had already embarked on. As a writer accustomed to sitting alone in my study rather than to working creatively with others, it was, without exaggeration, a life-changing experience for me. I felt vulnerable, I felt raw, I felt exposed – and I have rarely felt more alive. That description could stand, too, for the whole experience of working with Kathryn.

Kathryn's album, *Songs from the Novel Greatest Hits*, is, then, both for those who have read, or would like to read, this novel;

and for those who know Kathryn's music, or would like to know it; and for anyone who is interested in music, or in literature, or in the rarely-explored borderlands between the two.

It is produced by Romeo Stodart, of the band The Magic Numbers – a man of great charm and astonishing musicianship. Romeo has also, along with singer-songwriters Michele Stodart and Polly Paulusma, contributed lyrics to several songs. I am grateful to everyone for their belief in this project, and above all to Kathryn, who provided a soundtrack to my life all those years ago – and has now done so again, both for me and for my character, Cass Wheeler.

LB

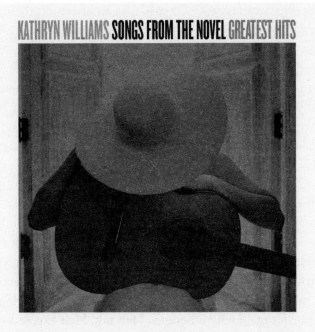

To purchase *Songs from the Novel Greatest Hits* visit:
http://bit.ly/SongsFromTheNovelGreatestHits

Discover Laura Barnett's

NO. 1 BESTSELLER

THE VERSIONS OF US

'The beautiful love child of David Nicholls's *One Day*
and Kate Atkinson's *Life After Life*'
The Times

'I simply adored this wonderful novel' Jessie Burton

'A triumphant debut . . . a thoughtful, measured book about
the interplay of chance and destiny in our lives'
Sunday Telegraph

'Three love stories seamlessly intertwined . . .
its very scope is a joy' *Guardian*

'Will keep you gripped until the tear-jerking conclusion'
Daily Express

'Exciting and clever' *Red*

blog and newsletter

For literary discussion, author insight,
book news, exclusive content,
recipes and giveaways, visit the
Weidenfeld & Nicolson blog and
sign up for the newsletter at:

www.wnblog.co.uk

For breaking news, reviews and exclusive competitions
Follow us 🐦 @wnbooks
Find us 📘 facebook.com/WNfiction